CW01263102

Help Me If You Dare

By Makiah Bullock

3

4

Copyright

Copyright 2023 by Makiah J. Bullock All rights reserved.

This Novel is a work of fiction. Although settings and locations are based on fact, the characters, dialogues and instances portrayed are either the work of the author's imagination, or used fictionally. Any resemblance to actual persons, living or dead, are entirely coincidental.

No part of this book may be reproduced in any form or by any electronic or mechanical means, including information storage and retrieval systems, without written permission from the author, except for use of brief quotations in a book review.

Scriptures used in this book whether quoted or paraphrased are taken from; The Evidence Study Bible, copyright © All rights reserved.

Dedications

FIRSTLY, I WANT TO START OFF BY GIVING THANKS TO MY LORD AND SAVIOR FOR PLACING THIS STORY IN MY HEART. A LITTLE BACKSTORY - WHEN I FINISHED THE FIRST DRAFT OF THIS BOOK, I WAS STILL IN THE WORLD, BUT UPON RETURNING TO THE LORD, HE MADE ME REWRITE THE WHOLE BOOK. I WAS HESITANT AT FIRST, BUT AS THE LORD GUIDED ME THROUGH THE PROCESS, IT ALL CAME TOGETHER. ;)

SECONDLY, I WANT TO GIVE A SPECIAL THANKS TO A WONDERFUL SISTER IN CHRIST, DELFINA DIAMBUILA. THIS NOVEL WOULD HAVE NEVER SEEN THE LIGHT OF DAY IF IT WASN'T FOR YOUR ENCOURAGEMENT. YOU HAVE BEEN MY BIGGEST MOTIVATOR AND I LOOK FORWARD TO GOD USING YOU FOR GREATER THINGS. ALSO, CONGRATS ON YOUR AMAZING CHRISTIAN ROMANCE NOVEL,
"IT ALL STARTED WITH A PROMISE."

8

Table Of Contents

Copyright	5
Dedications	7
Table Of Contents	9
Chapter One; Sidell	12
Chapter Two	20
Chapter Three	29
Chapter Four. JJ's POV	34
Chapter Five. Sidell's POV	45
Chapter Six. JJ's POV	56
Chapter Seven. Sidell's POV	65
Chapter Eight. JJ's POV	71
Chapter Nine. Sidell's POV	75
Chapter Ten. JJ's POV	84
Chapter Eleven. Sidell's POV	86
Chapter Twelve. Sidell's POV	98
Chapter Thirteen. JJ's POV	102
Chapter Fourteen. Sidell's POV	119
Chapter Fifteen. JJ's POV	128
Chapter Sixteen. Sidell's POV	134
Chapter Seventeen. JJ's POV	144
Chapter Eighteen. Sidell's POV	152
Chapter Nineteen. JJ's POV	157
Chapter Twenty. Sidell's POV	163
Chapter Twenty-One. JJ's POV	167
Chapter Twenty-Two. Sidell's POV	171
Chapter Twenty-Three. JJ's POV	175
Chapter Twenty-Four. Sidell's POV	180
Chapter Twenty-Five. JJ's POV	185
Chapter Twenty-Six. Sidell's POV	193
Chapter Twenty-Seven. JJ's POV	204
Chapter Twenty-Eight. Sidell's POV	216
Chapter Twenty Nine. JJ's POV	218

Chapter Thirty. Sidell's POV	222
Chapter Thirty-One. JJ's POV	233
Chapter Thirty-Two. Sidell's POV	240
Chapter Thirty-Three. JJ's POV	246
Chapter Thirty-Four. Sidell's POV	256
Chapter Thirty-Five. JJ's POV	267
Chapter Thirty-Six. Sidell's POV	274
Chapter Thirty-Seven. JJ's POV	287
Chapter Thirty-Eight. Sidell's POV	300
Chapter Thirty-Nine. JJ's POV	303
Chapter Forty. Sidell's POV	308
Chapter Forty-One. JJ's POV	313
Chapter Forty-Two. Sidell's POV	320
Chapter Forty-Three. JJ's POV	332
Chapter Forty-Four. Sidell's POV	336
Chapter Forty-Five. JJ's POV	342
Chapter Forty-Six. Sidell's POV	354
Chapter Forty-Seven. JJ's POV	367
Chapter Forty-Eight. Sidell's POV	369
Chapter Forty-Nine. JJ's POV	373
Chapter Fifty. Sidell's POV	381
Chapter Fifty-One. JJ's POV	390
About Author	401

II

Chapter One: $idell

I sighed loudly, my patience wearing thin as we crept along the highway in our beat-up van. I usually didn't mind being on the road with my dad behind the wheel. He always drove well, but today his slow and cautious style felt like some kind of punishment for leaving our comfortable life in Massachusetts. For hours, we'd been stuck in this metal box, rolling through various states as we made our way to our new home in Chicago. And I swore, at this rate, we may as well have walked there! My dad had insisted on driving instead of taking a quick flight like a normal person - all in the name of saving money. Well, it wasn't worth it to me.

Thirteen hours of this torture and I was about ready to pull my hair out. I longed to stretch my cramped legs and breathe in fresh air instead of the stale, musty smell of the van. But nope, my fate was sealed for at least another thirty minutes confined to this tiny seat, feeling like a prisoner in my own skin.

My little sister, Cayest, sat beside me in the back, shooting irritated glances my way. I knew exactly why. My constant fidgeting grated on her nerves. Can't say I blame her though, being trapped in this confined space with each other wasn't exactly our idea of quality bonding time. But even if we weren't in this car it wasn't like I could escape her even if I tried - she was a master of manipulation who found ways to stick close by, whether by stealing my stuff or blackmailing me into letting her tag along wherever I go.

In the front seats, my Russian-speaking Bukharian Jewish mother chattered away while my father listened attentively. Her curly brunette hair was pulled up into a tight bun. Her head bobbed with each hand gesture as she repeated her list of instructions for the billionth time. Apparently, once we got there, we're supposed to unpack immediately according to her royal highness, because you know...who needs rest after a 13-hour drive?

Clearly not everyone was raised the same way as my mother who thought cleaning was some kind of hobby. This woman would literally transform into a cleaning maniac at the mere sight of floorboards. I imagined she was already envisioning herself scrubbing down the pristine surfaces of our new kitchen! I may have been born in America, but my parents' old-world traditions ran deep. Chores were ingrained in me from birth, and as a 17 year old girl, my personal freedom was nothing but a distant dream. Socializing outside of our church community was forbidden and any hint of rebellion was met with fierce resistance. I wouldn't be surprised if my parents were already arranging an "appropriate" marriage for their "respectable virgin daughter". No wonder I spent years looking for a way out of this restrictive life.

Don't mistake my words; I loved my parents dearly. Yet, they're so stuck in a routine that it worsened my depression at times. Dad used to work part-time as a pastor in the community church. These days, when he's not being a tool for the Lord (as he liked to call it), he's a writer. My mother's distaste for his line of work was well-known, but she did her best to not let it show. She had her own passion—a perfect fit for her personality. A scrub nurse who traveled the world, ensuring everything was spotless and sterile. It was no wonder we were uprooted yet again when she accepted an offer to work in Chicago.

"And your father has already set up the alarms in the house. I will not tolerate any uninvited guests or strangers snooping around. Do you hear me?" Mom said, turning her body in the passenger's seat to face me.

"Sidell," she hissed, snapping me out of my daze. I yanked out my earbuds, replacing my favorite worship music with the awkward silence of our car.

"What?" I blinked, pushing a strand of hair behind my ear.

"You're not listening again," she scolded, smacking her thigh in frustration. Dad sighed quietly as he rubbed his hand over the steering wheel, clearly wanting this never-ending car ride to be over as much as we did. Yet here we were—still going nowhere fast.

"I was," I insisted, motioning vaguely toward where the earbuds had been. Cayest snorted beside me, seemingly ready for an argument to erupt between Mom and me—a common occurrence whenever I allowed my mind to wander during her monologues.

"Mama? Sidell must have earwax because she can't hear you," Cayest giggled. With every fiber of my being, I clenched my fists, fighting against the sudden urge to grab the little girl by her neck and wrench her out of her seat.

Ignoring Cayest's comment, Mom turned her fury back on me. "Go on, what was I saying?" Mom challenged, daring me to prove her wrong.

"Uhm..." My palms started to sweat as I struggled to remember anything Mama had said in the past hour. This was it - the moment of truth. Nervousness washed over me as I scrunched up my face. "Forgive me, Mama?" I pleaded, hoping for some mercy.

"Utterly disgraceful," she hissed darkly, before turning her cold gaze straight ahead and crossing her arms tightly across her chest. I could see her sending a murderous glare Dad's way, undoubtedly blaming him for my lack of attention span.

From the rearview mirror, my father exchanged a knowing look with me. Clearing his throat, he tried to diffuse the situation. "You should pay more attention to your mother when she is talking to you, Sidell," he stated calmly. I huffed and folded my arms across my chest, sinking deeper into my seat.

We always did this; she and I would argue, and then she would inevitably drag Dad into it, blaming him for not being strict enough with me. Naturally, I channeled my pent-up frustration onto my little sister, even though she was innocent in this chaos. It felt like living in a madhouse until dinnertime or Bible study or going to church. We were just like those dysfunctional families you watch on TV shows – utterly crazy and disorganized.

"It wasn't intentional… I'm sorry, Mama," I apologized, drawing my words out in a groan so the underlying, 'let's please not get into this,' was clear as day.

In the hushed stillness of our car, Cayest's swift tapping on her phone keyboard disrupted the peace. At just thirteen years old, she was already a social media sensation. I couldn't help but roll my eyes and flinch at the incessant clicking that bombarded my ears.

"Well, that's quite impressive," I murmured, searching for something to say.

Without even glancing up from her screen, she casually replied, "It's not that difficult."

I rolled my eyes at her snobby response, but deep down, I couldn't deny that I yearned for the same sense of normalcy she seemed to possess. I yearned to fit in. I craved an identity that didn't revolve around battling spiritual demons or striving to be the perfect Christian girl everyone expected me to be. But how could I achieve that when the church constantly celebrated how "holy" and "blessed" my upbringing was? It felt as though no matter how loudly I screamed from within, no one could hear my plea for freedom.

That's why leaving our suffocating neighborhood filled me with such joy. In Massachusetts, we had lived in a small community reserved for people like my family – people considered Russian refugees. Due to our cultural similarities, everyone there felt like family. And as you know, when you live in such close quarters, families tend to keep a watchful eye on one another. So naturally, every move I made was judged and scrutinized – by relatives, store owners, and everyone in between. Even the dogs and cats seemed to have dirt on me. But here in Chicago, no one knew me. No one knew my family or our reputation. It was a clean slate, a fresh start – an opportunity to begin anew!

"It's never intentional with you, is it, Sidell? You never listen!" Mom snapped in her favorite irritating tone that always triggered me. I narrowed my eyes at the back of her head, unable to believe she still wanted to go on about this. But just as it seemed like Mom was about to ruin this special day, our new neighborhood came into view as Dad turned a corner.

I rolled down my window to catch the breeze, pleasantly surprised by the different scent in the air – far from the polluted and chaotic depiction often portrayed in the news. Then again, we were in the suburban part of the city, where everything appeared polished and purified. As Dad effortlessly maneuvered past the security gates, which swiftly closed behind us, it felt as if I was traversing sanctified streets. I couldn't help but close my eyes, inhaling deeply as a silly grin danced across my face.

"You're so weird," Cayest remarked, but I paid her no mind as I fully absorbed this precious moment of serenity.

Finally, Mom fell silent, and it's remarkable how much one can ponder within mere seconds of stillness. The U-Haul truck ahead of us veered into our new driveway and parked. Squinting through the thick shrubs that blocked our view, I strained to make out any details of our new home. Dad had been the only one who had seen it before, and it surprised me that Mom hadn't voiced her opinion. Then again, I understood why – Mom could be extremely picky when it came to house hunting, whereas Dad simply lacked the patience for it.

Despite that, upon first viewing, Mom seemed slightly impressed by the architecture. The off-white brick adorning the soft blue concrete and tall columns formed an archway over an extravagant golden knobbed double-door. I gazed at this remarkable design in sheer astonishment.

"Hmph. You got lucky, Garren," Mom remarked to my dad as she peered out the passenger window, scanning the area for anything distasteful.

Dad let out an awkward chuckle as he switched off the engine, which purred to a halt a short distance away from our mailbox.

"Finally," Cayest exclaimed with an exaggerated eye roll as she dramatically stored her phone away. Being the youngest, she was Mom's favorite and a tad spoiled. More outspoken than I was at her age. We were both reflections of our parents – she was practically a carbon copy of my mother, with light brown eyes and wavy brown hair. While I took after my dad, inheriting his vivid blue eyes and blonde tresses, though he sported a few strands of gray at the front, a testament to his maturity.

As soon as we came to a complete stop, we scattered out of the car like a pack of wild animals. It was my family's first time in another state, and the unfamiliar sights stirred a strange mixture of anticipation and fear within us. The locals appeared nice enough; walking their dogs, jogging along the block, engaging in friendly conversations with one another in the neighborhood.

But then we felt someone's gaze boring into us from across the street – an elderly couple perched like statues in their lounge chairs, observing our every move. My dad initiated contact with a friendly wave.

"Privet! How's it going?" he called out enthusiastically, his Russian accent slicing through the silence. The couple eyed him suspiciously, before returning his friendly wave. Shaking my head, I chuckled to myself. I should've known that my dad would've already introduced himself to our new neighbors.

Back in our previous residence, Dad had been the captain of the "Neighborhood Watch." Personally, I hated it. Why? Because it provided an excuse for everyone to judge my every action and forced me to maintain a facade whenever I stepped outside.

The sound of my flimsy cardboard box ripping open interrupted my thoughts as its contents scattered across the front lawn. "Shoot!" I muttered under my breath. Mom breezed past me, clutching a green vase between her fingers.

"Make sure you clean that up," she called over her shoulder as she entered the house, Cayest trailing behind her. I let out a deep sigh.

Duh, obviously, I'm not going to leave it here.

Dad grabbed a crate from the moving truck, assuring me, "Sidell, don't worry about it, darling. Take your time." His words offered solace as I bent down to gather the scattered items.

Straightening up, I replied gratefully, "Thanks, Papa," clutching the bulky objects close to me as I made my way toward the house. The moment I stepped inside, the scent of pine and fresh paint enveloped me. The layout was just as I had envisioned – an inviting entryway leading into a living room and dining area, a straight staircase ascending upstairs, and a cozy nook at the far end of the house that served as a den. The well-equipped kitchen nestled at the back. The countertops adorned with modern appliances made my mom giddy.

"This is beautiful," Mom beamed with an enormous smile as she wandered through the kitchen and exited through the glass door that led to the backyard. I couldn't help but agree – the house possessed a distinct charm. The open space felt far more expansive than our previous claustrophobic townhouse. Here, the walls bathed in a soothing light beige hue, made it feel welcoming and comforting.

As I soaked in my newfound environment, my gaze unexpectedly locked with Cayest's from across the living room. Without exchanging a single word, we sensed an unspoken connection between us. Abandoning the items clutched in my arms, I sprung up the stairs in a frenzied dash.

"That's not fair, Sidell, you got to choose last time!" Cayest yelled, her voice ringing in my ears as she frantically chased me. The competition to claim a bedroom electrified the air as she closed in on me, but managing to reach the top floor before her, I lunged forward and slammed my hand on a random door.

"Room's mine! Better luck next time," I reassured her with a sly smile while breathless. Cayest began to whine as she charged into the room.

"Be quiet, I don't care. I'm telling Papa," she threatened, drawing out her words as she stormed past me like a tempest, tears welling up in her eyes before racing back downstairs.

"Always so dramatic," I mumbled as I proceeded into my room. It was spacious, the walls painted a serene off-blue with white trimmings adorning the edges. Recessed lights embedded in the ceiling bathed the room in a gentle glow. A closet with sliding doors and two wide windows offering lovely views complemented the light wood flooring.

"Jackpot," I declared with utmost satisfaction, clicking on the light switch.

Several hours passed before we managed to transport everything inside the house, though we were far from fully unpacked. Only the furniture, electronics, and a handful of pots and pans had found their rightful places.

My room fared slightly better than the rest of the house. My modest desk now occupied a cozy corner next to the sliding door closet. My bed sat elegantly in the middle of the room near one of the expansive windowsills, adorned with a new spread and plush pillows that gave it an exquisite appearance. It was a bed made just for me.

Exhaustion weighed heavily upon me, but I was determined to complete the task at hand so I could witness my room's transformation once everything was in order. I positioned my fancy suitcase in front of the closet, beside the bed at the far end of the room. It was the same suitcase I had acquired for summer camp, containing a few of my Dawned clothes and simple footwear. As I looked up, Dad entered with his hands on his hips, scanning around the room for whatever parents do in situations like this. His face was passive, and I couldn't tell if this was a proud Dad moment or what.

I gently patted my slightly weathered Bible, the one I'd been using since I had learned to read, as I debated whether I should put it on the study table or up on a shelf.

Dad was silently flicking through my music CDs that were still in one of the last boxes left to unpack as if he was considering jamming out to them or something.

"Papaa..." I said, jogging over to him as he pulled out one album after another. "Eto moya sobstvennost," I added with a slight attitude.

He raised his palms up as if in defense. "I was just checking to see if your music options glorify God," he stated as if he's not the parent and don't have the right to touch my stuff without asking me first.

I laughed nervously. "Da, Papa, they do," I said, gathering the discs and quickly stashing the box away in the closet.

"Alright. Well...your mother insists on cooking dinner, but I'm hungry now, so I'm on my way to pick up a pizza for the time being," he said, setting a baseball cap on his head. "You wanna ride?"

"Net, spasibo," I responded, avoiding direct eye contact with him. "Please, no onions, though."

"Ponyatno. I won't be long; your mother and sister are already in the kitchen getting things started," he said, patting my head with a light thump, which was so dad of him. He was definitely a man's man—hardened exterior, battles won and lost—but beneath the surface of his bravado was an intangible softness that could crumble in the wake of any risk to his family. I watched him go with the knowledge that he'd tear this world apart if it put us in harm's way.

Chapter Two.

The aroma of a piping hot pizza filled the air, tempting our family as we finished saying grace. It was around 6 p.m. and our father, sitting at the head of the dinner table, posed a seemingly innocent question, "How are you two liking your new rooms?" Little did he know, it would trigger big emotions from my little sister. Cayest's eyes narrowed into thin slits, her long brown curls cast shadows over her face like a veil. I took a bite of my pizza, trying not to smirk at her over-the-top reaction. My room was bigger, with a view of the leafy oak tree in our new backyard. Hers faced the neighbor's brick wall.

Mom tapped the table's wooden surface. "Girls, pay attention to this," she urged, nodding towards the bulky box tv resting on the countertop. I shifted my gaze to the screen as Mom cranked up the volume, ensuring that the sounds of gunshots didn't go unnoticed.

The grainy image showed a reporter standing in front of yellow police tape, her voice tense as she described a robbery gone wrong.

"Two teenagers shot in a convenience store holdup downtown," the reporter announced. "Witnesses say the suspects opened fire before fleeing the scene."

Mom shook her head, swallowing the reporter's words as absolute truth "This neighborhood may be safer than the rest of Chicago, but don't think you can wander around unchecked like you did in Boston, Sidell," her eyes locked onto mine. "Or they'll shoot you too."

I nearly choked on my pizza, the cheesy bite sticking in my throat. Does she really have to make everything a lecture? Avoiding her stern gaze, I reached over to my glass cup and gulped down some water. I wondered what else she would throw at me.

"I've found a church with a great youth group," Mom continued, her tone leaving no room for debate. "You'll be there every Sunday. It will keep you safe from the temptations that come with being young."

Dad shifted uncomfortably in his chair but said nothing. Cayest's scowl had transformed into a smug grin, clearly enjoying my discomfort.

I nodded, resisting the urge to roll my eyes as I took another bite. The sweet and salty flavors danced on my tongue, briefly distracting me from Mom's cryptic statement. I knew this was just the beginning of a long battle for independence in this strange new city. But for now, I'd have to pick my battles carefully. Starting with finding a way to wipe that smirk off Cayest's face.

Since that dinner on Friday two weeks ago, it's been pretty non problematic. Those first two weeks I stayed in the room most of the time. The only time I interacted with my family was when we had our routine Bible studies or during unpacking and mealtimes. I guess I just needed the isolation. My family can be a little overwhelming sometimes. So, it felt good to be able to jam to my music in secret and just have some room to breathe. As I enjoyed the peace and quiet, I also had the opportunity to pray and worship God. In the serenity, I began to realize that he was the only person I could stand to be around most of the time.

Outside looking in, people would often say that religion was forced on me by my parents and that I was indoctrinated. But, even if I was, how would it hurt to be led by God and be guided in the right direction?

I think people are shallow and judgmental. People usually don't attempt to understand spiritual things, nor do they even want to try, and if they do, they only remain open-minded for a short period of time before they start finding faults with how you're living.

"Oh, that's not very Christian of you."

Like gah! I'm a human being! I'm not perfect! And God knows this, as he's been patient with me despite the many times I backslid and became lukewarm.

Some people are so biased and narrow-minded that they are unwilling to know God or his love because they believe he is a cruel, vindictive, unforgiving entity with no redeeming virtues.

Later in the day, a notification pinged on my phone. It was a message from Elemai, an acquaintance from my old church. She wasn't talking about anything, really. She was just repeating recycled lines like, "I couldn't believe you really moved. I'm going to miss you."

I just replied with a *lol* because that's honestly all I could say. May the Lord forgive me if this comes off rude, but we weren't really even friends to begin with. I had just hung out with her for the sake of my parents, who constantly praised her and wished their daughter was more like Elemai. Shallow convos like that got old really fast. In fact, her text only reminded me how much I craved *real* friendship.

★ ★ ★ ★ ✝ ★ ★ ★ ★

The sharp scent of detergent filled my nostrils as I shut the washer machine lid with a soft click. I had spent hours fussing over sorting the items by color, desperate to appease my mother's OCD. She had a habit of micromanaging everything, including laundry. She stood there with her arms crossed, watching me like a hawk to make sure I didn't get too wild and crazy with the settings as I prepared to turn it on.

Glancing up at her, I couldn't resist being cheeky. "I'm truly grateful that you have instilled in me this profound love for doing laundry! The world truly needs more individuals who value the importance of clean clothes."

My mother rolled her eyes, but I could see a hint of a smile on her lips.

"I need it done right," she said in a matter-of-fact tone. "You're lucky to have me standing over you. I can't afford any stains or colors bleeding and ruining my clothes."

The machine hummed with a low resonance, echoing through the whole house. I carefully transferred the neatly folded clothes from the dryer into a wicker basket beside me. The soft touch of warm fabric against my fingertips brought a sense of comfort and accomplishment.

With my task completed, I hoisted the laundry basket on my hip and began climbing the stairs to put away my clothes.

Passing by my father's study, I heard him softly muttering something in Russian as he sat engrossed behind his laptop. Intrigued, I peeked through the slightly ajar door. His brows were furrowed in concentration behind black-framed reading glasses, his fingers pressed thoughtfully against his chin.

"Everything okay, Papa?" I inquired, leaning casually against the door frame. A smile graced his face upon noticing my presence, his eyes crinkling with affection.

"Yes, fine. Just brainstorming, my dear." He checked his wristwatch. "I have approximately another hour before I take a break and resume my work."

"Want me to bring you something? Water, maybe?" I asked, offering my assistance.

He shook his head. "No, I'm good. However, could you do me a favor and check our mailbox? I submitted a change of address form, but it usually takes around five business days to process." He groaned softly. "I would hate to make another trip if it didn't go through."

I laughed lightly. "Sure thing." As I turned to leave, I heard his frustrated sigh and the clatter of his glasses being tossed on the desk. Being a writer must be stressful.

Out of consideration for my mother's preferences, I threw on a light sweater before venturing outside. Not only was there a slight chill in the air, but my choice of attire was also dictated by the fact that my pajamas consisted solely of a tank top and pajama pants—and challenging my mother's standards of modesty was never an option.

I opened the mailbox to find nothing inside, not even the regular sales papers. I closed it and started to make my way back to our house when the screeching sound of tires from a nearby car startled me. Turning around, I observed as the car came to a halt at the curb of the neighboring house, blaring heavy metal music from its open windows. Intrigued, I found myself captivated by thoughts about the driver. *Who would be crazy enough to drive like that?*

The car settled into place as its engine was switched off. A middle-aged redhead woman stumbled out from the passenger side, clutching a drink in each hand. Every staggering step she took, it became increasingly apparent that she was drunk. Circulating around the opposite side, the driver followed behind her. I assumed he was her son—with fiery red hair, adorned in dark clothes and an array of jingling chained accessories. As they made their way up the driveway, a third passenger emerged from the backseat. This young girl, around my age, possessed honey-brown hair that fell to her shoulders. She was casually dressed in a cropped, Metallica short-sleeve shirt, sweatpants, and sandals.

"Roxen! You're supposed to be helping me, you sloth!" the girl shouted as she unloaded groceries from the trunk.

Roxen blatantly ignored his sister's plea, which resulted in the girl hurling a bag of groceries at him. He ducked just in time, the bag crashing into the side of their house instead. I stood frozen, unsure of whether I should intervene or continue pretending not to notice. But as I took a deep breath and made up my mind, I started walking along the sidewalk towards her.

I wasn't typically a social butterfly, preferring to be befriended rather than be the one who makes friendships.

However, this time, I couldn't ignore the glistening droplets of sweat on the poor girl's forehead. It was agonizing to witness her struggle without offering assistance.

Lost in her own world, she seemed unaware of my presence until my timid voice broke through the silence. "Hey, uh, hello there?" I stammered. "Um, can I help you put your groceries in your house? You seem to be having difficulty."

Startled, she paused from her relentless pacing back and forth then turned towards me, her eyes widening as she saw me for the first time.

After eyeing me skeptically, a small, embarrassed smile appeared on her face. "Oh my goodness," she exclaimed in relief. "I would truly appreciate that. Thank you so much. Today's been such a crappy day for me!"

I nodded with an understanding smile as she handed me a few bags of groceries.

Upon closer inspection, she was really pretty. Her grayish-green eyes framed her face perfectly with its thick lashes. Her brown hair had been stylishly chopped just below the neckline of her shirt. Besides her eyebrow and belly button piercing, she looked sort of sophisticated in a way.

"I'm sorry, I didn't catch your name. I'm Dawn," she said as we walked up the driveway, weighed down by the grocery bags.

"Nice to meet you. I'm Sidell. I just moved in next door two weeks ago," I replied, nodding in the direction of my house.

"Oh yeah? Well, welcome to the neighborhood. FYI, it's usually not this chaotic." Dawn chuckled nervously, " Just a little bit of bad luck today."

I chuckled, "Good to know."

We stepped into her house, and she gestured towards the kitchen, where the boy with the dark clothes was rummaging around in the refrigerator. "You can set the bags down anywhere," she said as the boy noticed my presence. Dark eyeliner outlined his green eyes, as he gave me a quick, uninterested glance. His nose and ears were adorned with multiple piercings. The female ghoul printed on his shirt matched the skull and coffin rings on his fingers. But what really caught my attention was the upside-down crucifix ring he wore on his middle finger. It made me slightly uncomfortable.

"Ah, Sidell, this is my older brother Roxen. Roxen, meet our new neighbor Sidell," Dawn said as she calmly introduced us.

Roxen gave me another glance before chugging orange juice directly from the carton.

Dawn scoffed. "So disgusting, no decency at all. Don't mind him. He's been like that since he was eleven," she said, rolling her eyes at her brother's behavior.

I smiled faintly, hoping it wouldn't betray me by showing my discomfort with the situation.

As we walked back to the car, I caught sight of the old people across the street again. They were back in their lounge chairs, staring. Dawn smiled at them and proceeded to shout, "Hi there, Mrs. and Mr. Moore! How are you doing? I'm thinking of getting my eyeballs pierced this summer!" She flailed her arms around as she spoke. I cringed while she chuckled mischievously, clearly getting a kick out of winding them up. I wondered if this was a regular occurrence.

The couple leaned in and murmured to each other while giving Dawn side-eyed glares. But she just kept on going. "Oh yeah, I got my tongue pierced yesterday," she cheered, sticking out her tongue to show off the diamond stud.

I managed an awkward smile, standing off to the side like a frozen vegetable. It was obvious that Dawn was bold and outgoing, while I, on the other hand, was always trying to process my next awkward hand gesture.

Dawn giggled and turned to face me. "Don't let your guard down around them, and don't let their "I'm too old to know any better" routine get to you; they snitch better than yapping shoes. I would've been caught in some deep trouble if it wasn't for my mom being an alcoholic," she laughed.

I stumbled over my own thoughts as I tried to process what she had just said. "Um, sorry?"

"Don't worry about it," Dawn assured. "My mom won't be offended, she's so dazed she laughs at anything. You kinda get used to it after a while." She shrugged.

"Oh...I see..." I said, not sure how to react. All of a sudden, Dawn gasped and glared at a mark on the car. She huffed as she began polishing the indented scratch near the tail light.

"My doll is already getting scratched up." She pouted.

"Is this your car?" I asked, my eyes widening. Dawn finally gave up on the scratch.

"Yep. I've been saving since freshman year, babysitting, sucking up to old people, stacking any small change I could get my hands on. I counted my money religiously every night, and when I got to the magic number, I made a mad dash on Black Friday and bought it." She said this all like a proud child. "I would have driven today if it weren't for Roxen willing to offer me money to drive instead," she added with an eye roll and a slight shake of her head. "His car was impounded and he's desperate to get back into the driver's seat."

I laughed in response. "I can't wait to have the freedom to drive my own car. I've tried carpooling and taking driving lessons with my mom, but it's enough to make me drive off a cliff." I exhaled deeply.

"Girl," she said, "one of these days, I can teach you if you want."

"Really?" I asked excitedly.

"Yeah, I'll teach you the basics, and I'm sure once you get the hang of it, you'll be a natural. I just know it," she gleefully laughed, making fun of my nervousness.

"Yeah? Well, that would be awesome!" I replied, secretly hoping that she was serious.

"Peachy keen, we can make it a Saturday thing," she said, closing the trunk of her car.

★ ★ ★ ★ ✞ ★ ★ ★ ★

I leaned against the kitchen door frame as I watched Dawn chug an entire water bottle before proceeding to remove the store-bought goods from the bags we had brought in.

"Give me a moment. I'm so horrible with names. You told me that your name was Si-dell... right?" She furrowed her brows, hoping she hadn't mispronounced it.

"Yes," I answered.

She sighed in relief. "OK, good. Sorry, would you mind if I just called you Sid?"

"Sure, I sometimes go by Sid also," I said with open hands. That was a lie. I've never gone by the shortened form of my name. It just never occurred to me or anyone around me to ever use it. But it sounded cool in the moment

"So, Sid, do you think you could hang for a bit? You don't have a curfew, do you?" Dawn asked in a jocular tone as she put away the items.

"Ugh, not really, but my parents are so strict. They would have to approve of you first, and I 'd rather not put you through that agony." I chuckled. "Though I should probably start heading home before they send out a search party," I said with an eye roll, shrugging nonchalantly.

"That's a pity," Dawn said with a mock frown, placing a can of beans on the counter. "Welp, maybe we can run into each other at school or something. If you're not enrolled yet, you should convince your parents to let you go to Westwood High School. It's near downtown Chicago, but trust me, it's not a bad school," she suggested brightly as her blue-painted nails tapped the counter.

A small grin spread across my face as I contemplated her offer. "Mmn...I'll definitely try."

"Here, take my number down." Dawn pulled out her cell from the pocket of her yellow sweatpants. "Do you have your phone on you?" she asked.

"Uhh...oops, I forgot it at my house," I uttered sheepishly. Taking a breath, I continued, "Do you happen to have a pen and paper?"

"Ummm..." Dawn began rummaging through the kitchen drawer, eventually retrieving a lonely crayon and a pre-opened envelope. "Better than nothing." She snorted as she hovered over the counter and scribbled the digits down.

"Thump!"

Before we knew it, Dawn and I were shaken out of our little world by a loud sound coming from the living room. We shot each other nervous glances before peering out the kitchen to find the source of the noise. Suddenly, Dawn's mother swayed into view, wearing a silk bathrobe with a cigarette in her hand. She had just clumsily tumbled down the stairs. With as much grace as she could muster, she dusted herself off before slipping away into a nearby room.

I glanced back at Dawn with my hand clasped over my mouth, unsure if it was okay to find it funny or not, but to my surprise, she too was trying her hardest to stifle a laugh.

CHAPTER THREE.

Dawn and I got to know each other over the next two weeks.

Unbelievably, we had become fast friends. Thankfully, my unpredictable mother had taken an instant liking to her as well, which scared me to be honest, because Dawn, of course, had piercings. But it was like Mom saw past it entirely and just accepted Dawn's cheerful personality. Also, and I am not judging by any means, but surprisingly, Dawn was Christian and had values, which easily earned her a spot in my mom's heart. As a result, it was amazing to observe how Dawn just knew how to win my mom over. And somehow, with her captivating personality, she managed to bewitch my mother into allowing me to attend Westwood High School. The day we moved into our new home, Mom had made it quite clear that I shouldn't venture into Downtown Chicago on my own. But for some reason, she didn't seem to mind me going to school in said forbidden zone.

Moving on past that, I will not deny that I was ecstatic when I officially became enrolled today. When my mom and I first stepped foot on the school's campus to meet my counselor, she was in awe of the architecture. The school had a distinct gothic style with obvious Christian undertones. The cruciform-shaped buildings gave that away. Mom knew she couldn't resist the school's religious foundations and signed me up. Classes were to begin tomorrow—a Tuesday.

★ ★ ★ ★ ✞ ★ ★ ★ ★

Mom grabbed a hanger off the rack, beaming as she held up a horrendous plaid skirt and matching blazer. "Oh, honey! This one is perfect for you! So prim and proper."

We were now at Fevaron Clothes in search of my school uniform. Dawn leaned against the basket, barely containing her laughter as she surveyed the monstrosities my mom had picked out.

"No way! It's tacky, Mama!" I screeched, batting away her hands as she fussed over me unnecessarily.

"Yep, I agree," Dawn piped up, standing upright from her laid-back posture. "What's even up with the checkerboard and zippers? It's straight out of the 90s."

Mom pursed her lips, annoyance flashing across her face. "Well, why don't you girls pick something out then?" She waved her hand towards the expansive racks of clothing.

Finally, some freedom. I immediately started scanning through the clothes myself, searching for an up-to-date style of school clothing. The rule for the school uniform was the same for all ladies. As long as you possessed a skirt, a blouse, a tie, and tights that coordinated with the school shades of Silver, Green, White or Black, You'd be all set.

"Come on, Sid," Dawn implored, lightly knocking on the dressing room wall.

I peeked my head out and whispered to her ear, "Act surprised when I walk out so my mom doesn't suspect a thing," I said, adjusting the skirt around my waist.

"I got you bestie babes," she replied, her voice filled with mischief. "So strut your stuff!"

With a deep breath, I swung open the dressing room door, revealing my chosen outfit. I playfully began posing like a fashion model on a runway, my back toward them.

"Hello there," I spoke in a falsetto voice. I flaunted off the edges of the short-medium cascading black skirt.

"Whew! Now who is that sophisticated young woman?" Dawn teased, nudging my mom with her elbow. "Looks like someone's ready to hit the books, wouldn't you say Mrs. Evermost?"

"It's beautiful," Mom replied, studying me intently. My fingers fidgeted with my emerald-green belt buckle under her thoughtful gaze until she rewarded me with a tentative smile. "I must admit, Sidell, this outfit suits you remarkably well. It's quite elegant."

I exhaled a breath I hadn't realized I was withholding.

"Yesssss! It screams classic chic." Dawn chimed in as she approached me to insist on a twirl. I did so, delighting in the shimmer of the plain, white-collared shirt as it caught the glint of the glittering silver, green and gold tie. Without delay, Mom tucked away the items and two pairs of tights. She scolded us with a playful smirk, reminding us not to tell my dad about how much she had spent.

She was saying it more so towards me as if I couldn't keep a secret from my dad, but unbeknownst to her, I had taken a couple of twenties from his wallet before.

Later that night, I prepped my backpack with the supplies I would need for the new school year. I was so thankful Dawn had offered to drive us in the mornings. It sure beat taking the bus. I carefully hung my brand-new uniform inside my chaotic closet and treated myself to a steamy shower. Once I was cozied up in my pajamas, I knelt beside my bed and said a silent prayer.

"Lord, thank You for Your grace, Your patience and Your love in my life. Please, be with me as I start this new school. Anoint me so that I may be a blessing to my teachers and classmates. Let me excel in all of my studies and surround me with positive people. If there is someone out there who is meant to enter my life, let me be an open vessel so that Your will is done. In Jesus' name, Amen."

★ ★ ★ ★ ✞ ★ ★ ★ ★

The school courtyard bustled with students and staff, all murmuring their own conversations. That said, we seemed to be the noisiest. A hush fell over everyone in the courtyard as they stole peeks in our direction.

"Leave me alone, Tony!" Dawn squealed, using me as a shield from her dark-haired admirer who had highlights. With a determined glint in her eye, she firmly declared, "I'm with my friend," though he continued to persist despite my presence. My hastily placed messy bun did nothing to hide the two flat ironed curls falling onto my cheeks. I lazily blew them out of my face as I played the spectator, just watching as Dawn and this mysterious *Tony* bickered back and forth, playfully ribbing each other.

This was certainly not how I had imagined my first day at a new school to start, being a third wheel in someone else's popular world. I tagged behind Dawn everywhere she went that morning. She attempted to introduce me to her group of friends and incorporate me into their conversations, but I couldn't seem to find my voice.

She must have sensed my shyness at some point because she leaned in and whispered in my ear, "You can talk too, you know? My friends are now your friends." Her kind words were a much-needed reassurance that she wasn't trying to exclude me and that she wanted to welcome me into the fold.

Ding!...Ding!

Thank you, God, who created the heavens, the earth, and the lovely sound of the bell! I felt relieved. Everyone suddenly broke away like ants to go to their first-period class. I hastily reached into my small purse, hoping to find my schedule before I got too far behind.

"I'll catch you later, Sid. You'll be fine, right?" Dawn asked as I began to look up, but I didn't even get a chance to respond because Tony swooped in and affectionately whisked her away. I patted down my uniform and sighed as I pressed out the creases.

They disappeared into the crowd and I muttered a quiet, "Yeah," into the empty space ahead of me. As my eyes danced around the many buildings surrounding me, I mentally considered which way I needed to go as everyone brushed past me.

Being map blind is an actual thing. Finding it extremely difficult to locate places I've never been before is an adopted disability of mine, and unfortunately, my severe social anxiety makes asking strangers for help nearly impossible.

Except for earlier when I tried asking the school's Head Master, Ms. Kyepher — the scary woman with coke-bottle glasses and a bun so tight her forehead looked stretched. Dressed in a Victorian-style buttoned-down dress, she looked as welcoming as Christabella from Silent Hill.

Anyone who got to know me soon realized I was a sweetheart. But this Ms. Kyepher lady almost tested my salvation with God. I simply asked her in the softest tone possible, "Do you know where room 843 is?"

I noticed the slouch in her neck and back that had likely been caused by very bad posture. Her large brown eyes flicked in my direction, and she looked at me as if I had ruined her day as she ignored me completely.

That's alright, because God doesn't like ugly, and I hope her body stays like that, I thought spitefully.

The only good thing I could be grateful for at that moment was having ditched my backpack in my locker earlier.

Dragging that thing around would've pushed me over the edge. I was already pacing frantically between buildings, on the verge of a meltdown. Late, lost, trying not to cry. One more building to check before I swallowed my pride and asked another human being for help.

The building I entered was called Psalms Hall. Breathing a prayer, I turned into the empty beige hallway.

There were just two doors on the ground floor, and I chose the one on the left, begging God to end this nightmare.

Chapter Four: JJ

"Yes, Grandma, I hear you!" I hollered towards the bathroom door. My right hand, enclosed in its fingerless leather glove, had a hold on my pick comb. I gazed at myself through the mirror as I combed out my recently trimmed flat top. The single, golden, hooped earring that hung from my left ear glistened and caught my eye. I ran my fingers along the sides of the small hoop with a gentleness that's typically reserved for live creatures instead of accessories. It's just something about gold jewelry and how it looked so mesmerizing against my brown skin. It simply gave everything a more personal touch, you know?

I got the flat top three days ago, and it turned out pretty good. However, it was starting to get a little nappy from sleeping on it, so I had to style it again. I set down my pick comb and then picked up a small bottle of face oil. I applied it to my washed face, rubbing it into the premature stubble of hair on my chin. It's my senior year of high school and puberty has already peaked, so I had to take preventative measures before I got that distressed wild-man beard.

Grandma knocked again. "Hurry up, boy, I don't like being late," she said impatiently.

"Alright. I'll be out in a minute!" I bellowed again. Finishing up, I stepped outside to meet her. I didn't want her coming into the bathroom and nitpicking about this and that, from the shower curtain dripping onto her perfect hardwood floors to the mess scattered over the counter. It would be no use giving her any excuses.

She thrusted her ancient Android phone into my hands, demanding I turn it to silent mode. Grandma was never one for technology, which often embarrassed me when I was around people. But who could blame her? She'd seen enough of life without having to learn how to navigate a touch screen.

While I silenced her phone, I swiped closed her open apps in the process. As I did so, she teetered on her toes, her head covered with her usual brown bobbed wig that was far away from the hue of her natural gray afro. Her bright red lipstick marked her lips as she spoke.

"You've been in there since early morning, all quiet. What's up with you?" she curiously asked. Knowing how intent she was on getting to where she needed to go on time, I played along, hoping my humor would distract her from probing me about my self care routine.

"You know it takes me a while to get ready. What's that thing you be saying? Remember, cleanliness is next to godliness?" This earned me a slight smile. Grandma was devoutly religious and tried in every way to ensure that I followed suit—and yet here I was, an atheist attending a Christian high school.

It had been torturous two years ago when I was a sophomore. Felt like I'd been hit by a train of faith-driven culture that I had been purposely avoiding since I was fourteen. At age fourteen, I witnessed the demise of my childhood innocence due to the death of Donica—my best friend, girlfriend and summer companion. Back then, yeah, I was resentful towards my grandma, who believed enrolling me in this school would transform me and bring me back into the light. By "light," I mean the church, God, religion, and all of the ideology that had so far escaped me.

Grandma began fixing the pearl buttons on her purple and gold fleece dress jacket. "Okay. I'm going to my doctor's appointment, then the women's society meeting. I should be back by evening. There's leftover black-eyed peas and chicken stew in the kitchen. Take care of yourself while at school. Don't get into trouble now, you hear?"

I rolled my eyes. "Don't trip Grandma, I haven't been getting into too much trouble. At least not in recent years, and the type you're referring to. And you know that. All that is behind me, promise."

"I guess it's because I always remind you not to. And one can never tell with you young ones of today. You could spring a surprise on me." She chuckled. I think she's just grateful that I didn't get caught by any authorities, unlike the unlucky ones she heard about on the news.

Even though I was tall and slim, towering over her in height, she still managed to kiss me on both cheeks.

"I'm locking the door as I step out. Hope you've not lost your keys again. Or you'll be outdoors for the rest of the day till I return," she said, walking away, her heels clicking against the hardwood floors.

I smiled as I went back into the bathroom. I'd lost my keys a couple of times and my grandma never quite seemed to forget. On one occasion when she had gone out and locked the door, I didn't know that I had left my keys in my locker at school and was therefore locked out all day until she returned in the evening. I had been left to fend off the little neighborhood delinquents, or kids I should say, who wouldn't stop bugging me for quarters to buy candy.

My iPhone suddenly rang, and the caller ID told me that it was my friend Tony. He was probably wondering what was taking me so long, considering I hitched a ride with him to school most days. Well, whenever I could, because Tony was either suspended or getting in some one-on-one time with his girl, Dawn. In other words, I usually rode the school bus.

"Yo, just wait for me, bro, I'm on my way out right now," I spoke with the phone to my ear, prancing around the living room, looking for my elusive backpack. I could imagine my grandma right now instigating, with her hand on her hip, still dressed in her night clothes, "I told you now, didn't I? Look at you scarpering about like a headless chicken. This generation thinks they know it all when grown folks tell them something."

I rolled my eyes, annoyed by the fact that she was *mostly* always right. Eventually, I found my backpack hiding between the ancient couch that nobody sits on and the dusty granddaddy clock.

Locking the apartment, I shuffled through the nearby playground, nearly twisting my ankle as my shoelaces came undone. *Just my luck.*

Bending down to tie them, none other than Rayo caught my eye, puffing a blunt with his usual spaced-out look. He was posted up on the green box with the rest of his gang friends, no doubt plotting their next act of juvenile delinquency. They called themselves "The Serpents" which I thought sounded ridiculous. Rayo and I grew up together in this neighborhood and he's been terrorizing it for years. He'd often look after his cousin Khyree, who I hated with a passion.

As kids, Rayo and I never really crossed paths outside of mine and Khyree's explosive beef sessions, probably because he was too mature for his age. He joined The Serpents at ten while I was still learning how to ride a bike without training wheels. Rayo was well aware of my utter disdain for his cousin, but as long as I minded my own business, he kept his distance. An unspoken truce I appreciated.

I met up with Tony, whose sleek, gray sedan was parked next to the foreboding wired fence wrapped around the apartment complex. I nodded, though I couldn't tell if he noticed me because of his tinted windows. We had an odd friendship, for sure. Unlike me who grew up in the abandoned ends of Chicago, Antonio Mayez, or Tony as he insisted I call him, was raised in the privileged Heights in a well-off two-parented household. How we ever became friends was a mystery, but we met at school and have just been tight ever since.

37

I climbed into the passenger seat of his car, our hands clasping briefly with a subtle shake. His strong black hair, accentuated with golden streaks, was shaved close on the sides and kept longer on top. He donned a forrest green blazer and pants that matched mine. Before putting on my seat belt, I immediately reached over to the radio, scoffing at the heavy metal streaming from it.

"Bro, every time I get in your car it's like someone is trying to scream their way out of hell. When are you gonna play something good?" I teased him, knowing all too well of his deep-rooted love of aggressive music.

He just smiled. "You just don't appreciate good lyrics, man." His light brown eyes quickly scanned his phone for any messages before setting it back down on the armrest.

"I appreciate good lyrics, but this is just noise," I chuckled, twisting the knob until I heard something closer to my taste.

I came across a mellow country rock tune and cranked up the volume violently. "Nah, see this here? Now this is *my* kind of rock," I declared with a smirk and raised my hand for a high five. But he only smiled wider, leaving me hanging as he shifted the transmission lever into drive. We both burst into spontaneous laughter as we sped away from the parking spot.

"What's the deal with the biker gloves, man?" Tony asked as we shifted our way through the entrance of the school about fifteen minutes later.

"You sure are bold to speak with peach avocado ChapStick on. Yeah…I see it glistenin' off your lips," I shot back as he tried to clown me.

Tony rolled his eyes but couldn't help but smirk.

"At least I don't look like I'm about to invade a medieval castle," he retorted, gesturing at my studded leather.

I cackled. "Why you hating? It's a classic look, man. Plus, I'm not trying to look like every other mindless drone in this prison,"

"Truth," Tony said as we walked towards our lockers. "But you know what they say, 'when in Rome, do as the Romans do.'"

"Yeah, well, I'm not in Rome and I'm not about to conform just because everyone else is," I said as I opened a piece of gum.

"Fair enough," Tony said with a shrug. "Just be careful not to ruffle too many feathers. You don't want to get suspended."

"Oh, you mean like you?"

"Hey, that was one time!" Tony protested, though there was a teasing glint in his eyes. "And I still maintain that Mr. Johnson was asking for it."

I knew the story all too well. Tony had gotten in a fight with a teacher who had been picking on him for weeks. Eventually it escalated into a physical altercation that got him suspended for a month.

I lightly punched his shoulder. "Hey man, I don't mean to intrude on whatever you do in your personal time or whatever. But what was the deal with you not getting in on the game last Friday."

"I was looking for Dawn. She's got a new friend or whatever and has been ignoring my calls. But that's okay because I'm going to get her today," he said with a devious grin. "I'm just pissed that she's acting like she couldn't hang."

"But that's how most girls are to tell you the truth. They will cling to you like a leech, but when someone more interesting comes around, they forget all about you," I said with a shrug.

"Yeah, well, Dawn and I have been together for three years now. She knows not to play games with me," Tony grumbled.

"Her friend, it's not a dude, right?" I asked.

"No way! It's some chick from Russia or whatever. Well, Dawn said she's from Massachusetts, but the girl sounds Russian."

I nodded, still not sure why Tony had to be so possessive of Dawn. But I knew better than to question it. A message pinged on Tony's phone, which he immediately unlocked and read. He then looked up and scanned the bustling courtyard, saying, "She said she's here. I'm gonna go find her."

"Well, I'm not gonna hold you. Ima head to my locker," I said, not really wanting to stick around for their love fest. "See you later, dude." His knuckles bumped my shoulder before he began walking briskly away.

I stowed my backpack in the locker, spinning the combination with a satisfying click. I then turned to face the crowded hallway where swarms of my peers moved around. With a sigh, I merged into the flow of traffic, instantly irritated by the constant jostling of elbows and shuffling of feet.

"Yo what up JJ." El-Train hollered, his familiar white teeth sparkling as he approached.

I managed a nod as our hands clasp, snapping our fingers together out of habit. We used to be partners in crime - stealing, fighting, going to church together. That's until grandma shut that down, then we've grown apart. We were raised in the same apartment complex and have one class together, but even then we only talk in the halls. I guess people just change.

"Look who's out here serenading the hallways this early morning," I teased, as he handed me a small brown bag. I inspected it immediately, "What's this?"

"My moms figured you dashed out without breakfast again. Ham, egg, and cheese. Eat up, lover boy."

I inspected the contents: a ham, egg and cheese sandwich, still warm. My stomach rumbled.

"Tell Auntie I said thanks," I muttered, peeling back the wrapping. The delicious aroma hit me instantly.

El-Train leaned in, "What you been up to fam, any new conquests? C'mon, spill."

I took a savage bite of the sandwich, chewing slowly. "A gentleman never kisses and tells."

El-Train guffawed. "Yeah, whatever. I'll catch you later, playboy."

As he walked off, I savored the flavors in my mouth, but it didn't last long. Out of my peripheral vision, I saw Destiny, a girl with box braids gliding towards me with a note in her hand.

Here we go again, I thought bitterly. Not that I minded attention from females - in fact, I'd cultivated my reputation as a legendary ladies man on purpose. But lately, the thrill had faded. Each flirtation tasted stale, the conquests blurring into an endless reel of mindless repetition.

"My friend Cherish said this for you." Destiny said, handing me a note with a playful smile.

As I read the perfumed-drenched love letter from Cherish, I couldn't help but smile. "Where she at?" I asked, scanning the bustling hallway for this mysterious Cherish, but she was nowhere to be found.

"She hiding in Ms. Johnson class." Destiny sassed, running her fingers through her braids. "Cherish! He's looking for you!" she shouted dramatically towards the open door of a classroom.

I licked my lips, "Tell your girl to stop playing games," I said, tucking the note in my pocket as I walked away backwards. When I turned to face forward, that's when the bozo of all bozos came barreling his shoulder into mine, scuffing up my fresh sneakers without so much as an apology.

"Yo Khyree, you got a problem?! Whassup?" I snapped, pulling up my uniform pants and puffing out my chest as I sized him up.

Khyree just smirked arrogantly and adjusted his outdated Pikachu beanie, that he didn't know how to take off.

"My bad, Jamison. I didn't see you." he winked, before sauntering away.

I sucked my teeth and gave him a dismissive wave. "Aight." I played it cool, but inside, my blood boiled at the injustice. Khyree Latimore had always been in my shadow, constantly trying to one-up me no matter what I did. It's like he's obsessed.

Watching him walk away, I couldn't help but how cool we could've been if he wasn't so insecure. Khyree a foster kid and like me we both came from hard places, so we should've had some common ground. But no. He got "adopted" by the hoity-toity Latimores, who smothered him with money and attention just to make themselves look good. Their 'caring family' act made me sick.

I saw their true manipulative colors years ago, when this feud started in middle school. I had become romantically involved with Donica Williams, who you'd come to know was my best friend and was now the ghost queen of my night terrors. Of course Khyree had a thing for her too. That boy never could handle rejection well. Mommy and Daddy Latimore knew it too, and they used Donica's family's money troubles to try and bait her into choosing Khyree. They put fancy jewelry and big wads of cash right in Donica's hands, promising more if she picked him over me. But the crazy part was - she still chose me in the end! Not that it mattered...

Now we're here in our Senior Year of highschool, locked in this never-ending feud. The tension between us only grew stronger with every passing day. It was only a matter of time before things came to a head.

When the bell rang, I headed to my first-period class, French. I had no idea how this class was going to benefit me in the real world when the ideal foreign language was Spanish. But hey, at least I finally got a place to sleep—hint; reason for me being secretly quiet this morning.

Last night's dream was a vivid replica of my usual night terror.

A piercing scream echoed through the air. She looked at me with terror-filled eyes, her mouth agape, releasing a sudden gush of thick red liquid. Our memories forever tainted with her blood.

The memory of how she had fallen into a heap at my feet, heart-wrenching sobs gutting her as she choked on her blood that morning, still haunted me.

Silence wasn't a trait of our bustling neighborhood, but in that moment when that stray bullet struck her, it felt like the city held its breath.

I watched as she crumpled like a puppet with torn strings. Panic clawed up my throat, as she grabbed onto me, causing me to fall and press my hands against the cold concrete. "Donica!" My shout echoed off the brick walls that lined the alley we'd claimed as ours since we were kids.

A halo of dark kinky curls framed her face, her skin was a smooth dark complexion. This wasn't Donica who outran me at every sprint, who could talk her way out of any trouble with a sly grin. Blood continued to spurt from her lips, staining my shirt and hands. Fear surged through me as I tried to unlatch her fingers from me.

I was confused, asking her why she wouldn't let go of me because I… I was afraid. Selfish. Even after three years, my nightmares reminded me of that singular moment every night, just like clockwork. The sound of guns firing, and her knees buckling as she fell from my life will haunt me forever. Donica's death was still chasing me, and it always will.

I slumped into my seat, staring blankly at the whiteboard as the teacher droned on in French. Once again, my thoughts wandered back to that fateful day, the day my life had changed forever. The day I lost the only person I ever truly loved. I shook my head, trying to push the memories away, knowing that I couldn't dwell on the past forever. It was already driving me crazy. I needed to focus on the present, on school, and on my future. But it was so hard to focus when the pain felt so present, so raw, and so fresh as if it had happened yesterday. How was I supposed to cope when the memories kept flooding in, threatening to drown me in sorrow?

"Bonjour, comment ça va?" The teacher interrupted my thoughts, causing me to jump in my seat.

"Uh, ça va bien," I replied automatically, my mind still elsewhere. After that, the lesson dragged on, the teacher's voice becoming a distant hum. My classmates chatted amongst themselves in French, but I couldn't bring myself to join in. I was too lost in my own thoughts.

I recalled seeing the lights of an ambulance turn onto our block. Donica's parents were sobbing on the doorstep while the paramedics approached, and Grandma was trying to comfort her. I just stood there frozen, unable to budge.

They tried their best as parents to keep her safe in this cursed city, but I just had to beg her parents to let her hang on a school night. She was only fourteen years old, and will forever be. And I was at fault for it.

That day at the hospital was my first long and truly miserable night. It was long and the chaos was scary. She had doctors and nurses in and out of her room, but I still felt strained. She was my best friend and I felt obligated to care for her. I loved her. I remember pacing back and forth in the waiting room, sitting on the cold dirty floor without a care. Keeping an ear out for anything unusual so I could rush to her aid. Nothing ever happened, just silence... haunting silence every single minute. Sitting in that waiting room, my grandmother prayed longer than usual, spending the little time she could worshiping God, just hoping for a fiery miracle to act as a flaming fire to consume Donica's wounds until she was completely healed. Some people who came to visit from the church we attended all said the same thing. The women hugged me tight and whispered in my ears that there was gonna be a miracle, and I believed. I believed everything then. Because it was just unfair that my best friend of all people would be reduced to this miserable, dying state. I believed and hoped and prayed for a last-minute miracle.

Until that dreadful hour. The wailing cries of her grieving parents greeted me as I lifted my head from my knees. I hadn't even realized I'd fallen asleep. A shiver went through me as I stood up off the ground. My grandma took my hand and looked at me with bloodshot eyes, and I saw how much older and worn out she looked at that moment. The ordeal had really taken its toll. Donica was like a granddaughter to her, and I could see that her anguished eyes said what her mouth could not.

I shook my head, convincing myself that Donica was asleep. But when my grandmother whispered those two heart-wrenching words into my ear - "She's gone." - That made it final, and I ran out of that hospital, through the busy streets. I wasn't sure how many miles I ran but it didn't matter. When I made it back to the apartment, I locked myself in my bedroom. My whole body shivered uncontrollably. There was a lump in my throat and tears in my eyes, but they wouldn't fall. I couldn't breathe because my chest felt painfully tight.

I stayed like that until an hour later, when Grandma broke the door's lock in a panic after repeatedly hollering my name but received no response. She flew inside and held me tightly as she cried bitterly into my shoulders. My tears finally came out then, free-flowing, making my chest constrict even more painfully. I wasn't breathless anymore. I felt a heaviness. I didn't have a name for the feeling and I don't know how long we stayed like that, but I remembered the aftermath all too well.

Numbness.

I went through the funeral in a haze. Staying out of conversations, getting polite hugs from church members, the pastor, friends, everyone. I weaseled out of giving a speech after Grandma gave hers in between sniffling and dabbing her eyes. Eventually, I lost touch with everything—sports, school, and especially church.

I was never really a devout churchgoer to begin with, but Donica was always able to convince me to go along with her. I attended Sunday school and was generally an average teen churchgoer. I thought I had a relationship with God, but with Donica gone, it didn't make any sense to continue. I couldn't stand the sympathy and condolences I got when I went. Grandma kept going, and that was when our rift started growing. The rift grew even wider when I started hanging around with the wrong crowd. I became affiliated with gangs and hung out on street corners. Grandma would pray and lecture me, which I now know was out of love. But back then? I was so eager to get out of the house because I was so suffocated by the constant arguments and quiet, lonely nights.

Grandma played her hand and soon I ended up in the one school I would have never chosen if I had a choice. The religiousness was not only restrictive but also extremely suffocating.

I could never return to how I used to be, even if I tried. I tried to pave a new path, starting with identifying as an atheist. After the funeral, I turned agnostic for a long time, unable to believe in the God that took my best friend away from me like that. I couldn't understand the reason why I had to go through that trauma, and finally it became clear that I could never go back to the church. After the religion part of my life was sorted, the next thing was school. I had to think about my future, and I needed to be independent. My new path in life couldn't accommodate my grandma and her praying warrior groupies. I would have chosen to quit school altogether, but I couldn't deny that the nerdy part of me enjoyed burying my head in dozens of books and scientific material.

Click, click.

Alerted by the heavy class door opening, I lifted my head. *I had fallen asleep... again.* I rubbed my eyes and sat up as an unfamiliar girl passed my desk. Normally, I couldn't care less about my classmates - I barely even recognized half of them with my constant napping habit. But this girl was different. She could have been new, or maybe she was just quiet and I had never noticed her before.

44

It was a double period, so there was no need to move, so my eyes followed her across the class as she timidly circled the room. I concluded that there was no way she belonged in this class. How did I know? Well, she just followed a few random students who had just come in for the second period before nervously sitting in the chair next to me, which everyone knew was reserved as my makeshift footrest. Plus, she avoided the teacher completely instead of handing him her schedule, so she was definitely lost.

I yawned as the teacher re-addressed the class, and I noticed a few funny expressions around me. My classmates were looking at me like I knew this girl. So, I tried to play it cool like I didn't even notice her sitting next to me. But then the girl's pen flew out her hand, and the whispers and snickering grew louder like something was genuinely funny. I rolled my eyes and sighed, deciding to help her out since most of my classmates were being jerks and making it obvious that they were talking about her. I also noticed some other boys plotting. So, being the gentleman I was, I decided I'd be the first to strike up a conversation with her before any of them could get a word in.

Chapter Five: Sidell

The heavy door slammed shut behind me as I entered the stuffy classroom. It reeked of cheap deodorant and fresh pencil shavings choked my senses. Row after row of uniformed teenagers jostled and elbowed each other for space. The teacher at the front, wearing a silver blazer over his collared shirt, was surrounded by about thirty students who were eyeing me like detectives examining a suspect. My heart thudded in my chest as I scanned their unfamiliar faces — staring back at me with curiosity and judgment. I was definitely in the wrong class and, worse, maybe the wrong building entirely. My mind reeling, I scrambled for an excuse that would sound authentic. But I told myself no! I was not about to admit defeat and walk back out of the room with my tail between my legs just to continue aimlessly wandering around the school corridors.

The teacher adjusted his eyeglasses before casting an impatient glance my way. I automatically assumed that he wanted me to take a seat because I was prolonging his lecture. So without another glance his way, I hurried to find an empty chair.

My heart raced as I searched the aisles, but every chair seemed to be taken by someone with a scowl or a disinterested look. Just when I thought I was doomed to stand for the entire class period, I spotted an open chair next to a boy slumped over his desk, barely awake as he scribbled in a notebook. Avoiding eye contact at all costs, I pulled out my pen from my bag and pretended to be engrossed in the lesson. But it wasn't long before I noticed people whispering and openly staring at me.

"Who's that girl?"

"Is she new or something?"

My face flushed as I sank lower in my seat. Great first impression, I thought sarcastically. I was already the subject of gossip on my first day. I sighed, wondering how long it would take for the rumors about the bumbling new girl to spread through the halls. Struggling to drown out the murmurs, I focused on the teacher, who was droning on in French. The clock above the door ticked by slowly - 9:15am. If I escaped now, I could still make my actual second period class. But it was like I was glued to the chair, which was oddly comfortable. I wanted to melt into the material and disappear. Then my sweaty hand decided to betray me, as my pen slipped from my fingers and clattered loudly on the linoleum floor. I cringed, feeling all eyes turn to me as the snickers and giggles grew louder. And there it was, my pen mocking me from halfway across the room. Cupping my hands over my flushed cheeks, I desperately tried to cool them down. *Could this day get any worse?*

"Pst. Pst." The boy beside me used his fingers to drum a soundless tune on my table. The gesture took me by surprise, and I was scared to look up at him. His hands were covered by black fingerless gloves, leaving his brown skin visible. I took a few deep breaths to bring my face back to its normal color before looking up and facing the mystery boy who had been trying to get my attention.

My gaze flicked over to him, and I was met by his dimpled smile. His eyes burned into mine, but they were warm and striking despite the ordinary brown shade. His Afro-textured hair was shaped in a perfect low flat-top, and the single gold hoop earring in his left ear glinted under the classroom light.

His lips barely moved as he whispered his tempting offer. "If you wanna make a getaway and don't know how, I can help you..."

I looked away from him, my attention snagged as if by a fishing hook, and glanced at the teacher who was still droning on in French. I then shifted my attention back to the boy who had just offered me a chance to escape.

"I've had the time to come up with plenty of excuses, so you don't have to worry," he continued, smiling, and I realized that I've not said anything in response to his small talk. I've just been staring wide-eyed at him like the scatterbrain that I was.

"Oh, uh, that's nice. Uhm, sorry, I meant that'll be great. I do want to leave… Thank you. I guess. Sorry, my head is not in its best state right now," I said in one breath, kicking myself for stuttering like an idiot. He stared at me so intently, like I was some sort of science project and I couldn't help but feel even more flustered. Oh god, was my face turning red again?

"First day fever?" he said and his eyes crinkled at the edges as he smiled.

Blinking slowly, I was unable to string two words together, like I had suddenly lost all ability to speak.

"Just follow my lead." He winked and my blush deepened even more. "Mr. Auclair, I need to help out the new girl, she's got an appointment with her chaperone," he said, getting out of his chair as smoothly as a feline, and before the teacher could even look our way, he was already on his way out.

I looked at the teacher as he did a slight eye roll in my direction as though the situation was nothing new and he didn't care if I stayed in his class or not. My charming escort already had his hands on the door, looking back at me impatiently, which was what got me out of the chair and moving fast. Every head in the classroom turned in my direction as I made my way to the door. Within five seconds, I was in the hallway with my new friend. He motioned for me to follow him. His strides were long, while mine weren't, so he slowed down multiple times to match my pace. The simple gesture tugged at my heart. I'm generally clumsy, but I had to put in extra effort not to bump into him even though we were walking very closely together. He pushed through the double doors leading outside, holding them open for me. They closed behind me with a bang.

"Did you actually mean you had an excuse to get yourself out of class rather than for me to get out with less embarrassment?" I threw the accusation at him even though my mouth curled into a smile. The fresh outdoor air helped untie my tongue and bring my flushed face back to normal.

"Ah, you got me. You were my ticket to get out of class," he said, pinching his bottom lip. It was the most effortlessly attractive thing I had seen in a while. I rarely stared at men this way, so it took me by surprise. All the men in my life could be counted on one hand, and they included my dad and my pastor. Male friends at church were kind of out of the question.

"I think you owe me then," I said, taking a fleeting look around. It was like I was in the middle of nowhere again. I really needed to start doing better with locations.

"Hm. Do I? You got out of the class. I think we're fair." He shrugged his shoulders, and I had to tell myself to stop taking note of every single gesture he made with his body.

"I need to get to my class or at least familiarize myself with the school so this doesn't happen again." The morning sun was out, causing me to squint in his direction.

He stared at me openly as he rocked on the balls of his feet a few times. He's probably deciding if I'm worth his time.

I hope I am.

He leaned in as he finally asked, "What was your first period?"

"Uhh...." I unzipped my flat small purse and began rummaging through it for my folded schedule. Once I found it, I skimmed through it nervously as I could sense him watching me. "It's uh...geometry....843," I said, slipping the creased paper back into my purse before zipping it up.

He let out a low whistle. "Geometry first thing in the morning? Cruel and unusual punishment if you ask me."

"Gee thanks," I muttered.

"But yeah, uh, you're right over there. You don't want to pass when the time comes around and be late." He pointed at the castle-like building on the other end of the courtyard and I sighed in relief.

"Ohh. Right, I hope not." I almost did a facepalm, feeling dumb because now I had a reputation of walking around the school like eight times.

"Come, I'll take you." And with that, he gestured for me to continue walking with him.

We got into stride walking side by side, close but not touching. I stole a glance at my phone. It was now past 9:45 a.m. My class would end in fifteen minutes, so any hope of making it in time was dashed, but I wasn't about to mention that.

"My government name is Jacky Jamison, but I go by JJ or just Jacky," he said as I turned to peer at his side profile. I took a moment to analyze his uniform. He wore a dark green blazer, a thin gold chain necklace over a black T-shirt with dark green dress pants. With his hands deep in his pants pockets, he caught my eyes lingering on him for a moment too long. I cleared my throat as I couldn't even hide my smile.

"Sorry." I laughed bashfully. "My mind was elsewhere; I go by Sid."

"Sid? Hmp. Is that a shortened form of Sidell?" he asked and I felt as if a bubbly joy was about to spill out of me. I couldn't explain it, but him being able to guess my name so quickly gave me a warm feeling in my chest.

"Yea!" My grin was brighter than the sun.

"Delighted to make your acquaintance, Sidell." He paused in front of the white two-story building. "And, we are here," he announced before breaking into another broad smile.

"Thank you. I must have been daydreaming this morning."

"Don't trip. It happens. This school may be small, but it can still be hard to navigate."

For a moment, we just stood there with nothing to say or do, both awkwardly taking in the surroundings but refusing to make eye contact.

"Anyways, thank you once again, JJ. I think I missed the class already," I finally said, filling in the silence.

"Want a proper tour of *Chi-Town*?" he asked with his easy half smile. "I wanted to leave the class so I could ditch school completely, but I think I can give you a tour on my way. Are you familiar with the city?"

"Here, Downtown? No. I live in the Uptown area, you know, the stereotypical suburbs with picket fences," I said with a stupidly proud grin. He laughed at my faux modesty.

"Oh yeah, you're royalty. You know many people who attend this school live in that area and are stuck up, prancy people, like most of the chaperones here. Have you met the Head Master by any chance?" he asked with a laugh.

"Unfortunately, yes. And she definitely put a bad taste in my mouth. I met her earlier while trying to get directions. She looked like a Victorian librarian, Ms. uh..."

"Ms. Kyepher," we both said in unison, and I couldn't help but laugh out loud.

"Yooo, she gets on my nerves. She is so cutthroat and preachy. You don't even have to say nothin' to her and she's still gonna study you as if you live on the wild side," JJ rambled in a patronizing tone.

"That is hilarious because that's exactly what she did to me!" I managed to say through my laughter while wiping real tears from my eyes.

JJ inhaled deeply and blew out his breath loudly. "That lady is something else, man."

I yawned. "Oh boy!" I sighed as my laughter subsided. Out of the blue, I began to feel hungry.

"Hey, do you know if the cafeteria is still open? It's an emergency," I said with dramatic despair in my voice, really wishing that I hadn't starved myself that morning.

"There's a vending machine in the teacher's lounge but that's off-limits most of the time. Other than that, the cafeteria doesn't stay open during lessons. It opens again at lunchtime, around 12:30 p.m.," JJ said with a hint of understanding in his voice. "There *is* a diner outside of the school grounds though, but we may have to dodge a few security guards. That's if you're up to it. I don't want to drag you into anything and get you in trouble."

My pulse flared with excitement as JJ suggested the risky option. I hesitated, thinking of the possible repercussions if my parents were to find out I ditched class. Especially with a boy. However, I was captivated by the idea of a daring escapade with JJ. His wide grin had already won me over.

"Sure, I'll go." I grinned back at him. I then quickly added, "But wait, will we be able to get back in?"

"Oh yeah," JJ assured me. "I have my ways, I never pass security twice."

"Well, then I should probably warn you now. I can be very anxious at times, so please forgive me if I panic when we see the guards the first time."

"Nah, you good. I don't mind. Trust me, I'm patient. See, I already dedicated the whole morning to you," he said with his infectious smile. "Since you did help me get out of class," he added, nudging me playfully.

"Oh yeah? Great. I guess I can try to show out since you're dedicating the morning to me and all." I flipped my bangs off my cheek playfully. It made him laugh out loud, showing off that perfect smile.

After successfully sneaking past the school's security guards and chaperones, we soon walked into the lively city. JJ led us to a diner called "Janda's Kitchen," which was his favorite spot. He shared that he was raised by his grandmother and that Janda's Kitchen was the closest thing to his grandma's cooking. The diner was a small-cozy room flooded with warm indoor lighting, comfortable booths, old-fashioned dining tables, and a long counter, with circular swirling stools. A jukebox was tucked in the corner and behind the counter were photos of some famous people who had a meal in the establishment; It was retro and I liked it.

The friendly middle-aged African American woman with the pixie haircut must have been Janda herself. She was a heavy-set woman though she floated gracefully around the room as she manned the place, the brace on her leg not seeming to hinder her at all. As she greeted us with her warm Southern drawl, you could already tell the food was going to be delicious.

After serving another customer, she approached our table with a notepad and pen, ready to copy down our orders. She was smiling widely at us like she had a special little secret.

"Hey how you doing, Jacky? It's good to see you again. How's your grandmama doing?" Janda asked him with a smile and a slight nod of her head.

"Oh, she's still smacking me silly. You know how she is." JJ grinned, making Janda swat at him playfully with a dish towel.

"Oh, hush up now!" She laughed boisterously, her voice resonating in the diner.

Their interaction captivated me; I couldn't help but crack a smile. Janda turned to me and lightly tapped my shoulder. "How you doing there, young lady? I don't think I've seen you here before."

"...No, this is my first time," I answered shyly, my blue eyes averting from her brown-eyed gaze.

"Me and Sid go to school together," JJ chimed in as if trying to extinguish any notion that we were dating. Janda grinned as her eyes shifted between me and JJ, perhaps suspecting something else.

"Okayyyy, if you say so," she drew slowly. "So, what can I get for you two this early in the morning?" she beamed.

JJ courteously extended his arm, showing me the menu and allowing me to place my order first. His politeness bemused me. Having male friends was new to me, as I had only ever been acquainted with a few while in the youth group at my family's old church. And from my observation, all the guys acted like immature brats, but with JJ, it was different. We had just met an hour ago, and yet I already felt like he really respected me.

"I'll have the cinnamon French toast with extra butter..." I murmured, my gaze shifting away from the menu.

"And for the sides?" she inquired, her pen scratching rapidly across her pad.

"Bacon....and scrambled eggs," I answered.

"Drink?"

"Cranberry juice," I replied. JJ's eyebrow quirked but he said nothing, turning his attention to his own menu.

"Alrighty, and for you?" she asked JJ, her smile radiant despite her worn-down face.

"I'll have the three stack waffles with the spicy sausage and orange juice," he replied, meeting her gaze with a warm smile of his own.

"Oh, and can we get two straws, please?" I chimed in.

"No problem, hun, it'll be right up.... I'll put a rush on your orders." She reassured us before scooping up the menus, then disappearing behind a door that led into the kitchen.

I drummed my fingers on the table, biting the inside of my cheek. I could feel JJ's eyes on me as he asked, "Do you have something against normal breakfast beverages?" His tone was jovial yet curious as he leaned in.

I bit my lip. "Well, people don't usually choose cranberry juice as their first choice, do they?"

I knew my mother despised me when I replied to a question with a question, but it wasn't my mother that I was talking to. Instead of a disapproving frown, JJ rewarded me with a cute smile.

"Nah, not really, but it's probably not your fault you've got funky tastebuds," he teased, making me laugh at his easy-going nature.

"For your information, cranberry juice is healthy. It helps flush out toxins in the female-" I stopped in my tracks right before repeating what Mom had said about cranberry juice. It would be wildly inappropriate to elaborate on a topic like that with a guy I barely knew.

"What were you going to say?" JJ wondered, challenging me with a mischievous grin on his face. I felt nervous all of a sudden. The butterflies in my stomach did a nosedive as I started to turn red. I should've just kept my mouth shut.

Thankfully, my awkwardness was interrupted by Janda's voice. "There we go, one cranberry juice and one orange juice! Here's your straws."

"Yay, straws! I love straws!" I said, trying to act natural.

JJ chuckled as he scrunched his face up. "Yeah, me too," he said as he ripped the paper off his straw.

★ ★ ★ ★ ✞ ★ ★ ★ ★

The second our dishes were placed on the table, I clasped my hands together and bowed my head to pray. JJ clearly did not have the same thought, already claiming the syrup to drip over his waffles.

I muttered a quick blessing under my breath before taking a bite of bacon. I chewed slowly, watching JJ wolf down his food, stopping only when he noticed my judgmental stare. I smirked and he sheepishly slowed down.

He's cute.

JJ wiped his lip with the back of his hand. "Ask me a question," he demanded, leaning closer with a roguish grin.

"Like what?" I asked, scooping a forkful of eggs.

He smirked. "A better one than that."

"Wait, that wasn't my —! You're impossible. Fine. Why don't you like being in class?" I challenged him, with a hint of a smile.

"Because ditching is more interesting," he answered like it's obvious. "Why did you follow me, Ms.Sidell?"

"Because you promised food," I sassed, arching my eyebrow.

JJ threw back his head and laughed. "Fair enough. Still, you don't know me."

"I know a little more now," I said. "Though not enough to determine if you're actually worth my time."

I blushed, immediately regretting my bluntness.

He chuckled, a smug grin spreading across his face. "Oooooh, aight then." He nodded.

I leaned over and playfully tapped his fingers while laughing. "No, seriously though, it's my turn to ask a question."

"Alright," he grinned and I relaxed back into my seat.

"Hmm... let's see... what do you think happens when we *die?*" I asked.

He raised an eyebrow and visibly pondered this, accepting the challenge. "I think . . . everything just goes black and quiet, and then our bodies return to the earth."

"Oh," I said, a little disappointed. *Shoot! He's not a man of God.* At that moment, every Bible verse I'd ever memorized flooded my head. Specifically the verses about being unequally yoked with unbelievers. But then I remembered that I wasn't looking for a man to spend my life with. I was just looking for a friend. I think?

He shrugged nonchalantly. "Who knows? Why, do you believe differently?"

"Mmn, differently," I muttered while aimlessly moving my fork around on my plate.

We lingered in comfortable silence, and I thought of Philippians 4:7: "And the peace of God, which surpasses all understanding, will guard your hearts and your minds in Christ Jesus." The words echoed through me like a mantra, propelling me to speak them aloud, but I settled for letting them simmer in my soul.

"So," JJ's persistent smile asked for my attention, "do you want to enjoy my magnificent company some more?"

My own smile stretched across my face as I nodded.

"Uhm, yeah." I took a sip of my drink, batting my eyelashes back at him.

He gave a mock bow and cheesed. "Cool."

I laughed at his goofy nature. We sat there in a daze as we finished our breakfast, completely absorbed in our own world.

I wasn't sure what it was about him, but it felt like I'd known him for a very long time, much more than these last few hours we've spent together. And I wanted to know everything about him, about his family, his life; anything he was willing to tell me.

Well, that's a scary thought. Why was I so interested in knowing him? How did I already care so much? I didn't even know that I was capable of letting new people into my heart, but if every conversation with Jacky was like this, learning more about each other and talking like this, I knew that he was about to nudge his way right in there.

Chapter Six: JJ

Maybe I'm a bad influence. Or maybe I'm just a teen who's willing to do whatever to have fun with someone new. I'm surprised this girl, Sid, agreed to tag along with me on my little escapade. I would've painted her as the goody-two-shoes type, always running off to her next class without a second thought.

It couldn't be a coincidence she had decided to sit by me, considering she's the "Russian chick" that Tony was talking about earlier. The same one that happened to be friends with his girl Dawn. But I didn't mention it at all to Sid because it didn't feel relevant to what we had going on. But I could definitely see why Dawn liked hanging with her more than Tony. For some reason, I liked spending time with Sid too. I wanted to get to know her better. She's a pretty cool miss, down-to-earth sort of girl, unafraid to laugh at herself, even at her own expense. She's the kind of girl who could keep up with my humor, but she could sometimes be a bit gawky. But it was the kind of awkwardness you had to love. But most of all, I respected the way she listened to me like I was the center of her world.

By now, we were crossing at the streetlight to get back to the school. Even though we had just left Janda's kitchen, the new memories of the time we spent there stuck in my mind. It made me think about the serenity I used to feel so long ago when Donica would come to watch me play football. We used to offer up a quick prayer before sealing it with our secret handshake. I can still hear her voice cheering for me from the stands, louder than anyone else's. Back then, I felt embarrassed, but also happy, and privileged all at once, but most of all, I felt at peace.

I shook off the nostalgia as my eyes caught sight of something glimmering on the ground.

"Oh, look, a quarter!" I exclaimed, snatching the money off the pavement.

Sidell giggled beside me, finding amusement in almost everything I did or said.

"Seriously? Didn't you just pay for our lunch? What do you need that for?"

"No one's ever too rich to pass on a quarter," I shot back with a smirk. "Plus, we can share a Mike and Ike's or something. There's a corner store right there."

The entrance bell to the liquor store echoed in our ears as we stepped into the murky establishment. I moved slowly, assessing my surroundings as Sid followed me with her gaze. The store clerk, a bronze-toned man with an unruly rich black beard, lurked behind the protective glass window, pretending to read a magazine while keeping one eye on us as if we were about to commit a crime. He was acting as if I didn't shop there all the time.

I let Sid get anything she wanted.

"Do you work? Is that how you were able to pay for my lunch and all this stuff?" she asked as I grabbed a variety of candy from the shelves.

"I've tried a few different jobs here and there, but no employers are exactly hot for me at the moment. So nah, I get an allowance from my grandma every month. You know, doing all the manly stuff around the house, like taking out the trash."

Sid's lips curled into a smirk as she pointed a pack of starbursts at me for emphasis. "A girl can take out the trash too," she said coolly. "It's not exclusively a man's duty. I've done it plenty of times before."

My trademark grin spread across my face as I teased her. "Yeah, but y'all do it with disgust. We boys do it so we have an excuse to show off our sweat and muscle shirts." I winked as I threw a bag of M&Ms into the air and then caught them in one hand with flair.

"Oh God." Sid laughed as we moved towards the checkout counter. We exited the store after purchasing our items, but not before I made sure to count the three crispy twenty-dollar bills in full view of the store clerk, a smirk on my face.

I'd gotten pretty crafty when it came to ditching. So, as we snuck back on campus, security wasn't an issue. I led Sidell through what I called "a safe cut", escorting her through the football field. There was a small, damaged area in the wired fence in which we used to enter the school grounds. The sun beamed brilliantly in the sky as we walked over the spray-painted numbers printed on the field, and I retold an old story of how skeletons still walked the school grounds and haunted the halls. Sidell giggled, of course, not taking me seriously at all.

Since it was lunchtime and we had already eaten, I insisted that I continue giving her a tour of the school, just so she wouldn't get lost again.

"Let's start with the legendary Disciples Den. Slight side note, when I was a sophomore, I didn't really get the hype," I said as we walked towards the popular student hangout.

"Okayy..." Sid's reply sounded overly excited and I figured she was having a good time with me. I smiled at her as I continued to lead her on our little impromptu tour.

"Of course, the main attraction is the famous medieval large red door, which leads to the ancient atrium with an open-air sanctuary, once frequented by a secret society known for their magic potions," I spoke with a spooky charm and Sidell laughed lightly in response as I pushed open the large red door to the Disciples Den. She looked up at the gothic stained-glass ceiling while I led her through, and when she stepped onto the main path of the courtyard, she turned around to smile at me in awe as if she finally understood why this place was so popular.

The place was pretty dope. The trees formed an archway on either side of the pathway. The weather was still warm at this time of year, so the trees were a vibrant, flourishing green. There were loads of students traveling back and forth, some pausing to take pictures and others lounging on the benches or just chatting with friends. I matched Sidell's slow pace, taking small breaks as I skimmed my finger across her schedule..

"Dang. It's too bad that we don't have any classes together.." I said, gripping her schedule as the wind threatened to snatch it away.

"Really?" She asked excitedly, her gaze bouncing between me and the schedule as she came closer to take a look. A beautiful blush bloomed on her cheeks, making my heart skip a beat.

"Yep, it would have been cool to have you as a study partner." I said regretfully, licking my lips.

Our eyes met and locked in an unceasing gaze. I could feel my face flushing under the heat of her blue stare. With a slight tremble, I gulped and slowly turned away, embarrassed of how I had become so consumed by her in such a short time. My throat became dry, and I cleared it. After a minute or so, I smoothly changed the subject with a weak attempt at humor.

"And now I present to you the most legendary Holy Ghost Hall!" I gestured grandly towards the magnificent building before me, bowing low in front of her with mock fanfare.

"I wouldn't have guessed that you'd have a goofy side to you because you don't look goofy at all," she said, playing with a lock of her hair. For some reason, I found her faint Russian accent calming.

"Danggg! Is that a good thing?" I teased, pinching my bottom lip in amusement.

"Yeah," she laughed and smiled warmly at me. "I mean, like, if I'm being honest, your features don't match your personality."

I laughed but started to doubt myself slightly. Maybe she thought this was a front, a faux personality that can be switched on and off.

As we continued to make our way throughout campus, I gave her the details on the buildings we came across. It was like something out of a futuristic yet urban picture. "This legendary masterpiece was built ages before we were born."

"I suspect your vocabulary is limited to sentences with only legendary in them," she said, laughing and raising her head to look up at the building before shooting me a playful smirk.

"Sheesh, you just keep on calling me out today." I huffed out a laugh, pressing my hand to my chest.

Before either of us could say a word, two girls approached us with a digital camera and asked me to take a picture of them with the Hall as background. I wanted to refuse but obliged with a smile and positioned the camera for the shots. The whole thing took about a minute, and the girls thanked me, giggling. They both gave me a lingering look before walking away, but I decided not to acknowledge it.

"So, you want to go in?" I said to Sidell as if the distraction didn't even occur.

"Yeah!" she said, following me into the building. Her eyes lit up as soon as we got inside, awe filling her face at the first sight of the cathedral-like structure. "What is this Hall used for?" she asked breathlessly.

"Hm. That is the million-dollar question. There are lots of classroom spaces and departments, and it is also used as a venue for the 'Crispy Fishers of Men Club,' whatever that is. And other times it's used for academic parties— with chaperones of course. And sometimes it's just a kick back spot." My hands were back in my pockets and I was staring at the ceiling, my brows furrowed together, focused.

"Hm, that's interesting." Her lips parted as though she was about to say something else, but she was interrupted by the sharp chime of the bell.

The sudden sound made her jump and bump into me. I got my hands out of my pants pockets fast enough to steady her.

"Sorry, that caught me off guard." A little giggle escaped her mouth as she pulled herself away from my grip, embarrassed.

I smirked. "Yeah right, you just wanted to hug me,"

"Oh shoot, you got me, that was my plan all along," she chuckled.

"Really!?" I replied, surprised to hear her confession. She rolled her eyes and smiled.

"Of course not," she said under her breath before giving me a playful shove. We grinned at each other and I gently shoved her in return.

We began walking up the staircase of the cathedral. "Thank you for taking your time to do this. I really appreciate it." Sid's voice echoed behind me as we were making our way to the second floor.

"You can pay me, if that will make you feel better," I said, getting to the top of the stairs before her.

"What?" she said as she reached me slightly out of breath, and I laughed at her expression.

"Nah, I'm playing. But I wouldn't mind hanging out with you some time. For free..."

She smiled at the thought. In return I gave her a cheeky grin and she got all bashful again.

"Whoa, hold on, what's that?" I asked, pointing randomly at her white collared shirt.
"What's what?" she asked, falling into my trap by looking down. I took my finger and wiped away a nonexistent piece of lint from around her chin.
"I think it's gone now," I said, flashing a wink her way.

"You're corny, you know that?" She lightly swatted my arm.

"If I show you something cool, will you promise to be my girlfriend?" I asked boldly, hoping that this playful banter between us would continue.

She batted her eyelashes as a deep grin spread across her lips. "I just met you," she said, suddenly adopting a poker face.

"But when you know you know! You know?" I shot back with a determined grin.

"Well, you still haven't won me over yet."

"Ah, so you're playing hard to get?" I tried to sound casual and let my gaze drift away. She pushed her shoulder against mine playfully, making me fake a stumble. I backed into the staircase railing, pretending to grip it for support while I groaned in pain.

She sputtered with laughter. "You're such a dork, oh my gosh."

Breaking character, I stood up and smiled.

"No, but for real cool whip, let me show you my favorite hot spot." I gently touched her elbow to guide her back down the stairs. We'd only known each other for two hours or so, and I knew that she already felt safe with me. She had told me about her Russian parents and how strict and reserved they were. And I felt for her because what teenager would want to be limited on what they can and cannot do?

"I think by the time we part, I would have incorporated legendary into my everyday vocab," she teased as we left the building.

"That would be legendary," I said, unable to stop smiling. She burst into a fit of giggles. We walked through the courtyard, the beauty of the girl I'm walking with and the surrounding scenery not lost on me.

"So far, this day has turned out way more positive than I could have imagined or even prayed for. If every day goes like this, with me being able to interact with random people, build bonds, talk freely and genuinely enjoy myself outside of my parents' peripheral, then I'm up for a prosperous first semester," Sid said in relief.

I smiled even though I didn't share her sentiment. I was only here at this school to graduate with high honors and make my grandma proud. I'd do almost anything to accomplish that. "Phew, we made it but it is packed," I said, observing the area.

The area was crowded. It looked like everyone in the whole school was in one place, as if they had planned this. Then it hit me: it was the back-to-school fall art exhibition, a chance for aspiring artists to show off the pieces they had been working on all summer.

The school's art gallery was an old industrial building, with towering windows and high ceilings that gave off a glow of creativity. Most of my peers were there, though not to paint or explore the various works of art.

They were there to flirt, make out, and create a facade of productivity instead of going to class. The chaperones were in the background, observing the scene with silent vigilance. I shifted my body to face Sid, standing close enough for her to hear me as I gave her a secretive smirk.

"Alright, if the place is too stuffy and we start smelling body odor, we'll dip. Fair? That way I'll have more time to win you over," I joked.

Her lips curled into a small smile. "Hah, we'll see about that," she replied teasingly as she crossed her arms.

"Oh, we will!" I said confidently, spinning around on the balls of my feet.

Thankfully, a painting station was still available. I made my way to the art supplies shelf, grabbing two palettes, a couple of paint brushes and various tubes of paint. I tried to grab too many things at once and began dropping several items. Without hesitation, Sidell helped me out. Her fingers gently brushed against mine. It was enough to set off a spark of fireworks in my chest, a sensation that spread all over my body. I caught her eyes brighten and a light blush appear on her cheeks.

As we made our way through the thick crowd, friends and acquaintances greeted me. Eventually, we found a vacant table with less activity. It looked like the perfect spot to set up. With paint trays and tools in hand, we sat down to work on creating some art. My arm brushed against Sidell's as we got comfortable, giving me that feeling again and I knew that I just wanted to be next to her.

We began competing against one another, trying to create the best versions of the same scenery. Sidell decided to paint the most beautiful mountains while I chose to depict a field of flowers. Then, I thought of combining our efforts and suggested Sidell help me add color and texture to my painting. We were sitting very close as I spoke gently to her and showed her how to change colors and use different techniques. That's when I found myself taking Sidell's hand in mine and guiding her with a paintbrush as I taught her how to create texture on the wooly lambs in the background of my painting.

"Here, I'll go again. What's the first thing that made you really happy today?" I asked as our hands moved in tandem, my brown eyes following our intertwined hands.

She thought about it. "Dawn. My friend, when she hugged me." she smiled to herself. "She was so excited that I was coming to school with her today. When she came by my house to pick me, she yelled my name and basically tackled me."

"Why wouldn't she?"

Sidell shrugged. "I don't know. I never really had a friend like her before," she admits freely. "She matters to me and I know I matter to her, even though she has a million friends and I'm literally nobody. It makes me happy."

"Nobody?" I echoed, looking up at her.

"It's not a bad thing," Sidell backtracked, meeting my gaze. Her entire body blushed when she noticed how intensely I watched her. "And before you say anything, I have plenty of self-worth, okay? It's just that sometimes I feel like a nobody." Sidell maintained her challenging eye contact.

"Well, you're not to me," I said with such certainty.

She forcefully laughed as she returned her gaze to the canvas. "Thanks, but I think you're missing the point."

"No, I get it. I just disagree."

She turned her head, her eyes only inches away from mine. "Fine," she said quietly. "I'll allow it."

Lost in each other's eyes we remained close, our entwined hands stopped dancing across the canvas. For a moment it was as if we were alone, and we were magnetically drawn to each other. I moved in closer, our lips almost touching, until my phone lit up and vibrated the table. I let go of Sidell's hand and shuffled away on the steel bench, embarrassed. She swallowed dryly and apologized. "Sorry."

Shaking my head, I replied reassuringly, "Nah you good." Although neither of us said a word about it, we both knew what had almost happened. She played it off well by looking around the room to make sure no one had spotted us.

As I read the message on my phone, my eyebrows furrowed upwards. The message that came in was not positive and I think Sid caught on to my change of demeanor, so I reassured her by turning off the screen and nestling the phone into my pocket.

I paused to think to myself before looking up at Sidell to address her. "That was my alarm. I have football practice today, so I need to go home and grab my gear. I totally forgot about it!"

"Oh, you play football?" Sid asked, seemingly interested. I didn't want to confront the sadness creeping up on me at the realization that a perfect day was coming to an end.

"Yeah, I just picked it up this school year. I used to play for a bit in Freshman year. But I, uh, had to quit for a while." I let my voice drift away.

"That's cool." She attempted to lighten the mood, jabbing the paint brush into the glass of water. I smiled in response even though I was having an internal dispute. I switched my focus elsewhere, so she didn't think that it had anything to do with her.

"Yeah," I said, deep in thought. The silence that followed was slightly awkward and laced with uncertainty.

"You do have the physique for football," Sidell said as she stood up from the bench.

"Come on, let's get out of here." She smiled encouragingly as if she could sense that my energy had changed. I stood up before staring at her as if she had suddenly grown a pair of horns.

"Thanks for the compliment," I said, a little more at ease. I flashed her one of my dazzling smiles as I followed her out of the crowded hall.

Chapter Seven: Sidell

The crisis was averted and thankfully, we didn't part awkwardly like strangers who hadn't just experienced the best few hours together. We made it back just in time for fifth period and JJ kindly walked me to my class, but we hung out by the lockers until the bell rang, geeked out by each other's presence.

"Share your contact with me? You might need help getting around. Who knows what class you might end up in without my help?" His eyes brimming with mischief, he whipped out his phone and looked at me expectantly.

"Oh please. That was a one-time mix-up," I said, sinking my hand into my purse.

"Yeah right," he said. I handed him my phone. As he gave me his, our fingers touched briefly and I felt a wave of electricity sizzle inside of me for the second time today. I think he felt the same, but I couldn't be sure. He returned my phone to me. I looked at the screen to find out he had saved his contact as "Legendary JJ."

I laughed and rolled my eyes.

"I'll catch you later, Sid," he said as soon as we reached my classroom.

I released a hopeless breath. "Okay." I forced a smile even though I desperately wanted him to stay. "I'll call you — whenever I get lost again, I mean. I promise."

He gave a single nod as he flashed me a warm, reassuring smile before turning on the heels of his sneakers.

As he slowly drifted down along the hallway, I peered into the class I was about to enter. I paused at the door and looked back to see him from afar looking over his shoulder at me, his hands in his pockets. I couldn't see his smile. I hurried inside my class, knowing then that I wouldn't have the courage to contact him first. I could only pray that he would try to contact me.

The remainder of the school day went surprisingly smooth. I only met my fifth and sixth period teacher as most of my day had been spent ditching. But none of my peers dared to introduce themselves; I think they found me strange because I kept randomly smiling. I blamed JJ for my behavior as I constantly replayed our time together inside my head.

When Dawn and I met up with each other in the parking lot after school, she noticed right away that something was different. Dawn gasped in amusement as she caught me blushing from ear to ear.

"Sidelllll, I wanna know." She laughed as she started her car. "Tell me, which one of these uniformed boys has got you whipped."

"Stopppp," I giggled, covering my burning cheeks with my hands and peeking at my reflection in the visor mirror. "Is it that obvious?"

"We're not leaving until you spill the beans, miss shyness!" Dawn joked, leaning back in her seat.

"Oh, my goodness, you are not going to let me…. Alright." I grabbed my phone, unlocked it and pulled up JJ's contact info. I placed one hand over my mouth as I held up the phone for Dawn to view.

"JJ!" She let out a high-pitched squeal, her eyes widening in excitement. She started bouncing up and down in her seat, which made me chuckle and break out into an awkward two-step dance against the car's floorboard. I couldn't help but join in her jubilation— it felt almost contagious.

★ ★ ★ ★ ✞ ★ ★ ★ ★

I bent over the kitchen sink, scrubbing my hands vigorously and trying to sneak a peek at my vibrating phone. Dawn had sent me a flurry of texts, wanting to know what JJ and I had discussed when we had been skipping class. I inconspicuously silenced my notifications.

The kitchen bustled with energy. The air was flavored with the sweet aroma of Makaroni Po-flotski and wafting steam from the simmering tomatoes. My father tended to the bubbling pot while my mother chopped fresh vegetables for salad at the dining table nearby. Cayest hovered close by, pestering my parents for help with her eighth grade math homework. Dad's deep voice reverberated through the kitchen as he asked me, in Russian, how school had been that day. His steely blue eyes held mine, searching for something deeper.

"It was good actually. Wasn't as stressful as I'd thought it would be. I definitely learned a lot," I answered his question in English, struggling to find the right words. Although I understood most of the Russian language, and knew a few words, I couldn't quite express myself in it yet.

"That's good," Dad said. "I trust in God that my daughter will stay away from any troublemakers." He dusted off my chin, his expression one of both pride and concern. I forced out a laugh, knowing it was already too late for that. Not to say JJ was trouble, of course.

"Have you made any new friends?" Mom asked, her voice stern and unwavering. I could feel her piercing eyes on me from across the room, daring me to lie. I didn't want to look back because Mom could always see right through me. I hesitated, not wanting to tell my parents about how my first day really went. From meeting a boy that ultimately led to ditching most of the day with him. But I was aware that if I ran away from the truth, I'd suffer the consequences.

I began drying my hands with a paper towel. "Yes, I did," I answered, terror scorching through my veins.

Mom's eyes brightened as she said, "Oh that's great–"

"My new friend is a boy…" I added hastily in an effort to avoid their judgmental assumptions.

My mother arched an eyebrow as she said, "Oh dear, it's a boy!"

They knew of my history when it came to trying to develop friendships with boys. I was very determined to make sparks happen whether it was with a boy I'd known for a while or a short time. But those friendships never seemed to crossover to the dating scene because my parents never allowed it.

It felt like an eternity of ensuing silence before I followed with, "He was kind and helpful."

My parents shot each other fearful glances, likely picturing a juvenile delinquent who had already polluted my innocence. I even caught Cayest gasping, her widened eyes dancing between me and my parents.

"I know what you're going to say," I said, hoping to console them, "but please believe me when I say that he's nothing like you're probably imagining. It was purely innocent. He helped me when I had gotten lost. I was trying to find my class and by mistake I ended up in his class… So he showed me where I had to go. And that was all."

One of Dad's eyebrows arched skeptically as he asked, "And he only escorted you straight there? Nothing else?"

My stomach sank. I replayed the day over in my head: departing school to grab a bite downtown, flirting on the staircase of an empty building with a strange boy, and nearly kissing him! *Yeah*, my parents would ship me to my grandparents in Russia in the blink of an eye. But then to my surprise, a feeling of relief inundated me when Dad didn't ask about it explicitly, meaning that I wouldn't have to lie.

"No, Papa. That was it."

Mom remained quiet as she chopped a cucumber and turned her gaze back to Dad. Cayest pretended she was still working on her math homework, but I could sense that she was eagerly waiting to see how my parents would react. Dad tightened the top cover of the pot and spun the knob to adjust the flame. He shifted his gaze away from me, avoiding eye contact as if I was sinful.

"Go do your homework upstairs," he commanded, dismissing me coldly. "I'll let you know when dinner is ready." His voice was hollow and unemotional, like he was forcing himself to be a disciplinarian. He winced once the words left his mouth.

An overwhelming feeling of shame settled in my heart, but I left the kitchen and shut the door to my bedroom. My emotions threatened to bubble over. Even though Dad's words were not harsh, his dull tone was enough to make me feel like I had done something wrong— something deserving of his disconnected reprimand… but had I?

★ ★ ★ ★ ✞ ★ ★ ★ ★

It was now 2 a.m. and everyone in my house was asleep except for me. Dinner had been tense and awkward, as I had expected. My parents were still clearly upset, probably blaming each other for allowing me to attend that school instead of the all-girls private high school that was closer to our house. I was on my bed, lying on my belly with my phone lit up. I held it up to my face as I told Nireska, an old family friend about my first day at the new school. I reverted back and forth from English to Russian as we talked. Even though she and her husband were the known gossipers in our family, I felt like she was the only one that seemed to be reachable.

I sniffed and wiped tears from my eyes as I spoke, "I know, I wasn't being honest to say that, because yeah, I ditched with him. But I couldn't tell them that! My mom, at dinner for instance, kept insisting that I needed to join some Christian youth groups or whatever, because she fears I'll be led by my 'flesh'. So, imagine if I told them what really happened! Not only that, but she is constantly reminding me that I'm reckless, which is a lie. I barely even left the house back in Massachusetts, so why doesn't she just admit that she and my dad are overprotective?"

"Well let me just say this. JJ, you said his name was?" Her accent thickened as she began to reprimand me. "Anything could have happened to you after leaving the school grounds with him. You don't know this boy, or if he had good or bad intentions. So, I do agree with your parents on that." I rolled my eyes before she quickly added, "I do understand where you're coming from, because I was seventeen once. Just because I'm saying this, don't think I don't understand; I grew up under the same traditional, Christian, Russian standards too. That's why I went through a rebellious phase with boys. Nevertheless, I encourage you to be wise and extra careful."

"Yes, I know. And I will be," I said as my eyes moved away from the phone and glanced around my dimly lit room.

"All I can say is I love you hun, and your parents do as well," Nireska said. "Yeah sure, it sucks that it may come in this form of do's and don'ts. But the fact that they care enough to correct you when you're wrong or protect you from danger... That ought to mean something. Some teens don't have that and end up with many issues."

"Yeah." I sighed before clearing my throat. "Sorry again, for calling you so late," I said. I rubbed my eyes, hoping that was a good enough hint for her to realize that I was sleepy and ready to get off.

"Oh no, I don't mind. Anytime." She paused, smiling through the silence. "I'm not going to hold you from your beauty sleep. I'm sure you have to get up early. But do give me a call sometime," Nireska said warmly as my sigh of relief released the tension that had started to grip me tightly.

"Alright, I will. Love you." My voice was layered with guilt and some regret.

I knew my parents meant well and they didn't always support my decisions, but sometimes I felt their behavior was too much. They liked to stand in the way of everything in my life and it's depressing. Every time I'd make a first step towards life beyond them, they seemed to revolve around me even more.

I tapped the red button and tossed the phone away from me. My only source of light now was the moonlight that was gaping through my window. Rolling over onto my back, I fastened myself beneath my polka dot comforter. My hair fanned out loosely across my pillow and purple tank top.

Dead air filled the atmosphere as I laid there, almost still. Gazing up at the ceiling, I whispered to the heavens, *"God, was I wrong today?"* I listened for some kind of answer, but none came. I valued God's opinion more than anyone's really.

"Lord, if JJ is what my parents assume, please don't allow a friendship to proceed any further. But if by Your will, JJ and I can be friends, I pray that You will work it all out. And as confirmation, if it's meant to be, please let me see him again." - Amen.

Chapter Eight: JJ

My cleats dug into the earth of the expansive football field as the summer sun ate at my back. I waited for the football to touch my hands but it never came. I honestly regretted coming to football practice today because no matter what I did, I couldn't concentrate on the field. That's probably why my teammates weren't gonna risk giving me the ball. Even if they did, I wouldn't have noticed because her light blue eyes were stuck in my head. And all I kept doing was berating myself for having acted weird during our last few minutes together.

With a clipboard in his hand and a whistle hanging around his neck, Coach Davis immediately noticed that I was distracted. "Mr. Jamison!" he called and signaled with two fingers for me to go to him.

I removed my helmet, relieved as a cool breeze drifted across my sweat drenched face. I jogged over to where he hung by the water cooler next to the wired fenced bleachers. "Yes Coach?" I asked, tugging at my jersey to fan myself from the heat.

"I can't have you daydreaming on my field when we have a game in a few weeks." He nudged his head over to the bench for me to sit down.

I nodded, obeying his unspoken command. I was aware that he could have just kicked me out of practice altogether, but he knew how well I could play when I was on the ball, so sometimes he went easy on me. I sat down on that bench, watching the other guys play passionately. I was wondering if I should call her right away for a chance to slip away so we could hang out some more. But it had not even been two hours since we last parted ways. I wanted to see her again, but I didn't want to seem pushy… or crazy.

What the hell was up with me? I didn't even know her last name.

It wasn't like I hadn't dated girls before. I was used to just going with the flow, so why did it feel different this time? That question kept nagging me during the rest of practice. As I came out of the locker room with the guys, I considered how I was never really interested in forming any type of relationship with the girls in my class. In fact, my nonchalant attitude and laid-back vibe had earned me a reputation. A lot of girls in school mistakenly thought I was a player.

I exited the sweaty locker room, my body and mind exhausted from practice. I wanted to take a cold shower to wash away all the sweat and grime of the day before heading home for an evening of rest. But as soon as I arrived in the two-bedroom apartment, I knew it would not be an ordinary night. When the droplets evaporated after my icy shower, I crashed onto my mattress, hoping for a restful sleep. But as usual, it was not to be.

I had the regular nightmare: Donica sobbing at my feet, her voice going from heart-rending sobs to cackles as she started pulling my legs. Terror took over my senses as I started sinking into the wood floor. Over the years her face has stayed the same, and it felt weird because I kind of expected her to age in my dreams also. But it was always the same thing, the terror of trying to scream but being unable to move. It was always the anchor to know when to wake up, and as per usual, I always woke up covered in a cold sweat. Would I ever find closure? I just wanted her ghost to leave me alone. But I was also afraid to forget what she had looked like in person, before that bullet ate into her flesh. I was conflicted. In a dark twisted way, I was sort of grateful for the nightmares… They kept my memory fresh.

It was cutting close to 7 p.m. by the time my grandma arrived home from her women's bible study at the church. She's now adorned in her floral nightgown with her signature gray afro tucked neatly in a bonnet. In the sanctuary of her bedroom, she sunk into her covers, devouring a bag of trail mix while watching "Steve Harvey's Jeopardy" on TV.

"Hey, Grandma," was all I managed to choke out as I shuffled into her bedroom, carrying with me a light throw blanket over my shoulders.

Climbing onto her bed and laying on top of her blanket, I wanted comfort; security. So, I sat as close to my grandma as possible and then folded myself into a tight ball. I probably looked silly, a tall dude curled into a fetal position. But I didn't even care. Without looking down at me, her calloused fingers ran through my hair and she smiled warmly. Even though I had barged into her space yet again, she didn't seem to mind. These kinds of nights had become frequent whenever those cursed nightmares came. No one knew about my nightmares, not even my grandma, and I intended to keep it under wraps with the hope that they would one day just vanish.

★ ★ ★ ★ ✞ ★ ★ ★ ★

In the following few weeks, football practice was a success. I didn't play at my best but at least I didn't get benched again. I had formed a sort of brotherhood with a few of my teammates. Probably because none of them were devoutly religious like the rest of my peers. Jocks and religion just didn't mix, and I was glad I had chosen to get back into football. Wrapping up our recent match, most of the boys planned to go hang out at the park and impress some girls at the basketball court. But I took a raincheck and went to Janda's Kitchen for apple pie. As soon as I entered the diner, she beamed up at me and before she even said it, I knew what she was going to ask.

"How is your beautiful girlfriend, the one you brought over last time?" Janda was the most delightful middle-aged woman I'd ever come across. She always had a twinkle in her eye, and she seemed to have taken a peculiar liking to me. Maybe it was because I reminded her of one of her grandsons, or because I always brought friends who turned into loyal customers.

"Oh, she's not my girl. Just a friend," I said. We both looked disappointed. I wanted to laugh at the weirdness, and that was when I realized I had to see her again… like a need… I yearned to see her again.

"Your regular, scallops and steak?" I nodded and she went to work.

The front door opened, and I whipped my head around to see who was coming in. A gaggle of girls, one of them hoisting a digital camera, all chattered away as they filed in. I slumped back into the vinyl booth, cursing my ridiculous obsession. What did I expect? For her to show up out of the blue when she hadn't called me once in weeks? I pictured her getting lost on campus again and some eager boy coming to her rescue. I grimaced as the very idea put a bad taste in my mouth. I didn't like it, not one bit, but it felt strange to feel that way. I wanted to call her, but it got harder with every passing day.

For the first time ever since I had discovered Janda's Kitchen, I couldn't enjoy my food. Partially because the girls were being too loud, and I had to ask them not to be filmed multiple times. Then there was the persistent irritation I felt at the thought of some cheesy guy getting close to Sidell. They were crawling all over campus, cringy, somewhat sheltered dudes, with rich parents and large amounts of disposable cash.

My meal went even more downhill when I received a text from my mom inviting me to her engagement party. Now my mood was in the sewer, and I reluctantly opened her text as I pushed my half-eaten plate of food across the table.

"You might not see or feel it, but I do love you, Son. I know that we've had our differences and we dealt with the huge curveball life threw at us differently. I may not be able to make up for lost time, but I am able to find solace in Devin and the

church. I can only pray you are able to move on and make peace with me. I want to start over with you, my son, and it would mean the world to me and Devin if you would grace our engagement party with your presence."

Fury flamed inside me as I got up and flung open the door of the diner, leaving Janda behind without so much as a goodbye. I only opened the text message again once I was back in my bedroom and trying to get some homework done at about 9 p.m. I threw my head back against my bed's headboard while Tony made himself comfortable nearby. We held a light conversation as I reopened the text message. The darkness of the room was illuminated by a soft yellow hue while Tony flipped through a magazine, filling the air with its rhythmic sound.

"What is it dude?" he asked cautiously.

My jaw dropped at the sight of the words on the screen. Anger boiled up inside me and I gripped the phone tightly.

"You good bro?" Tony asked, adjusting himself in the bean bag chair that rested lowly on the ground. His light eyes watched me intently for any sign that something was wrong. "You were talking for a moment but then you ended up zoning out."

"No," I replied, trying to keep my composure. I grabbed the can of dark soda off my dresser to quench my thirst. Though I was unsure if it was healthy to drink it with a throbbing headache. "I'm sorry Tony, but I think we should call it a night." Our conversation was now cut off, though Tony understood and took the hint.

He nodded. "Alright. I'll catch you later bro," he said as he collected his backpack and headed out. The stuffy atmosphere in my room was suffocating and I desperately wanted some fresh night air, even though it had grown colder recently as the month passed by. But still, I craved the cold, hoping it would help clear my mind.

Chapter Nine; Sidell

The piercing shrill of the first-period bell cut through the symphony of adolescent chaos that was my high school hallway. The scent of drugstore perfume battled against the aroma of sweet mint chewing gum, while the thrumming rhythm of a thousand conversations echoed off locker-lined walls. Amidst this sensory battlefield, I threw in the combination on my locker while Dawn stood beside me, already mid-scandal. Her rapid hand movements indicated that she was deeply invested in her dialogue. Her voice demanded attention like a spotlight in a crowded theater. I could always count on her for an Oscar-worthy teenage melodrama before classes. Today's episode: The Wrath of Tony's Laughter.

"So I told that anorexic witch straight to her Botoxed face, keep laughing at my man's jokes and I'll ram my fist so far down your throat, I'll be working you like a ventriloquist dummy.' Dawn spat the words out rapid-fire. "And don't say I was rude, because it's true!"

Dawn talked so fast that I often had a hard time trying to catch every word she said. If there's anything I've learned from being a best friend to an extrovert, it was how to wittily keep up with a lively conversation. So naturally, my mouth caught up with my mind as my brain began to formulate an appropriate response at the end of her sentence.

I clicked my tongue. "Uhm, violence solves nothing, Dawn. And policing his laughter isn't exactly a sign of a healthy relationship." I paused, softening my tone. "But I get it. When you're sprung on someone, jealousy creeps in."

Dawn rested her hand on the locker beside mine and sighed. "I know…" She turned her head to face me. "But he's my man, and I just can't stand anyone else drooling over him." She smiled, causing me to shake my head. She was clearly head-over-heels for this guy.

"My stomach hurts but at the same time I'm so hungry," she exaggerated.

"Well, have you eaten anything today?" I asked, knowing she tended to forget basic human functions like eating when immersed in her daily dose of drama.

"Of course not!" She exclaimed, placing a hand on her forehead as if she might faint. " I'm too busy dealing with everyone else's problems."

I chuckled under my breath. Dawn fancied herself to be the therapist of our high school, listening to classmates spill their woes whether they wanted her advice or not."Okay, let's get some food in you before you waste away," I said, shutting my locker.

In the cafeteria, I sat at one of the giant, round tables alone as I waited for Dawn to come back with the syrup for our waffles. But somewhere along the way she had gotten distracted and started talking to whoever she knew. It suddenly felt like the school chose these lunch tables, big enough to seat fifteen students, just to make the students who sat by themselves to feel even lonelier.

I jumped when Dawn slammed her tray down across from me. "I swear, my stomach is touching my back right now, " she moaned. I couldn't help but chuckle at her dramatics.

"Well eat up then, can't have you fading away on us."

As Dawn handed me a syrup packet, I heard a nervous voice over my shoulder. "Hey Sidell."

I cringed internally, knowing that voice anywhere. Khyree Latimore, my admirer who was constantly trying to get my attention. I looked up to find the brown skinned, uniformed boy with dark brown eyes standing above me.

"Oh. Hi Khyree," I grumbled. He hesitated, opening and closing his mouth several times. I watched as he glanced back at his friends several tables away, who were all nudging each other and snickering in anticipation of what they expected to happen next.

I rolled my eyes. "Please, sit, give them something to pat you on the back for," I said, averting my gaze away from his longing expression.

He complied and sat across from us, tugging down on his pikachu hat. I could tell he was psyching himself up for his next attempt to woo me.

Dawn slurped her juice box loudly, eyeing Khyree up and down. Then she leaned close to my ear and whispered mockingly, "What did you do to him Sidell, you got him under some sort of spell?" She giggled like an idiot and I darted my eyes at her silly accusation.

"Will you stop it?" I spoke through clenched teeth. Dawn just giggled gleefully in response.

She had this ongoing joke that Khyree had been taken aback by my *flirtatious ways*. But to be clear, I didn't like him at all. Dawn knew that, but she often made fun of him for her own amusement.

I nodded my eyes at Khyree as a cue for him to speak since he was just staring at me. He flashed me a bashful smile before throwing one more glance over his shoulder. "S-sorry," he chuckled nervously, "I bet the last thing you want is me trying to hit on you first thing in the morning."

I raised an eyebrow. "Is that what you're doing?"

"Eh, no. I mean yeah, uh —" He awkwardly nodded towards his companions behind him. "My friends and I are having a bonfire after, ah, school and I was just wondering if you'd want to stop by."

"With you?" I asked, biting open my syrup packet.

His brown eyes widened as he stuttered, "Uh, yeah, no not necessarily, I mean, we can definitely call it that if you want, but I just thought that, you know…" He let his gaze linger on me as he fidgeted with his expensive watch. It was clear that he was losing himself in my presence.

I didn't know how many times I've had to tell him no, but I decided to soften my response this time. "I appreciate the invitation, Khyree, but I can't. Thanks though." I gave him a small smile, hoping to let him down easy but he didn't seem too convinced.

"So, you like my friend huh?" Dawn chimed in with a mischievous grin, causing me to glare at her.

"What makes you say that?" Khyree sputtered, trying not to let us catch onto his deepest desires.

Dawn shrugged nonchalantly. "Oh, I don't know. My friend is a pretty hot blonde, don't you think?" She winked.

I cleared my throat, giving a subtle hint that I was feeling uncomfortable with the direction the conversation was going.

"O-kayy. Khyree, I think we're done here, right?" I said pointedly. "Listen, this interaction was nice and all but my food is getting cold. So yeah. I'll see you in class."

"That's alright. See you later," he mumbled as he reluctantly got up and left.

When he was finally out of our sight, I shot a daggered glance at Dawn. "I hate you, you know that?" I asked, scooping up my tray as I got up to leave.

"Oh, come on Sid, I was joking, you little stick in the mud." She giggled at me apologetically as she walked beside me. I threw away my food in the trash and eyed her suspiciously.

"I don't get why you keep making jokes about this," I hissed quietly. "He literally got on one knee the other day in front of everyone and shoved a real diamond ring in my face. Not only did I have to reject him, but then he followed me around school all week like a lost puppy! If he hasn't gotten the hint by now then he never will. And you keep making it worse by leading him on."

We exited the cafeteria and Dawn elbowed me and smiled.

"Awe Sid, I couldn't help it, he's so funny! Besides, I think you should give him a chance. He's been pursuing you for a hot minute. Unlike JJ, who you only knew for one day before he went ghost rider on you. I bet you he transferred schools."

Running my fingers through my hair, I stopped walking abruptly. I gave her an exasperated look before sighing in defeat. "Don't say that, okay?" I warned her. "He's probably going through something right now, who knows what or why. Plus, he doesn't owe me anything…" My voice trailed off.

Every day I thought about the encounter I had with JJ. A constant nostalgia coursed through me as my daily thoughts replayed the adventure we had experienced just over a month ago. I hadn't tried to call him, and he hadn't contacted me either. After we'd met, Dawn had challenged me for a while to call him, but I always chickened out with the flimsy excuse that he might be busy. Moreover, I had only promised to call him when I was lost at school or needed help with something.

Dawn finally dropped the conversation after a week or so, but I still had not been able to fully pay attention in class, my head constantly swirling with theories as to why he hadn't even texted me. Maybe the bond only happened in my head. Maybe he was just being nice, and it meant nothing. I even started fabricating a plan to get lost on purpose so I had an excuse to call him for help. But I pushed those thoughts away and focused on hoping to run into him by accident maybe. I even hung around his French classroom, but after the first time, I decided that it seemed stalkerish and obsessive, so I never went back. I also went to the school's art studio before the exhibition ended, with the hope that he might show up. Nothing. No success. I guess if God willed it… then it would be done.

"Mmm hm," Dawn said flatly, knowing full well that I was hurt by his absence, but didn't want to admit it. "Welp, I'm still hungry. Come on—let's go to the gym. I bet cheer coach wouldn't mind sharing some snacks."

For the past few weeks, I had been living on the wild side ever since I had enrolled at Westwood High. After summoning the courage to audition for the school's cheerleading squad, I was shocked when I had been selected. Together with Dawn, I had taken my confidence to a whole different level. My once timid and uneasy Russian persona had been transformed into a slightly extroverted, more social member of society, who's found the most joy in expressing herself through cheerleading. Although my parents were against the idea of me wearing skirts above my knees - without tights - they eventually caved in after acknowledging my eagerness and enthusiasm for the sport and how it helped to ease my battles with off and on anxiety.

Speaking of anxiousness, It wasn't easy to avoid Khyree during the day. Our AP classes overlapped thanks to the sadistic curriculum coordinator who clearly hated me. I tried my usual tricks - slow walking to classes so that I got there after him and I could choose a seat far from him, but it never worked for Spanish. I always got there first no matter how much I delayed, and he always came in after and plopped down right next to me.

I pleaded with our Spanish teacher, Ms. Montez to rescue me from Khyree's escalating weirdness - the arrogant flaunting of his family's money, the unsettling love notes stuck inside my textbooks, the invasive questions blurted out in front of the class.

But my words bounced right off Ms. Montez and her oblivious smile. She probably thought Khyree just had a harmless crush. The one time I tried to switch seats, she made me move back, claiming I needed to "give him a chance." Give him a chance to do what? Annoy me? Because he's done that.

Khyree turned to me in his seat, his eager eyes burning into me. "Hey Sidell. Have you heard about the big football game happening this Saturday? The whole school is talking about it." his voice echoed in the already quiet classroom causing several students to turn and stare

I plastered a polite smile while suppressing an inward grimace. "Yep, I've heard. Should be a fun time."

"So... you'll be doing your cheerleading thingy at the game?" he asked with an awkward chuckle that suggested he already knew the answer. "I told my parents all about it. They're super excited to come and support you."

I cringed, heat flooding my cheeks. His parents didn't even know me. Why were they so invested? I steadied my voice, saying, "That's really sweet of them, Khyree. But I'm just one of many cheerleaders, so they really don't have to come just for me."

He didn't seem to hear me, his mind already racing ahead. "And if our team wins, my parents want to take you and your family out for dinner. They're really looking forward to meeting you."

I broke out in a cold sweat, hearing our classmates muffled giggles and whispers around us. I just want to crawl under my desk. I couldn't believe Khyree sometimes. It was like he lived in his own world.

"Wow…I-, Thank you for the offer, Khyree," I nervously giggled. "But I think my family already has plans if the team wins. I hope you and your family have fun, though."

Khyree's face visibly deflated at my words, but he quickly tried to recover by forcing an awkward grin onto his face. "Oh... yeah, sure! No biggie! Enjoy the game, Sidell."

"Thanks, same to you," I muttered as he turned back towards his desk with an uncomfortable shuffle and began fiddling with his papers.

I let out a breath. Why did he have to be so clueless? I almost felt bad, but mostly I just wanted him to stop with his awkward attempts at friendliness that bordered on something more. I wasn't interested in Khyree in that way, and I didn't want to give him or anyone else the wrong idea. His social clumsiness was exhausting.

★ ★ ★ ★ ✝ ★ ★ ★ ★

That Saturday night was the school's football game and I was over the moon to know that my parents and little sister would all be there to show their support for me. My dad even went as far as creating a vibrant and glittery banner for me, making me feel overwhelmed by his childish creative side. Plus, my mom, who would still be dressed in her surgical nurse uniform, would take time out of her daily routine to help me practice and even my little sister wanted to join in on the fun. In a way, my cheerleading had brought my family closer together and I was deeply thankful for their support.

The girl's locker room was filled with the boisterous noise of a dozen teenage girls from my cheer squad. We were all wearing the same outfit—green and silver uniforms, with white shoes, and bows in our hair. I had even put a little bit of makeup on: silver glitter eyeliner, mascara, and lip gloss, but my parents hadn't seen that yet.

"Dawn, can you fix my ponytail?" I asked, my voice quavering. I sat down on the bench, feeling the constriction of the tie on my scalp. Dawn stopped her conversation with some of the other girls and stepped over to me.
"Sure, bestie babes," she said. As she released my blonde hair from its captivity and it cascaded down my shoulders, I closed my eyes, releasing a breath of relief. In the background, the faint sound of a crowd cheering from outside echoed and rumbled off the walls.

"Are you okay?" Dawn asked, sitting in front of me once she finished pulling up my hair.

I glanced at her short curly mane styled in a wet and wavy look with glitter spray.

"Well I'm better than your hair right now. What's with the whole drowned noodle look?"

Dawn laughed and smacked my leg. "It's called style, maybe you've heard of it?"

I rolled my eyes dramatically. "Oh yes, nothing says style like crusty hair gel and split ends."

Our banter eased my nerves slightly. Dawn always knew how to make me laugh, even when I felt two seconds away from puking. Still, this was my first game ever. What if the crowd realized I didn't belong out there? That I was just an awkward, clumsy girl who could barely do an aerial cartwheel.

Dawn tilted her head, her face serious. "But really what's going on?"

"I just…I don't know. I'm feeling kind of nervous, you know?" I said, trying not to pay attention to the butterflies wrecking my stomach.

"That's natural, you haven't cheered at an actual game before. Just try not to worry," Dawn reassured me, patting my leg. I could see the excitement in her eyes. "I am proud of you, you know Sid? You've really come out of your shell. Don't doubt yourself now."

I smiled and slipped my arms around her. "Thank you."

Dawn took a deep breath and shook her head. "Alright, let's get out there before Mrs. Sherrie comes looking for us. Are you going to be, okay?"

I nodded and tightly gripped my pom poms.

"Well, let's just do what we came to do. We are the best, right? We got this." Dawn smiled and winked at me. She marched out of the room, the rest of us following behind. The stadium was overflowing with students and parents, all wearing shades of green and silver. Even from a distance I could pick out my family in the crowded bleachers, and I offered a wave before turning my attention back to the field. A feeling of dread filled my stomach the moment my feet touched the turf, but I skillfully followed the rhythm of the music as I moved my body in sync with the others.

We shouted our calls with strong, loud voices as our school's football team burst out of their tunnel and cut through the banner showing our school logo. I recognized every face, but one figure was missing… JJ. So much for hoping he'd reappear.

"What's wrong?" Dawn asked after our first cheer. Snapping out of my thoughts, I shook my head and forced a fake smile.

"I'm okay," I lied. I quickly changed the subject. "I think I'll go get some water." I tucked a stray lock of hair behind my ear.

"Kay." Dawn gave a concerned nod. I tossed my pom poms and picked up my small purse that was hidden under the bleacher before jogging and weaving past the crowd without bumping into a single person. I stopped when I exited the wired fence, to let my heart rate return to normal.

Though there was a cooler filled with water for us on the field, I just needed to be by myself for a minute.

Heading for the water fountain, I trudged in the direction of the empty school hallway. Suddenly, there was a blur as someone ran past me. If I had not been thinking about him at that moment, I probably wouldn't have recognized the strange boy running frantically through the school, shrouded in dark clothes and looking dangerous. But I recognized his familiar scent of aftershave as he whizzed past me, and I didn't think twice before zipping after him.

Chapter Ten: JJ

Luckily, the Westwood campus was small, so my sprint around it took less than thirty minutes. Not satisfied or exhausted enough, the hate and anger still coursing through my veins at full velocity, I headed to the alumni stadium to run more laps. I was so pumped with adrenaline and anger I could have burst a blood vessel if I kept up that pace but I didn't care. The campus was still lit up and even though it was nearly 10 p.m. there were still some people about, mostly on the football field to prepare for the big game, a game that I should have been at. My heavy-footed running and breathless panting seemed to be an unwelcome rhythm to the calm, quiet night's atmosphere. I didn't mind the stares I got. I had my hoodie covering half my face and I was moving at a blurring speed; it was hard to care.

How could she do this to me? I thought, once again recalling my mom's text message. How was she just able to leave me when it benefited her. How could she be happy without me, and fall in love with another man just like that? How could she even think of building a life and home with him... and a whole new family? Did I mean nothing to her? If she had stayed and knew of the bond I had with Donica, would she have comforted me when she passed away?

I always hated being an only child, especially with how lonely I felt after losing my best friend. Even though my grandma always showered me with love, I still had bouts of loneliness. I felt extremely jealous when my friends talked about their annoying siblings, and after Donica left me, I was the loneliest I had ever been. It just seemed as if all the women I desperately clung to eventually left me, besides my grandmother... First my mom, then Donica... And deep down, I knew the fear of abandonment was the reason why I had ghosted Sidell. Disappearing on her before I could get my hopes up was way easier than losing her in the long run.

My feet were pumping against the ground as I pushed myself even harder. The field was now in view and that was when I heard it: running feet in sync with mine. I slowed down instinctively to make sure I wasn't imagining it. The sound slowed down also and I picked up my pace, ignoring whoever was following me. I was not in the mood to socialize. Misery might need company, but I just wanted to be left alone.

"JJ."

The voice was heavy with panting. I came to an abrupt halt. Turning around slowly, my stewing brain caught up with my senses and registered the voice before I even saw her. She was bent forward, breathing hard and swiping at the sheen of sweat on her brow.

"Sorry, ah, I need to catch my breath. Goodness gracious. Ooh." She was still panting and I was dumbfounded, standing about twenty feet away from her and watching her chest heave in and out. *Is it Sidell, in the flesh, or did I conjure her up?*

"Sidell?" My voice croaked when I spoke. She smiled that familiar wide smile that made her look like a child given permission to raid the cookie jar. All the pent-up tension in my body pooled to my feet. I walked up to her as she's still bent forward, trying to catch her breath. I didn't know how long she had been running after me and trying to get my attention. It was a bit of a shock to see her in a cheer uniform. Not that she didn't look good… I just would've assumed that cheerleading wasn't her sort of thing.

If you asked me now, I still couldn't tell you why I had done it… I suppose it just felt right at that moment. As she straightened up and flashed another triumphant smile, I grabbed her and pulled her to me. A sigh escaped her mouth as I held her against my body.

Maybe I wanted to make sure she was really there. Or maybe I just needed to feel her touch. She felt stiff against me as I clung to her. I held onto her as tight as I dared. Her body was aligned against mine perfectly and she smelled of earthy floral freshness. Her body relaxed after a few seconds and finally, she started slowly embracing me in return. She rubbed my back gently, patting. That was when I realized I was crying.

Chapter Eleven: Sidell

"Shh, it's okay. You're okay," I said in my best soothing voice. I used my free hand to run up the nape of his neck, then rubbed his shaking shoulders in a back-and-forth motion. His musky scent infiltrated my senses, reminding me of wet earth after a storm. I'd never been in such an intimate situation with someone before. This was new, uncharted territory.

JJ's body was quivering as he tried to steady his raw outflow of emotions. He was still holding me close to him. I had settled into the hug and I was not complaining. It's awkward and delicious at the same time. I was more worried that he might get ashamed of crying in my arms and try to distance himself from me tonight. But I wasn't going to let him… not this time, God help me.

"Okay, I think I'm cool now. But I still need to hold you for a bit. I hope you don't mind," he whispered into my ear and a cold shiver ran down my spine as his lips grazed my ear. His voice was low and throaty. His arms tightened around my waist, pulling me even closer—there was no space between us now—and in that moment, I knew I wouldn't let him go.

"Of course not," I replied softly, "take all the time you need." Then I added with a sheepish smile. "It's a bit of an awkward way to meet again…"

"No doubt." His laugh rumbled through my soul like thunder, possessive and commanding, despite his vulnerability.

His body relaxed in my embrace and his face nuzzled into my shoulder; I could feel his weak smile against my skin, making my heart flutter. We remained like that for what felt like an eternity before he gently detached himself from me, yet he remained close. My heart resumed its insane pounding as he held me in his intense gaze… his dark brown eyes were like two pools of ink. I was entranced by their depth, lost searching for something beneath the surface… but I'm the one who broke the stare first. Again, I tried to keep eye contact with him for a moment, but it was too hard to bear such close scrutiny, and my eyes darted down after a few seconds. I tried once more. His stunning eyes didn't even blink, and I failed a third time.

"Thank you," he finally said, his voice an unsteady whisper. "Would you mind...chilling with me?" He held out his hand, and after a moment's hesitation I took it, my skin tingling at the touch.

It was like we connected through some kind of telepathic communication as we moved in comfortable silence until we reached a spot in the middle of the street, away from the school grounds and far enough away from the glaring light of the lampposts.

We strolled together into the seemingly infinite parking lot, his fingers intertwined with mine. The lamps atop the school provided an ethereal glow to the street, creating a serene environment that was otherwise void of life. We settled on the curb, both of us still silent, his gaze glued to the pavement beneath us. Faint echoes of whistles and cheering from the football game sounded in the distance.

I fought the urge to stare up at his heartbreaking allure, trying to connect the dots of what had just happened. It didn't make sense for someone to skip a game, only to go running around the school campus in tears at ten o'clock at night.

 I wanted to ask him what was wrong, but I didn't want to press. I just offered my presence and comfort, hoping that was enough. My mind briefly turned to God— wouldn't He have been the best source of comfort? But I quickly dismissed the thought. I barely knew this boy and I had no idea what was going on in his life. All I could do was sit there with him. Looking out into the expansive parking lot, I wondered why I'd never noticed how it looked under the twinkling stars. It was breathtakingly beautiful… He was breathtakingly beautiful, the scattered beams of light illuminating his dark mysterious eyes as he gazed down at me.

"I'm sorry if I weirded you out," he began after a while. "Hell, I weirded myself out. I didn't know my pent-up emotions would come out that way. I needed an outlet and I'm grateful it was your hug." His voice was calm and it sounded like he had been taking deep breaths to steady his emotions. The strong urge to hold his hands almost overpowered me, but common sense and the fact that his hands were buried deep in his pockets kept me in check.

"It's alright," I assured him, the corners of my mouth forming a small smile that he faintly reflected on his face.

"Did you miss me?" he asked with a smile still lingering on his lips. But I noticed the traces of deep hurt etched into the fine lines of his handsome face and it tugged at my heart. The smile didn't reach his eyes, and I yearned to know what had made him so upset.

"Maybe a little," I chuckled lightly. "I mean, you're off the hook now, since you're playing me with the damsel in distress bit..." My joke went too far, I know, but anything to bring light back into his eyes. It's clear that he was dealing with something deep here. I didn't know what he had going on, but it was clearly not something shallow. I've never seen anyone look this devastated, angry, pained and lost. Yet still he was able to put up a front of coolness.

He chuckled calmly. "Ah. You're far too mellow, Sidell. I feel better already. Thank you." He held my eyes for longer than I felt was necessary and that alone sent the same delicious chill down the entire length of my back. I fooled myself into hoping that the back chills were due to the cold…

I wanted to respond, to tell him that his dimpled smile was maddeningly hot — but the words died in my throat. He's been through something that has ripped him apart, and I doubt he wanted to hear declarations of his attractiveness when his heart was still in pieces. We slipped back into our comfortable silence, which spoke volumes without either of us having to say a word.

My phone buzzed in my purse, and I looked at it as a wave of déjà vu settled heavily in my chest. This had happened before. A phone call, a text, an interruption...ending a moment we were attempting to enjoy together. I unlocked my phone and Dawn's nickname illuminated the small screen with a text that read:

Dawn: "Where are you at???!"

With a deep exhale, I quickly typed back.

Me: "In the Twilight Zone. I'll be back soon, MOM."

Oh right. I had ditched the cheer squad mid-routine a few minutes ago. My parents were sure to have noticed my disappearance from the stands...They'll probably be okay though...Here's to hoping that the game will remain fascinating enough for them to forget about my whereabouts. I put the phone away so I wouldn't disturb the mood, but it seemed as if I already had because JJ was staring at me, and when I looked at him, he didn't look away. Feeling the warmth of a blush spread across my face, I explained the interruption.

"My friend. She wanted to know why I'm taking so long to get a drink of water. That's what I told her before running into you…"

A slight grin touched his lips, though his eyes remained guarded. "Oh snap. Yeah, sorry I dragged you out here. Come on, let's get you back to the game, *cheerleader*."

He rose and offered his hand. The faint heat radiating from his fingers was like a warm embrace. I hadn't noticed how cold mine had grown in the night air, but they were soon warmed by the gentle circles of his fingers upon my palms as he escorted me back to the game.

"It's okay," I said. "I'm glad I ran into you." The night was quieter now, with less people around, and JJ was still holding my hand even though they had both sufficiently warmed up by then.

"I don't know what you're dealing with, but I can always be here as a shoulder for you to cry on," I offered as we took the path that winds down toward the other side of the bleachers. "No pun intended," I said quickly, but he only responded with a slight pressure that enclosed around my hand, a quick nod, and a faint smile that didn't touch his eyes. "You better contact me this time around..."

"I will…" JJ said, letting go of my hand as the football field came to view.

"Ok…" I said. A heavy weight caused my shoulders to slump. The feeling took me by surprise as I watched him pull his hoodie over his face as he walked off. No goodbye hugs or anything. Not that I was expecting it, but our goodbye left a sour taste in my mouth. This was kind of becoming a habit.

CHAPTER TWELVE.

Somehow, I'd managed to get away with my secret little rendezvous, which was a small miracle really. I guess Dad and Mom had been too preoccupied with the excitement of the game, being that it was their first-time experience and all. But I still had to bribe Cayest for her silence on the drive home. She had noticed my disappearance and wasn't buying the excuse that I had to sit out of half the routine because I couldn't remember the steps. I sighed loudly. *Why must she be so observant*? Little sisters were so troublesome.

As soon as I got into the house, I showered quickly and then transitioned into my night clothes. I then proceeded to the kitchen to grab some snacks before I headed back upstairs to my room.

"Miss girl, you missed the majority of the game," Dawn said once I returned to my bedroom, closing the door behind me. Even though it was Thursday and a school night, my parents had granted her permission to spend the night. Perched on the air mattress my dad had so thoughtfully supplied for her, she shifted her gaze from her fingernails and the opened nail polish bottle to glare at me.

A few beats of silence went by, then she spoke, "So, what's up? You don't look... What's the word I'm looking for? You don't look like you. What's up?" Although her words were gentle and intuitive, I couldn't help but feel like I was standing before a jury, awaiting a verdict.

I tossed her a Rice Crispy Treat that landed on her thigh before slumping onto my bed. I wasn't physically exhausted, but the hurt in JJ's eyes was heavy on my heart and I felt emotionally drained. I kicked off my flip flops and threw my pillow across the bed. I dragged the covers up to my chin before I looked at Dawn who's patiently waiting for a reply. "Nothing. Just tired. It's been a long day," I said, with a small smile to convince her.

I didn't know what to say to her about JJ, so I didn't say anything. I couldn't fathom what he was going through. I just knew that he was dealing with something tough enough to make him burst into gut-wrenching sobs in the arms of a girl he barely even knew.

"Hm," Dawn said with a raised brow. Then she went back to painting her fingernails.

"Yeah, thanks for covering for me with the cheer coach. Emily was being a pig hole," I said, grateful that Dawn was a good talker.

"No worries." She smiled conspiratorially. "And yeah, Emily needs to mind her damn business—like I didn't see her sneaking off to the quad with Kyle…" She leaned in closer and whispered, "He's so ugly." A choked giggle escaped me, and I tried to hide it behind my hand. Dawn was right, but I didn't want to add anything to her statement as I always tried to be nice and avoid gossip, since it was a sin.

"But anyways, I was just worried in case you'd gotten lost. Again," she said. A sly smile highlighted her face in the brash lighting of my dresser lamp. I rolled my eyes, and we both laughed, hers louder than mine.

"Yeah right. Well, I'm crashing for the night. Goodnight." A yawn escaped my mouth and my body felt a hundred times heavier as she replied, "Goodnight."

My body shut down as I drifted off into dreamland. JJ's face, his scent, and the weight of his body pressing against mine lingered at the back of my consciousness as I settled into a comfortable position, my chin snuggling the soft pillows as I recalled the smoothness of his skin.

★ ★ ★ ★ ✞ ★ ★ ★ ★

I woke up around 4:30 a.m. to use the bathroom. After returning to my room, I picked up my phone from where it had fallen off the bed. I scrolled straight to his name, and I tapped the text icon.

me: Heyy, goodmorning. This is me checking up on you. How Are You? I meant what I said about being a shoulder when you need one JJ.

I didn't think twice before pressing send, because I knew that any second thoughts would make me overturn my carefully contemplated decision that I'd been ruminating on since he'd left me at the bleachers. I dropped the phone like it was on fire and laid my head back down on my pillow. *So much for waiting for him to text me first...*

Bzzz* I hesitated, surprised that he was even awake. Biting my nails, I took a slow deep breath before snatching up my phone with a quickness.

Legendary JJ: Sidell! Heyy, look who finally decided to contact me. I'm doing better than yesterday. Thank you.

My heart skipped a beat as a smile quickly spread across my face. Then a second message came in.

Legendary JJ: And uhm, I owe you an apology for last night. Er, something I thought I'd dealt with came up again, and it upset me more than I thought it could. I'm not sorry about the hug though. I'd appreciate it more, if you're feeling generous. 🖤

The smile on my face was threatening to split my jaw in half. I tried to think of something witty to reply, but I kept coming up with nothing, partly because Dawn's sporadic snores were so loud, and partly because I'm just generally a bad texter.

me: Glad to hear you're doing better. About the hug, you're gonna have to earn those, lol.

I chuckled to myself as my fingers suddenly adopted a mind of their own. He replied immediately.

Legendary JJ: Oh yeah? Okay, I'll take that as a challenge. Mind You, my charm is irresistible. Fair warning.

I couldn't believe that I was flirting at 4 a.m. on a Friday morning with JJ after he had cried in my arms only a few hours ago. But I didn't really know what constituted flirting. Was I reaching? I'm sure texting each other at 4 a.m. in the morning counts, right?

me: Ha-ha. Bring It On.

Legendary JJ: Don't say I didn't warn ya.

me: Ok, we'll see if that charm of yours lives up to hype.

Legendary JJ: Ha-ha. Oh, we definitely will! Anyway, what are you up to today and why are you up so early?

me: Well, I got school obviously lol and I erm, just couldn't sleep.

Legendary JJ: Same... I hope you dreamt about me lol...

My stomach turned as I read his words, making me sit upright in bed. I panicked, not knowing how to respond but thankfully another text appeared before I had the chance.

Legendary JJ: Wanna hang out again? Continue our unfinished day of fun?

Me: Sure. What did you have in mind?

★ ★ ★ ★ ⛧ ★ ★ ★ ★

"Good morning!" I yelled at a drowsy Dawn as soon as she opened her eyes.

JJ texting me back had given me a spring in my step and there was no way I could fall back asleep after that. Him saying that he wanted to hang out with me again was as far as I've ever gotten with any guy. About an hour ago, I had to stop myself from hyperventilating as I quietly came to terms with the fact that I might like JJ in a way that was beyond platonic. I desperately needed Dawn's advice, and I was in her face as soon as she snoozed her alarm. She usually got up way before me, annoyingly coming over to my house every so often to get me up in the mornings. But now it was my turn.

"Get up, Naughty Dawn!" I sang, removing her pillow from under her head. That prompted a reaction, which was an eyelash flutter before she went right back to sleep. I decided to leave her alone for a few minutes and headed downstairs to the kitchen.

"Good morning." I greeted my dad as he tended to the coffee pot. He was dressed in a blue t-shirt and khakis with his reading glasses above his forehead and Newport sneakers on his feet.

"Morning slugger." He planted a kiss on my head. His gruff, golden beard with hints of gray stubble tickled my skin.

"Where are you heading?" I asked.

"As you have probably heard already, Nireska and Vestor are in town today. I'm heading over to the airport to pick them up."

Oh gosh….I forgot they were coming.

Nireska was visiting with her husband, Vestor. I had eavesdropped on my mom's conversation with her last weekend. I had heard her trying to arrange a stay with us, telling us a sob story about Nireska's living situation.

My parents were too kindhearted and offered her the two guest rooms—which aren't even completely finished. I'm not going to be a selfish liar and say that I didn't respect Nireska for being emotional supportive in our phone calls. Because I'm grateful for them, I was just uncomfortable knowing guests were coming, and I didn't know how I'd be able to handle it.

I blew out a breath. "Mama leave yet?"

"Yeah, she has already left for work, and as for your sister, she's in the car. I'm about to drop her off," he said, pouring a cup of coffee.

"Dobre."

I looked on the countertop to find that my mother had made some Draniki, which are thin, crispy potato pancakes that were more savory than sweet. I placed four of them on a plate, shoved the plate into the microwave, and pressed the button for a minute. Then I waited.

"Well, I'm out of here. Make sure to lock up the house before you and Dawn head out," he said with a pat on my shoulder before he exited the room. "Remember the key goes under the mat."

"Yes sir, have a good day, Papa," I said. I listened to the sound of his jingling car keys and heard the creaking of the front door as he left. The microwave dinged, and I scooped my breakfast out. After taking a little tempting bite, I set the plate on the counter while I poured some cranberry juice. Then grabbing my plate and drink, I fixed the bottle of feta dip under my arm and trudged back upstairs to my room.

Dawn was sitting up on the air mattress when I walked in, her brown hair was pressed on the side of her face and her eyes were still heavy with sleep. I pushed my steaming breakfast in front of her nose, knowing that the aroma would do the hard work of waking her up completely.

"Ugh. What time is it?" she groaned, feeling around for her phone blindly.

"Early o'clock," I answered, taking a sip of my cranberry juice.

"Blah." Dawn got up from the air mattress like an elderly lady with aching joints. "Why are you up so early anyway?" Her voice was acidic as she snatched a Draniki off my plate and began to nibble on it. I grinned as I thrusted my glowing phone screen in her face and she flinched at the sudden light. Still half-asleep, she grabbed my device and squinted to read what was on the screen. I sat my plate down on my dresser as I watched, curious and intrigued, while she scrolled up to read every message.

Legendary JJ: Maybe we can meet up before the first bell? Possibly in the courtyard?

As Dawn read JJ's messages, her eyes widened, and it seemed like the sleepiness had evaporated from her body in that instant.

"Girl, why didn't you respond back to him, you weirdo," she said with an amused smirk. "You do know that he can see that you've read the message, right?"

My cheeks burned as I nervously bit my nails, trying to come up with a response. I managed to muster a sheepish smile. "I know... I don't know why, I just got kinda flustered. That's why I wanted you to help me."

"Help you with what? You want me to look over your shoulder as you text your new boyfriend?" Dawn wiggled her eyebrows suggestively.

"Come on, he's not my boyfriend," I replied defensively.

"I'm only teasing you, maxi pad." Dawn cackled in delight. "Okay, so this is what you'll say," she began as she opened the phone's keyboard.

"Ahm....What are you doing?" I asked as Dawn began typing out a response.

"Trying to help you! Like you wanted, remember?" Dawn chuckled. "If he's going to be in the courtyard and you're planning to run into him, then let the Lord's will be done and accept the divine opportunity." Dawn hit the send button and tossed the phone onto my bed while looking at me with hopeful eyes. For some reason I didn't trust Dawn's sneaky response.

"Let me see," I said, picking the phone up from where it dropped on the corner of the bed.

"Pardon my death breath, I'll be in the bathroom luv, thank me later." Dawn made a peace sign on her way out of the room. My thumb scrolled straight to JJ's name and I tapped the text icon.

Me: I'll be there. And if you don't mind, my friend Dawn will be tagging along too. We're kind of inseparable.

It wasn't my message that had set my heart racing; it was the moment JJ read it. I took a long sip of my juice in an attempt to keep the butterflies in my stomach at bay. I was so excited to see him.

After several minutes, Dawn returned, escaping the bathroom's thick mist of steam. Her hair was up in a ponytail, tightened with a rubber band, and she had a towel around her body. I averted my eyes as I went over JJ's messages, still in disbelief. I heard her making noises while gathering her things and applying her sweet-smelling lotion. Then selecting clothes, she sang off key, "Show us your glory, show us your glory," from the worship song featuring Melodie Malone called 'Holy Ground' by Passion. Her loud antics were nothing new; she always made sure to announce her presence wherever she went.

"Turn on your TV or something," she said, as she had advised countless times before. As usual, I replied, "I don't watch TV." Not out of lack of interest, but because there were much better ways to fill your head than with government programming.

This was our routine on mornings like this. On some days, when I would have my bible laying out and about, I'd meditate on God's word, using her loudness as a challenge to see how good I am at tuning out the noise. Today, I was too distracted with my thoughts to even try meditating. My phone lit up with a buzz and I almost spilled my juice on myself as I scrambled to pick it up.

It was a text from Mom, reminding me to head straight home after school. Her order pretty much confirmed what Dad had already told me. I shook my head, scoffing.

I'm literally dreading Nireska's presence, especially her husband, Vester Lenkov, who I'm sure still has a crush on my mother, which both my dad and mom are too naive to notice. And when I had made it known to my parents a while back, they had gotten mad at me. It's not my fault I called him out on his adulterous tendencies. Even long after my parents had been married, he's been trying to swoon my mother with flowers and desserts or whatnot, which was so weird. Now I had to be around these people all night and then some.

"Please God." I spoke silently as I begged the heavens. "There's got to be something. Extra credit work? Needed tutoring? Heck, even detention sounded more inviting. Anything to delay my return home."

★ ★ ★ ★ ✞ ★ ★ ★ ★

After being deterred in the girl's bathroom for five minutes, Dawn and I headed towards JJ. My heart pulsed like a drum as I stepped into the sun-drenched schoolyard. The sea of students, all in their green, black, and silver uniforms, parted at the sound of Dawn's loud voice, opening a path for us. We were on a mission.

Our destination, JJ's bench. He was there alright, his neon pink cap worn backwards to stand out from the crowd. Even from where we sat, I could make out his signature black fingerless gloves that clung to his hands. The sight of him sent ripples of wildfire through my belly and I gasped - involuntarily - under my breath.

"Oh gosh, that's him." I exhaled. *As if I wasn't just texting him earlier.* My cheeks burned with heat, and I wanted nothing more than to turn away, but Dawn's mischievous grin and gentle prodding egged me on.

"Come on," she said, her voice laced with the thrill of danger. She pulled my arm, urging me to follow her lead.

My feet dragged behind me as I stepped closer to what felt like an abyss. My skin prickled with sweat as I approached him and my breath became shallow and quick. I felt a presence before me, and with Dawn's gentle nudge, I turned to face him. JJ was absorbed with his phone, unaware of the world around him. He had one foot propped on the bench and one hand tucked in his pocket. His posture oozed confidence and swagger.

My mouth suddenly felt dry, words eluding me. "H-Hey," I murmured, my voice a mere whisper in the open air. He finally lifted his gaze from the phone and our eyes met for the first time today.

The corners of his lips curved into a devilish smirk. "Yo, whassup?" he drawled, his voice dripping with confidence. He stood up from the bench in one smooth motion, never breaking eye contact.

"Nothing much really," I replied, my fingers nervously running through my hair in an attempt to distract myself from his magnetism. He adjusted his backwards cap and flashed a knowing smile before throwing a glance at Dawn. Her hazel eyes twinkled with delight as she took in our shy exchange.

"Oh," I said, finally shaking off my trance. "JJ, this is my friend Dawn. Dawn, this is JJ."

"Yeah, we already know each other," JJ said casually. My eyes darted from one to the other as JJ nodded and Dawn smiled affectionately up at him.

"Yeah, he's Tony's friend," she said.

"Really?" I blurted. I knew that they have known each other but Dawn hadn't told me that Tony and JJ were friends. It was really cool for them to know each other, and I beamed at the thought of us all getting together for some sort of double date.

Dawn turned her attention to him with a curious look. "So how are you doing, Jacky?"

JJ flashed a confident smile at Dawn. "Good and you?"

"I'm good," she replied with a hint of amusement in her voice. "You've certainly made quite the impression on my friend Sidell here," Dawn said coolly, her tone slicing through the air. My eyes immediately sought out Dawn, my smile attesting to what she had said without uttering a single word.

"Really?" he said, flattered, his ego swelling with each passing second. My cheeks grew flush with embarrassment, so I rushed to respond before Dawn could expose me further.

"Yeah," I stammered quickly, my eyes finding Dawn's before meeting JJ's gaze again. "I mean, I told her you're really cool to hang out with."

His brown gaze dazzled me, pinning me in place with a riveting intensity. "Well, I could say the same for you. That is why I couldn't wait to hang with you again." He spoke in a deep, throaty voice, his lips curling into a teasing grin, making my heart thump with thrill. "Are you still up to hang?" He laughed, sending shivers of anticipation and delight through my body.

"Umm," I stuttered, my mind refusing to process the implications of his question. "I mean I can't risk ditching again…"

"Nah," he softly interjected before I could finish my sentence. "I mean like after school." Before I could respond, Dawn piped up.

"Sure, she can. She's totally free." She said with enthusiastic hand gestures. I shot her a questioning look, as if to say, 'Am I really?' but was secretly pleased that she had spoken up.

He showed his gratitude towards Dawn before turning his focus back to me. "I ain't tryna pressure you or nothin', I'm just askin'," he explained.

My mother's voice echoed in the back of my mind. *Get home straight away*, she had said. But I wasn't ready to go home right after school. Not with the looming threat of having to entertain unwanted company.

I suppressed my urge to groan in displeasure and simply responded with a, "Yeah. Yeah I can make it," soothing JJ's ego with a frail smirk. "Where do you wanna meet?" I asked. Right then, the school bell chimed, reverberating throughout the courtyard. Everyone started to disperse.

"Do you usually take the school bus after class?" JJ asked me, his voice almost drowned out by the commotion around us.

"I mostly rely on Dawn for a lift…" I whirled around to look for her as I spoke, but she was nowhere to be found. "Who just ditched me!" I sighed, my eyes tracking down her figure that was slowly disappearing into the horizon. I called after her as she walked arm-in-arm with Tony. She briefly turned back, throwing a fleeting wave over her shoulder.

JJ removed his cap, his hand grazing his coarsely textured haircut. "I don't have a car at the moment, but we can ride the school bus to my apartment. I live just a few blocks away. It'll only take a minute. Do you mind?"

I arched my eyebrows and cocked my head inquisitively at him, my eyes alight with enthusiasm. "Your apartment?"

"Yeah." He gestured to his uniform. "I was kind of hoping to change before our outing."

"Where will we end up after going by your apartment? Will my parents approve?" I asked slyly. His enigmatic smirk containing a million secrets was enough to enchant me.

"Now, why do I gotta spoil the surprise? Just know when we get there—you gon' love it. As far as your parents are concerned, you'll be studying." The bling from his single earring glowed in the sunlight as he spoke. My heart raced and my face flushed red as I felt the anticipation of the day ahead. Yeah sure, I might have been preparing to step out of the comfort zone of my Christianity, but I would only be a teenage girl once.

"Okay then, count me in," I spoke coyly, batting my eyelashes. "See you after school."

JJ nodded as he smiled with his eyes. "Cool beans." He beamed, his voice brimming with excitement. "I'll text you." And just like that, we were off. JJ to his first period class, while I went to mine in a state of wonder, my mind spinning with intrigue over what JJ had in store for us.

Chapter Thirteen: JJ

It was definitely a date. Right? Did I just ask a girl on a date after such a long time? However, did I manage that? When she had texted me so early in the morning, that was the green light I needed. I could hardly sleep last night, so when my phone buzzed at 4 a.m. I heard it immediately. Before her message, I had been envisioning another horrible day, and I had already ruled out going in for classes, or football practice, or anything that would get me out of bed in general. I had the nightmare again last night, the same one as before. It woke me up at 3 a.m. I couldn't go back to sleep so I laid down, responding to Sid's messages and waiting for the light to spew in through my window. I could hear my grandma singing worship songs and praying in tongues as she started off her day.

I didn't want to think about how I had behaved last night with Sid, and I decided against replying to my mom's text with enough bile to make her call off her engagement in shame. I chose to ignore her instead, and I knew that running into Sidell last night contributed to that uncharacteristic peaceful approach. Her undeniable peaceful aura had rubbed off on me, and it was like hugging her transferred some of her energy onto me. It's crazy, I couldn't explain it. I managed to fall asleep way past midnight with the smell of her Ocean Spring scented shampoo lingering in my mind.

When her text had come in, my whole mood took a 360-degree turn. I went from down on my luck with the whole world against me to an excited boy who was enchanted by the pretty girl he was talking to. I was just glad no one was around to see me smiling like an idiot. I also had to make a concerted effort not to infuse my texts with too much enthusiasm. I didn't want Sid to think I was desperate. Or plain loony.

Throughout the day, I counted the hours and waited for the end of the day. It was the most excruciating few hours of my life. Waiting. I hated it, and I rarely waited for anything.

Finally, the shackles of the school's prison-like walls burst open, granting us our hard-earned freedom, and I practically flew to the school bus pick-up zone to wait for Sidell. I texted her as I waited, breathing heavily. The school bell had barely rung, but I didn't care about seeming desperate anymore. All the hours sitting uselessly in class not paying attention to the teacher, daydreaming and waiting had caught up with me. She didn't respond for a few minutes, and chances were that she wasn't even out of class yet. Finally, my phone rang with her name as the caller. I answered on the second ring, nearly forgetting to maintain my cool composure.

"Yo, what's up?" I answered the phone, trying to sound nonchalant and manly.

"Sorry, can you hold the bus, I'll be right out. I'm just waiting to collect some make-up work from my teacher."

"No problem… you're good, the driver hasn't even opened the doors yet," I replied. My heart was swelling with anticipation.

Not long after ending the call, the open double doors to the school's entrance revealed the dynamic duo Sidell and Dawn. They were giggling and playfully roughhousing their way towards me. "Don't do anything I wouldn't do…" I managed to hear Dawn say as Sidell's shy smile met mine. I wore a sly grin, with one hand casually posed in my pocket as I waved them over with my free hand. Sidell looked like an advert for those health supplements companies you come across everywhere nowadays. It might've been the white teeth, glittering eyes or even the long blonde hair, but she always looked stunning.

"You better take good care of her, Jacky!" Dawn warned, jabbing a finger at me even as she grinned. "I've known this girl for a hot minute now, and forewarning you, I hand out beatdowns before filing missing person's reports."

Sid shuffled closer to me with a smile on her face and I wanted to embrace her like I did the night before, but this was hardly the spot for all that. There were too many people around and it didn't take a rocket scientist to deduce that Sidell had a very shy side to her, so public attention may do more harm than good. Why was I so quick to engage in public displays of affection anyway? It was still unclear to me what exactly I wanted with her.
"You can chill, she's all good with me," I said with a half-smile, both hands held up in mock surrender.

Sidell cackled with glee as she looked over at her friend. "Bye Dawn!" she called as her friend left with a grin. She then turned to me with a light-hearted smile.

"Hey." She finally addressed me. Her eyes still had that glitter to it like she had been handed the secret to the universe and was excited to share it with the whole world. I didn't know how a person could manage to exude so much positivity. This much awesomeness without knowing it, and also be totally unaware about her effect on people… Her effect on me…

"Hey." I touched her arm, and I saw her eyes react to me in the slightest way. I caught it because I was staring straight into them. "I'm guessing that you don't normally agree to hang with mysterious boys, and then follow them home," I said as my mouth lifted into a lopsided grin that I had no control over.

"Ah, so you read minds?" she asked, cutely shielding her face from me.

"Yep. It's kind of something that was passed down to me," I joked, hoping to make her laugh. And she did, the sound of her carefree laughter giving me an unexpected surge of nostalgia. It had been so long since I'd enjoyed the company of someone like this, and I was glad that I was able to make her laugh, and hopefully feel special. It was a feeling that made me very content.

"So…You ready? My bus is right there." I motioned to the school bus parked off to the side. Its sliding doors had just opened, inviting my peers inside with a loud hydraulic hiss.

She nodded and replied, "Yeah, let's go."

"Alright, follow me." I touched her arm again; I couldn't resist the insane urge to touch her at every possible opportunity. We hopped onto the bus and took a seat near the back as we waited for the bus to fill up.

"Can I sit by the window?" she asked shyly. We gazed at each other.

She shimmered like a dream as I held back a chuckle and replied, "Dang…I really like the window spot. Y'know?" My fingerless gloved hand gripped the seat in front of us as I spoke.

She smiled teasingly, "Please…" she purred, batting her beautiful blues. My grin was now broader than a city block, but I tried to keep cool by licking my lips.

"Alright, I got you," I replied, and we rose simultaneously to switch seats.

"Thanks," she said, gazing out of the window as the bus pulled away from the curb. Even though this was only our third time together, I could already feel the connection between us growing stronger.

As the school bus moved along, our conversation flowed with ease, as if we were reading pre-written dialogue from a movie script. I stared into her eyes and tried not to get lost in their depths for too long; I wanted her to know that my attention was focused solely on what she had to say. Even the brief moments of silence bound us together like an unbreakable thread, underlining our connection. She glanced at me from below her lashes and her voice was a bit timid as she asked, "Can I try your hat on?"

I chuckled and leaned closer to her. "You really wanna wear my hat?"

"Yeah," she softly replied. "I just want to try it on."

I removed my neon pin cap from my head, my fingers tracing the edges with reluctance before handing it over to her.

She put it on and then looked up at me, her face softening into a coy smile. "How do I look?"

"Looks dope." I grinned, nervously glancing around, wondering if anyone was watching us as she stuck out her tongue playfully. I shook my head in awe. She was too cute for words. She grinned back at me. She then carefully removed the cap from her head and placed it back on mine, gently grazing my forehead with her fingertips as she did so. I flinched internally at the unexpected contact, my feelings towards physical connection having been numbed ever since my best friend - the love of my life - had passed away. Sure, I'd flirt and converse with girls, but anything beyond verbal communication was usually completely off limits.

Sidell leaned back in her seat, her eyes and smile never leaving me. The silence was too much for me to take and I nervously bit my lip, wondering what I could say or do to break the tension. I opened my mouth to say something, but nothing came out... I was suddenly tongue-tied.
Real smooth, Romeo.

Her smile widened as she watched me squirm.

The school bus finally screeched to a stop, unloading us and some of my Downtown peers in front of the rusty metal gates that guarded my neighborhood. Sidell seemed anxious by how close she kept to me. I guessed she was out of her element here, being from Uptown Chicago and all. Everywhere I looked brought back a flood of memories, both good and bad. A wave of shame swept through me at the thought of Sidell being exposed to the harshness of this neighborhood.

The buildings loomed around us, their dull red bricks marred by graffiti. Sickly green trees dotted the neighborhood, not an oasis but a reminder of how even nature couldn't thrive here. There was the clatter of rolling dice on the pavement and music blasting from windows and street corners as wafts of cigarette smoke mingled with the smell of spilt liquor. The only brightness in the area came from the children who ran around, laughing and playing, despite the grimy surroundings.

As we walked down the cracked sidewalk, I couldn't help but notice the way Sidell's eyes darted around, taking in the sights and sounds of my neighborhood. She was used to the clean streets and fancy shops of Uptown. Here, she stuck out like a rose blooming in a junkyard. Guilt gnawed at my stomach for bringing her to this place. But another part of me was glad she was seeing it—the good, the bad, the ugly truth of where I came from. She needed to understand if we were ever going to really be friends.

"Are you alright, Sid?" I asked softly.

"Huh?" She paused, nearly tripping on an overturned trash can. Her lips parted in a contemplative expression. "Yes…I think so… Why do you ask?" she eventually replied, her voice revealing her uncertainty.

"No reason, it's just…I thought with this being all new to you…" I trailed off, allowing the unsaid words to hang heavily in the air between us. "Ah, this is my place, right across from the playground. Shall we?" I quickly changed the subject by guiding her towards the apartment. We arrived at the door and I started untying my sneakers.

She stared at me and sniggered. "Why are you taking your shoes off outside?" she asked, tucking a loose hair strand behind her ear.

"Oh uh, we gotta remove our shoes before we enter the house. Since a day or two ago, my grandma has been tripping on me about it, because supposedly she just learned that people can carry spirits with them and what not. I paused for dramatic effect. "But really, she just got the floors deep cleaned and doesn't want our nasty shoes mucking them up." I winked and chuckled. She nodded understandingly before starting to do the same.

"I wouldn't be shocked if that was true," she remarked as I removed the house key that was tucked inside my sneaker.

"I suppose it requires a bit of faith, right?" I said, shoving the key into the lock, hearing it click loudly. The door opened easily as I pushed it inwards and we both stepped inside.

Upon entering the apartment, we intruded on the bible study taking place in the lounge with my grandma, Bernadette, and her three friends, Aris, Monnie, and Tedra. I internally huffed, because why today out of all days! They couldn't have done this at the church? Grandma and her ever-present hospitality! This was going to be awkward…

"Oh, look who just came in the door. We were just talking about you, Jacky. How was school?" Grandma greeted us warmly, her eyes zeroing in on Sid.

I tossed my backpack on the ground with a strained smile, resisting the urge to drag Sidell back out the door. "It was alright. This is my friend Sidell. We're gonna hang out for a bit."

Sidell offered a slight wave, her shyness very apparent. I couldn't blame her; my grandmother's friends' presence was overwhelming.

One of grandma's closest friends, Aris, beamed at us. She was a sweet older woman with curly gray hair, warm hazel eyes and caramel-colored skin. Her smile widened as her gaze darted from me to Sid. "Ain't she a beauty? My oh my."

"She sure is," Grandma enthusiastically seconded before addressing Sidell directly with a friendly smile. "Hello there, I'm Jacky's grandmother. How are you dear?"

"I'm good and you?" Sidell replied in a soft voice, throwing me a brief glance.

"I'm doing alright." Grandma nodded in her recliner chair as she glanced at me again. "You're bringing her through the front door, what a refreshing change."

I hissed a sharp "*Grandma*," before redirecting an awkward smile towards Sidell, who raised her eyebrows, clearly wanting to laugh.

My grandma eyed both of us in that cautious parental way before she inquired curiously, "So what was y'all teens planning on doing on a school night?"

I prepared to answer, but Aris interrupted by flicking her thinning curls. "You know these kids today. They just wanna Netflix and chill." She nodded confidently, pretending to understand teens.

Monnie, the eldest in the group, raised an eyebrow, her wrinkled face contorting into confusion as she asked, "What do you mean? *Netflix and chill*? Is that some kind of game on Facebook?"

Tedra cracked open a soda pop and attempted to offer an explanation. "No? If you are talking about the one with puzzles, that's OnlyFans."

I waved my hand in the air to reject the notion. "Okay, no. That's not even..." I paused and pinched the bridge of my nose as I held in the muster to laugh. I then turned my attention back to my grandma. "Grandma, we were just gonna hang out and do some homework. Is that okay?" I asked, trying to convey my innocence.

"That's alright," she answered sternly, "as long as y'all hit the books first." Grandma's eyes burned through me as she spoke.

"No doubt, we were just getting to it," I replied assertively as I motioned for Sidell to follow me. Sidell acknowledged the elderly woman with a grin before following me.

I opened my bedroom door and flinched at the unexpected sight of the annoying kid in my room.

Kaluna, a snot-nosed and sassy nine-year-old girl who frequently violated boundaries when she visited, had made herself at home on my bed, where she sat watching my television.

If she hadn't been so irritating, she would have passed as a cute little kid. Her thick dark hair was neatly braided and full of brightly colored barrettes that matched the yellow t-shirt she wore under a pair of overalls. Her brown eyes were glued to the Looney Tunes cartoon on the television.

Thoroughly absorbed by what she was watching and the pile of jellybeans she was blissfully devouring, Kaluna still hadn't even noticed us in the doorway.

"Why are you in my…" I paused, then directed my voice toward the hallway. "Grandma! Why is she in my room?!"

"Let her watch her cartoon, she ain't hurting nobody," Grandma's distant voice yelled back.

Kaluna and Sidell locked eyes, and she smiled before waving at her. "Hi," Kaluna chirped in a sing-song manner as if she were already aware of my disdain for her presence.

"Hi." Sidell returned the greeting with a small wave.

"You're really pretty," Kaluna started with a twinkle in her eye.

"Aww so sweet, you're pretty too," Sidell replied softly as she smiled down at her.

"She can do that at her mama's house. They don't got cable?!" I asked my grandma, quickly crashing Sidell and Kaluna's interaction. I grabbed my remote and switched off the television. "Get out of my room Kaluna," I said firmly. Kaluna nonchalantly stood up on my bed with her dirty sneakers still on before hopping off with a smirk on her face.

"Your room is ugly anyway," she mocked out of spite before skipping out.

"Grandma! How come you let the spawn of Satan wear shoes in the house?!" I said but got no response in return. I sucked my teeth as I grabbed the door, ready to slam it. Then I remembered Sidell was here so, I just settled on closing it lightly, leaving it cracked. My head shook of its own accord as I turned to address Sidell.

"My sincerest apologies," I uttered.

"It's okay, I definitely get it. Was that your sister?" Sidell asked, taking off her backpack.

I narrowed my brows. "Hell nah." I slid off my school uniform blazer and tossed it onto my bed. "She is just some kid from the neighborhood. And she'll keep coming around if Grandma continues to feed her."

A soft laugh escaped her lips and she smiled as she perched on the edge of my bed, watching me rummage through my drawers for an outfit to wear. My room wasn't up to par, and I automatically assumed it wouldn't meet her expectations; posters were strewn about the walls, little cars cluttered every corner and CDs were in high, disorganized piles. It was basically a hoarder's dream come true.

"I wonder what my parents will think when they find out I'm not coming home anytime soon. I don't even have a legitimate excuse yet." She sighed, glancing away from me. My shirt and jeans hung from the crook of my arm as I searched through the dresser for a pair of socks.

"Why don't you call them and let them know you're at my house?" I tried to give her a reassuring smile. Sidell snorted.

"That would be a death sentence. My parents would flip if they knew I was lingering around this side of town—at a boy's house. They already gave me hell when they found out about you."

I raised an eyebrow at her and joked, "You told them about me already, like my name and everything?"

Sidell smiled back and rolled her eyes. "Pft, oh yeah," she said, voice dripping with sarcasm. "I gave them your social security number and dental records. They're practically planning our wedding as we speak."

I chuckled as I rummaged through my dresser, sensing she needed to vent.

"All I needed to say was a boy helped me, and they filled in the blanks themselves right before immediately going into protective overdrive mode." she sighed. "I might as well be under house arrest."

I nodded understandingly. "I get it. But you're not a child anymore, Sidell. You don't need their permission."

"I wished it were that simple, but it's not. They have such high expectations for me. It's suffocating." She traced a finger over the faded blanket, lost in thought.

"What do you want?" I asked gently.

She looked up at me, "Freedom. To make my own choices without disappointing them."

"Then take it. Claim your freedom. It's your life to live, not theirs—"

"*Jacky!*"

I was abruptly interrupted by my grandma's voice, which echoed from the living room. I could tell that her company had just left by the way her tone of voice had reverted back to normal.

"I'm coming," I responded, setting my outfit down on top of the dresser. "I'll be right back," I informed Sidell before turning out of my bedroom door.

I approached my grandma, who was now in the kitchen with no wig on, her short white afro now on full display. "Yes ma'am?" I asked her, my fingers hanging on the archway of the kitchen entrance.

"I had put some rice and cabbage on the stove. Go on and ask Sandy if she wants something to eat," she said with a hand on her hip as she removed the foggy lid.

"Her name is Sidell, Grandma, and anyways, we're getting food while we're out."

"I didn't ask what you were doing," she said. "Now go ask her, child, before I smack you silly."

I huffed, walking back to my bedroom.

"Sidell?" I whispered, peeking my head into the room. She put her cell phone aside as she looked up.

"My grandma wants to know if you'd like some cabbage and rice,"

"No thank you." She smiled. I was determined to keep my grandmother from imposing on my visitor, so I raised my voice slightly for maximum effect. "See, Grandma? She doesn't want any…" The words caught in my throat as I was startled by a looming figure in my peripheral vision. I spun around to find my grandmother standing directly behind me.

"Hush up child," she said, barreling past me to get into the room. "Young lady," she said sweetly as she addressed Sidell directly, "would you like some cabbage and rice?"

"Uh, yes, yes please, just a little bit," Sidell said as her eyes caught my bulging ones.

I mouthed, "Seriously?"

Sidell responded back with a shrug that said, "What else was I supposed to do? Sorry?"

"I got you beloved," Grandma replied, turning out of the room but not before smacking the back of my head.

"Ah! What did I do…" I began rubbing my head as she disappeared down the hall. As soon as she was gone, I left the door ajar again and placed my hands on my hips.

"You could've still declined it you know?" I said to Sidell, feeling uneasy that Grandma had pressured her into accepting food. It's not that I wasn't comfortable with what we ate, but I didn't want Sid to have second thoughts about coming over again.

"I know, I know," Sidell said, trying to reassure me. "But it's okay, really. Besides, it's free food."

My lips turned up slightly, but the uncertainty still lingered in my expression. "Just don't feel like you have to say yes to everything she offers, okay?" I reminded her softly.

She nodded, balancing her arms at her sides as her gaze roamed around my room.

She looked so beautiful just then that I couldn't resist wanting to understand what was going through her mind. The football on the shelf beside my door caught my attention, and I started tossing it up and down a few times as I changed the subject. "So, what do you think?" My eyes locked onto hers, searching for an answer to a question I hadn't even asked yet.

She smiled as her eyebrows flashed up, "About?"

"My room?" I gestured around us with my hands, hoping that she would give me her true opinion. She grinned mischievously and pointed one finger towards the floor in front of us.

"Not bad," Sid said, seeming to enjoy the subtle shade that passed between us when she added, "your dirty laundry doesn't look too bad on the floor."
"Oof," I coughed as I quickly scooped up the mess forming a circle around us. "My fault," I apologized sheepishly as I threw some of it into a pile next to the closet. "Excuse the miscellaneous mess. I haven't gotten around to summer cleaning…or winter or spring…"

Sid snickered and rolled her eyes at my poor attempt at humor. "So, apart from football, what else do you like?" she asked, her voice soft and melodic.

I shrugged. "Well I uh…It's not the manliest activity but, I love to paint. Not sure if you can tell from the last time we met."

"Oh yeah, I remember. When you taught me how to paint the lamb. We should do it again sometime." She chuckled, a pleasant sound that made me feel a little more relaxed.

"Right…" I trailed off before my memories could paralyze me, quickly suppressing the memories of my best friend Donica before they could rush through my mind like a tidal wave. We'd spent our days exploring nature and its beauty; picnics and painting, sharing our emotions about the world around us. But then she was gone, and suddenly this world felt oppressive and hollow without her.

"Do you have any artworks here with you?" Sidell asked, looking around for clues. I had my cds and tapes tucked away beneath a mound of teen fashion magazines. They were mostly paintings that I've created with Donica, and… I wasn't ready to take the journey back there just yet. Revisiting them would mean letting go of Donica all over again. It was a darkness I didn't want to dwell in any longer.

"Not right now... I er… would have to find them in this mess." My voice wavered as my emotions threatened to overtake me. "But if you remind me, I could show you the next time you come around..."

"Of course, I'd love to see them." Sidell's eyes shone with warmth and understanding, as if she knew exactly what was going on in my mind without me even saying it. "I'll hold you to that."

I smiled at the thought of her making a return visit. "I hope you do…" I was still talking when I noticed a small figure peering through my window. *This girl is definitely testing me!*

"What?" Sid asked, noticing my sudden silence and change of expression.

"Kaluna's outside. The same troublesome little girl from earlier," I explained, wondering why this annoying little girl was eavesdropping on us. Sid slowly turned her head towards the window and arched a skeptical eyebrow.
"Oh? Where outside?" she asked, the corners of her mouth tugging up into a friendly smile. I hoped she wasn't taking a liking to that miscreant. I strode over to the screen-less window, determined to put Kaluna in her place.

Just as I parted the curtains, Kaluna's voice reverberated from the bushes where she'd been hiding. "I wasn't peeping at you," she said with an impish grin. The Jellybeans rolled around in her mouth like marbles.

I slid back the glass window. "So what was ya doin then?" I scoffed, narrowing my eyes at her as I folded my arms across my chest.

"Mmm." Kaluna paused for a moment, an immature grin covering her face. Then she sang mockingly, "JJ and blonde girl sitting in a tree, lockin' lips like a pack of fleas!" She darted away, laughing maniacally.

Chasing after her would be a wasted effort and embarrassing so instead I closed my window as I watched her sprint away with no repercussions.

Swiveling around to meet Sidell's gaze, I chewed on my lip, feeling a wave of embarrassment swell within my chest as I couldn't help but chuckle at Kaluna's antics.

"Sorry again," I said apologetically as I ran a hand through my hair nervously. "I didn't know she was gonna hit us with that musical number."

Sidell smiled shyly. "Oh, it's okay really. That was kind of funny." She chuckled, her eyes gleaming with amusement as she watched me. "You know, I kind of like the fact that your neighborhood is so lively. It's refreshing."

I couldn't help but sigh and shake my head in disbelief. "You won't be saying that when she starts throwing rocks at your window at five in the morning," I joked.

Sidell's laughter filled the room, and I couldn't help but feel like I'd made the right choice inviting her over. She really had a way of making me forget about all the troubles that had been plaguing my mind.

"You never know, I might like the wake-up call," she joked.

I grinned back at her, feeling a warmth spread through my chest. It was moments like this that made me grateful for the people in my life who had brought me joy and laughter. It was moments like this that made me forget about the pain of losing my best friend.

Placing my thumbs in my pants pocket, we fell into a comfortable silence as I looked around my room randomly. That's when I spotted a black pouch on my dresser. I unzipped the bag and pulled out a glass bottle colored with a light blue liquid. It was my cologne— my favorite fragrance at that. Playing off my genuine need for a distraction, I unscrewed the lid and breathed in its beautiful aroma.

"This is my favorite cologne..." I murmured as I walked over to Sid so she could take a whiff too.

"Really nice. I can see why it's your favorite. What scent is that?"

I examined the bottle as if I was seeing it for the first time. "It's called aqua di gio?" I looked at her as if she knew the perfume, but she shrugged.

"I guess it's a really popular men's cologne," I said, returning the bottle to its pouch before dropping it on my dresser. I leaned against it. I sighed, changing the subject. "So, how are your gaming skills?"

Sid looked at me curiously and echoed my words. "My gaming... skills?"

"Yeah."

"Um.... They can be described as adequate."

I nodded. "Hmp."

She smiled, "Why?"

Trying to conceal a smirk, I answered vaguely. "Oh, nothing. Just asking." Gathering my clothes, I spoke again. "Listen, I'm gonna go to the bathroom to change. If someone knocks on the window, just ignore them. I'll be right back."

Sidell chuckled. "Okay, I'll be here."

A few minutes later, I stepped out of my steaming hot shower, the steam drifting into the hallway. I grabbed my long sleeve purple t-shirt and slipped on my dark jeans, spritzing some cologne onto myself as I finished dressing. Threading my gold hoop earring through my ear, I ran a pick comb through my flat-top. I then strided out of the foggy bathroom.

I made my way to my bedroom, but Sidell was nowhere to be found. Then I heard Grandma's voice coming from the dining room, peppered with laughter amidst the savory smell of cabbage and rice. I peeked around the corner to see them seated at the table, chatting pleasantly while they ate. I was surprised to find Sidell in deep conversation with my grandma, who was animatedly telling her a story about her youth.

I politely stood off to the side, expecting their convo to cut off at some point, but they kept on. Then somewhere in between her rambling, Grandma mentioned her testimony on how she found Jesus. And knowing Grandma? Yeah, she's not going to stop yapping about him. So, I took matters into my own hands.

"Alright Grandma," I said, pushing in a chair at the table, "it's getting dark out so we need to get going."

Grandma's attention turned to me then back to Sidell. "Jacky's always in a rush." She chuckled heartily.

I raised my eyebrows with a smile as I couldn't deny her statement... like I said I hated waiting.

"Okay, you two have fun now. Don't be out too late."

"We won't." I bent down to give her a kiss on the cheek before turning to Sidell. "You ready?"

"Yep." Sidell stood up with a smile. "Thanks again for letting me stay for dinner, ma'am. That was delicious."

Grandma waved off the gesture and replied, "You're welcome anytime sweetie." Then Sidell offered to take both plates to wash them up but Grandma stopped her. "It's okay baby," she said with a smile and a gentle pat on Sidell's arm. "I need to keep moving or else these legs will give out on me."

"Alright, I'll be back later." I waved at Grandma before we stepped out of the door.

The distance to the place I had in mind required hitching a ride on the bus, but I wanted to spend as much time with Sidell as possible, so we opted to walk. It would take longer, but the walk would act as part of the tour of Downtown Chicago. Sidell made herself clear as soon as we left my apartment.

"Even though I agreed to walk, I have to warn you, I'm not a very athletic person. So, if I faint on the way, you'll be held accountable."

I looked at her mischievously for a second before she burst out laughing when I kept staring at her. I sensed that she might laugh like that when she was nervous. I needed to quit staring openly at her like a creep, but I couldn't help myself. She pulled me in with her mysterious beauty.

"Then I'll just have to carry you…" I finally said, the smirk still apparent on my face. "If you want..." I added quickly. "Only a suggestion... "

"No chance!" she replied insistently as she blushed. "I think I can keep myself from turning into dust before we get there." She smiled and then laughed nervously again as I blatantly continued to stare.

★ ★ ★ ★ ✞ ★ ★ ★ ★

We got to know each other better as we walked and talked. It felt like we were creating our own little world in the midst of the bustling city. We marched down each street with a youthful boldness, playing our childish games like *I spy with my little eye* and then *truth or dare*. I was caught off guard when Sid had first suggested the last game, and I just nodded in agreement with curiosity boiling inside me.

"Truth or Dare?" she asked and I was hesitant before settling on "Dare". Unfazed by my choice, she smiled deviously and challenged me to shout at the top of my lungs, "I'm a maniac!"

I sucked my teeth at her request but couldn't help but laugh along with her when I declined. "Hell nah," I said, still smiling.

Sidell went into a laughing frenzy. "Why not? It's not like I'm asking you to do something dirty."

I laughed. "Ain't no way in Soho. What I look like, embarrassing myself like that in public?"

She shrugged. "Suit yourself." Then she gave me a sly grin. "But you know there's always a consequence for backing out."

I raised an eyebrow. "Consequence? What consequence?" I said, knowing full well about the compulsory forfeit of refusing to go through with a dare.

Sidell just smirked and avoided my question, clearly trying to think of something to punish me with. Luckily, we arrived at our destination right on time, and I pointed at the sign as we got closer, hoping to distract her. Then I turned and stared at Sid, my thumbs shoved in the pockets of my jeans as I leaned against the wall of the graffitied building.
"The arcade?" She smiled brightly. "And you couldn't tell me?" She pinched me playfully as I backed away slightly.
"I wanted to surprise you," I replied, holding up my hands in defense.

"Well, you definitely succeeded," she said, her eyes sparkling as she looked at me. She then focused on the arcade like it was the most fascinating place on earth. Her gaze fixed on the flashing multi-colored neon lights, floating bubbles, and live karaoke that could be seen through the windows. I swallowed a chuckle as I directed her to the entrance.

"Just so you know, it's on now. I'm a champ so there's no way you're gonna beat me in any game."

"Oh yeah? I assure you, I learn fast so we'll see about that." She smirked at my confidence. But I knew she had no idea what a real pro-gamer I was.

"Hmmm. Just don't cry when I repeatedly beat you." I smiled boastfully.

"I feel like you're being overconfident. You mind toning it down a little?" She smiled.

"Why? Feeling intimidated?" My mouth transformed into a lopsided grin that I had no control over.

"Pulease! I'm just saving my energy," she said, shielding herself from my fiendish face with her dainty hands. A carefree laugh sprung from her and the sound of it made me feel nostalgic. It felt like such a long time ago since I've genuinely enjoyed playful banter, or just being in the company of an attractive girl.

Chapter Fourteen: Sidell

The Arcade was located way out in downtown Chicago. The whole place was packed with excitement! They had laser tag, air hockey, bumper cars, and obviously the classic gaming machines. If I kept hanging with JJ, I may as well forget about going home. The sounds of joy, laughter, and blaring music was fused into a lively chorus of white noise. We continually bumped into people as we tried to get by. The floor was absolutely flooded with teenagers.

"So, this is a daily occurrence for you, huh?" I asked as I took in the entirety of the whole place as we weaved our way through the crowd.

He laughed before answering. "I'ma be real with you, I *do* actually come here almost every day."

I gasped at his admission. "So, this is where you've been hiding!"

His infectious lopsided smile that spread across his face always managed to make me melt. "I'm kidding," he said playfully. "I come here once a week max, Fridays and Saturdays mostly."

"Whew, I was going to say. I might have to tell Ms. Kyepher where to find you. That way I'd see you in school more." I flashed a cheeky smile and he chuckled at my sass.

"So, where do you wanna start?" he asked slowly, lingering on the last syllable.

I was still distracted from the movement around us, that I didn't even realize that I was bouncing my leg.

"Sidell, are you okay?" He asked, puzzled. "You look like you're going to break out into a break dance."

"I actually need to go to the bathroom first."

A nervous laugh escaped JJ's lips as he scratched the back of his head. "Oh right...." He paused and gestured towards the door with the word *Women* written in bold print on it. "It's over there."

"Ok, I won't be long," I said, making a dash for the door.

"I'll be at the Pac Man Machine," he called out as I entered the bathroom.

The bathroom was spacious, fitted with marble tiles on the floor and walls. There were stalls on each side, and a cool looking sink was fitted on the marble wall next to a full-length mirror. I quickly did my business, washed my hands and headed back out.

Amidst the throngs of laughing teens and whirring sounds of arcade machines, there was JJ — just as he'd promised — playing Pac Man. A fluffy pink Barbie keychain now hung from his belt loop, clashing hilariously with his rough-and-tumble style.

"I didn't know you had a soft spot for Barbie," I teased, sliding up next to him. He looked down at his keychain briefly then back to me, smiling.

"Yeah, dem chicks bad," he laughed as I playfully rolled my eyes. "Nah I'm playing, this is for you. I won it at that claw machine," he said, unhooking it from his belt loop.

"Aw thanks," I said, taking the keychain. "But I'm more of a Bratz kind of girl."

JJ squinted his eyes and brows. "The big-headed dolls?" He laughed.

I gasped with mock offense and tried to keep a straight face as I said, "Their heads are not that big."

JJ chuckled. "Nah. Have you seen their eyes? They take up half their face!"

I couldn't help but laugh at his observation. "I hate that you even pointed that out."

★ ★ ★ ★ ✟ ★ ★ ★ ★

JJ's fingers flew across the buttons in a frenzied blur. I was barely keeping up. He rolled up his arched back and punched the air in frustration each time I managed to land a hit. But I knew he wouldn't go down easy.

The screen flashed - Player 2 Wins! I threw my hands up with a victorious yell. He laughed to mask the saltiness that he must've been feeling. I loved it!

"Now you're just spamming!" JJ joked, trying to cover my hand movements with his fingers.

"You are too!" I laughed, clinching another win. JJ pulled back his hands from the machine, balling them into fists as he grinned. It was impossible to ignore how handsome he looked. His charisma was electric, igniting a fire in me I'd never felt before.

"Victory is starting to look good on me huh?" I teased, flipping my hair back confidently.

"Psh, I'm still just warming up," JJ scoffed. "Thought I'd take it easy on you at first."

"Yeah, yeah," I said, making an L with my fingers.

"That's it. The Legendary JJ needs to give his royal hands a rest," he said, putting on an exaggerated British accent and shaking out his hands dramatically.

"You've barely done anything," I said, pointing to the four simple buttons. "Not like this ancient thing requires much skill."

"Excuse me, I am a gaming legend," he declared, puffing out his chest. "We artists need to pace ourselves, preserve our instruments."

I laughed and playfully punched his arm. "You big baby."

"Nah but forreal though, I do need a break. My thumbs are starting to cramp."

We walked to the upstairs sitting area. Our steps echoed off the steel-covered steps as the dance music from below died down and the scent of wings and fries hung in the air.

The dining area had a nice view of the outside, a small open kitchen, and several booths that lined the large window, covering a whole wall. The countertops were covered in every kind of chip you could imagine, and it was topped off with glass tubs of blue and red ribboned candy.

We settled at a vacant booth and were immediately attended to by an energetic girl who was obviously a highschooler as well. I watched as she bounced from booth to booth with infectious enthusiasm. She took our orders attentively. I requested a serving of the special wings, plus fries on the side, and the medium sauce instead of high. I didn't want to drink too much water and make a fool of myself if I couldn't handle the heat. JJ ordered the same thing, but with the spicy buffalo sauce instead. I raised a brow at him and he just grinned. The girl went on her merry way and quickly came back with water and a fancy basket full of buttery bread as we waited for our food.

The booths were designed to be family-friendly, so they're spaced out, leaving a lot of room for a group of at least four people. With just the two of us, it's like having too much space, but no space at all. Most of the other booths were occupied and soft jazz music was playing from the corner farthest away from us.

"So..." I didn't really know what I wanted to say, but I desperately wanted to fill the silence as we watched the waitress skip back toward the kitchen. For some reason, something urged me to bring up what had happened that night during the game. I'd never been that close to a boy before, and I still felt like I needed to know what warranted such a reaction. But I didn't want to push him too much, I didn't want to seem too nosy.

"Yeah, this is the point when we ask each other questions about ourselves. But the twenty questions thing is somewhat cliche. Don't you think so?" JJ asked.

"Yeah, it might seem lame, but you can get to know a lot about someone, you know?" I countered softly, because I didn't want to push him away. He seemed like the kind of guy to shut you out to deal with whatever he's dealing with in private.

Placing his elbows on the table, he leaned forward. "Okay, you go first. Ask away," he said, his hands resting on his face as he looked directly into my eyes.

"Okay, do you mind if we, um, well, if we started with what happened last night? Uh, and, like if you don't want to answer that, it's okay. You can ask me your question instead."

I was out on a limb here, but I needed to know what I was getting myself into. I watched him as his eyes glazed over quickly. It happened almost too fast, but I caught it and kneaded a piece of bread in my hand as he took his sweet time to reply.

"That's a long messy story. Hardly fit for discussion over a dinner date, Sidell," he said, and even though his eyes have gone dark, his mouth quirked up into a half smile.

Then it hit me. I replayed his last words and I almost choked on the bread in my mouth.

So, it is a date! I knew it!

Containing my excitement, I dusted off my fingers and proceeded to say, "You don't have to tell me if you don't feel comfortable, but I want to help, however I can."

He looked like he was gathering his thoughts. My hands stretched across the table and touched his fingers as they nervously tapped the wooden top.

I could tell that he really didn't want to talk about last night, but as soon as my fingers touched his skin, I seemed to forget that I was trying to comfort him. I only knew that I wanted to continue touching him. His eyes relaxed and went back to the enchanting warm brown they usually were, the dark cloud drifting away as he sighed. He was so achingly beautiful at that moment that I had forgotten myself and started caressing his hands in gentle, lazy motions with my thumb. Watching him visibly relax and enjoy my touch, tugged at my heart. It's like the whole world melted away and we're locked in this beautiful moment where all the sensations to be felt were peace and companionship.

"And here is your order. Enjoy!" the young waitress yelled, dropping the contents in her hands on our table.

Her sudden intrusion made me pull my hands away from his and hide them under the table like I'd been caught doing something distasteful. She smiled at me with a wink and it only irritated me because the magical moment I was sharing with JJ was gone. He didn't seem as fazed as I was. He was totally cool, like we were already at the stage where touching each other was completely okay.

I tried the famous deep-fried wings, and to my surprise, they were well-seasoned, melting in my mouth in a burst of flavors. We both ate in silence for a few minutes, until JJ paused to drink a glass of water, and then cleared his throat. I took a glance at his plate and his food was already half finished.

"My mother abandoned me when I was five," he revealed with a sudden solemnity. I instantly felt terrible for pushing him into telling me about last night. Why did I think he was going through a breakup? *How shallow!*

"Oh, I'm so sorry," I said, slightly taken aback. My hands stained with sticky sauce kept me from reaching out to touch him again.

"No, no. It's fine. Don't feel bad for asking. I'd be worried if you weren't curious after my episode last night. Don't feel bad." His voice was quiet and soothing. He seemed to be reassuring me, and himself.

I nodded, dropping the fries in my hands because the mood was now sober. It would be insane to keep devouring wings while he's reliving a traumatic experience I practically pushed him to recount.

"I guess she didn't have the strength to stay, so she left my grandmother to raise me. She had visited me once when I was ten, but she left again without as much as a goodbye. After that, everything went downhill from there."

"Downhill? What happened exactly?" I asked.

"What happened?" he repeated, my tone biting. "I'll tell you what happened. I felt rejected and worthless, like I wasn't good enough for my own mother to love. I struggled every day just to get out of bed. The pain was so intense I wanted to end it all because the one person who was supposed to love me unconditionally didn't even want me." He paused, shaking his head. "She thinks it's so easy to forgive, but it's not. It feels like she ripped my heart out and stomped all over it. So now we remain more like strangers than mother and child. Irreconcilable differences and all that..." He trailed off.

"But last night, she texted me again with an invitation to her engagement announcement party. And I just kind of lost it. I got so angry I smashed my phone against the wall... Then I saw you and everything just boiled over... For years she's been trying to erase the fact that I'm her son, hiding me like her dirty little secret. And now she hides behind religion and her perfect new life to justify abandoning me, like none of it matters...." He said in one breath, as his right hand gripped the edge of the table in a vice-like hold.

"Oh JJ." I could only say those two words before I trailed off. That was a lot. He was dealing with a lot of conflict and I saw that it had taken a chunk out of him.

I cleaned my fingers with a napkin before reaching out for his hand. I couldn't possibly hold off any longer. I pushed him to talk about something very hurtful and I felt terrible because truly, I was not expecting that. But I was also grateful that I was able to do what I knew how to do best: listen and provide comfort. However, he snatched his hands away passionately as he thumped the table with his fists, making the silverware jump.

" She didn't care then, she doesn't care now. And I'm supposed to just show up to her stupid ceremony and smile for the cameras like everything is okay? Like she didn't ruin my life and leave me to pick up the pieces all by myself?" JJ's voice risen to a shout. I could feel eyes on us but I didn't care. Let them judge. They didn't know his pain.

"No, JJ. You don't have to do anything you don't want to," I said, searching his eyes. "You have every right to feel angry and hurt. But don't let her control your emotions like this. You're stronger than that."

He let out a bitter laugh. "Stronger? I'm barely holding it together. But you're right about one thing. I won't give her the satisfaction of seeing me like this."

He took a deep breath. When he spoke again his voice was calm. "I know this isn't me. I just need to come to terms with the fact that my mother will never be the parent I need her to be. And that's okay, I have people in my life who love and support me...like you."

The way he said 'you' sent shivers down my spine. It's like he said it with so much depth and meaning, like he's trying to convey something that words couldn't express.

"I'll always be here for you, JJ," I said softly, my hand tentatively reaching out to touch his once again. This time he didn't pull away, he simply leaned into my touch, his eyes closed as if savoring the sensation. We sat in silence for a few moments, lost in our own thoughts and emotions. But then JJ spoke up again, breaking the silence.

"You know what's weird?" he asked, opening his eyes to look at me.

"What?" I asked, intrigued.

"The fact that we haven't known each other for that long, yet we're already talking about deeper stuff," he said with a small smile. I couldn't help but smile back.

"Yeah, I guess it is weird. But I'm glad we're able to have these conversations so quickly."

We sat in silence for a few moments, the weight of JJ's story still heavy on both of us. Though, there was also a sense of comfort in knowing that we had each other to lean on. And underneath it all, there was a deeper connection forming between us. One that I couldn't quite explain, but I was excited to explore further.

He chuckled, his voice hinting at something he wasn't saying.

"Oh, and Sid? I understand how you feel about me, but could you not scuff up my sneakers?"

My gaze dropped to his expensive shoes under the table. I had not realized my feet had been resting on his for the past few minutes. "Oops. Sorry about that." I tried to cover up my embarrassment with a joke. "And FYI, I'm not feeling you yet. Not in the slightest, so, so much for that irresistible charm..."

He gave me an exaggeratedly wounded expression, then flashed me a heart-stopping smile. "Dang it," he said wryly, arching an eyebrow playfully. "All that hard work I put into smiling." The laughter spilled out of me before I knew what was happening.

We quickly finished our food and headed back to the main floor of the arcade. JJ was a complete gentleman; he didn't mind spending his hard-earned cash. He paid for two hours' worth of gaming, and in between rounds, JJ would flirt with me and make jokes while I tried my best not to blush too much. He seemed to forget about all his worries as he challenged me to different races or duels. Even though I rarely won against him, it was still fun trying to beat him, and watching him enjoy himself after everything he had just told me he'd been through.

"You up for a movie?" JJ asked as we fed our tickets into the prize machine. He settled on a Rubik's Cube while I opted for an expandable ball fidget toy. Then my phone pinged. I glanced at the time before scrolling through the missed calls and messages.

"Shoot." I grimaced, already knowing what the messages would be about. Then I directed my attention to JJ, playing it off with a smile. "A movie? This late?"

"It's only 8 'clock. The theater is right next door to here."

"JJ, I'm sorry. But…I think I have to go," I informed him. He frowned as if he hadn't expected me to leave so soon, even though we had literally spent hours together.

"Why?" His deep voice wrapped around me like silk.

I sighed and looked away, wishing this wonderful night wouldn't end so quickly. "My sister just messaged me asking where I am. I guess my parents are pretty heated, and I don't want them to worry."

"Please?"

"Why do you want me to stay so bad?" I joked as I watched him pinch his bottom lip. His sudden nervousness was almost adorable.

"Maybe it's because I like you."

Just when I thought this guy couldn't steal any more of my heart for the night, he goes and says something like that. "Okay. I'll hang longer," I told him.

Chapter Fifteen: JJ

The lobby of the movie theater was a bustling hotbed of activity. Muted conversations rode on a wave of nauseating popcorn and nacho cheese aromas as patrons meandered across the grandiose, brightly lit hall, movie posters lining the walls. Sidell and I were purchasing some snacks at the movie theater's concession stand. That's when I was immediately caught off guard as I spotted my friend Tony and his girlfriend Dawn. Damn! Of all the days we could cross paths, why on my first date with Sidell? There they were, standing outside the restrooms, Tony's hands in Dawn's back pocket, murmuring something in her ear.

"Gosh, this is just silly," I mumbled under my breath. Trying not to look in their direction again, I caught sight of Sidell for a moment. She gasped, then beamed with delight at the sight of Dawn, but all I could do was offer a wistful smile— a feeble attempt to hide my frustration at having our evening disrupted by their presence.

"Aww I can't believe they're here," she said softly before adding, "they're so cute."

Cute wasn't the word I'd use to describe them. No, it's more like the two of them were five minutes away from wild kissing. I forced a tired smile and echoed her sentiment. "Yeah, cute."

It took a few minutes for Tony and Dawn to notice us as we got our popcorn and moved away from the busy lines. It was Sidell's idea to acknowledge them. Personally, I wanted to avoid them at all costs. It was hard not to feel like bozos as they approached us, their clasped hands swinging like an established couple. While me and Sidell kept a good foot of distance between us, and every time she smiled at me, I felt my throat grow dry. It was no use—confident Jacky Jamison was long gone, replaced by this dorky dude with no swagger whatsoever.

I was literally trying to figure out how to hold Sidell's hand without being awkward about it. My game was weak, and I blamed it on the fact that Tony and Dawn spawned out of nowhere and turned our date into multiplayer mode.

Dawn and Sidell practically erupted in jubilation as they raced towards one another, the enthusiasm of their reunion palpable. Tony and I, however, opted for a more subtle display of brotherhood— a special handshake known only to us.

"What are you doing here, bro?" Tony asked, his eyes widened at seeing me with Sidell.

"Uhh...just chilling," I began, coughing nervously. "We were just at the arcade."

"The arcade huh?" Tony chided, eyebrow arched teasingly. I scowled back in reply.

"Looks like Sidell's testing the waters tonight, hanging out all late. I am shocked," Dawn cackled as she looped her arm around Sidell's. Her free hand dug into Sidell's popcorn.

"Yeah, it's a surprise," Sidell laughed stiffly at the awkwardness that had infiltrated the conversation. We locked eyes for an eternity, my guilt skyrocketing as I wondered whether I had tricked her into staying out too late. Was I making her feel obliged to stay out with me against her parents' orders?

The question rang in my head where it hung for a moment before Dawn interrupted. "So what movie are we watching?"

"Jacky really wants to go see the new Rom- Com," Sidell said, and I shot her a glare that only lasted until she started smiling again.

"I really think we should go see the new gore fest with the orangutans and the alien babysitter," Tony chimed in.

"Dude, this is why nobody asked you. Wait," I paused, scrutinizing him with a careful gaze. "We? Who said y'all was joining us?"

"Since we're already here, we might as well tag along with you guys. Maybe it'll help prove to my parents that I have friends."

"You don't have friends," I pointed out, tilting my head as I stared at him, hoping this dude could read between the damn lines.

"How about we not see that twisted fantasy movie," Dawn told Tony, and he frowned and pursed his lips, pretending to be upset.

My eyebrows furrowed as I looked between them. "So, we're just going to roll past the part where y'all just invited y'all selves to join us?" I asked, but with no response from either of them as they continued their conversation.

"Babe, I'm not saying that you're sadistic." Dawn mocked a whine as she moved over to Tony. He then leaned in to whisper something in her ear that made her giggle. I pressed my lips together and ducked my head, and when I looked out of the corner of my eye at Sidell, she was just as disinterested. Her eyes were glued to her phone with a fixed gaze.

I took a chance and softly tapped her elbow. "Are you good?" I whispered. Her head snapped up from the illuminated screen and we locked eyes for an instant.

"Yeah, sorry about that." She smiled, quickly putting her phone away.

"Whatever." Dawn giggled, pushing away from Tony's intimate grip on her. "Sid, do you want to watch Clown Mansion?" she asked. "The thrill is mellow, I promise."

Sidell blinked a few times before redirecting her eyes from me. "No, clowns freak me out," she giggled.

Tony immediately displayed two thumbs down while shooting Sidell a disappointed glance. "Weak Sauce, Sidell's obviously on her Church girl mode tonight." he scoffed, earning a playful punch from Dawn.

"Bro," I interjected coldly, "how about you and Dawn go see it, and Sidell and I can go literally watch anything else," I replied with a hint of defensiveness in my voice, directing it at Tony, who was as clueless as ever.

Sidell absentmindedly glanced around the lobby as she twirled a lock of hair between her fingers. I used that opportunity to give Tony a full-on death stare.

"You don't want us coming with you for any particular reason?" he asked in a hushed tone as he tilted his head.

I kept silent, my eyes fixed on him until he realized what was happening.

Tony's gaze flicked to Sidell before quickly returning to me again. "Oh—!" he started to say.

I let out an exasperated sigh before he could finish.

"All the good seats will be gone soon. Let's just all go see the Rom-Com you were talking about, JJ," Sidell said, her voice breaking through the tense moment. I shot her a grateful smile, relieved that she had diffused the situation before it escalated any further.

"Aight. That works for me." I raised my shoulder in an indifferent shrug.

Sidell looked at Dawn expectantly as Tony's eyes kept darting back and forth between me and Sidell. "Uh, ok yeah," he stuttered, and I bit down on my tongue to keep from groaning.

"Yay! It's a double date." Dawn beamed as her fist pumped the air. And to make it worse, I chose that exact second to make eye contact with Sidell, whose eyes widened slightly.

"Well, not like double date as in two dates, but like you two plus us two…" Tony said. "Just like, four friends hanging out at the movies, but two of them are dating and the other two are you guys . . . who are not. I think."

I stared at Tony as he word vomited. He had an apologetic look on his face.

"This is so nice, the four of us hanging out. Isn't this nice babe?" Dawn said, beaming at Tony before leaning in for a kiss.

I rolled my eyes.

This was getting old real fast, and the movie hadn't even started yet.

"O-kay, me and JJ are going to book our seats," Sidell announced before pulling me by the arm toward the line. "Thank you, Jesus. I couldn't take another second of that," she whispered.

"Twenty bucks says they'll be making out the entire movie." I threw my head back with a groan.

Once we were all in the theater, I led Sidell up the steps and snagged four seats in the dead center. I ended up between Tony and Sidell, which wasn't a problem until the trailers started and Tony began making out with Dawn.

I rested my head on my hand and turned to look at Sidell, obscuring Tony's make out session from my view. "I'm going to kill him," I whispered, and Sidell sank down into her seat with a giggle.

She shrugged. "We could just ditch them." That would be a jerk move but so was Tony and Dawn inviting themselves onto our date, making it definitely not a date as they then spend the whole time making out with each other. Sidell nodded to the very back row that was completely empty, and before I had time to tell Tony I was ditching him, Sidell was pulling me by the hand.

My fingers interlaced with hers as we snuck up the steps, my heart pounding at the contact.

She let me hold her hand until we took our seats, but she gave me a grin like we had just gotten away with something. "Think they'll be mad?"

"Most likely, but who cares. They probably won't notice until the end of the movie," I whispered, leaning close so she could hear me.

Sidell looked over at our old seats, where Tony and Dawn were still going at it, before looking back up at me, her blue eyes piercing even in the dark. "They are kind of cute, though."

I rolled my eyes and slumped back into my chair. They weren't cute. They were nauseating.

"You can tell they really love each other," she murmured.

There was something so wistful and sweet in her voice, something that made me wish I could just put my arm around her and pull her close. After a beat, she ducked her head, and I swore I caught a shy blush on her cheeks.

Before I could overthink it, I grabbed her hand. But then, my thoughts caught up with me and I panicked that it was a step too far. When I tried to let go, Sidell interlaced her fingers with mine, holding on tight enough to keep me from letting go.

I relaxed my hand back into hers, pulling my arm in so she had enough room on the armrest too. Sidell's eyes were fixed on the screen, but every now and then, she'd sneak a glance in my direction. Those were the moments where I felt like my heart might beat itself out of my chest.

CHAPTER SIXTEEN: SIDELL

I was only vaguely aware of what was going on in the movie. It wasn't as good as I thought it was going to be, but that's on me. Most Rom-Coms always left me disappointed, so I should have expected this. But I couldn't blame my inability to focus on the weak storyline entirely. To start off, I just couldn't relax. In the lobby, my phone had kept blowing up with messages and phone calls from my parents and my nerves were shooting through the roof. Even in the darkened theater, I kept scanning the crowd to see if my parents may have someone spying on me, because that's what strict parents do. Heck, I jumped at the opportunity to ditch Dawn and Tony, but it was more so I could snag a seat in the very back, that way I didn't have to worry about being snuck up on from behind.

And of course, I felt that whatever this was between Jacky and I, that it was personal. And I didn't want anyone's instigating eyes intruding on an intimate moment between us, even if we were just talking.

JJ's hand was still firmly holding mine, a constant reminder that he was there. I was surprised earlier, at the arcade. When he allowed himself to be vulnerable and open up to me about his past trauma. And now that I knew, I could see that behind his smiles, he seemed jittery, nervous, and at times, he even seemed to be stumbling over his words. Compared to when we first hung out when he was energized, cool, and collected, a sharp contrast to my anxious, nervous rambling. But not tonight.

Something had shifted between us the moment he pinched his bottom lip and said, "that's because I like you," and waited a beat too long before clarifying what he meant. Once I realized that he liked me more than I had realized, I couldn't stop noticing the signs. I went back and forth trying to rationalize that I was just seeing what I wanted to see, and I was almost convinced of that until Jacky grabbed my hand. And kept holding it throughout the whole movie, even if it meant jerking his other arm uncomfortably to get a handful of popcorn from between our seats.

I stared intently, through hazy eyes, at the glossy screen. But my attention wasn't on what was playing. Instead, it was focused on Dawn and Tony, who, despite my better judgment, kept snagging my attention. Seeing them together had been awkward and uncomfortable. Like dangling a donut in front of someone on a diet. Their PDA was obnoxious, and I was just waiting for them to ditch the movie all together so they could go be unbiblical in the parking lot or something. But as nauseating as they were, I couldn't look away. They just looked so in love. Like they just couldn't keep their hands off each other. Both of them were so happy to just be here together, all smiles and giggles. Giddy, even.

I'd never had that. And as I watched them whisper to each other in the dark with soft smiles, it finally clicked.

I wanted that.

With a new determination in my heart, my eyes flickered up to JJ, the mysterious guy who had appeared in my life. The guy who helped me after I was lost and confused on my first day of school. The guy with buried trauma and turmoil, who felt comfortable in my arms. The guy who seemed to know how to make me smile no matter how corny his jokes were, and the person who lingered in my dreams - apart from God himself - whom I thought about endlessly without even realizing it...

I held my breath and leaned my head on his shoulder. I stayed very still as his muscle twitched beneath my cheek and Jacky sucked in a sharp breath. But then, he gripped my hand a little tighter and rested his head on top of mine, and I buried my smile into his sleeve before he saw it.

★ ★ ★ ★ ✝ ★ ★ ★ ★

"You guys ditched us," Dawn groaned. Jacky and I exchanged an exasperated look. We went back to our one foot of distance in the lobby, but the stammering of my heart remained.

"You two were just making out the whole time," I replied, and it was kind of cute how both Dawn and Tony blushed.

"Oh blah." Dawn giggled, as she hugged me. "I'll see you tomorrow, bestie. I pray for traveling grace. And grace with your parents, knowing how they get down."

I huffed a breath. "Don't even remind me."

"Alright, peace out my guy," Jacky told Tony with a handshake. "We'll see you tomorrow. Dawn, keep him out of trouble," he added.

Then his hand found the small of my back and started nudging me toward the doors. I almost missed Dawn saying "Like anyone could" with how overwhelmed I was by the warmth of his hand. I nearly ran into the glass door.

"Oh my God. I can't take you anywhere," Jacky snorted, letting go of me to push open the door. I waited for him to return his hand on my back, or even grab my hand, but he didn't. He just walked next to me, keeping a distance of one foot.

We left the theater's parking lot and took the bus back to his apartment complex so I could retrieve my backpack. After doing so, JJ and I stepped back out into the cool night air, and thankfully, he had some money left over so he paid for an Uber. We stood near a wired fence, waiting for the Uber. The street was dark and quiet except for a few passing cars. JJ nudged me and uttered a single word. That one word completely melted me.

"Sidell?" His voice was like velvet in the night air. I turned to face him and noticed how close he was standing to me now; how his brown eyes were boring into mine as if searching for something — something only he could find.

"Yes, JJ?" I barely managed to get the words out, feeling suddenly very vulnerable in front of him.

He hesitated for a moment before asking, "Can I have a hug?" His request was almost timid as if he was afraid of hearing my response.

But all fear vanished when I smiled at him. In an instant, he was holding me in an embrace so strong that it took my breath away, making everything around us blur into insignificance as peace overcame us, like a wave crashing onto shoreline rocks and spreading its tranquility far and wide.

"I'm going to miss you JJ," I said softly against his chest as reality began settling back into our consciousness.

"I'll miss you too," he replied before reluctantly pulling away from me, once more giving me a look filled with longing that stole my heart.

Beep, Beep.

We both looked over to see the Uber driver roll down his window as he impatiently waited for us to finish our farewells — had he been here this entire time?

"Uh, I have to go now," I mumbled awkwardly before gathering up enough courage to turn away from him and make my way towards the car. I slid into the backseat, the horror of reality slowly creeping back in ever so subtly. I waved goodbye until he disappeared out of sight.

On the ride home, my thoughts raced as fast as my heartbeat as we sped through the dark streets, the lights of downtown faded behind us. I sighed, already missing JJ's smile and the way his eyes crinkled when he laughed. Sure my parents are going to kill me, but oh, those few stolen hours with him made me feel alive in a way I never had before.

I was finally approaching my house and I could see Dawn's mother, Ms. Tipton, outside smoking a cigarette with a wine glass in her hand. I tried to slip by unnoticed, wondering how Dawn was so happy living with a mother that was barely sober. *Does Ms. Tipton worry about her daughter being out this late?*

My heart began to race widely as I noticed the family car in the driveway. My parents would know that I had gone somewhere, and the traditional Russian blood in them would not truly approve of my friendship with JJ. If only they could see past their dictatorship to see the real JJ — thoughtful, charming, and so much more than just some kid from the wrong side of the tracks.

And I know for a fact that, no matter how I'd try to explain that JJ and I were just friends, I doubted they would listen. But the thought of lying to my parents didn't sit well with me. If I told them one lie tonight, I would have to continue lying and my father would go berserk if he found out that I'd started keeping secrets from them.

"Please, God. Help me," I muttered under my breath as I made my way up the driveway. After a short while, I reached the door and rang the bell twice. Cayest, who was dressed in her spongebob pajamas opened it swiftly with a bossy glint in her large brown eyes as her brown curly hair cascaded past her shoulders.

"Where have you been?" she spat. I didn't answer her because she's my *little* sister. I brushed past her into the house in search of my parents. I found them in the dining room, seated at the table.

"Hi Papa, hi Mama," I said hesitantly.

"Where have you been?" my father demanded. His voice was low and angry, an unfamiliar tone that sent a shiver down my spine. His eyes burned with disappointment. I'd never seen him so upset. Especially not with me.

I blinked and took a small step backward.

"Don't you dare lie to us, Sidell," my mother chimed in. "I checked with Ms. Tipton as if she would know. But why did I ask the drunk woman when she couldn't even explain the whereabouts of her own daughter? So, I want you to tell me right now, where have you been?"

A wave of panic washed over me. I had been caught this time, and without an alibi to make excuses for me. There was officially no way out.

I mean, I was with Dawn. Partially. But if I say that, I'll probably mess up Dawn's good graces with my mother.

"I was...I was studying with a friend," I stammered, cringing at how unconvincing I sounded. "We were studying together… For a test." Somehow, I hoped that making this about my academic pursuits would make my mother go easier on me. But she was made of sterner material, like all other Bukarrian Jewish women before her.

My mother arched a thin brow. "Studying? At 12:45 in the morning?" Her tone dripped with disbelief. "Let's try this again. Who were you really with, Sidell Evermost?"

I took a deep breath. I couldn't keep lying to them. Apart from the fact that, as a good Christian, I was supposed to tell the truth, lying to my mother would only infuriate her further.

The words felt like lead in my mouth. 'I...I went out on a date after school,' I confessed. They all froze and looked at me like I was speaking a foreign language. "He is harmless. He goes to school with me," I added.

Complete silence followed. Cayest stared at me angrily, her arms folded across her chest. I was pretty much convinced that Cayest's annoyance had nothing to do with me. It had everything to do with the aftereffects of my actions and how they would affect her. I tried to ignore her the best I could. It was not the right time to complain about her attitude.

The ticking of the clock on the wall echoed in the room, suddenly magnified by the quiet. My father looked at me as if he wasn't sure whether to yell or cry.

Realizing that I could not let them think the worst of me, I kept talking. "We did have a chaperone. His grandmother was present the whole time. We didn't do anything inappropriate," I said. As if that was supposed to count. I had disobeyed my parents. Stayed out late with a boy they didn't know. Let alone approve of. Knowing them, they would never approve of him.

My father didn't make a move or say another word. It made me sweat. If I had an ally in our family, it would most likely be him.

"What's his name?" he began to ask. "Is he a Christian? What Church does he attend?"

"His name is JJ. Jacky Jamison, and he is the one who helped me locate my class on the first day of school. He lives in downtown Chicago, and that's where I was. With him. And his grandma," I replied. I did realize I was blabbering at this point. But I hoped that keeping the conversation going would give Mom less time to attack. Or remind me how much of a disappointment I had been.

I glanced over at my father, hoping the details I had shared would soften the blow. It did nothing. He was frozen in place like a mannequin, continuing to stare at me. Shocked and angry.

Nireska chose the wrong moment to re-enter the house from the back patio. Her husband, Vestor, was right on her heels as he closed the sliding glass door behind them.

"Ah, Sidell," she said, smiling at me mischievously. "We were just talking about you. Where have you been all evening?"

Her pitch black hair swung in its ponytail as she sailed smoothly past my mother and towards me, unaffected by the tension brewing in the room. "Zdarova, Sidell. Kak dela?" she asked, her blue eyes seeking mine.

I replied to her greeting in English. "I'm fine. How about you? It's nice to see you again." I could feel beads of perspiration forming beneath my arms as she pulled me in for a hug. This was one of the few times I welcomed Nireska's intrusive habit. It wouldn't make this mess I had created go away, yet it was something. A chance to get my thoughts together.

Vestor, who cradled a wine glass, leaned against the back of my mother's chair. "Teenagers running wild in a new city, eh?" he chuckled, cut off sharply by the motion of Nireska softly tapping her index finger on her lips.

"Go to your room, Sidell. We'll talk about this later," my dad said coolly, the warning hidden beneath his words.

Just as I turned to leave, my mother held out her hand towards me. "Your phone. Let me have that."

I clenched my phone protectively against my chest. "Mama?"

"Day eto." Mom spoke more sternly now.

Suppressing an irritated breath, I shoved my device into her hand, careful not to be too rough with her Jewish temperament.

★ ★ ★ ★ ✞ ★ ★ ★ ★

I laid up in bed, staring at the ceiling. I couldn't shake off the feeling that I'd made a huge mistake. My mind was tangled in thoughts of JJ. For the first time, I let myself confront the possibility of letting him go. It would be for the best, anyway. There was no way my parents would ever accept him. Dawn had been a stretch. Her gender and bubbly personality made it easier for my mum to overlook the other aspects of her life.

The sound of conversation from the living area floated up to my room. I pressed my ear against the locked door to listen in on what they were saying but without any success.

For the first time, being cooped up in my room was maddening. Not knowing the verdict my parents had decided on or what was being said about me downstairs made me want to scream.

I had returned to slump on my bed for the second time when I heard a knock on my door. Sitting up straight, I watched my father slowly open the door and step inside. The moonlight seeping through my window highlighted his face, which seemed to be set in a permanent scowl.

We stayed in our fixed positions for what felt like forever, neither of us mustering up courage to address the situation. My father's unkempt, salt-and-pepper hair fringed his forehead worriedly. I had never seen my father look so upset.

I slowly drew my legs up to my chest that was tucked under the sheets, giving him space at the end of it to sit down beside me. He settled himself tentatively at the foot of bed, its fabric dipping underneath him as I nervously tucked a strand of hair behind my ear, awaiting to hear what he had to say.

He sighed heavily and ran a hand through his thick beard where it settled determinedly upon his brow. "Your behavior reflects on the rest of this family, Sidell," he said quietly yet sternly. "We have guests staying over in our home, and you've just embarrassed us in front of them."

"I'm sorry," was all I could muster up in return. I couldn't bring myself to say the words I was sure he was desperate to hear. I couldn't bring myself to say it would never happen again.

"Where were you, Sidell?" he asked with chilling gentility.

I was about to speak, I wasn't sure what was going to come out of my mouth, but I had hoped it would be something that could alleviate my mess.

My father suddenly raised a finger to silence me. "Hold on, Sidell, I want you to think carefully about your answer before spilling it." he warned softly.

My heart could as well be a pumping machine because it began thundering loudly right beneath my chest.

"I told you guys already. I went out on a date," I stammered.

"And doesn't the place have a name? He asked with a slightly arched brow, his thoughts unreadable. Whenever dad got like this, you can never tell what was going on in his mind and that was really scary. Again, I had never seen my father this displeased with me. Should I tell him the truth? Should I not?

"I went to the movies," I whispered.

"With?"

Lord please, just save me this one time. I already told mom and him so what more do they want?

"Sidell, I'm still waiting," it was clear Dad wasn't going to leave without an answer.

I swallowed, then said, "I went out with JJ." I supplied softly, hoping he hadn't heard me, but he did.

He swung sharply to face me, "That was the boy you met in school, right?" He asked.

"Yes Papa." I replied in a hushed tone.

Dad didn't do anything for a minute, then he faced me with so much disappointment in his eyes, I felt like crawling into myself.

"You've started this school for what? A few weeks? And within this same short time, you are already going out with him? What has gotten into you, Sidell?" he asked rhetorically.

I could say nothing, I could only look at my feet in shame. I didn't mean to bring shame on anyone, especially not my family. I know Nireska and Vestor were probably having the best gossip on how I had turned waywords and that was absolutely not the case. I summoned some courage and tried to pacify my father.

"Papa, I promise you it was nothing like that, I only went to the movies and just-"

Dad interrupted, "Did you inform anyone, did you ask for our permission?" he asked sharply and that quickly shut me up.

Dad rose to his feet, facing me, he said, "This is the way it's going to be, I don't want to hear anything about that boy, Jax or whatever he calls himself. You will go to school and return home when due. Whichever of your friends who wants to visit can come see you at home. You are not permitted to go anywhere but home, school and church," he said with a note of finality.

I quickly scrambled off the bed as he rose up, "But Papa, I'll want to visit Dawn-"

"No. No, Sidell, not anymore… It saddens me that your mother might be right, I have been too easy with you and that was what gave you the green light to go out on a date without our permission. The Sidell I know would never do that," he spat.

He could as well, punch me on the chest and it would have the same effect.

"Don't let me catch you with that boy. And if you dare disobey my instructions, Sidell, "he warned in a very imposing manner, "You are going to see a side of me you've never seen before." He warned and then swept out of the room.

I looked into the empty space my dad just vacated and thought of how fun today had been and how sad it ended. What was I going to do because I really enjoyed hanging out with JJ.but I hated disappointing my dad. What should I do?

Chapter Seventeen:
ψψ

My eyes fluttered open to the offensive glare of sunlight filtering through my curtains. I realized that for the first time in ages, Donica's vacant stare had not haunted my dreams. Small victories, I guess.

I heard Grandma's soft knocks at my door, calling me for morning prayer. which I had long stopped attending since Donica's passing. But oddly enough, this morning, I didn't feel angrily resistant like I usually did when I heard her calling my name.

But I was still frustrated with God for taking Donica away from me. *Why couldn't he save her from the clutches of death?* I'm sure he could have if he had wanted too. It was clear that *we* just didn't matter. Even so, the disdain I normally felt towards Him was a little less than usual.

I reluctantly peeled back the blankets and dragged myself from my slumber. I never got a chance to text Sid last night, thanking her for spending the evening with me. But I was sure I was going to see her again. Maybe we could even spend more time together at school. Describing what I felt as sparks would be a gross understatement. It was a downright explosion. A wildfire had erupted in my belly. There was only one person to blame for it.

Since Donica, I'd never felt so alive. I couldn't keep still, fidgeting and pacing around my room. Nervous energy and excitement bubbled up inside me. When I caught my reflection in the mirror, I startled myself with the ridiculous grin plastered on my face. How had I gone this long without experiencing all of these sensations?

Scratching my armpits, I yawned as I made my way to the kitchen for breakfast. Setting a glass bowl down on the table, I dumped my cereal out. Just as I was pouring the milk into the bowl, I saw the front door unlocking itself out of the corner of my eye. I froze mid-pour.

Who could that have been? My grandmother was in her room and I was here so...who else had a key?

The sound of her hair barrettes clinking together gave it away. Kaluna, the neighborhood delinquent, came skipping in with a backpack on her shoulders, dirty shoes untied, worn out jeans, and a bright orange t-shirt. My face twisted into an expression of disbelief.

"Grandma! You gave HER a key?!" I yelled before I could even register my own thoughts. I found myself rubbing my forehead in confusion. "Ain't no way. I'm still asleep. I just got to be."

My grandmother waltzed out of her room to confront my bewilderment. "Relax boy, she just went to the mailbox for me," Grandma said calmly before turning to Kaluna and saying warmly, "Thank you baby. You have a good day at school, young lady. Make sure you tie dem shoes up before you trip and bust your head."

"Yes ma'am." Kaluna smiled slyly before sticking out her tongue at me and darting back outside. I shook my head in frustration and turned back to my bowl of cereal. "Anyways...Good morning, Grandma."

"Mornin'," she said, flipping through the mail, her face beaming. There was a mischievous glint in her eye as she looked up at me. Even before she spoke, I could guess what it would be about.

"Well, well, well. You never told me you were seeing someone, JJ. And here I was, thinking you were too busy with schoolwork to make new friends," she teased, a twinkle in her eye. "I think I like this one."

I rolled my eyes but couldn't help chuckling at my grandmother's teasing. I didn't doubt for a second that she would approve of Sidell, but it did matter to me that they had gotten along so well. The last thing I wanted to deal with was the tension between two women in my life.

"She's a good friend, Grandma. I mean, she is different from the other chicks at school. She's really cool, you know? I like— I mean she could light up a place without even trying. And I just think that's really cool, you know? Her being herself."

My grandmother nodded thoughtfully. "I can see that. But what else do you know about her? Who are her parents? Where is she from? If she is going to be coming around often, I'm pretty sure her parents would need to know where she's at."

Swallowing hard, I hesitated for a moment before responding. "Uhh, I'm not sure that is a good idea. At least not right away. Her family is pretty uptight, and I'm not sure what they would think of her being around me, much less one that's outside of their tradition or whatever."

Grandma nodded and pulled a chair out from under the dining table. "That's a tricky situation. I've been in one before, and it did not end so well. Maybe invite her or her folks to my Bible study. Just see it as one of the smaller efforts you'd be making for someone you care about. Take it from me, her parents are likely to go easier on you when they realize that you are not a heathen bent on stealing their daughter away from the truth."

"Yep. They couldn't have that, right?" I shrugged with opened palms.

"Listen Jacky, I wanted to talk about something with you..." Her eyes searched mine like a vulture scavenging for a meal. The kitchen clock read 6 a.m., only moments away from Grandma's daily devotion. And there it was on the table; her tattered Bible along with several other devotionals sprawled across the mahogany tabletop.

Frowning, I scanned the items atop the furniture. "Yeah? About what?"

"Sit down, JJ." Her words were muffled like a whisper in the wind.

"Wait…Grandma what is this even about?" I asked.

A wave of panic swept over me as I wondered if this sudden discussion had anything to do with church or religion. My belief in any sort of deity had vanished, and I wasn't about to let Grandma try to talk me into believing otherwise. She inhaled deeply, pressed her palms together and closed her eyes. With lips moving in silent prayer, she opened her eyes again, they landed straight upon me like an arrow striking its target.

"Laussie called me." She spoke patiently, but her tone was still strict. I scoffed and leaned back against the wooden dining chair.

"What does she want this time?" Despite knowing better, I feared she might've manipulated Grandma into talking me into visiting her. But I didn't care about whatever scheme she was cooking up. That woman had ditched me like yesterday's news; how could I ever forgive someone who had done that to me?

"JJ...I know how you feel, how hurt you are. But she is still your mother."

My voice rose as anger surged through my veins. I shouted, "I don't want to talk about her!" *Just the thought of her annoys the hell out of me!*

But Grandma kept talking. "She's gonna get married soon and I think we should be there to support her." I couldn't believe I was sitting there listening to every word coming out of her mouth. *Is this a joke?!*

I shoved my bowl away. "I ain't comin'. Nuh-uh. When has she ever supported me, huh?" I spat, standing my ground with unyielding firmness. "Answer that." Grandma was silent as she broke eye contact with me. "That's what I thought, case closed!"

There was a beat of silence as I swished the spoon around in my cereal. Then Grandma's voice cut through the silence like a shard of glass. "This could be your sign for you to go back to church. It's about time, JJ. It's not as bad as you think."

I stared blankly at the wall behind her as she spoke. It had been years since I had set foot in a church, and the thought of returning made me feel uneasy. However, her concern for me was palpable, and I couldn't bring myself to dismiss her suggestion outrightly, even though it annoyed me.

"I don't know, Grandma," I answered, my voice barely above a whisper. "I haven't been to church in so long. It just doesn't feel like the right place for me anymore."

She reached out and placed a wrinkled hand on mine. "I understand that, but sometimes, when we're feeling lost, it helps to return to the things that once gave us comfort."

Sighing, I leaned forward with my elbows on the table and pretended to consider her words. She had been there for me, ever since I was a child. Her wisdom and kindness had guided me through many difficult times, and I trusted her advice, but this was different. Her words were dripping with affection but lacked conviction.

"I don't think so. Nothing about the place or the deity that refused to help me at my lowest could ever possibly bring me comfort. All the imperfections in the universe, or the human body to start with, would not exist if he existed and cared about his people half as much as they care about him. I mean, he could fix it all with a hand wave or something since he's all-powerful, right? But each time someone somewhere genuinely needs the old man, suddenly, he is nowhere to be found. He reminds me of her in so many ways."

Surprisingly, she listened patiently to my outburst instead of hurriedly trying to prove me wrong like she had always done before.

"I understand your anger and your pain. But trust in God. It isn't just about getting what you want. It's about believing in something greater than yourself, something that guides you through the darkness and helps you find your way. God never promised us an easy life, JJ. It's the trials and tribulations that we go through that make us stronger and bring us closer to him."

"So, all the adversity is supposed to draw me closer to him, right? Does he even care if it breaks me first? Isn't my well-being supposed to be his priority?" I watched her skeptically, unsure of how to point out all the holes in her religion.

She kept at it, undeterred by my questions. "You might be angry with God, but have you ever stopped to consider why you're angry? Is it because God didn't give you what you wanted, or because you feel like you've been abandoned?"

"Maybe both?"

"I see," she said, nodding. "Well, I can't promise you that everything will work out exactly the way you want it to. But I can promise you this: if you lean on God, if you trust in him and let him guide you, it does get easier. He asked that we should bring our burdens to him because he cares for us, and he never allows us to carry a burden we cannot handle."

I was growing agitated and had no intention of arguing any further. I stood up abruptly while keeping my gaze on her. "No. I can't do this again Grandma. I'm going back to bed. I've got school in two hours," I spat before storming out of the kitchen in a huff. I slammed my bedroom door behind me, not caring what the rules were, just eager to find solace in the familiar confines of my own space.

Stripping off my shirt, I tossed it carelessly onto a nearby chair before adjusting my blue plaid pajama pants. Setting my alarm for an hour, I flopped onto my bed with a deep sigh before haze clouded my eyes and I fell asleep.

★ ★ ★ ★ ✞ ★ ★ ★ ★

I jolted up from my pillow at the sound of my phone alarm, clutching at the sheets, gasping for breath. Just when I thought the nightmares had escaped me. Cool stickiness of sweat clung to my skin as I suddenly felt hot. This nightmare felt so real. Donica's agonized face still lingered behind my eyelids, her mouth open in a silent wail as she reached for me. And right behind me stood Sidell who was twisting my shirt and yelling her head off at the sight. I groaned, pressing the heels of my palms against my eyes. This was new. My subconscious was getting creative, weaving Donica's ghost together with my living friend. I didn't have the slightest idea what that meant, and it scared me.

My head throbbed and I felt heavy as goosebumps spread across my skin. It seemed like a dark unseen presence was there in the room with me. I shook my head sharply. "Get a freaking grip, JJ," I muttered under my breath. Still, I couldn't entirely shake the bone-chilling terror that lingered.

Instinctively, I reached for my phone on the nightstand, silenced the alarm with an aggressive stab of my finger, and then went to dial Sidell's number. Maybe hearing her voice could chase away the unease from my nightmare.

Voicemail. I tried again. Still nothing.

"C'mon, Sid, don't do this to me," I groaned, raking a hand through my tangled hair as I climbed out of bed and paced back and forth in my dimly lit room, the sun shadowing through my curtains as my eyes stayed fixated on my phone. My heart pounding with every unanswered call. The morning had taken an unexpected turn, and I couldn't shake off the feeling that something was wrong.

Has something happened to her? I should have called her before going to bed to find out if she had gotten home safely last night. I fired off a string of increasingly frantic texts, my thumbs flying over the keyboard. When she still didn't respond, I threw my phone onto my bed in frustration. "Real mature, JJ," I grumbled. But I couldn't help it — I needed to know Sidell was okay. The dream had left me rattled.

I paused by the window, glaring out at the hazy morning sunlight that filtered through the curtains. Last night, Sidell had mentioned needing to leave early, her voice tinged with a hint of urgency. But I made her stay. And when we departed, she had assured me that she would be fine, but the lack of any response from her now was heightening my apprehension.

Fear consumed me, whispering doubts into my ear. Was she hurt? Lost? Why wasn't she picking up her phone? I didn't want to overreact, to jump to conclusions, but the gnawing worry ate away at me like a relentless beast.

"That's it." I snatched up my phone again, scrolling through my contacts until I found Dawn's name. She'd know if something was up with Sidell. And if she didn't...well, then it would be time to alert the authorities. I only hesitated for a moment. My finger hovered over her name, unsure of what her response might be.

Summoning courage, I pressed the call button. Each ring echoed in the quiet room as my heart raced. Finally, Dawn answered groggily. I could tell my call had abruptly awakened her from a deep sleep. Good, now she can share my misery.

"Dawn, it's me, JJ," I said in a breathless rush. "I'm sorry to wake you up, but... have you seen or heard from Sidell since last night? I've been trying to reach her, but she's not answering and I'm freaking out over here."

There was a brief pause. I held my breath, listening to the silence on the other end. Come on, Dawn, give me some good news here. Dawn's voice, still laced with sleep, broke through the line. "JJ, calm down. Sidell... She's okay. Well, physically, at least."

My heart sank at her words. Physically? What did that mean? "What do you mean, physically? Did something happen? Where is she?"

Dawn exhaled a breath. "No, she's not hurt." Her voice trailed off as if the words tasted sour in her mouth. She continued. "It's just... her parents found out about her little trip with you yesterday. I guess her mother came over to ask my mom where she was when she didn't get home on time. I think she's been grounded."

I struggled to process the words. Grounded? That seemed like nothing. But the weight of Dawn's tone suggested that it was far from it.

"Why... why didn't she tell me? Why isn't she picking up her phone?"

"Obviously she's in a lot of trouble. Most likely they took her phone away. Um, it's really best if you stay away from her for now," Dawn explained.

"Alright whatever." I ended the call. Of course they had taken away her only way to reach out to me. Because I just had to convince her to stay out longer last night for my own selfish reasons. Some freaking friend I turned out to be.

Chapter Eighteen: Sidell

My heart pounded against my ribs as I slipped out of the foggy bathroom and tiptoed back to my bedroom. It was still early in the morning, Dad had left to drop Mom at work and Cayest at school, giving me time to get ready. After the talk we had in my bedroom last night, my dad made it clear that he was dropping me off at school himself. "Don't let me catch you with that boy." His voice echoed. But I wasn't some lovesick addict who couldn't control herself. Annoyance flared within me.

I rifled through my closet, grumbling. Where was my uniform skirt? Ah, there it was - wadded in a ball under my pom poms. I shook it out and yanked it up over my hips, hopping on one foot. Come on, come on...I grappled with the zipper. The loud honk of a car horn made me jump. I scurried my stocking covered feet across my room to the window. Peeking through my yellow and silver curtains. Yup, it was Dad, right on time.

I slipped on my shoes, took one last glance in the mirror and groaned. My uniform was wrinkled and my hair was a mess. Today was not my day.

With a defeated sigh, I trudged down the staircase. Each step I took across the tiled stairs seemed to echo louder than usual through the empty house today. It was a reminder of the discord I brought into our home.

Tension lingered in the car as my dad drove, making it difficult to breathe. I couldn't really face him or my mom just yet, not after what had transpired. Rolling down my window, the cool morning air enveloped me, providing some respite from the suffocating atmosphere inside. But there was still a heavy weight on my shoulders, a burden I couldn't shake off. It wasn't just the disapproving glares and stern words from my parents that haunted me. It was the knowledge that I had disappointed them, that their trust in me had been shattered.

When we pulled up at school, I nearly leapt from the car in sweet relief. My sanctuary! At least here, freedom awaited me within its walls, even if it was only for a few hours.

I slumped my back against the lockers, banging my head back against the cold metal. ***Thunk. Thunk.*** Maybe if I hit hard enough, I could knock some sense into my foolish brain. Clearly all my common sense had dried up, based on the insane decision I'd made to stay out with JJ last night.

My stomach knotted. I couldn't possibly avoid him forever? But I also couldn't bear the thought of explaining to him how my parents had overreacted to our date. How would I rationally explain their fussing over something as normal as a movie date? I pictured it: "Hey JJ, just wanted to let you know my parents have basically disowned me and sentenced me to a life of misery over our date. But other than that, I had a great time! Let's do it again soon!" I rolled my eyes at my own sarcastic inner monologue.

"Hey Sid, you okay?" A familiar voice broke through my spiraling thoughts. I opened my eyes to find Dawn standing in front of me, concern etched across her face.

I managed a weak smile and shrugged. "I'm trying to be. Last night was... intense. My parents are still furious about the whole date thing."

Dawn's eyes widened, and she leaned in closer, her voice barely above a whisper. "I had no idea. My mom said your mom came over to ask about you. But we both know that my mom was drunk off her head; that poor woman was probably caught off guard. Dazed mommy didn't even bat an eye when I told her that I spent most of the night at Tony's." She chuckled lightly before regaining seriousness. "So, what did they say?"

I managed a weak shake of my head.

"They haven't even spoken to you yet? Is it that bad?"

I nodded, a lump forming in my throat. "Let's see...they took my phone, banned me from leaving the house, My mom's been giving me the silent treatment for over 24 hours now, so yeah, I'd say we've moved into hostage situation territory."

Dawn sighed. "I'm so sorry, Sidell. That's tough. What do you plan to do about it now?"

"I have no idea. Keep a low profile, maybe. Clean the house top to bottom? Maybe if I become the perfect daughter until this whole thing blows over," I said quietly.

Dawn studied me, chewing her lip. "Have you spoken to JJ since then?"

At the mention of his name, my stomach dropped. "No, and I don't plan to. I mean, how humiliating would that conversation be? 'Hey JJ, remember that fun date we had? Well, my parents have lost their ever-loving minds over it and now I'm under house arrest. But let's definitely do it again soon!'" I laughed harshly.

Dawn squeezed my arm gently. "Aw Sid, I know it's hard, but you have to talk to him. You can't avoid him. He needs to know what's going on. If you want to keep things going, you both need to be more careful."

I fidgeted with the handmade bracelets on my wrist, contemplating Dawn's words. She was right, of course. Keeping JJ in the dark would only lead to more misunderstandings and unnecessary complications. But a part of me had already made up my mind, I couldn't let him get entangled in this mess. There was no way it would work out.

"I appreciate your advice, Dawn," I said softly, my voice tinged with sadness. "But I think, um, I think it's better if I break things off with him. It's not fair to drag him into this chaos." I blinked rapidly to keep the tears at bay.

Dawn let out a chuckle, trying to lighten the mood. "Break things off? Whoa, Sidell, you are taking this too seriously. I'm sure your parents will realize nothing comes in the way of true love. You should speak to him. JJ's probably stressing over this. He called me earlier this morning, worried sick about you. I don't want to imagine what he is going to be like when he finds out that you're dumping him after y'all fell in love and held hands three times in a span of twenty-four hours."

I gave her a look regarding the shade she just threw.

She held up her hands defensively. "Hey, I'm just saying, I don't want to have to deal with his melodramatic heartbreak or be caught in the crossfire."

I forced a smile, grateful for Dawn's attempt at humor. "Yeah, I'm sure he'd be devastated. But maybe it's for the best. At least this way, he won't have to deal with my family."

Dawn placed a comforting hand on my shoulder. "I'm pretty sure it is going to be fine."

Before I could respond, Dawn stiffened in front of me, panic washing over her face. She then leaned in and whispered harshly, "Whatever you do, don't turn around. JJ is headed this way!"

My heart stuttered wildly in my chest. I wasn't ready to face him yet. My flight instinct kicked in and I darted forward without thinking, weaving between students to avoid detection. In a moment of panic, I slipped behind a stone pillar, pressing myself against it as I struggled to steady my breathing.

From my hiding place, I strained to catch snippets of their conversation. Meanwhile, Dawn, being the loyal friend she was, stepped up to cover for my sudden disappearance. The sound of their voices floated by, and my heart sank as I heard JJ's frustrated tone. *This was a disaster.*

"Have you seen Sidell?" He asked calmly.

Dawn acted clueless as she tried to ramble for an explanation. "What - like, here?"

He huffed. "Yes, here."

"Oh, she's not here. She's, uh, not feeling well today. She's not in school."

I silently thanked God for the existence of Dawn in my life as I heard JJ huff in annoyance. "Not in school? Is she just sick, or did they lock her up at home or something?"

Dawn had another lie ready. It was surprising how she never missed a beat. "Well, she is not sick. Sidell couldn't come because she has been crying and has weighty eye bags under her eyes and a face full of stress pimples. Oh, and killer cramps too. Yeah. So, she just wanted to sleep in today."

I snuck a peek to catch JJ scratching the nape of his neck. "Can you convince her to come tomorrow? Maybe help her cover the eyebags in the bathroom or maybe give her some ginger ale or something."

Dawn shrugged. "I can't make any promises, but I'll see what I can do, okay? Just give it a bit more time."

"Well, you have to tell her I need to talk to her, cool?" As JJ stormed off, I slipped out on the other side of the pillar. Dawn's concerned eyes met mine as I rejoined her in the blessedly JJ-free hallway.

"Sidell, we can't keep doing this," she whispered, her voice filled with worry. "It's only a matter of time before JJ figures out what's going on. You need to face this head-on."

I nodded, realizing the truth in her words. "You're right, Dawn. I can't keep hiding forever. I'll figure out a way to talk to JJ later and figure this whole thing out. Thank you for being there for me."

Dawn smiled, "You know I'll always have your back, bestie babes." The bell rang, signaling the start of first period. Dawn sighed. "You might want to get to class before JJ appears out of nowhere with another request."

I chuckled despite the heaviness in my heart, grateful for Dawn's ability to find humor amid my emotional rollercoaster. With a renewed outlook, I headed in the direction of my first class, willing myself to forget about all that had transpired.

Chapter Nineteen: JJ

I sucked my teeth. "What is their issue?" I mumbled to myself as I caught sight of an old white couple staring at me from the safe distance of their well-kept suburban neighborhood. They appeared uncomfortable with my presence and pretended to be admiring the rose bush surrounding their lawn. But the elderly man was clearly hacking away randomly while his wife instructed him in hushed tones. I could feel their eyes burning holes in my back as they sneaked a few glances my way. Their discomfort with my presence was as clear as day.

I almost laughed. This wasn't my first rodeo with racist geriatrics.

I was currently standing at Sidell's doorstep, my shoes resting on the Welcome mat on the wooden surface. Her address had been easy to find; all I had to do was search the Uber receipt from the night we went out. A cool breeze toyed with my ears, urging me to abandon this foolish plan. But I couldn't leave, not when Sidell was suffering for my mistakes. Sure, showing up unannounced to a white girl's house could end badly, but it was my fault she got grounded. As a man, I had to own up to the consequences of my actions. Even if her parents slammed the door in my face, at least I tried.

I hesitantly raised my arm, ready to knock, when the door swung open and Dawn emerged from the house. Her face contorted in shock when she saw me, her hands frantically flapping as if she's motioning for me to step back.

"JJ? What the hell are you doing here?!" she whispered as we both stepped off the porch steps. She had closed the front door behind her.

"To make things right," I retorted with a raised brow.

"Jacky, pleaseee. Sidell's parents cannot see you!" she pleaded, her voice tinged with desperation. "It'll only make things worse. You need to go. Now!"

Confused by her anxiety, I paused to study her expression. It made no sense why Dawn was trying to get me away from here.

"I have to see her parents, Dawn. I need to apologize and explain everything," I stated in a gruff voice, anger rising in my chest. "Sidell doesn't deserve to be punished; I'm the one that made her stay out late."

Dawn took in a deep breath, her eyes darting anxiously towards the door. "JJ, please listen to me," she muttered, her voice trembling. "Sidell was only grounded. She wasn't absent from school either. I lied. She's been at school all day. There is no point in seeing her parents. You can just talk to her in school tomorrow, I was barely allowed inside and I dropped her off!"

My heart skipped a beat, and my mouth went dry. Each statement Dawn made just kept on getting weirder. "Why the hell would you lie? Are you for real right now?" I couldn't fathom the thought that Dawn had gone out of her way to stop me from seeing Sidell and was doing so again. How did I know that she wasn't concocting lies right now?

"Get out of my way, Dawn. I'm not trying to deal with you right now," I said as I attempted to walk back up the porch steps. But Dawn grabbed my shirt, scrunching the fabric in her fist.

"I'm so sorry, JJ. I thought I was protecting her. I thought it would be easier if you thought she was still grounded. I didn't know you would come here today."

Anger surged through me. My voice rose involuntarily. "Protecting her? From who? From me? You're crazy, and I wonder if Tony knows that. The only person Sidell needs to be protected from is you! You lied to me and most likely lied to her as well for whatever reason! Dawn! On my grandma, that's not cool. Why are you even doing this! Be forreal, are you jealous?"

Dawn's eyes widened for a second. "*Jealous*! Trust me, Sidell made the decision herself. I was only trying to help her because she asked me to." She sighed, her eyes filled with sympathy. "Look buddy, she just wasn't ready to have the conversation with you."

Our raised voices must have alerted the household, because Sidell's whole family emerged out the front door like ants fleeing a flooded hill. I didn't know Sidell had a little sister. The curly headed young adolescent girl clung to her mother's side, eyeing me curiously. Another couple followed after them. They looked much younger than Sidell's parents, and I imagined that they were her relatives.

Sidell was the last person to walk out of the open door. Her head hung low, and she refused to meet my eyes. The expressions on everyone's faces ranged from confusion to concern. I cleared my throat noisily, trying to figure out the best way to explain myself, but I didn't get the chance to. Sidell's dad gave me a hard look, piecing it all together.

"JJ, I presume?" he said. "So, you're the one Sidell went out on a date with? And you thought it was a good idea to come here after both of your actions led to her being grounded."

A wave of guilt washed over me. I understood why they were angry, but did they have to be so judgmental right off the bat? "Yes, sir," I replied quietly. "I had to let you know that I deeply regret my actions. What happened was wrong, and I take full responsibility for it."

Sidell's mother watched me like a hawk, her brows scrunched in dissatisfaction. "Mistake? How convenient." She scoffed. "You took our daughter on a reckless adventure, exposing her to danger and distracting her from her studies. Sidell was supposed to come straight home after school, but we had no clue where she was for hours after she was supposed to be home. We do not want you around here or around Sidell either. Your attitude doesn't align with our values, and you influenced our daughter to disobey more than a few of our rules and God's commands. You are not the right person for Sidell to be around."

My frustration boiled over, and I could no longer keep my thoughts from spilling out of my mouth. "I get it. I messed up, and I'm sorry for that. But I'm not finna stand here and let ya'll talk to me like I'm trash! Sidell is mature enough to make her own decisions. Her mistakes are hers alone. I take responsibility for mine, but don't pin everything on me!"

Sidell's father's eyes narrowed into slits. "You might want to reconsider your tone when you address my wife." he warned, his voice low and dangerous.

His threat bounced off me like rain on a tin roof. "My tone? That's rich coming from the man attacking a teenager to make himself feel big."

Sidell's mom gasped, immediately turning to their two house guests and whispering conspiratorially, no doubt spreading lies about my character.

"I swear ya'll church people ain't nothing but hypocrites. The moment someone doesn't fit your perfect little mold, you cast them out like lepers. Sidell is old enough to think for herself, her mistakes are her own. Stop trying to control her!"

"That's enough!" Sidell's father thundered, taking a menacing step forward. His fists were clenched and ready for a fight. "You best start walking before I make you limp off my property."

"Why you balling up your fist?" I challenged, stepping forward, meeting his gaze without flinching. "Who you think you finna touch?'"

Dawn jumped between us, holding up her hands in a calming gesture. "Okay let's all just take a deep breath here." She turned to me, her eyes pleading. "Come on JJ, be the bigger person and walk away."

I avoided her gaze, too stubborn and pissed to back down. The damage was already done. "Nah Dawn, he ain't scaring nobody." I wasn't about to be intimidated by this bully.

I risked a glance at Sidell who was being comforted by her little sister. Tears flowed freely down her cheeks as she bit her trembling lip, trying to hold back sobs. It was painful to see her like this. Not being able to do anything about it made the pain much worse.

"We need to leave," Dawn said firmly, her fingers squeezing around mine for stability.

My flesh turned to Jell-O and my legs wobbled beneath me as she led me away from the chaotic scene. Dawn must have sensed my imminent breakdown as she wrapped her arm around my waist, bearing some of my weight. "It's going to be okay, JJ," she soothed. "There is nothing anyone can do at this point but give Sidell and her family time to process the whole thing. I'm sure they'll come around eventually."

I looked at her through blurry, tear-filled eyes. "Did Sidell put you to this as well? It seems you have gotten good at expressing her thoughts." I choked out.

Dawn took a deep breath before responding carefully.

"JJ, I think she was scared. Scared of what that conversation might mean for your relationship." She hesitated but continued on bravely. "Sidell probably didn't want to hurt you."

Though it pained me to admit it, I knew Dawn was probably right. I finally accepted that Sidell wanted space, even if her methods were less than ideal. With time, I hoped we could rebuild what was broken. But for now, all I could do was walk away.

★ ★ ★ ★ ✟ ★ ★ ★ ★

When I got home, I dragged myself to my room, the weight of the world resting on my shoulders. I was hurt at the thought that Sidell had asked her friend to lie to me, just so she didn't have to speak to me. All the anger I had felt at their deception and her parents had yet to drain away.

I closed my bedroom door, falling face-first onto my pillows. I vaguely remembered my grandma coming in a few times to ask me if I was ill. I mumbled an incoherent response and shooed her away. Kaluna even came by, not to pester though but to offer me a drawing she had made. And as if me ignoring her wasn't enough to not be bothered, she decided to tape the picture on my wall before skipping out.

When I finally woke up, the day had turned to night, and someone had thrown a blanket on top of me. I felt peaceful, wrapped up in the cocoon of the covers and rolled over to go back to sleep when I heard my phone buzz on the nightstand. I sat up with a jolt, and unlocked my phone. I'd missed three calls from Tony, two from Dawn and a handful of text messages from both. Dawn must have told her boyfriend what had transpired earlier. I threw the phone back on the nightstand, not ready to deal with any of them just yet.

Chapter Twenty: Sidell

My throat felt like it was closing up as I shuffled through the bustling school hallways, keeping my eyes glued to the floor. The gnawing pit of anxiety in my stomach over last week's blow up with my parents and JJ was threatening to swallow me whole. I clutched my textbook tighter to my chest with each step, as if it could shield me from the guilt pressing down on my shoulders.

The once lively halls now seemed dull and muted without his infectious laughter echoing off the walls. I sighed, my breath shaky. I had gone through all the stages of heartbreak without ever having been in a relationship. My luck at keeping things platonic between us had finally run dry, while I pathetically tried to ignore the hollow ache in my chest every time I thought of how he might despise me.

I shook my head, swallowing back the lump in my throat. It couldn't just be bad timing anymore; we'd hang out, have the best time, then something would happen to make him pull away again. But I knew deep down I was partly to blame for driving this wedge farther between us. When my parents had confronted him, questioning his intentions and casting doubt on his character, I just stood there mute, paralyzed by my desire to be the perfect daughter they expected. I was so afraid to disappoint them that I failed to stand up for my friend - no, the guy I was secretly falling for.

I blinked rapidly as tears stung my eyes, weaving through the crowd of oblivious classmates. I replayed the confrontation in my mind, the flash of hurt on JJ's face as he tried to defend himself, only to be bombarded by more criticism as my parents refused to listen. A quiet sob escaped my lips as I realized the gravity of my mistake - I had betrayed not just JJ, but myself too. More than anything, I wished I could take it all back, to try and repair things before it was too late. Before I lost my chance at...at what, exactly? Happiness? Love? I pressed my palms to my eyes in frustration, earning a few weird glances from passing students.

"Get it together, Sidell," I muttered under my breath. Crying in the hallways isn't going to magically make JJ forgive you. But I had to try...I had to find him and apologize, even if he rejected me.

★ ★ ★ ★ ✞ ★ ★ ★ ★

By the time the bell rang for lunch, my legs felt weak. I lacked the willpower to head to the cafeteria. I always sat with Dawn for lunch. I had skipped lunch these last few days, but today, I was tempted to head in the direction of the cafeteria, and it's not just because I was famished.

As I walked in, I was sure that everyone was staring at me. Dawn and Tony were at their usual table, but JJ was nowhere near of course. Dawn saw me first. She waved at me then whispered something to Tony that was surely another lecture about being nice to poor, pathetic me. I continued bravely, crossing the room until I reached them, resisting the urge to dramatically crawl on my hands and knees.

Tony's shoulders tensed up like he was expecting a punch as I pulled a chair to join them. Dawn shot Tony a look that clearly said "Be Nice or I'll tell everyone about your secret girl band obsession." My lips quirked. Bless her protective instincts.

"Hey guys. How's it going?" I greeted them with false cheer, but they were already distracted, their gazes fixed on something behind me like cats hypnotized by a laser pointer. Curious, I smoothed my hair from my face, took a deep breath, and turned my head to follow their gaze.

My breath caught in my throat. JJ was making his way toward our table. My mind raced. I was unsure of how to react. We haven't spoken since the argument. Tension hung heavy in the air. Part of me wanted to make up some excuse and flee the scene, sparing myself from the awkwardness of sitting at a table with him after our nuclear fallout of a breakup. But the other part of me, the part with a backbone, refused to scurry away like a frightened mouse.

Before I could decide, JJ arrived at the table without so much as a glance in my direction. He pretended I didn't exist, greeting Tony and Dawn a bit too cheerfully. I wondered if the connection between us had been completely ruined. At the moment, it was almost as if I were a ghost, an unwanted presence haunting the space between them.

The atmosphere became suffocatingly tense as JJ put his soda can down on the lunch table before sliding into the chair next to me. His stupidly alluring cologne heightened the butterflies in my stomach, which fluttered angrily against my will. He unknowingly reawakened the yearning ache in my chest, a confusing desire, longing, and sadness. I couldn't fight off the sensation. I tried to catch JJ's eye as we ate, but his gaze remained fixed on his pizza, ignoring me purposely. The pain intensified and I bit my lip to keep from crying. Begging for his attention would be pathetic.. I had sufficient ego to not sink that low.

I took a deep, calming breath, trying to steady my nerves before attempting a civil conversation. "JJ, can we please talk?" I whispered politely.

JJ's reaction was a mere flicker of his eyes. But before he could respond, Dawn interjected, "Guys, maybe it's best if we all talk it out. We can't keep avoiding this."

Tony nodded in agreement, and I felt grateful for their support.

Inhaling and Exhaling a breath, I look at JJ again. My heart pounded against my ribcage as I mustered the courage to speak my truth. "JJ, I'm sorry. I should have spoken up, defended you, and shown you that I believe in us. I let fear and the desire for approval cloud my judgment, and I hurt you in the process. I am genuinely sorry."

The words hung in the air as I waited for his response. *Please just say something, even if you hate me. Anything is better than silence.*

He shrugged, glancing at me. "I don't think my silence has got so much to do with what you did or did not do that day as compared to our reality now. There is nothing you could have said to make either of your parents change their minds. It is probably best this way."

Dawn jerked her chin at JJ and gave him a dirty stare.

I returned my focus on the pizza rolls on my plate, pretending not to be hurt by his nonchalant response. I apologized. I no longer needed to justify myself or tiptoe around him. I belonged there as much as anyone else.

When the bell rang again, I stood quickly, the metal legs of my chair scraping loudly against the floor. "I've got to go. I'll see you guys later." I turn sharply, my ponytail whipping around. I immediately started counting the sound of my footsteps on the linoleum floor to keep my mind off JJ.

Thirty-two steps. Thirty-two steps and a full dose of determination was what it took to walk away from him. Outside the door to the cafeteria, I stopped and released the breath I had been holding.

If this was what my father wanted to protect me from by restricting my dating, then he hadn't been wrong.

Chapter Twenty-One: JJ

Stepping onto the football field, my nerves coiled tightly within me. It's another day of practice, and I was determined to give it my all. Though, as I joined my teammates, I couldn't help but feel a heaviness in my chest, a distraction that lingered in my mind. Thoughts of Sidell flooded my mind, and I couldn't shake off the guilt that gnawed at me.

Coach Davis blew the whistle, signaling the start of our practice. The sound cut through the air, jolting me back to reality. I positioned myself on the field even with my mind still clouded with remorse. The ball was passed to me and I watched it sail through the air, but I failed to react in time. It slipped through my fingers, and my focus was shattered.

With every missed pass, frustration builded up inside me. I could hear the disappointed murmurs from my teammates, their eyes darting in my direction. But my mind was far away, replaying the lunchtime conversation with Sidell over and over again. I remembered her tear-filled eyes as she apologized for something I had caused without thinking. The nonchalant attitude I wore that day now felt like a heavy burden.

As practice continued, my performance deteriorated further. I caught glimpses of my coach's expression, his brows furrowed in disappointment. He eventually called a timeout, and the team gathered around him, huddling close. I braced myself for what I knew was coming.

"JJ," Coach began firmly. "What's going on out there? You're not playing like yourself today. You didn't give us your best during the last practice either. What is going on with you?"

I met his gaze, "Coach, I'm sorry. I'm just... I have some personal stuff on my mind."

He studied me for a moment, gripping his clipboard. "Football is about focus, JJ. I understand that life can be challenging, but when you step onto this field, you need to leave your worries behind. Your teammates are counting on you."

Guilt and frustration rushed through me. "I know, Coach. I messed up. I let my thoughts get the best of me. I'm sorry."

His expression softened and he placed a hand on my shoulder. "We all make mistakes, JJ. But it's important to learn from them. When you walk out there, make a conscious effort to leave your worries at the gate. Use the game as an escape, a chance to channel your emotions positively."

His words sunk in, realizing he was right. I needed to regain control over my thoughts and emotions. I took a deep breath, feeling a renewed determination welling up within me.

"Thanks, Coach," I said, my voice laced with gratitude. "I'll give it my all. I won't let my personal problems affect my performance."

He gave me a nod, pointing his pen at me. "That's what I like to hear. Now get back out there, and let's see what you're truly capable of."

I smiled before putting my helmet back on. Jogging back onto the field, I blocked out the noise of my thoughts, focusing solely on the game at hand. This time, as the ball was passed to me, I reacted swiftly, my movements precise and determined. I felt a surge of exhilaration as I caught the pass, my teammates cheering me on.

At that moment, I understood that football was more than just a game. It's a refuge—a place where I could leave my worries behind and become the best version of myself. And as practice resumed, I immersed myself fully in the game. The weight of my personal troubles began to lift, replaced by a newfound energy and focus. Each pass was a chance to prove myself, to show my teammates and my coach that I could rise above any distractions.

The crisp autumn air filled my lungs as I sprinted down the field. My feet moved swiftly as my mind cleared. The game was like a dance—a symphony of coordinated movements and calculated decisions. I started to regain my rhythm, catching passes with ease, dodging defenders effortlessly.

My teammates noticed the change in me, their encouragement echoing in my ears. Their faith in me ignited a fire within, pushing me to work harder to exceed my own expectations. I saw the smile on Coach's face, his pride evident in his eyes. It's a stark contrast to the disappointment he had been showing just moments ago.

With practice drawing to a close, I approached him, with a mix of gratitude and determination coursing through my veins. "Thank you, Coach," I said, sincerely. "You helped me realize the importance of focus and leaving my personal troubles aside when I step onto this field. I won't let you down again."

Coach smiled, placing a hand on my shoulder. "You're a talented player, Jacky. But talent alone isn't enough. It's the mental strength and the ability to rise above adversity that truly sets great athletes apart. I believe in you, and I know you have the potential to achieve great things."

His words resonated deep within me. The sun was setting, casting a warm golden glow across the field, and I took a moment to savor the beauty. The sound of my teammates' laughter and the thud of the football against their hands echoed in the distance. It was a reminder that football wasn't just a game—it was a bond, a shared passion that had brought us together.

★ ★ ★ ★ ✝ ★ ★ ★ ★

Locking the front door behind me, my fatigue from practice quickly dissipated when I saw my grandma seated in her recliner chair, her piercing eyes fixed on me. I couldn't help but smile at the sight of her, but I knew she wouldn't be fooled by my attempt to hide what was truly going on inside me. She wanted answers, and she deserved them.

She beckoned me to sit beside her, and I complied, my heart heavy with the weight of the truth I was about to share. "Grandma," I began, "there's something I need to tell you. But promise me you'll understand that I'm fine, really. It's just... complicated."

178

Her gaze intensified with concern. She had always been fiercely protective of me, and I knew she wouldn't let this go easily. So, I took a deep breath and mustered the courage to reveal what had been troubling me.

"Mom... she... she wants to meet up with me," I stammered, the words catching in my throat. I could see the surprise flicker across my grandmother's face, quickly replaced by a composed expression as she processed the information.

"And she sent you a text, I suppose?" my grandmother asked with both curiosity and restraint.

I nodded. My eyes fixed on the floor. "Yeah, she did. But Grandma, please understand, I can't see her. It's... it's just too much for me to handle."

Silence hung heavy in the air as my grandmother absorbed my words. I could feel her disappointment, but she surprised me with her response.

"You know, child, it would mean the world to me if you went. Not for yourself, not for your mother, but for me," she said softly, her eyes glistening with unshed tears. "I haven't seen my daughter in years, and I fear time is slipping away. This might be my last chance, my final opportunity to hold her and tell her how much I still love her."

Her words struck me deep in my core, tearing at the walls I had erected to protect myself. My heart ached for her, for the pain she had endured all these years, silently longing for a reunion that seemed out of reach.

I reached out and gently held her hand, my own voice trembling with emotion. "Grandma, I... I didn't realize how much this meant to you. I'm sorry for being so stubborn. If it brings you comfort, if it gives you a chance to see her one last time... then I'll do it. I'll do it for you."

A tender smile graced my grandmother's lips, and she squeezed my hand. In that moment, I realized that it wasn't about guilt-tripping me. It was about granting her the closure she desperately sought.

171

Chapter Twenty-Two: Sidell

Fainting under the weight of my eyelids, I stifled a yawn as I sunk into my chair at the dining table. Gazing downward, my eyes were glued to my homework that was spread haphazardly across the wood surface. My mother was in the background kneading the yeast-based dough on the counter-top behind me.

In the past, she would have insisted on my little sister and I to help her with the baking or at least hang around to watch what she did. Mom wanted the routine to be imprinted in the back of our minds already, just because she wanted to prepare us for marriage. But now, she had managed to chase Cayest out of the kitchen in a grumpy tone that had given me pause, her patience wearing even thinner when I'd insisted on doing my schoolwork in the kitchen.

Clearly, she was still bent out of shape over me dating JJ. No matter how many times I told her nothing happened between us, she refused to believe me. Sometimes I wished Mom would trust me half as much as she trusted God's word. But no, I was the permanent black sheep who could do no right.

I bit my lips nervously, debating whether to push her buttons. She was being so unreasonable! I knew I shouldn't, but the urge to stir things up was strong. The aluminum foil crinkled as my mother spread it over the pan before placing the dough on top. She moved around stiffly, intent on shutting me out, at least as long as she didn't have to say the first word.

I turned around in my seat. "I didn't realize that baking is your hobby, Mama. There's so much that I don't know about you."

"Yes," she hissed, sliding the pan into the warm oven without mittens. A part of me wanted to call out a warning as I watched, but I held back.

"Is there something you'd like to talk about?" I asked.

She dumped the utensils she had used in the sink with a noisy clang and turned the water on. "Did you finish your homework?"

Mom was slowly easing out of the silent treatment she had been giving me, but her questions remained closed ended, without any warmth or emotion attached to her voice. I would rather have her yelling at me than continuing this way much longer.

Without another word, I hopped down the stool and strode towards my mother with purpose. I wrapped my hands around her waist, and she stiffened in place. "Mama?" I whispered with my arms tightening around her. "I love you." She peeked at me over her shoulder in bewilderment. "Sidell, what has gotten into you."

Embarrassed, I quickly let go and walked away, stung by her rejection.

"Good afternoon family." Nireska greeted as she floated into the kitchen along with Cayest. "Yaheli, do you mind? I was thinking about going with the girl's to bible study." Nireska asked my mom. I glanced back at my mother, who gestured nonchalantly. "Fine with me, you girl's grab a coat."

I tried not to cry as we strolled through the neighborhood to reach the church, the early evening air crisp and peaceful mocked my inner turmoil. I walked ahead briskly, and Nireska hurried to catch up until we were marching in sync, the rhythmic taps of our shoes magnifying the tense silence between us.

"I couldn't help but notice the tension between you and your mother," she said, her black hair flowing in the wind. "Is she still angry about what happened with your friend? Do you want to talk about it?"

I hesitated. Opening up about my personal business felt both frightening and intimidating. Could I comfortably trust *Nireska* of all people?

I sighed quietly, finally answering. "Without any evidence, my Mom believes whatever fits her narrow worldview best. And as for my friend?

I tried to talk to him… but he was very closed off about it, so I guess that's all that there is to it."

"But is that all you believe there is to it? The boy I saw seemed very much interested in you. He's probably hurt and still reeling from being told he wasn't good enough for you."

"I know… and I think I like him a lot, but it feels impossible! I'm torn between my parents' wishes and my own desires."

"Well, love has a way of challenging our beliefs and pushing us to question what we have been taught. If you truly love him, don't be afraid to push for it, Sidell. Some of the greatest joys in life will come from taking risks and following your heart."

I looked at her, confused. "But isn't it wrong to disobey my parents? To go against their wishes?"

"Sidell, there are times when parents, despite their love for us, may not fully understand our heart's desires or the depth of our emotions. Blindly following their rules can lead to a life filled with regret and unfulfilled dreams. You deserve happiness, and if that means pushing for what you want, then you should consider giving this boy another chance." Nireska said, lost in her own thoughts before meeting my eyes again. "Sidell, sometimes we have to question what goes on behind closed doors. My own experience has taught me that obedience does not guarantee happiness. I wonder if blindly following my parents' rules has brought me the fulfillment I truly desire."

I'm taken aback by her honesty. I realized there's a story hidden beneath her words, a story of battles fought and compromises made. It sparked a curiosity within me, a yearning to understand the complexities of her own life and what demons she wrestled with.

"What about you, Nireska?" I asked softly, my voice filled with a mixture of curiosity and concern. "What goes on behind closed doors? What do you sacrifice for the sake of your marriage?"

A flicker of sadness passed through her eyes, a veil of unspoken pain.

"Sidell, marriage is a journey filled with ups and downs. I've gotten used to it. You don't have to go through the same trials and tribulations just to please your parents… or anyone. It's easier going through it when it was solely your decision. Because then you wouldn't wonder what your life would have been like if you'd said *no* and followed your heart."

The street lights flickering one by one, as we finally approached the old church building where our bible study meeting was taking place. Walking up the steps, a swirl of emotions churned within me. I was torn between loyalty with my parents and self-discovery with JJ.

"God, I need your help. How do I make choices that follow the needs of my own heart and soul without disobeying you or my parents?"

In the midst of my prayer, I felt a gentle breeze blowing, as if a reassuring hand was guiding me toward the right path.

Chapter Twenty-Three: JJ

I stepped into Janda's Kitchen, my sanctuary from the chaotic city life.

The worn wooden floors squeaked under my weight as I navigated to my usual booth, passing familiar faces, nodding at regulars and exchanging casual smiles with weekend visitors. The light from the morning sun streamed through the large windows, casting an inviting glow on the polished table as I settled in. Before I had the chance to whip out my phone, a new waitress approached with a stutter and a contagious grin. Was she laughing at something or just nervous? When she brought me my food, I noticed her name tag read "Cherish." *Why did that name sound familiar?*

"I dig your shirt," Cherish said playfully, as if we were old friends. But for some reason, my mind was drawing a blank on what shirt I had thrown on this morning.

I looked down. The Clash? Seriously? I wouldn't know punk rock if the artist himself came back from the dead to give me a personal tutorial.

"Oh yeah, The Clash," I said, scrambling for something to say. "They're one of my favorites. Classic punk rock."

Cherish raised an eyebrow, a smirk playing on her lips. "Is that so? What's your favorite album of theirs?"

Damn. I was sinking fast. "Uh...you know, I like all their albums. Too hard to pick just one favorite."

She let out a laugh, her eyes glinting with amusement. "It's okay, you can admit it's not your shirt. I won't judge."

I felt my face flush. She had seen right through me. "Alright, you got me. I borrowed this from my friend Tony. He's the real classic rock fanatic."

"Nothing wrong with branching out from your usual style," she said. Her voice was kind, not mocking like I expected.

I looked up and noticed how striking she was. Her afro hair was dyed a dark red and styled in tousled twists, complimenting her warm brown skin. Expertly applied makeup highlighted her natural beauty. A subtle gold septum ring glinted as she smiled.

Cherish shrugged, "You should still give The Clash a listen. They ain't half bad."

The playfulness of her response made me wonder if she was flirting with me. It made me stop. It made me think of another time, with another girl. A girl who I couldn't be with. A familiar coldness swept over me.

"Yeah, maybe I'll check them out," I mumbled, avoiding Cherish's gaze.

"Mm. Your change is 10 dollars and twenty-five cents." She handed it over, and I put it into the pocket of her apron. She smiled and looked at me, giving a little pause. "Have a good day, JJ."

My pulse jumped a bit until I realized I gave my name for the order - that's how she knew it. I laughed under my breath at myself, then smiled in return. "Thanks. You too." I said unwrapping my silverware from its napkin.

I didn't know what's wrong with me. She was gorgeous, friendly and my type. She'd probably give me her number had I asked for it.

It wasn't completely foreign to me to have girls act like this around me. The ones at school stayed far away from me, of course - everyone there knew enough about how I used to be and was scared enough to leave me alone. In public, however, I could sometimes get attention. Girls who knew nothing about me saw a tall, smooth, charming guy and none of the damage underneath. They might be drawn to my intensity, but none seem to actually like it once they get close enough. It's too scary, too real. It becomes less hot and more *'yikes,'* if not outright terrifying.

But Cherish looked like she could be intense, too. She looks like someone I would theoretically get along with. *And she's a baddie, I* mentally shouted at myself in frustration as I watched her take another order. I could still ask for her number now, if I wanted.
But I wouldn't.

I knew I shouldn't. Besides that wasn't what I came there for.

My heart was pounding with a mix of excitement and resentment. It's been years since I last saw her... my mom, and now she wants to meet up. Part of me longed for that connection, that missing piece in my life, but another part was filled with anger and hurt for all the years she abandoned me.

I took a sip of my drink before glancing at the clock on the wall, and the minutes seemed to slip away too quickly. Each passing second felt like an eternity. My anticipation grew with every tick. I tried to push down the doubts and the nagging voice in my head that told me not to get my hopes up, but it was hard to ignore.

The minutes turned into an hour, and I began stress eating. When my favorite apple pie started to taste bitter in my mouth, that's when real life kicked in to torment me. She wasn't coming. The disappointment taunted me like Donica's ghost, washing away the excitement and leaving me broken. How could she do this to me? Again! How could she build up my hopes, only to let them come crashing down?

Anger welled up within me, fueled by the unanswered questions, and the broken promises. Heat rose in my chest, my fists clenched involuntarily. I had given her a chance, against my better judgment, and she had once again fallen short.

Janda sauntered over, pity in her eyes. "Sorry hun, but we gotta close up. Want me to box that food for you?"

I scowled, shoving the offending drink toward her. "No thanks, I've lost my appetite."

She offered an understanding smile but I didn't need her sympathy. With a huff, I jumped up from the table, my footsteps heavy with frustration as I made my way out of the diner. I didn't look back, refusing to let pain overtake me by glancing back at her empty chair. The resentment weighed on me, a burden I had carried for far too long.

I stormed out of that disastrous excuse for a reunion, the door slamming loudly behind me. So much for closure. What did I expect - that she'd actually apologize for ruining my life? Hurrying down the busy street, I caught my reflection in a storefront window. I let out a sharp, bitter laugh that made a nearby pigeon flutter away in fright. Some naive part of me still hoped we could hug and cry and she'd be the mother I wanted, but the rusty padlock sealing my past shut just clicked permanently into place.

I pushed the apartment door open with more energy than needed and slammed it behind me as hard as I could. The loud noise was satisfying. That's when I saw Grandma and the three disciples from Church gathered around her. I was caught off guard for a second, but I recovered quickly.

"JJ, what's going on with you boy?" Grandma asked, her face filled with concern.

"We are not going to that damn wedding, and if you insist on it, you'll have to go alone!" I stormed off to my room, leaving Grandma and her guests with their mouths agape. Slamming my door, I faintly heard one of them shout "Jesus!" followed by speaking in tongues.

I fell back onto my bed, staring at the familiar patterns on the ceiling as my mind was consumed with disappointment and anger. It felt like every sliver of hope and trust I had, had been shattered once again.

The sound of footsteps approaching my room interrupted my thoughts, and I turned my head to see my grandmother standing in the doorway. Her face was etched with concern, her eyes filled with a mixture of love and disappointment. I sensed that she knew exactly what had happened.

She entered the room, her steps cautious and deliberate, as if she's treading on fragile ground. I could hear the women from her fellowship waiting in the living room, their hushed voices lingering in the air. But at that moment, it was just the two of us.

"What happened, Jacky?" she asked softly. I viewed the lines of age engraved on her face, and all I felt was the ache in my heart and anger at my mother for putting her through turmoil as well. For putting *us* through it.

I took a deep breath, trying to steady myself as I struggled to find the right words. "She... she didn't show up," I managed. "I waited, Grandma. I gave her a chance, and she let me down. Again!"

Chapter Twenty-Four: Sidell

Coming home from Bible study, the walls of my home felt like they were closing in on me. The peace I felt in the cathedral evaporated as soon as I stepped through the front door. Depression then picked up from where it left off, dragging me into its dark embrace once more. Determined to distract myself, I grabbed the broom from the kitchen closet. Starting downstairs, I swept with furious intensity, as if I could push away my troubles with each bristle stroke. The rhythmic motion provided some brief peace, until I reached my parents' closed bedroom door. My grip tightened on the broom handle as I strained to listen to their heated argument.

Suddenly, Cayest pushed past me, nearly knocking the dustpan from my hands.

"Can you move instead of just standing there?" she hissed at me before storming off to her room and slamming the door.

I huffed and closed my eyes, refusing to let her attitude get to me. It was clear that the tension in our home extended far beyond my parents' bedroom. Cayest's outburst only added to the oppressive atmosphere that seemed to consume every inch of our house.

I should intervene, but would my actions backfire and cause even more chaos? After all, it seems like everything I do only fuels Mom's anger. Am I the root of the problem? It sure feels that way, as even the slightest misstep on my part ignites her rage.

"Sidell?" Nireska's soft voice startled me. She stood in the guest room doorway, brow furrowed. "You've been sweeping that same spot for five minutes. Is everything alright?"

I forced a smile. "Yeah, why do you ask?"

I guessed she assumed that my behavior was related to my incident with JJ. To be honest, I'd had enough of thinking about him. But being reminded of him only made me think about him even more, which was exactly what I was trying to stop doing. I did not want to consider how much trouble my silly adventure with him had caused.

A small part of me wished that it was possible to wipe him from my memory or go back in time to undo what we had begun so that I could at least stop feeling guilty about the fracture it was causing in my family. But still, an even larger part of me wanted to race out of the house and head over to his place to talk to him about everything and make amends for what had happened.

"It's nothing." I said, finally answering Nireska's question.

She considered what I had said for a few seconds, then she smiled understandingly, and I quickly nodded at her as I went to dump the dustpan in the bathroom trash can.

"You've been thinking about him again, right?" she asked, winking at me.

"Huh?" Mortification washed over me; how dare she imply such a thing within these walls where my parents could possibly hear? Did she have a death wish? My parents couldn't discover that she approved of a relationship they disapproved of! How should I respond? What could possibly shut her up long enough for me to escape this interrogation?

"No…" The lie slipped easily from my lips as I moved into the bathroom.

"Tell me the truth, Sidell. You seemed…" Nireska paused, pursing her lips dramatically. "I might be wrong, but you've been a little different since we came back from Bible Study. More distracted." She glanced over her shoulder as she leaned on the doorframe.

"But it's not just that." I cut her off. "I've been sleeping less lately. And this thing about JJ should be forgotten - for everyone's sake." I walked past her, broom in hand, and she followed me to my room.

Bzzz.

I froze instinctively looking around for the source of the sound — I knew my phone wasn't in my possession. My mom hadn't yet returned it to me, and she wouldn't have suddenly forgotten and left it where I could easily find it.

As if reading my mind, Nireska extended the hand that had been hidden behind her back. "I was going to tell you about it," she confessed, biting her lip nervously.

"Where'd you get that?" I leaned the broom against the wall, its task momentarily forgotten. "Did you take that from my mother? She'll be livid when she finds out!" The normally calm hallways echoed with my hushed, panic-laden voice. " What are you even trying to do? Get me in trouble?"

I hurriedly approached her at the end of the hall, stretching out my hand for my phone the moment I stood before her. Nireska held the phone out, and I snatched it out of her hands. Her head dropped for a second, and she let out a little sigh. I felt like a horrible person, but I just couldn't deal with the possibility of her invading my privacy.

"Relax, Sidell." she smiled. "I'm on your side. JJ has been trying to reach you for some time. I just was not sure how to bring it up with you. You can see him, if that's what you want, Sidell. I'll drive you over there."

This conversation was continuing to get even weirder. I remained still, trying to gather my rambling thoughts. Nireska's eyes were on me, waiting for my decision.

"You would?" I asked faintly, my throat suddenly dry. I forced my lips to stretch into a small smile.

"Yes, I would, but you don't look enthusiastic about it. What is wrong, Sidell? Have you changed your mind about him?"

"No.. But, you know I don't want to cause any more trouble. What if my parents—"

"Find out? They wouldn't except, of course, if you tell them. Even if they do, it's not like you're going to do anything wrong. You've got a chaperone they approve of." She crossed the distance to place her hands on my shoulders, shaking me slightly. "Focus on all the things you want to say to JJ instead. Focus on fixing what's been broken and even if you don't get another chance at what you shared before, at least you would have a friend in school, aside from Dawn, to have your back. You can't go on moping around like you're doing now. It's only a matter of time before you snap and do something drastic. Trust me, I've been there before. I was once a teen too before I became a boring grown up."

"But what about Cayest? If she finds out about this, she is definitely going to tell on me and—"

"It would be our word against hers. Your sister is smarter than that. She wouldn't throw you under the bus unless it's to save herself, and that's completely avoidable if we leave right away and return before anyone notices your absence."

"I don't know? I mean, I could meet him in school—" I said hesitantly.

Nireska sighed, bringing her eyes into line with mine. "It seems that you have made up your mind about this already," she said, shaking her head with a half-smile plastered across her face.

I swallowed the protests building up in my throat, rearranging my features to look unbothered. Staring at her blankly, I mentally removed myself from the scene, losing myself in my thoughts.

Nireska inspected me for a moment longer before she released my shoulders. "I have to get my beauty sleep now. You might want to make up with Cayest. She actually tried to cover for you when you were out on your little escapade with JJ. Your mother almost bought her excuse too, until she called her bluff and went ahead to check with Dawn's mother. Unbeknownst to you, she got in trouble too, so you may want to spend a bit more time with her... You might just find that you're more alike than you think, and that being her older sister is not such a burden after all."

I was surprised to hear that Cayest had tried to cover for me. I had always thought of her as the tattletale, but maybe I had been wrong about her this whole time. I felt a pang of guilt for not trusting her.

"I'll try to make it up to her," I said softly.

CHAPTER TWENTY-FIVE;
ψψ

I wasn't a people pleaser.

Partly because I understood how important it was to control your life by constantly putting yourself first. No one else would do that for me if I didn't do it for myself. But mostly, I wasn't a people pleaser because my grandmother was one already. I'd watched her sacrifice her well-being for far too long, and I knew better than to fall into the same trap.

"You've gotta think of how your mother would feel," Grandma said. She stood in front of my dressing mirror, making finishing touches to her outfit even though there was a mirror in her own room. Her eyes occasionally found mine through the glass reflection. They were pleading and hopeful that I would change my mind.

"She didn't think about how I'd feel when she was a no show at the diner the other day." I shook my head, disgustedly. "She didn't think about how either of us would feel when she stayed away for years on end, acting like she didn't have a family back here."

Grandma stared at me with wide, sad eyes. She opened her mouth like she wanted to say something, but she didn't.

I was the exact opposite, unable to stop speaking.

"She didn't care about how I felt when she sent those texts, asking me to go watch her marry some man I'd never even met. Hell, I wouldn't even recognize my own mother if it wasn't for those dusty photo albums you insist on keeping around to torture me with false hope." I said, my hands curling into fists. "That's like all levels of messed up! Little Miss Bride has no feelings. There is literally no possibility that our absence will make her feel sad. She's been working on replacing us all, and I wouldn't want to get in the way of that."

Grandma crossed the floor toward my window, opening it to let in some circulation. It was the only sound in the room after my tirade. She sighed and shook her head like she couldn't believe what she had just heard. "That's a lot of hurt and baggage for one person to carry, JJ. If only you'd hand it over to Jesus. He truly cares about you."

"That's not gonna work. Your Jesus and I still got some squaring off to do as well. He might as well focus on all those prayers he refused to answer," I scoffed.

"You better watch your mouth, child. You can't talk that way about my Jesus." She defensively placed her hands at her hips. "Everything happens for a reason according to His plan, even if we don't understand it. You've got to let the Lord handle this in His own time..."

As she droned on with her righteous sermon, I slowly tuned her out, my chest burning hotter by the second. I rubbed my hands over my face in frustration. Any last shred of hope I'd been clinging to was utterly destroyed now. Those endless phone calls from my deadbeat mom, her pathetic attempts to make amends, and now her failure to even show up to our meeting—it was all too much. Maybe I should crash her wedding after all, if only to ruin her special day like she ruined mine all those years ago.

My grandma eventually strolled out of my bedroom, calling out instructions as she left. Without giving it a second thought, I grabbed my phone and scrolled through it. I couldn't help but feel a heaviness in my chest, as I saw Sidell's contact info. Clicking on our messages, nostalgia of her flooded my mind, and I couldn't shake off the guilt that gnawed at me.

My mind replayed the lunchtime conversation with Sidell over and over again. I remembered her tear-filled eyes as she apologized for something I had caused without thinking. The nonchalant attitude I wore that day now felt like a heavy burden. My fingers worked the keypad in a desperate attempt to apologize.

Me: Hey Sidell. I know you probably hate me. But, can we start again?

I stared at my message, wondering if I'd regret it when I hit send. Just then my phone rang as Tony's name flashed on my screen. I deleted my message and closed the chatbox. Swiping up on the call, I placed it to my ears, "Wassup Rockstar?"

"Where are you, I'm close by already," he said impatiently.

"Yeah..yeah my fault. I'll be right out," I told him, sitting up on my bed. After hanging up, I blew out a breath as I ran my hand through my hair, mentally preparing myself for what might go down tonight. Climbing into Tony's car in the parking lot of the school, I slammed the door shut while my eyes glazed over in a zombie stare across the windshield.

"What's up, man? Are you good?" Tony asked. He quickly glanced in my direction.

I sucked in a breath and turned to him. "Yeah. Just drive man."

Tony didn't need another prompt. His foot hit the accelerator, and soon enough we were flying along the main street.

"How is your grandma doing?" Tony asked, making small talk. "It's been a while since I saw her."

I cleared my throat, leaning back in my seat. "Praying up a storm as always and still nagging me to go to church, but I'm not into that stuff anymore. I just wished she would let it go and stop drumming faith into my ears."

Tony nodded understandingly. He had been around my grandmother only a few times, but that was more than enough of an introduction.

Silence reigned except for a soft hum from Tony and the purr of his car's engine. My gaze veered his way. "How is your girl, Dawn? Y'all still roughing it out?" I asked with a frog in my throat.

Dawn's well-being hardly concerned me. I silently hoped he had heard something about Sidell through Dawn and that he may bring it up in the course of our conversation. After my attitude towards her at school last time, I couldn't bring myself to ask about her outrightly.

"Ah, Dawn's great." He smiled. "We've been planning this awesome date night. You know, trying to keep the spark alive and all that."

"That's cool. Aye, doesn't Dawn live next door to Sidell? Have you heard anything about her lately?" I said, knowing that she probably still didn't have access to her phone.

Tony chuckled, peeping my game. "Nice try, my friend. But you can't avoid talking about your own problems by prying into mine. Sidell and you will have to figure things out for yourselves."

I scoffed, "Nevermind. I think it's over between us anyway, she just doesn't care enough to be straight with me. Might as well let bygones be bygones since her parents clearly run her life." I shifted the blame, desperate for some kind of justification for my feelings.

"Come on, man. At lunch you gave her the cold shoulder, but now you're begging for scraps about her life. Which one is it bro?" he asked, calling me out on my wack behavior.

I scowled at him, then shifted my gaze towards the window.

He was right and it annoyed me. "Alright, Tony. Let's go," I mumbled in defeat.

A short while later, Tony pulled up at the house party. We were a little early but Tony said that would be cool. Parked near the dimly lit sidewalk, I could hear the sound of distant laughter mingling with the bass-heavy beats that pulsated through the night air.

Tony turned off the car and locked the door before heading towards the house. With a mix of curiosity and anticipation, I followed after him, approaching the unassuming house, its windows illuminated with vibrant hues of red and blue.

The door swung open, revealing the chaos within. The air was thick with a combination of music, laughter, and the unmistakable scent of alcohol. The energy enveloped me, drawing me deeper into the already crowded room.

The room was a whirlwind of bodies, moving and swaying to the rhythm of the music. A kaleidoscope of lights danced across the walls, casting a hypnotic glow on the eclectic decor. Conversations meld together, voices rising and falling like waves in an ocean of sound.

My senses were on high alert as I pushed through the sea of bodies, taking in the vibrant tapestry of sights and sounds surrounding me. Each room I entered revealed a new spectacle—a makeshift dance floor in the kitchen, a group engaged in a spirited game of beer pong in the backyard, and an impromptu jam session in the basement.

A heavy hand immediately clamped down on my shoulder. I turned around to see that it was my football teammate, Nysear. "Yo JJ's here!" His squeaky voice roared into the crowded living room, as though amused by my presence.

"We haven't seen you hit a party in a while."

"Yeah, well. I'm here now." I tugged my shoulder out from under his meaty grasp.

"Yes you are," He agreed, tone slipping into strange, sudden seriousness. The silence lasted a beat too long. "Drinks are in the kitchen. Good to see you, man."

Nysear's always been a weirdo to me. I scoffed it off under my breath and headed to the kitchen.

A few people I didn't recognize were hanging in there but none of them acknowledged me, so I started pouring myself a drink without comment. I didn't recognize a lot of the drinks. I held up a can of soda to try and read the writing when suddenly a velvety voice hummed thoughtfully from right beside me. I jumped a little.

"I don't recommend that one."

I blinked down. The girl with the dyed - curly red hair, dark brown complexion, and light brown eyes. I recognized her - she worked at Janda's Kitchen. She complimented me once on Tony's Clash t-shirt, I remembered.

"Uh - and why is that?" I asked.

She squinted at it in thought and I noticed again how beautiful she is. Painted-beautiful. Her mascaraed lashes highlighted her brown eyes and her plump lips were marked with clear lip gloss.

"Mm, Tevin likes all these Japanese sodas, so I mean . . . you might. But most everyone thinks the flavors are too weird to casually enjoy. More of a novelty thing."

I looked again at the label. An illustration of strawberry cheesecake sat next to the Japanese brand name. *Huh.*

"I'll take your word on that." I nodded, placing the can back on the table.

She smirked. "Probably a good call. I'm Cherish."

"JJ. I think you—"

"Took your order. I remember."

I found it in me to smile. "So what would you recommend, then?"

"Doing a shot," Cherish says matter-of-factly with a throaty laugh. She leaned over the counter to grab the vodka. Out of respect, I looked away from her cleavage that was directly in my line of sight. She poured two shots. "Bottoms up."

The alcohol burned down my throat, but I welcomed its numbing effect. A few more couldn't hurt.

I kept talking with Cherish, our conversation getting louder and funnier with each shot. She was easy to talk to, without the pressure of forced flirts or awkward attempts at impressing one another. And with each giggle from her lips, I could feel my heart slowly healing. We moved from the kitchen to the dining room and eventually ended up on the makeshift dance floor in the living room.

The bass pulsed through my bones as Cherish's perfume enveloped me. "JJ," she purred, warm breath on my ear. "Wanna dance?"

When I met her eyes, they were filled with anticipation and a hint of mystery. And for a split second, I considered her offer, craving a distraction from my troubled mind. The pounding music reverberated in my chest. It urged me to let go and surrender if only for a moment.

A sly grin tugged at the corners of my lips as I took her hand. "Why not? Come on, let's dance."

We moved to the center of the pulsating crowd. Our bodies swayed in sync with the rhythm. The room became a blur of lights and laughter that momentarily drowned out my troubles. With each step, I felt the weight of my worries lifting as they were carried away by the party's electric energy.

As the music intensified, Cherish pulled me close, her hips moving in sync with the heavy bass. I let the rhythm guide me, losing myself in the music and the warmth of her body pressed against mine.

Neon lights flashed across her face, illuminating her mischievous smile. She spun around, her back now against my chest as we danced. My hands found their way to her waist, the fabric of her dress smooth beneath my fingertips.

But then, a familiar face caught my eye. It was Dawn, standing near the edge of the crowd, her gaze fixed on me. A mix of disgust and annoyance washed over her features.

I immediately jolted back to reality. Politely, I untangled myself from Cherish's, offering her an apology. "I'm sorry. I can't do this," I said, my voice barely audible above the music.

Her eyebrows perked upwards as she stared blankly at my retreating figure but I paid no mind. I weaved through the crowd, determined not to make any more stupid decisions tonight.

I made my way to Dawn. A mix of emotions passed through me as I covered the distance.

"Dawn," I said, reaching out my hand. "I had no idea that you would be here. Where is Tony?"

She hissed. "I'm supposed to be the one asking that question. You came here together, didn't you?"

I blinked furiously, struggling to get past the haze of alcohol that was clouding my mind to answer her question. "We did come together, but I have no idea where he is at the moment."

"That's rich and very convenient. You have no idea where he's at. Should have guessed that you'd stick to the bro code even if it caused harm to everyone else. Pretty sure he would have said the same thing about you if I'd caught him first." Dawn sounded more accusatory with each statement.

"Whoa, whoa, I have no idea where Tony is. I have no idea what is going on with y'all but what you saw earlier is totally unrelated, okay? I didn't do anything wrong. I was drinking, and it sounded like a good idea to dance with her at the time. It wasn't what it looked like. I would not intentionally set out to hurt Sidell, even though she's no longer interested in me," I mumbled, trailing after her as she navigated from room to room, searching for Tony.

Dawn's mouth flat-lined as she crossed her arms and turned to face me. "You're doing a lot of explaining for someone that's supposedly innocent, JJ. I don't care what you're doing here. I didn't come here for you either. But if you're going to act the fool and do stupid things each time you're not given enough attention, then it's best you stay away from Sid. She's not like the rest of us. She's almost normal, and I'd hate for anyone or anything to distort that near-perfect little life of hers."

Without as much as a goodbye, Dawn stormed off.

Chapter Twenty-Six: Sidell

The gymnasium echoed with the rhythmic thuds of sneakers kissing the polished wooden floor, underscored by Coach Sherrie's sharp claps leading the cheer squad through our drills. My ponytail swished back and forth as I struggled to mimic my fellow cheerleaders' movements. Each step felt like solving a puzzle, my brain straining to remember each twist and turn of the choreography.

"Five, six, seven, eight!" Coach Sherrie's voice boomed out, her usual motivational tone failing to keep my rhythm in tune today.

Where was Dawn and why didn't she come to practice? Did she ditch school without telling? All these questions buzzed through my mind as I desperately needed to talk to her. I got to know if JJ's okay. What if he's not?

I hesitated on a high kick, my balance wavering like a newborn deer trying to walk for the first time. Meanwhile, the girls around me were a blur of perky perfection, crisp and precise in their movements. While I constantly struggled to keep up, every step feeling like wading through thick mud, the other girls seemed to drift effortlessly on their feet, as though gravity had granted them a special favor.

"Again! From the top!" Coach Sherrie barked after a particularly messy transition. Disappointment settled on my tongue, sour and stinging. But I swallowed it down, determined not to let it show. We launched into the routine once more, bodies twisting and leaping in synchronized harmony, until we reached the pinnacle movement: the pyramid. This was where strength and trust were paramount, where every hand and foot had to find its place in the architecture of our collective effort.

I took my position at the base, bending my knees in preparation. Yet as the girl above me stepped into my interlocked hands, my arms quivered under her weight. The girl's foot slipped and frightened gasps cut through the air as we scrambled to avoid disaster.

"Timeout!" Coach Sherrie's whistle cut sharply through the chaos. "Sidell, over here."

"I'm so sorry." I apologized as I peeled away from my teammates', who aided the girl who had almost landed on the hard floor. Approaching my coach, I looked everywhere but her eyes as I waited for her furious lecture. But instead was met with her soft voice.

"Talk to me, Sidell. You're not yourself today. You're usually on point, but you're off. You're a hair away from an injury. What's going on?" She asked, genuinely worried.

I shuffled my feet, my gaze tracing the scuff marks on the floor. "I don't know, Coach. I'm just... out of it today, I guess."

Coach Sherrie narrowed her eyes, seeing right through me. "Alright," she huffed, shoulders sagging in defeat. "Take five, hydrate, and see if you can shake it off. We can't afford to have you out of commission."

I pushed through the gym doors, my shoes clacked against the stone floor, the echoes bouncing off the walls and grating on my already frayed nerves. The lights flickered as I pushed through double doors that led to the hallway near the locker rooms. I needed to find Dawn. Where was she?

Suddenly, I saw Dawn through the window that led to the coach's office. She spun lazily in the desk chair, fidgeting with trophies and trinkets that weren't hers. Why is she hiding out here?

I slipped inside, "Hey Dawn." I breathed. Dawn jerked violently, nearly toppling a teetering tower of trophies with a crash. "Goodness, Sidell!" she gasped, hand to her chest. "Give me a heart attack, why don't you?"

I forced a weak laugh, sitting ontop the desk beside her. "Sorry about that." I weakly chuckled, perched myself on the edge of the desk next to her. "What are you doing here all by yourself?"

Dawn's eyes darted shiftily. "Oh, nothing..." She trailed off nonchalantly. "Why aren't you at practice?"

"I'm just..." I leaned in close, dropping my voice to an urgent whisper. "Um..Do you have any idea how JJ is? I've been worried sick about him."

Dawn scoffed and then shrugged dismissively, refusing to answer my question. She seemed moody. "I guess he's fine," she finally muttered when she noticed my eyes boring into her. "There is no point worrying about him."

Confusion creased my brow as I pressed her further. "What is going on? Did something happen?" I asked.

Dawn huffed as she finally confessed. "I saw JJ at a party over the weekend," she admitted. "And bestie babe, let me tell you, he didn't seem too worried about you. He was all over some thick red dye girl, only stopping when he noticed I was glaring at him."

My heart sank. "JJ did that?" I whispered, my voice trembling. "Are you sure about what you saw, Dawn?" *He couldn't have moved on already, could he? I never responded to his messages, after all. Maybe this was my fault. Maybe I drove him away.*

Dawn ranted on. "And I was a fool to think Tony could ever be faithful to me. That toe fungus was supposed to be at that party as well. Can you believe that I couldn't find him even though his car was parked right outside? Searched every inch of that damn house too. Yet he wants me to believe he wasn't messing around with some girl. I asked JJ, and he told me he hadn't seen him even though they got there together. Ha!" She let out a humorless chuckle. "Honestly, Men lie easier than they breathe. I should've learned that from my cheating scumbag of a father."

Sighing, I closed my eyes and asked, "Did JJ speak to you? He must have said something. I mean, did he even try to explain himself?"

My heart squeezed in my chest as I contemplated all of his possible responses. Nothing I thought of made any sense.

Dawn kneaded her forehead with the ball of her hand. She turned to face me, "There's no use holding onto JJ," she said, frustrated. "Of course, the decision is solely yours to make but with the way it stands, I doubt if holding on is the right option. You're already threading on soft ice with your parents, Sid. You need someone who's solid in your corner, otherwise there's no point to any of the struggle."

Her advice stung, and I struggled to hold back tears. I was hurt, angry, and torn between wanting to end what I had shared with JJ and letting it go for my well-being. It's ironic that Nireska urged me to try again, and Dawn was now advising me to move on.

I swallowed hard and avoided Dawn's stare. "Well, if that's the way the cookie crumbles, nothing more can be done," I said nonchalantly as my hands trembled.

Dawn's eyes softened, and she opened her mouth to say more, but I quickly slid off the desk, and flashed a false bright smile. "I'll see you at lunch, Dawn." Before she could respond, I hurried out of the cheer office.

For the rest of the day, I forced myself to pay attention in class, but my mind was elsewhere. I barely registered what the teachers said, and when called upon, I couldn't muster the focus to answer their questions.

I ran out of excuses to give my teachers by the fourth period. The bell rang and I gathered my belongings. My chemistry teacher was standing beside his desk on the other side of the classroom, watching the students file out. His concern was palpable when he called out my name as I was passing him by.

"Sidell?" he called in a gentle tone.

I glanced up to find him frowning at me.

"Is there something you need to talk about? You seem distant lately," he asked.

"I'm fine, really." I plastered on a smile, but even I could hear the strain in my voice. "Just a bit stressed."

He nodded, though his expression told me my performance wasn't convincing.

Even so, I left his classroom without any further explanation. There was no way I could admit to one of my teachers that my low grades were all thanks to my obsession with a boy I'd been warned to stay away from.

By lunchtime, I headed to our usual table with a tray containing fries and a milkshake. The tension was thick at the table I sat at with Tony, Dawn and JJ. The conversation was strained, filled with silent glares and unspoken words. Dawn and I huddled together, muttering and forcing laughs between ourselves.

"I'm sorry for what happened at the party." Tony's voice was soft and barely audible as he spoke up.

I glanced across the table at him. His expression was filled with remorse and sincerity. I paused mid-meal, desperate to believe there was a genuine explanation for what had happened.

"I messed up by not following through on the plans we had made and not letting you know about it, babe," he continued. "Believe me, I wasn't doing anything but getting wasted and I forgot to meet you. It was also foolish and disrespectful, and I understand why you are angry."

Dawn assessed him through a half-lidded gaze. "I want to believe you, Tony, but I was at that party because I'd gotten a call from an unregistered number asking me to come pick you up because you were drunk. I roamed through all the rooms in that house and asked a dozen people, including JJ, but no one had seen you, meanwhile your car was parked outside. Where exactly were you? That's all I want to know. I need the truth!"

A hush fell over the cafeteria as more and more people turned their attention towards us. I returned my attention back to Dawn. Her eyes flickered between JJ and Tony expectantly.

"I've said it before. I was passed out in one of the bathrooms, Dawn. I was drunk, but I was right there. I hadn't gone anywhere," Tony continued, his voice strained with the effort it took to keep a level tone. "I promise you that it won't happen again. I want to make things right between us."

His words tugged at my heartstrings. I nudged Dawn gently, silently encouraging her to consider his plea. Tony's remorse and attempt to mend the rift was worth considering. Despite Tony's plea, Dawn merely crossed her arms over her chest and stared coldly at him.

"No one saw you go into that bathroom?" she asked, raising a brow. "No one used the bathroom and found you slumped there? You took yourself to a party without my knowledge. It would be pretty understandable if you hadn't already told me that you weren't going!"

JJ popped another crispy tater tot into his mouth then mumbled, "There isn't anything anyone can say to make you believe us if you've already made up your mind about what happened that night, Dawn."

"It's great to see that you've not lost your voice, JJ," Dawn said, her shoulders squared. "At least I didn't make up my mind without the hard facts. You were busy coupling up with that redhead." Dawn then pointed a finger in Tony's direction. "And your buddy over here was nowhere to be found. Now I'm just supposed to believe that he was stuck in the bathroom and no one had found him, not even you whom he'd gone along with."

JJ scrunched his face. "I'm pretty sure that dancing with strangers at parties is normal, Dawn. I'm not about to sit up here and endure this interrogation because I don't owe anybody anything. If you're not going to take my word for it, then I shouldn't even be speaking to you."

My stomach turned as I watched JJ push back his chair, ready to walk away again. Walking away seemed easy for him. As if it was second nature for him. The way he blatantly refused to even speak to me hurt more than I wanted to admit. It was like he'd just wiped me from his brain. I knew our relationship wasn't one-sided — he liked me. He'd said so himself. Despite that, he'd washed his hands of me pretty easily.

My sadness turning to anger, I glared at JJ and hissed, "That's the way it is, huh? You'd rather walk away than sit down to sort all this out?"

"Whose fault is it that there is something to work out in the first place, huh, Sid?" He spat out my nickname, his words clipped with a bitterness that threatened to engulf him whole.

Tony shook his head. "No, we shouldn't do this here. This is not the right time, JJ."

"No!" I shot JJ a pointed gaze. "We'll do it now. I'm tired of having to walk on eggshells around him. I am not going to keep apologizing for every single thing that goes wrong when it is much easier for him to simply walk away from all of it."

"You really don't know how to take a hint, do you?" He asked, approaching me head-on.

My mouth went dry as I looked up into his eyes. "What is that supposed to mean?"

"Take a wild guess."

My shock turned to fury. "Don't talk to me like I'm some sort of idiot for not correctly interpreting your *mood swings*. Use your big boy words, Jacky. I can't read your mind."

"Alright." He gets closer until there's no breather room between us. "Here it is - I don't want to talk to you. I don't want to listen to you. I don't want to look at you. I don't want to know you. That's why. Clear enough?"

Only adrenaline kept me upright, straight-faced, unyielding. "No. Not good enough."

"Don't push me, Sidell."

I gritted my jaw. This JJ had a disturbing undercurrent of volatility in his eyes. As much as I wanted to be tough and righteously indignant . . . it scared me. I hated that he scared me.

"If you walk away now, that's it." I whispered brokenly. "Don't bother coming back if you do."

"Then maybe putting some distance between us is for the best. I'm already dealing with enough bull**** from my own family. I don't need to add yours to the mix."

With that he stalked off, leaving an awkward silence behind. None of this went the way I'd thought.

★ ★ ★ ★ ✟ ★ ★ ★ ★

I was so lost in my sorrow that I didn't even notice I wasn't alone in the school's auditorium. Nor did I realize I was crying until a tissue appeared in my field of vision. I looked up, blinking through my tears to see Khyree Latimore's concerned face peering down at me.

"Are you okay?" he asked gently.

I took the tissue and dried my tears. "Please don't tell anyone about this," I begged.

Khyree raised one of his hands in surrender "I swear, I won't say anything. Do you mind if I sit?" He asked, signaling to the spot beside me.

I narrowed my eyes, still unsure if I could trust him. But the sincerity in his voice made me soften. "Yes. You can sit." I sighed, too emotionally exhausted to fight him off.

"So what's got you so upset?" he asked gently. His voice was soothing, like a warm blanket fresh from the dryer. I couldn't believe I was thinking this, but his presence actually felt...comforting. I was seeing him in a new light - maybe I'd never really given him a fair chance.

I opened my mouth to explain, but closed it again as a fresh wave of sobs rose in my throat.

"It's...it's a lot," I finally choked out, hating how weak I sounded.

Khyree hesitated a moment before placing a hand on my back, rubbing small circles. I stiffened briefly at his touch before allowing myself to relax into it. The warmth of his palm seeped through my shirt, easing some of the tension coiled inside me.

"I'm here for you…if you wanna talk about it." he assured.

I sniffled, debating on what I should tell him. "Do you know Jacky Jamison?" I asked.

He froze, "Jacky Jamison?"

"Yeah."

"I mean…" he trailed, brows drawing together in either confusion or something else - I couldn't tell. All I knew was that the question seemed to have tripped up his usual easy-going flow. "Why do you ask?" He paused, then leaned in seriously. "Is he bothering you?"

"No! Not at all. The reason I brought him up was because….he and I um…we got into an argument at lunch." I stopped myself before my voice broke.

"Are, are, you guys like friends or something?" He asked, hoping JJ and I were nothing more.

"I mean I thought we were, until he basically said that doesn't want to know me."

Khyree clicked his tongue in disapproval. "That's messed up. I'd never say anything like that to you, Sidell."

At his words, the dam broke and a fresh wave of tears spilled down my cheeks. I buried my face in my hands, embarrassed to be crying in front of him again but unable to stop.

"Oh Sidell, please don't cry," Khyree pleaded, wrapping an arm around me and pulling me against his chest. "I'm sorry, I shouldn't have brought it up again."

I clung to him, dampening his shirt with my tears but too distraught to care. "I want to f-forgive him but it still h-hurts."

Khyree gently tilted my chin up so I was looking into his kind, chestnut eyes. He brushed a tear from my cheek with his thumb, his touch so achingly tender I thought my heart might burst.

"I think it's best if you stay away from JJ from now on," he said firmly, though his eyes were soft. "I can't take seeing you cry like this."

I nodded mutely, unable to tear my gaze away from his face. My stomach fluttered traitorously. I ducked my head again, leaning into Khyree's solid hug wrapping my arms around his waist.

We stayed that way until the warning bell rang, signaling the end of lunch. I lifted my head from Khyree's chest, suddenly self-conscious.

"Sorry, I barely know you and here I am crying all over you." I mumbled, avoiding his eyes.

"Don't apologize," he said firmly. "I'm glad I could be here for you." He shook his head. "I never liked JJ anyway. He's always been kind of a jerk."

I let out a watery laugh even though I didn't fully agree. "We should get to class," I said briskly, reaching for my purse. But Khyree had already scooped it up and slung it over his shoulder. I opened my mouth to protest but he cut me off.

"We're going to Mr. Q's class, right?" he said with a playful grin. "I'm walking you to class whether you like it or not."

I rolled my eyes, but couldn't stop a small smile from spreading across my face. "Fine, lead the way then."

As we walked to history together, I felt the turmoil in my chest begin to settle. Maybe I'd been too quick to judge Khyree Latimore. Underneath that shy exterior, he was surprisingly sweet. And dare I say it - I was actually starting to like having him around.

"Goodmorning Mr. Q." Khyree announced as we entered the class. I took a seat at my desk, then Khyree gently placed my purse at the leg of my chair for me. "Thank you." I told him and in return he gave me a comically enthusiastic thumbs-up.

Mr. Q pinched the bridge of his nose, then sighed. "Take a seat, Mr. Latimore, before I'm forced to give you detention for your chronic tardiness."

Khyree jogged back up the aisle between tables, quickly fist-bumping his friend before giving me a heart-melting smile as he sat at his own desk.

I bit my lip and stared down at my hands in my lap. It's cute, but it didn't quite melt me. *He* doesn't quite melt me, but I still liked watching his effort. As I studied his reassuring smile, I felt a surprising flutter in my stomach. Was it admiration? Maybe even attraction? Or was it merely a rebound emotion from my fallout with JJ? I couldn't figure out how I felt or how I ought to, and while it was exciting, it's even more confusing.

CHAPTER TWENTY-SEVEN: JJ

I knew the deal wasn't about doing what felt good, but about doing what was right for me. That's the key to this whole thing. The key I couldn't hold onto, no matter how hard I tried. Stepping into my apartment, I kicked the door shut, dropped my beat-up backpack on the floor and made a beeline for the shower. Grandma wasn't home, so I cranked up my latest playlist on the little wireless speaker, letting the bass thumping through the thin walls loud enough to wake the dead. Or at least loud enough to piss off the neighbors again. Too bad, so sad. They could file another noise complaint. Wouldn't be the first time.

The freezing water crashed against my skin as I shivered violently in the cramped tub.

She despised me.

Sidell Evermost had nothing but pure hatred for me, and I made sure of it. Remember that look on her face during lunch today? It wasn't all an act. What I said to her was raw truth, something she needed to hear.

I didn't want to talk to her because she'd unveil who I really was. I didn't want to listen to her because she'd expect too much from me. And damn it, staring at her, hurt too much.

But one thing I said that had no room for twisting was that I didn't want to know her. I did want to know her. I wanted to know every detail about her life that consumed me day and night. If only I wasn't cursed with being myself, if only I wasn't painted by the dark strokes of her parents' perception... Can't have Sidell's halo tarnished by a delinquent like me.

No amount of fantasy could erase the hurt in her eyes today. I had put it there. Me and my jacked up way of coping. Pushing people away before they rejected me. Self-sabotage at its finest.

I shut off the water and toweled off roughly. Dragging on some ratty pajamas, I glared at my reflection in the steam-covered mirror as water dripped down my neck.

Seeing Khyree's smug smile as he walked Sidell to class today didn't help matters.

It hit me like a brick—Khyree had strolled beside her, playing the part of the charismatic fool. And when he locked eyes with me in the crowded hallway, his facade dropped for a moment. That disgustingly happy act morphed into a fake grin and sarcastic curtsy.

He wanted to provoke me, and damn it, he succeeded. I could've gone toe-to-toe with him right then and there, but I held back. Flopping down on my lumpy mattress, I scrubbed my hands over my face.

I shouldn't have said what I said to Sidell. None of this should've happened. But I couldn't bear the thought of her truly seeing me.

The one person I connected with—the one person whose opinion truly mattered—learning all there is to know about me and then stepping back. It's happened before, with everyone else. I wanted her to know everything about me, to have those conversations we never had. But the way things played out took that away from us both.

And now, all that's left is regret.

★ ★ ★ ★ ✟ ★ ★ ★ ★

The tall stained-glass windows cast colorful patterns on the polished stone floors of the school's main chapel. Sunlight filtered through the vibrant scenes depicted in the glass, creating a serene ambiance that contrasted with the turmoil within me. I hid out on the stage for a while, but my peace was short-lived as the custodian came and kicked me out like a stray mutt.

Since yesterday's lunch incident, distance was the only thing I needed at the moment. The bleachers seemed as far away as I could get from anyone. Weathered by years of use, the metal frames of the goal pole were a faded shade of green.

I found my spot amidst the row of seats. I was rewarded with a clear view of the green field and the white lines that marked the boundaries of the game. Lost in self-pity, I sat alone for hours, wondering how I always manage to screw up my life. I should apologize to her, but what's the point? She probably hates me now. The faint scent of freshly cut grass taunted me, conjuring memories I'd rather forget. My guilt mingled with melancholy, leaving a bitter taste in my mouth.

The spirited chants of cheerleaders practicing below were what drew me out of my thoughts. The vibrant pom poms being waved in the air was yet another reminder of Sidell. I'd almost forgotten that she had joined the cheer squad.

I searched the group of girls for familiar faces, hoping to see Sidell's, even if for a few seconds. I automatically found her. My eyes seemed to do that now whenever not given any other specific instructions by my brain. If she's around, if it's safe to look, she's my attention's default resting place.

Half of her hair was tied-back as the rest cascaded down her shoulders, revealing an unusually gentle facial expression, bright crystal blue eyes, her bright smile. I kept expecting her to look at me, but she wouldn't. For the first time in a week, I just wanted to look at her without pretending.

When I saw her saunter over to the orange water cooler, I decided to seize the opportunity to try apologizing. I silently crept down the bleachers, moving stealthily as a sloth through mud. With a cup tilted to her lips, she noticed me anyway then turned away, avoiding eye contact like I was a Jehovah's Witness.

"What do you want, JJ? I thought you didn't want to talk to me, remember?" She mocked. "I thought you didn't want to know me?"

Her words felt like a punch to the gut, knocking the wind and sarcasm right out of me. "I'm a liar. I do want to talk to you," I said earnestly, resting my hand on the cooler beside her. "I do want to know you."

Her attention remained averted as she ran her fingers through her hair. "Don't play games with me, JJ. You've made yourself perfectly clear."

I took a step closer, my heart pounding in my chest. "I know, but I didn't mean it. I was just trying to protect myself."

She finally looked at me, her eyes narrowed. "Protect yourself from what?"

"From getting hurt," I whispered. "From you."

Her expression softened slightly. "You can't protect yourself from me, JJ. I'm not going to hurt you."

"How can you say that?" I asked. "After what I said to you?" The memory of my cruelty stung like a fresh papercut doused in lemon juice.

"Because I understand why you said it," she said gently. "You're scared. You're scared of letting anyone get close to you."

I nodded, blinking back sudden tears. She saw right through me, straight to my damaged core. "Yes. That's why I push everyone away."

"But you don't have to push me away," she said, taking my hand in hers. "I'm not like the others."

I looked into her eyes and saw the truth in them. She wasn't like the others. She was good. And kind. And she cared about me.

"Hey guys! What's going on over here?" a carefully collected voice comes from across the yard. Sidell turned, but I already knew with a sinking feeling - Khyree. Why is this bozo even out here?

"Khyree, it's okay - go back to the field, I'll be there in a minute," Sidell called, smiling.

When she turned back to me, I saw the fear in her eyes. She knew me too well. The carefree JJ she loved was gone, replaced by something harder, deadlier. An icy rage simmered beneath my calm exterior.

Of course Khyree didn't listen. He edged closer, using Sidell as a human shield between us. "Is everything okay?"

"Everything's cool," I said, flicking my eyes between Sidell and Khyree. My throat bobbed with the effort of restraint.

"Sidell?" Khyree ignored me. "Is everything okay?"

"Yes, *thank you,* Khyree. I'll be right back to practice in a second." Sidell smiled, but I could tell from her posture she was just as irritated by his intrusion as I was.

Khyree didn't take the hint. "That's good." He scanned the running track to the left and right before resting his hands on the straps of his bulky camera. "Watcha doing here, Jamison?"

Sidell sat down her cup, ready to confess to Khyree but I beated her to it. "Just sorting out our differences."

"Huh. You guys are becoming friends again?" he asked.

"Yup."

Sidell watched us carefully, knowing this situation was like a grenade with the pin pulled. One wrong move could set it off.

"Why do it here and now? Did you not realize Sidell and I were in the middle of our photography session?" Khyree said in that condescending tone.

I snorted. *If this weirdo doesn't get out of here…*

Sidell volunteered. "Just supposed to be a quick conversation. Got sidetracked, I guess."

"Oh, okay." He turned halfway and nodded. "Adorable toxicity in a friendship… how nice." He turned around completely and, for a split second, I caught a glimpse of Sidell's face. She truly believed that the grenade would be put down. That all of this would've been okay. That was, of course, until Khyree decided to tear the pin out with his teeth and spit it in my face. He turned back around as though just remembering something.

"Oh - I saw your mom today, Jamison. Did you know she was in town?"

"*Stop,*" Sidell hissed.

I didn't say anything at first. Then, very calmly, I gave a simple, "When you gonna take that hat off? I'm tired of looking at it."

Khyree laughed as if he found my response amusing. It was as though this confrontation was merely the beginning.

Sidell intervened, "Both of you. Stop - right now, stop. Just leave it there."

"Nah, it's okay - I don't want to fight your little friend, Sidell," I said, sounding bored. "Are your parents calling you 'son' yet, Khyree? Or do you need a couple more years of filing paperwork to qualify for that?"

"Jacky."

"You know - I wish I could pity you, JJ. But I don't."

"Aw, damn."

"Normally I root for losers to change. Like underdogs, you know? But with you, I'm just hoping they pull you out of society as soon as possible. Jail, psych ward, makes no difference."

"What is *wrong* with you? Stop!"

"It's cool," I said to Sidell. "He's clearly been working on these for a while, let him use them."

"You think you're so *smart*, don't you?"

"Not particularly," I replied.

Sidell put her head in her hands.

"Oh yeah, so clever. How's that dark and witty persona working out for you?" he sneered. "Living off your grandma's retirement money? A mom who abandoned you? A dad who's nowhere to be found? Maybe it's because you're a psychopath."

"You don't know anything about my parents."

"Uh, I know I saw your mom with her new man on facebook. You're supposed to have your little special psycho visitation this week, right? Yikes. I'd run away too, if I were her."

"Whatever, Khyree. You're having too much fun with this."

Sidell attempts to console me, "JJ, look at me. Look at me don't listen to him. He's just trying to get a rise out of you."

"I know Sidell, but do you hear this dude?"

"Yes, I hear him. But you-,"

"Hey!" Khyree yelled. "Yeah, hello! Excuse me, but - what is this?"

Sidell braced herself and turned to face Khyree.

"Is this for real?" he demanded, gesturing between us with a horrified expression.

She didn't deny it.

"No, no, no. This has got to be a joke. I didn't take you as a idiot, Sidell," he groaned.

I leaned on the table behind me, and let Sidell do the talking.

"I think . . . maybe you should consider the possibility that you don't understand as much about this as you think you do," she said carefully.

"The guy is a psychopath. He's dangerous. What more is there to understand? You want him to get you gunned down too?"

Pushing myself off the table, I stood tall and confronted him head-on. "I want you to say that again," I warned through clenched fists. Sidell threw her body between the two of us, cutting off my advance.

"Okay guys, really. Just stop, I'm serious."

But it's too late. Khyree had found his winning trigger. "Me too, Sidell. I'm seriously worried for you. Hey, JJ - if you were to kill her like Donica, would they put you in prison? Or an institution?"

Khyree eyes widened at his own words just before I slammed my fist into his face. The sickening crunch of his nose breaking sounded oddly satisfying in my ears, but it did nothing to calm the rage coursing through me. I launched at him again, fists flying. His busted lip was payback for his smart mouth. Khyree shock wore off, and before I could land the third punch, my collar was wrapped up pretty tightly in his fists. We grappled, struggling for dominance.

I could hear Sidell screaming in the background as our teammates and bystanders rushed to break us apart. But their voices all blended together into one loud noise. That is until Coach Davis's voice cut through the chaos.

"Cut it out! That's enough! JJ, what the hell? That's enough from both of y'all!"

I took a deep breath, slowly loosening my fists as I stepped back. I straightened my disheveled blazer, ignoring the whispers and stares behind my back. Coach came over looking like he was ready to throw down too.

"Y'all wanna tell me what's going on here?" His voice was hard as stone, making both of us freeze up. He wasn't playing around anymore - no more smiling or pep talks.

With a metallic tang of blood in my mouth, I spat it to the side before speaking. "He was running his mouth when I was just having a normal conversation with him."

The sides of his mouth ticked up. "And?"

"And I threw the first punch. I'd do it again in a heartbeat," I assured, wiping my mouth with the back of my hand. Ain't no apologies coming from me today. Maybe for everything else but not for punching Khyree. He knew he was outta line.

Coach Davis's eyes lacked their usual warmth as he looked at me and said, "I appreciate you being honest. Otherwise, I'd have to rely on what other people saw, and that can be biased depending on who you ask."

"That's right." The words escaped in a breath before I gave a chance to think about them.

"You're benched for the entire term, JJ. You can't play on my team if you ain't got your stuff together. It's clear you still got some issues you need to work out. Best for you to take this time off and get yourself sorted. And it starts after y'all both do ten laps around this field. Startin' now!"

At the sound of the whistle, I broke into a run, circling the field. Sweat dripped across my forehead and slid down my back. It didn't help that I was still in my uniform. But I wasn't about to argue with Coach about that, not if I wanted to stay on the team.

A wave of dizziness hit me by my third lap. The cheerleaders had gone back to practice, and the rest of my teammates were doing their warmups. I heard Khyree right behind me, and even though I was breathing hard already, I picked up my pace.

My heart had moved all the way into my throat by the time I finished my seventh lap around the mammoth field. Tears burned at the edges of my eyes, and my legs felt like lead. Practice was over so the girls hung at the edge of the field, watching the jocks practice.

I caught a glimpse of Sidell watching from a distance. I was tempted to run off the field and apologize for what just escalated, but when I looked again in her direction, Sidell had retreated.

Desperation and regret gnawed at me, so I pushed harder, feeding my physical strength on the anger still simmering within. Panting like a horse after show jumping, I managed to walk off the field, my head hung low.

I knew my own damage. I knew what others thought, too, even if I walked around like it didn't faze me. The fact of the matter was that I'm a disappointment. The psycho of the school, the king of the deadbeats. I'm unstable, a liability, a loser, and allowing Sidell to discover this from a distance meant there would be no cord for her to cut.

Exhaustion pressed down on me as I neared my last lap. But my ordeal was yet to be over because Coach Davis was walking over to me.

"The principal wants to see you, Jamison. You might want to head there now."

I nodded and walked slowly towards the door that led to administration. It was not hard to guess what would come next. Ms. Tucker, the principal's secretary, sat behind her desk at the entrance, typing feverishly on her computer. The sound of a bell announced my entrance. She raised her head for all of five seconds before returning her attention to her work.

"May I help you?" she asked, being ignorant.

Holding an ice pack to my sore jaw, I answered, "I have a hot date with the principal, I'm sure."

She glared at me over her glasses. "What's your name?"

"JJ," I huffed. She's been at this post long enough to know every student's name. There was no way I'd be playing this game with her today.

"You got into a fight with Khyree? What were you thinking?" she asked, dropping the act. Her voice brimmed with accusation even though she had no idea what had actually happened.

I dropped the ice pack from my face, "That's the thing, I wasn't thinking with my big brain. Just my little one." I grinned impishly.

She pursed her lips. "The principal will see you now," she finally announced moments later. She waved me in the direction of the door. I sauntered into the office.

"It's nice to see that you are in good shape," Principal Baxster said as soon as I strolled in. "I was expecting that you would be a bloody mess. Or is that your opponent?"

I shrugged, slumping into the chair. "Khyree face broke my fall."

He motioned for me to sit down. "How is your grandmother doing?"

"Fine."

"Are you going through something you want to let me know about? There has to be a valid reason for you lashing out in that way, Mr. Jamison. This is so unlike you. What's happening?" he asked.

"Now that I have the time to think about it, I have no valid reasons for my actions. I was not thinking. I take responsibility for my actions and would love a second chance to fix things."

My circumstances have suddenly grown clearer now that I'm sitting face to face with the consequences. I don't want to imagine my grandmother's reaction to the news of my expulsion. It would not be right of me to put her through that or anything else for that matter. My mother had done enough to both of us.

"Mmmmm." He nodded, unconvinced by my little speech. Principal Baxster picked up a file and flipped through it carelessly. He knew that we both knew that he knew the content of that file by heart. The flipping and skimming were all part of an act that's supposed to have some psychological effect on me. And it did.

"Look, I'll cut to the chase and get right to it," he said. "JJ, we had hope for you, considering your background, and we still do. That's why you're still seated here. Your recent behavior has proven to be unruly and unobtainable. Hence your suspension for three weeks. Any further incidents will result in your expulsion."

The consequences of my actions seemed to be unlimited. Shame swelled within me and I struggled to keep my emotions in check.

"You'll resume school on the due date with your guardian and see the school therapist for the rest of the term for anger management sessions. Anything aside from this and you'll be forfeiting your admission. That will be all, Mr. Jamison."

Dismissed from the principal's office, I headed down the hallway to my locker to gather my belongings and empty my locker. It was surprising how a routine this simple still managed to symbolize my alienation from the school community.

Most of the school knew about my worst - or at least most public - incidents; it's never been a secret. Everyone knew to keep a safe distance from Jacky Jamison. Everyone knew about what happened in my past, the anger, the violent tendencies since grade school. My general reputation, my friends' reputations, and the fact that I've seen a million shrinks are common knowledge. Which means Sidell knew by now, too.

216

Chapter Twenty-Eight; Sidell

My insides were bouncing around like a pinball machine. How was JJ doing? Since that incident on the football field moments ago, I hadn't set my eyes on him. I wondered what the principal was going to say to him. Once we were back in the girl's locker room, changing from our cheer uniforms into our casual school uniforms, Dawn had noticed my demotivated mood. I immediately spilled everything to her in my desperation to talk to someone. I just needed to make some sort of sense out of the situation. This was my first experience with a boy I had found interest in. Dawn of course knew all about this stuff so she came in handy.

"Girl, stop tormenting yourself over that boy. You're too good for him - intelligent, beautiful. Don't waste your time on a man-child who can't even articulate his feelings," Dawn advised, nearly poking her eye out with her liquid eyeliner pencil.

I sighed heavily as I sat on my cheer bag. "It's deeper than that, Dawn. I know his reaction came from a place of hurt. I care about him."

She shook her head as she returned the cap onto her eyeliner. "You need to cut ties. He's bad news."

"Why? Because he made one mistake?" I asked

"Uh, he shattered someone's nose. That's beyond a little mistake."

"People make mistakes, Dawn. Even you." I regretted the words as soon as they left my lips.

Dawn looked like I had slapped her across the face. She pursed her lips. "What's that supposed to mean?"

I bit my tongue, watching the stall doors open and close. "Nothing, forget it. I'm just on edge."

"Clearly." Dawn turned back to the mirror, dabbing concealer under her eyes. "I'm only trying to help. But if you want to learn the hard way, be my guest."

I sighed, my shoulders slumping. She was right, as much as I hated to admit it. When he had assaulted Khyree, his volatility scared me, but it also drew me in. I wanted to be the one to soothe his soul.

"I can't just abandon him, Dawn. He needs someone." I fidgeted with the strap of my bag.

Dawn met my gaze in the mirror, her expression softening. "And that someone has to be you?"

I looked down. "I care about him. Underneath all that anger, he's hurting. I can't explain it, but I feel this...connection. Like I'm meant to help him."

Dawn turned around to face me, "I know you want to see the good in him, but some people are beyond saving. Don't let your kind heart lead you down a dark path."

I offered a small smile. If only it were that easy. My heart and my head were at war, each pulling me in opposing directions. I had to find the truth about JJ - who he really was underneath the volatility. I owed it to both of us to find out if he was worth fighting for, or if I needed to let him go.

Afterall, what Khyree had said to JJ earlier, now made me question everything.

"Who was the girl they were talking about? And why did Khyree say that JJ got her killed?" I thought to myself. *"Please God, don't let my mind go there...Is JJ capable of taking someone's life?"*

Chapter Twenty Nine:
𐂂𐂂

When I slunk back home after the fight with Khyree and the unexpected school suspension, I watched Grandma closely, searching for any hint that she'd heard about my latest failure. I expected a lecture to drop on me like a piano at any moment. But she just hummed cheerily over her crossword puzzles, oblivious. Maybe I was off the hook. Or maybe she was trying to lull me into a false sense of security before lowering the boom. With Grandma, I could never be too sure.

So when the next few school mornings rolled around, I went through the motions anyway, showering and dressing in my uniform as if everything was normal. Then I'd waste the days away at the arcade or wandering around the city like a vagrant.

After one of those hollow days, I dragged myself home exhausted, both mentally and physically. I shuffled into my bedroom, shutting the door firmly behind me. Collapsing onto my unmade bed, I stared up at the cracks in the ceiling, wondering how I had ended up here. Bitter thoughts swirled through my mind as I reflected on the unfairness of it all. Didn't they know I was trying, in my own messed up way?

A few minutes later, while I was still rolling on the bed, trying to get into a comfortable position, I heard a faint tapping at my bedroom window. The noise shook me from my concentration and I groaned in annoyance.

"Go away Kaluna!" I was sure it was her, so I ignored the knocking. Pulling the sheet over my head, I attempted to drift back to sleep. But the knocking persisted. I became more awake by the second until finally, with an exasperated sigh, I threw off the blankets and stumbled towards the window. Catching the curtains in one hand, I yanked them apart.

But when I saw her standing there—Kaluna with her toy stroller and favorite baby doll smiling at me on the other side—my anger dissipated. She was just a kid. An annoying one, but still a kid.

"What do you want?" I asked, softening my tone as I removed the locks and slid open the window. "Where are your friends? I don't got time to be playing with your baby doll today."

Kaluna scrunched her face. "I don't wanna play with you. You a grown man."

I had to laugh a little at her sass. This 8 year old had more sense than I did.

"Alright, fair enough. What did you want then?" I asked, leaning on the windowsill.

"Rayo said if he catches you at school again, he and his friends are gonna tear you up. Really bad." Kaluna snapped her fingers with a dramatic neck roll, imitating the tough kids from the neighborhood.

I clenched my jaw, fury rising within me. *Fun-ny*. So Khyree couldn't handle getting knocked down and sent his punk cousin after me, huh? Let Rayo keep talking big. I'd gladly put him on his back too if he came for me. The bitter taste of adrenaline flooded my mouth as I imagined the fight.

"Oh yeah?" I said, my voice low and dangerous. "Well you tell Rayo I'm not scared of him or his lil friends. And if he wants to come after me, I'll be ready to knock his teeth out."

"Okay." Kaluna laughed and turned to leave, blissfully unaware of the weight she had just dropped on my shoulders. I watched her skip down the sidewalk, clinging to a shred of childlike joy that I had lost long ago. Then I slid the window closed and turned back to my room, the darkness matching the anger I now felt.

"I wish Rayo would threaten me. I'ma knock him right out his shoes too."

★ ★ ★ ★ ✞ ★ ★ ★ ★

"Aye what up Jacky, haven't seen you in a minute brother." a gravelly voice called out. I looked up to see Mr. Baine leaning out his window, exhaling a cloud of thick smoke. "Long time no see, lil man. Where you off to with that heap of laundry?"

"Whassup Baine," I replied, shifting the basket's weight between my aching arms. "I'm finna wash some clothes. My grandma has been getting on me about it piling up on my floor."

"Oh, I see I see, well you know how she do. Can't have none of that stuff built up nor nothing. You know what's good."

"You got that right man, she wouldn't hesitate to come up in my room and throw it all out if I don't get on it."

"Hah! I believe it. Bernadette ain't no joke man. She raised you right though, don't forget that."

Lugging the overstuffed laundry basket through the apartment complex, I thought about what the old head had said. It was true, Grandma Bernadette had been there for me through thick and thin, raising me since mom dipped out on us, so she had stepped up without hesitation. Selfless as always, Grandma never complained about giving up her retirement to make sure I had a hot meal on the table each night. I made a mental note to be more appreciative of her efforts.

Rounding the corner, my eyes caught sight of the laundromat nestled near the second playground in our complex. Rays of smoke billowed out of the large glass windows. I paused and my heart jumped upon seeing Rayo and four unfamiliar people lounged inside, their raucous laughter pouring out. But Rayo's two main Lackeys "Juice and Smurf." were not in sight. And I just thought that was odd.

For a moment, It was like the little angel on my shoulder told me to turn back. But I swiped it off and straightened my spine, reminding myself - I wasn't going to let them intimidate me.

I marched into that laundromat with all the confidence in the world, determined to show Rayo that he didn't scare me. If he wanted to throw down, I'd give him a fat lip to match his cousin. But as soon as I stepped over the threshold, my ego crumbled.

The glint of metal tucked into all their waistbands made my blood run cold. *Guns. Of course, How carelessly for me to forget? They wouldn't be a gang if they didn't have those, now would they?*

My palms grew clammy as my pulse thundered in my ears. I thought I was done for. But luckily, they were too engrossed in their twisted reality to notice me. With quiet steps, I turned and retreated out the door, nearly tripping over my own feet in my rush to escape. When I was safely out of sight, I leaned against a nearby brick wall and took a shaky breath.

"Damn," I cursed under my breath. Looks like I'll have to find another laundromat, even if it means hauling my dirty clothes across town. As much as it hurt my pride, I wasn't about to take on a bunch of armed thugs.

Still, it bothered me that I'd let our neighborhood become so divided. If only we could get back to how things used to be, before the drugs and turf wars. I missed the old days, playing pickup basketball with Rayo and Khyree, back when our biggest concern was who got to take the game-winning shot. We were just kids. But these were no longer those days.

I sighed, pushing off from the wall. As Grandma Bernadette always said, "Tough times don't last, but tough people do."

She was right, and I also agree that a few quarters for the bus ride to that laundromat on Orchard Street wouldn't be so bad.

Chapter Thirty; Sidell

"That's too difficult of a style Caye, I'm not doing that." I said as my fingers threaded through her thick wavy brown hair. I bit the edge of my lip while Cayest shrugged and continued watching the DIY YouTube video playing on her upturned phone's screen.

"It was just an idea," she mumbled under her breath, "You don't have to do it," she said after a few seconds of contemplative silence.

"I can't get distracted, you already said two french braids. Will that be okay?" I asked.

Cayest clicked off the video and dropped the phone onto her lap, "Yeah. I guess. But leave out two curls by my ears." she giggled, before patiently waiting for me to finish with the braid.

We now spent countless afternoons like this, chatting about everything and nothing. Our post-hair style conversations had become a ritual, marking a closeness we never had before.

Even though I had no choice in being cooped up in the house because of my punishment, I didn't mind being around my little sister. For the first time I've actually witnessed her smiling– not her usual smirk that always seemed to challenge me but a genuine one. Perhaps Nireska had been right after all; our relationship was changing.

But before I could snap out of my thoughts, Cayest had already angled the hand mirror closer to her face as soon as I let go of the last French braid.

Her dimpled smile was all it took for me to feel absolutely accomplished.

"Wow, this is awesome, Sidell!" She beamed, posing from side to side to view the intricate style. "Can you do this again on Monday?

My lips curled into a smirk. "Uh . . . sure . . . but you're going to have to wake up a little earlier for that so we don't get to school late."

"Yay! I'm going to show Mama." She beamed, skipping out of the chair and out of my room.

I tidied up my dresser in the meantime, organizing my combs and hair ties into their individual jars. Not long after, I just happened to look up to see Cayest standing at my bedroom doorway with an amused but yikes face.

"What?" I asked concerned.

"Mama wants to speak to you. And she seems really mad." She warned, slipping away slowly.

Oh goodness, what now. My bare feet smacked against the hallway floor as I rushed down the staircase. *I wonder what mom was so worked up about.*

"Where did you get this? I don't remember ever giving this back to you?" Mom yelled, holding up my cell phone that she clearly remembered hiding away in a safe place.

I closed my eyes mentally hating myself for carelessly leaving it on the counter-top, knowing mom was going to do dishes. Even though our house guest Nireska was long gone, I still wasn't going to throw her under the bus. Even if she went against my mom's rules and snuck the phone for me. But if Mom kept interrogating me like this, I wasn't sure how long I could hold out.

"Mama, Why does it matter?! I'm seventeen and it's mine!" I justified. So what if I was being disrespectful? She was treating me like a child!

"Sidell Yovna Evermost— don't you dare use that tone with me!" Mom pointed my phone at me like a weapon, making me flinch.

"But Mama, this is so unfair! I've been grounded for weeks! Did I not do what you asked me too?" I replied, my emotions were getting the better of me.

"Your tail is so hot, you just couldn't wait to talk to that boy, right?" Mom accused in her jewish accent.

"Why do you always assume the worst about me?" I shot back. "I never did anything with him and I don't plan to!"

"Why try to defend someone who clearly has a questionable background?" Mom asked sharply. "You saw the way he tried to fight your father."

"He wouldn't have reacted the way he did if Papa didn't edge him on!" I yelled, no longer caring about staying calm. "And just because he's from the other side of the tracks doesn't make him a bad person! But you've already put him in a box labeled 'criminal' without even properly meeting him.""

"You're blinded by your feelings for him," she dismissed callously. "It's clear that he's making you act out like this."

I wanted to laugh and cry at the same time. "The only one acting out is you with your closed-minded prejudices. You don't know anything about him, so stop making assumptions! He's twice the person you'll ever be!"

Mom's lip curled. "I'm calling you're father right now, let him handle this." She dialed his number on the house phone with so much force I thought the buttons would break.

"Ugh! I don't care what he says." I groaned as I stormed out the kitchen and bounded up the staircase. Cayest leaned on the top rail with a genuine worried expression, "What happened Sidell? Are you okay?" she asked.

I didn't answer, instead I brushed past her and slammed my bedroom door hard enough to rattle the walls. Throwing on my blue jacket over my floral sundress, I hesitated before the mirror. The crystal blue eyed blonde girl with the low messy bun staring back looked timid and unsure, not at all like the bold spirit burning inside. But the trembling of my hands betrayed my false bravado. *Could I really go through with this?*

After slipping on strapped sandals, I descended the stairs with renewed vigor, each step echoing my defiance. Mom met me at the bottom, phone glued to her ear as she rattled off complaints about me in Russian to my father who was on the other line.

"And just where do you think you're going?" she asked me.

"I'm going out, and there's nothing you can do to stop me." My voice came out steady, despite my thudding heart.

Mom's eyes narrowed to slits. She grabbed my arm, her claw-like nails digging in. "You're not going anywhere, What you're going to do is turn around and march up these steps to my room." she warned.

I met her glare with one of my own, wrenching my arm from her grasp. "I'm going." The words slipped out before I could stop them. Shock splashed across Mom's face. We both knew I'd crossed a line.

Part of me wanted to apologize, to keep the peace. But a bigger part burned with resentment, tired of being treated like a child. I brushed past her, adrenaline coursing through me.

I paused, excitement and fear warring within me. I'd never blatantly disobeyed before. With a deep breath, I turned the knob.

Mom's frustrated yells to my dad on the phone faded behind me as I stepped outside. My heart pounded against my ribs—whether from exhilaration or anxiety, I couldn't tell. I couldn't believe I'd stood up to her like that. Part of me thrilled at this small taste of freedom, while my nagging conscience worried I'd gone too far.

Shoving the thought aside, I scrambled up the dusty porch steps that led to Dawn's house. I rang the doorbell repeatedly, trying hard to ignore the prickle of discomfort sliding up my spine. Inside the house came no response or sign of life. Where could she be? Wandering aimlessly now, I wondered where to go.

I didn't want to return to the house just yet. I know my father would be livid once he returned from the tool store but I couldn't stay in that stifling environment. In fact, at that point, I was simply tired of it all. I was tired of trying to be the perfect daughter, of abandoning things I want to indulge in because they wouldn't approve of it. Tired of listening to them preach what they don't even practice, just listen to how they speak of JJ!

I wasn't returning to that house, not now. I had some few bucks left in my purse, this should be enough to take me on a mini tour round Chicago, in fact, I'm going to the very slums of Chicago my parents were so afraid of.

Lord, you are probably speaking to me now, but I'm too blind by anger and hurt to listen, please help me.

This prayer was said silently and I took the city bus to school.

I had no intention of actually going to school. I'd just walk around the surrounding streets aimlessly until I either got tired or mugged, whichever came first. A few minutes later, I arrived in the neighborhood near campus. I picked a random direction and started wandering down broken sidewalks lined with liquor stores and dilapidated row houses.

My feet quickly started to ache - stupid choice to wear flat sandals. I knew this was probably the dumbest, most reckless thing I'd ever done. I had almost no money, no phone, and no real plan. But I pushed down the rising panic. As long as I could remember the way back, I'd be fine. I wasn't about to let my parents' paranoia ruin my taste of independence.

I passed shadowy figures hanging on corners - men drinking from crumpled paper bags, women in too-tight neon dresses, teenagers my age chewing gum and glaring. I stood out like a sore thumb in my orange and pink floral dress. I hoped I might find a cafe to slip into, but this area was a wasteland. And the worst part was? That I couldn't find my way back.

I felt eyes watching me as I wandered deeper into the urban maze. With each turn I took, the neighborhoods grew increasingly run-down. I knew I should turn back, but my stubbornness propelled me forward.

I somehow ended up waiting at a random bus stop, when someone slammed into me from behind. I turned to see a dirty man with missing teeth and tattered clothes. His age was indistinguishable in his drunken state. Fearfully, I moved away as he smiled at me with his decaying teeth. It was more than obvious it'd be a long wait before an actual bus came. As I turned to leave, my pace quickened in a desperate attempt to escape this forsaken street. But no matter how many corners I took, I seemed to only get further lost in this maze-like neighborhood. Panic began to set in as I realized I had no idea where I was or how to get out. And just as my thoughts became consumed by fear, two young men in black jackets with scorpion logos appeared out of thin air.

Lord, if you can just get me out of here safely, I promise I'll never leave the house angrily again.

"Aye smurf, ain't that the girl Jacky was with?" the short chubby one called out to his average heighted companion.

"Sure is, Juice. And she fine too." Smurf leered, exhaling cigarette smoke. "Hey baby you lost?"

I shook my head mutely, unable to find my voice.

"No need to look so frightened, cheerleader. We'll take good care of you," Smurf leered, undressing me with his eyes.

My mind became blurred with a jumble of thoughts.

The both of them were right in front of me, some paces away, I looked behind me to see there was another turning, I mentally calculated my chances of escape and saw that it was a slim one.

"I wouldn't have thought that if I were you, it would be such a bad idea." Juice said at the top of his lungs so I could hear him.

They didn't need to confirm my fear, I knew that already. There was no way I could outrun them. But I had no other choice, I either ran or surrendered and that wasn't an option so I ran.

"I love a good chase!" one of them exclaimed with delight as their heavy footsteps echoed behind me.

I stumbled out onto the bustling main street, grateful for the sea of faces swirling around me. My legs felt weak beneath me, but I forced myself to maintain a swift pace. I headed straight for the busiest laundry mat in sight, comforted by the thrumming press of people.

The bell dinged shrilly as I burst into the door, my heart pounding against my ribs. A mother sitting by the window shot me a judgy look, clutching her stroller like I was going to rob her of all she had.

Lady, I'm a 5'4 girl in a floral dress, not a hardened criminal. I raked my fingers through my hair, managed a tight smile, and bee-lined down the nearest aisle between the rumbling washers before my nerves got the best of me.

Just then, the bell clanged again. I risked a peek over my shoulder. The two goons prowled in, beady eyes searching for their prey - *me*.

Fan-freaking-tastic. I crouched lower, smooshing my floral dress against my thigh as I slunk between the machines.

Suddenly, I collided with someone unloading clothes. "I'm so sorry-," The words died in my throat. No way. It couldn't be.

"Sidell?" JJ gawked, yanking out his earbuds. "What are you doing here?"

I tried for a smile, but my nerves were shot.

"JJ, there's two guys following me."

I whispered, pointing towards the suspects with darting eyes. JJ's gaze snapped to them, and he shifted in front of me protectively as I shrank against the rumbling washer at my back.

He turned back, caging me between his arms. "Do you trust me?" He murmured, brown eyes melting my insides. Focus, I scolded myself, biting back the butterflies. Now wasn't the time.

"Yeah," I breathed.

His breath dusted my ear. "Put your arms around my shoulders and pretend to be my girl."

I nodded, looping my arms around his neck. His muscles tensed, then relaxed as I rested my cheek against his chest. He smelled like spice and leather and something uniquely JJ that made my knees weak. I inhaled deeply, losing myself in his scent until approaching footsteps jarred me back.

JJ's breath tickled my ear again. "I've got you, Sidell. Just follow my lead."

My pulse stuttered. But with his solid form pressed against me, his woodsy scent flooding my senses, focusing was impossible. I was hyperaware of his hands splayed across my back, his steady heartbeat under my palm. My nerves vanished, replaced by a giddy exhilaration I hadn't felt before.

"Yo, look who it is?" Juice said to Smurf, stopping just a few feet away.

"Looks like the cheerleader found her pretty boy."Smurf laughed, "Wassup JJ."

"Smurf." JJ replied, not budging from his protective stance.

"You know Rayo said when we catch you it's on sight." Smurf said, tucking his hand in his jeans. My heart spiked when I noticed the steel.

Shutting my eyes, I bit my bottom lip. *Oh no, what did JJ get himself into. Please God, I pray JJ has a plan that won't get us both killed.*

"So my understanding is that Rayo couldn't settle his own beef?" JJ asked. "Am I that bad?"

Smurf's harsh laugh bounced off the laundromat walls. "You think too highly of yourself, Jacky. Rayo's got bigger fish to fry than to corner you."

JJ's chuckle was low and dangerous. "If I'm such small fry, why send two goons to track me down?"

Smurf, who grew impatient, shifted his stance.

"Look," JJ began. "I'm not looking for trouble today. My girl here? She's got nothing to do with this. So how about you tell Rayo we chatted and decided to reschedule our disagreement for another day."

"I could bust a cap in you right now playboy." Smurf sneered. A toddler's giggle cut through the silence before her mother quickly shushed her.

"You really wanna do this here? In front of witnesses and cameras?" JJ asked.

Smurf glanced around, his bravado faltering. The laundromat wasn't crowded, but a couple of heads had turned at the mention of trouble, their attention now fixed on us.

Juice shifted uneasily next to Smurf. "Man, we don't need no heat," he muttered.

"Yeah Smurf, listen to your friend," JJ said. "Wouldn't want our little chat making its way to the cops now would we?"

Smurf scowled, but he slowly withdrew his hand from his jeans. "You better watch your back." he growled.

JJ's laugh held a sharp edge. "Yeah aight."

With a final glare, Smurf and Juice backed off as they sauntered out the laundromat, leaving us alone in the fluorescent glow.

I sagged against the washer, releasing a shaky breath as JJ gently unwound my trembling fingers from his neck.

"Thanks JJ," I mumbled, cheeks burning. "I owe you one."

"Nah you good." He said watching the door to ensure they didn't come back. "I always got you." he added, looking back at me.

Warmth flooded me head to toe as I searched his dark eyes, sensing a shift in our friendship's foundation. It was like God orchestrated this whole crazy mess just to mend whatever rift was between us. As we walked out under the flickering neon buzz of the 24-hour laundromat sign, I couldn't help but wonder - maybe there's hope for us yet? JJ and I now had a short, but complicated friendship that spanned betrayal, heartbreak, and now an uneasy truce.

"I don't see how you were able to walk down the street with that heavy basket." I said, watching as JJ fumbled to adjust the overstuffed plastic bin of haphazardly folded clothes in his arms, his biceps straining against his too-tight red t-shirt.

"Psh, this light work." he grunted, though I could see beads of sweat forming along his brow."Besides, I'm only around the corner.

I rolled my eyes. "Uh huh. Then why are you breathing so heavy? I thought big tough guys like you were supposed to have stamina."

JJ shot me a look that said he clearly wasn't amused by my teasing. "Hey, I've got plenty of stamina where it counts," he retorted with a smug grin.

I felt my cheeks flush despite myself. "Anyway," I said, quickly changing the subject, "I thought apartment complexes usually have their own laundromats?"

"They do. I was just being 50 cents cheap today." He joked. "And look how it worked out? I got a discount and I got to see you again."

I bashfully smiled before looking at the cracked sidewalk.

We walked in tense silence for a few seconds that felt like an eternity. The air between us was heavy with the weight of our unfinished business. I wracked my brain trying to think of something - anything - to break this unbearable tension.

But JJ beat me to it. "After the incidents in the cafeteria and on the football field, I thought you'd never speak to me again," he admitted.

My eyes widened in surprise. It was followed by a gentle smile. "Why would you think that? Everyone makes mistakes, JJ, including myself. I've gotten over it, and I forgive you. I hope you can forgive me too. I should have stuck up for you when my parents lashed out at you."

"I never expected it to be so easy for you to let go. I thought I had hurt you beyond repair," He said softly.

"My God taught me to let go of the past, and Tomorrow is a new day. As long as we both learn from our mistakes, right?" I offered my hand.

JJ paused his strolled and sat the basket on the ground. His hand met mine, his grip firm but gentle. "Truer words never spoken. Friends?"

"Friends," I giggled. As we walked the rest of the way to his apartment complex, the air between us felt lighter, like the weight of our past transgressions had been washed away with the laundry.

There was still much to work through, but it was a start.

Chapter Thirty-One:
ʯʯ

I couldn't believe I'd escaped Rayo's lackeys with my life yet again.

Barely made it out of that laundromat alive. But with Sidell there with me, I sure as hell wasn't letting her become their next victim. After her blowout with mom, she'd wandered straight into my side of town looking for me. I told her that was pretty unwise, considering if she didn't make it back home her parents would have my head on a spike. But speaking of unwise, bringing her back to my apartment complex probably wasn't too wise either. Especially with Rayo and his goons possibly still lurking the perimeter like vultures. I just figured Sidell would wanna see my Grandma again before I took her home. Grandma's been pestering me about Sidell's next visit.

I sat the laundry basket down with a thud the moment we arrived at my apartment door. Out of the corner of my eye, I caught Sidell unbuckling those prim gold sandals of hers. A smirk tugged at my lips. "Well look at that. She actually remembered the 'no shoes in the house' rule from last time."

I kicked off my sneakers and turned to her with a dramatic sigh. "Don't say I didn't warn you about my grandma. She's been asking about you nonstop since your last visit. Get ready for an interrogation."

Sidell let out a musical laugh and gave me a playful nudge. "Oh come on, I'm sure I can handle a few questions."

I raised an eyebrow as I fished for my keys. "We'll see about that."

I sniffed the air as soon as I stepped into the apartment. The scent led me straight to the kitchen, the aroma slapping my senses awake. My saliva glands went into overdrive as I locked eyes on them steak pies lounging on a platter. Locking the front door, my stomach growled like a jungle beast as I dashed across the kitchen, zeroing in on that juicy, tender steak pie that overflowed with mouthwatering stew meat and beef cubes. When that flavor hit my taste buds, I closed my eyes, savoring every second. "Oh, Grandma Bernadette, this is hitting."

"Get your hands out of those and come help me peel some potatoes." She cracked a wrinkled smile and I shot Sidell an amused look and mouthed "You see the theatrics".

Grandma stood at the stove to breaking up the browned drippings and fat with a whisk. "So how has your day been, young man? What have you been up to?" she asked with a small smile.

I ducked around her to snatch a beef cube from the pie. "Eh, nothin' much. Knocked the laundry out—and now I'm here to help you with this cookin'. Just another regular day if you ask me." I scurried over to the sink and gave the potatoes a rinse, a couple of times.

"So how is your little lady friend doing? She breezed through once and don't even want to see my old, wrinkled face again. Am I that bad?"

Putting in more elbow grease than necessary scrubbing the already squeaky-clean potatoes at the sink, I glanced at Sidell, betraying my true feelings with a foolish grin. Acting clueless, I replied, "Which little lady friend? Your memory must be fading, Grandma."

Sidell blushed and studied her finger nails. I smiled despite myself.

"Oh, don't play coy with me, boy." She glanced at her pot before sending an impish smile my way. "What was her name again? Sidney? Sandall? I can't remember right now. Can you jog my memory a bit?"

I laughed and replied, "Grandma, you know you worse than they give you credit for, right?"

"Why's that?"

I tilted my head toward Sidell lingering shyly in the doorway. Grandma followed my gaze and clapped her hands together gleefully.

"Well slap me sideways, look who's here! Come over child, let me get a good look at you."

Sidell approached with slow, graceful steps, her hands folded delicately in front of her. I bit my cheek, trying not to laugh at how much she looked like she was approaching a firing squad rather than my 5'0 grandmother.

"Yes ma'am, it's nice to see you again," Sidell said softly.

Grandma took Sidell's face in her hands, scrutinizing every inch of her like she was examining produce at the market.

"Mmhmm, still just as pretty as a peach pie on a Sunday morning. But you lookin' a lil peaky baby, have you been eating enough?"

Sidell smiled politely. "Oh yes ma'am, I eat very well, thank you for asking."

"Hmph, well you make sure to have some of these meat pies when I'm finished." Grandma turned to me. "Jacky, why don't you go ahead and set the dinner table for this young lady while I finish up here? Oh, and while you're at it, I want you to look over that letter you see sittin' on that table."

"A letter?" I asked, following her finger's point to a white envelope.

"Yeah. It's something I've been meaning to talk to you about. Got your name all over it," she said, giving me a stern side-eye.

I carefully unfolded the paper, and almost instantly, I released a long sigh as I skimmed over the fine-print details. Just my Luck. I wasn't ready for the lecture I knew was coming next.

★ ★ ★ ★ ✞ ★ ★ ★ ★

Halfway through my meal, I gulped down the leftover white wine in my glass, the crispy, fruity taste rinsing my palate. Couldn't this have waited? Grandma just had to bring up my suspension while Sidell's here sitting beside me. Not that Sidell wasn't aware of it anyway, she was there to witness the cause of my suspension. But I'm sure she didn't want to talk about it either, especially when it had to do with me beating down a boy who had a crush on her and who I felt was getting between what we had together.

I shook my head slowly, hoping against hope I'd somehow misheard her say I was going back to school. She'd talked with the principal, and just like that I'm reinstated. As if a simple talking-to could erase the threats and danger that Rayo and his crew posed if I went back. Don't get me wrong, I'm no punk. I used to thrive on that kind of drama. But things have changed, I've changed. Trying to find some peace in my life. The last thing I need is for my infamous nickname "Psycho" to gain any more traction. I didn't want to be known as someone who's always causing trouble.

I had to set down my cup. "You didn't have to do that, you know."

"With the alternative being you sitting around the house, disappearing and reappearing at will?" My grandmother asked with a stern lift of her brows. "Now child…I've let you have free rein for a while, hoping that you would come to it and realize that this path you're taking does not hold out much good for you."

I grabbed a stray bottle of water from the table, suddenly parched. Avoiding all eye contact from Sidell.

"I let your mother have the same free rein because I wanted to try gentle parenting. I wanted her to trust me enough to come to me with her issues and look where that got me."

"Grandma, why are you even mentioning that with Sidell right here. That was my mom's choice. I'm nothing like her," I retorted.

"Keep saying that until you believe it but you cannot expect me to let you continue this way. You've shown no sense of responsibility—fighting and sneaking out of school at will, sleeping around in my house instead of applying yourself to some useful hobby, and the lowered grades? I'm not taking none of that no more." Grandma folded her arms tightly against her chest.

"You make it sound like I was out there throwing hands with just anyone. It was just Khyree who I fought with and he said something—"

"Khyree? Latimore's little foster boy?" she asked. Of course she'd take his side - his rich parents funded her precious church that she cared more about than me.

"Yes." I replied, avoiding her eyes.

"And you fought him because he simply said something!"

"Yes grandma, what else do you want me to say?" I snapped. "That I'm an unhinged maniac who attacks people for no reason? Would that make you happy?"

She sighed heavily. "Boy you forgotten that Khyree got privileges that you can't even begin to imagine. He's got connections! All you've got apart from the God you don't acknowledge is that hard head of yours which you refuse to use. How do you think a mark on your record will look to colleges? Do you even think past high school, or do you imagine life ends at the school gates?"

I thought about getting as far away from her as possible. Oblivious to my boiling anger, she continued her tirade.

"What do you want to make of your life? There's only so long you can use having an absentee mother as an excuse! You hate how selfish she was, only thinking of herself, but here you are doing the same thing and breaking my poor heart all over again."

Silence enveloped us as I stared at my plate, blinking back furious tears. Sidell's fork scraped at her plate. With the knowledge of her being here to witness this, I couldn't break down. I swallowed the lump in my throat. "I'm sorry, Grandma. I didn't realize you felt this way," I murmured.

Her head tilted slightly, and a soft chuckle escaped from her lips, "Of course, you didn't. The more reason why I had to sit you down and properly communicate that to you. You gotta learn to do the same, Jacky. You gotta learn to speak about how you're feeling else all the pressure and pain you carry is gonna combust and explode one day, and innocent bystanders will get hurt. You know the reason God asks us to cast our burdens upon him is because he cares for us. He knows that we can't do it alone without being weighed down. He knows that we will go through things that will break our soul, spirit and bodies and that's why he assures us in Matthew 28:20, saying, "And lo, I am with you always, even unto the end of the World.""

A soft sigh escaped her lips as she absently caressed my hand across the table. "God wants you to let Him help you, JJ. He wants to hold your right hand, just as He promised in Isaiah 41:13. He has a plan for you, regardless of your current circumstances. He wants to journey alongside you, through the fire and the storm. Just like He did for Shedrach, Meshach, and Abednego. He is the God of hope, and He wants to breathe new hope into your life."

My eyelids fluttered shut as I contemplated her words. It was a lot to absorb, to process. Yet, within me stirred a desire to give Him a second chance. I yearned for a fresh start with Him, to experience the same joy and tranquility that enveloped Grandma.

"Remember," she whispered gently, "when you hear His voice today, don't harden your heart like Israel did when they rebelled."

I exhaled heavily, rubbing my fingers against my forehead in an attempt to release some of the built-up tension. "All right, Grandma. I will make another attempt at this. If it doesn't work out, then you'll let me be for the rest of my life," I muttered.

"No, JJ. That's not how it works. You're in need of God's help and he wants you to come to him with a contrite heart. He doesn't despise a broken and contrite heart. You open up to him because you need him and not because you want to prove something to me." Her tone was soft.

"Oh, and what happens to all the stories of the Shepherd leaving the ninety-nine sheep to go back for one that was lost?" I muttered, pushing my seat back. "I didn't see where the bible stated that the one sheep had to find his way back on his own. After all, there must have been a reason he left in the first place." I turned to Sidell as a way to escape, "You need me to drop you off at home?"

Sidell's eyes darted uncertainly between me and Grandma. "Yes. Please?"

Grandma's chuckle reeled me back in, "Or maybe the one sheep was the problem to begin with. Out of a hundred, why was it the only one that chose to go the other way? Surely if there was something wrong, then it would have had another sheep following it shortly after."

"Or maybe the one sheep was the only one with enough courage not to follow the multitude even when they were wrong?" I mumbled to myself, as I gathered my dishes and laid them in the sink.

"You ready Sidell? Because we can head out right now?" I asked, annoyed not directly towards her, but my grandma.

"Uh…yeah." Sidell replied innocently, getting up slowly as she gathered her dishes. She looked at grandma who didn't say anything else, but smiled amusedly as she sipped on her wine. The picture of grace, but I could see the fire in her eyes. That look said, "Ima be nice in front of your little friend, but when you get back, your getting hell."

But that's okay. I'd take the tongue lashing later if it meant escaping now. "A'ight, let's dip then." I took Sidell's plate and laid it in the sink with a clatter.

Sidell scurried after me, mouthing "sorry" at Grandma before slipping out the front door.

Chapter Thirty-Two: Sidell

Sitting in the backseat of the Uber, I glanced at JJ, who was staring out the window with a faraway look in his eyes. Bernadette was right, as much as I hated to admit it. But I couldn't bring myself to tell JJ that. He'd feel so betrayed if he knew I was siding with his grandma on this.

JJ was like a wounded fighter in the ring with God, battling it out gloveless, willing to get knocked down again and again before he'd let those divine fists heal him. That's just how JJ was - always turning everything into a grand epic struggle.

Seeing JJ's hostility and vulnerability, I understood that he really needed that tough love that his grandma gave him. But I also knew that sometimes his grandma's "tough love" could be suffocating, especially when you were gasping for air.

I reached across the empty space between us in the backseat and squeezed his hand. He looked at me with those intense artist's eyes, like I was the only thing anchoring him.

"Thank you JJ, for being such a great friend today," I said, infusing my voice with gentle affection.

JJ squeezed my hand harder, convinced as always that he was the one saving me. "No problem. Lets just hope that your parents will be able to see that," he said with an air of finality before sinking into his seat, and I knew that he wouldn't say anything else.

Oh right. I had forgotten about my rebellious tirade from early. When I stormed out of the house with that, "I do what I want energy". Ugh, I had to face my parents now. And it didn't help, that I asked JJ to come with me. I wanted my parents to know that JJ saved me today, in hopes it'll change their false narratives about him.

I sighed heavily, dreading the confrontation ahead. My parents were going to be absolutely livid. But it was too late to back out now. This whole situation was a disastrous mess. Why hadn't I just snuck out my bedroom window like a normal teenager? Why did I stand there and argue down with my mom?

JJ must have sensed my fear. He gave my hand another supportive squeeze. "It'll be alright," he said gently. "I've got your back, remember?"

I almost believed him. With JJ by my side, I felt like I could face anything. Even my parents' wrath. He was like a shield, protecting me from the storm.

Taking a deep breath, I prayed, "Please God, I pray that you'll supply grace so that my parents won't be rabid pit bulls ready to tear JJ apart when they see him with me."

Finally, my house came into view. Immediately the uber pulled into the driveway at the front of my house. The door bursted open and every single member of my nuclear family came tearing out the door.

Dad, with his long strides, ate up the ground in time. He took one good look at me and I almost saw him crumble for the first time. He immediately pulled me into his arms and hugged me tightly to his chest. Mom and Cayest joined in the circle. Dad gently pulled away. I could barely see him, because I was engulfed in hugs.

Suddenly, I heard the sound of a loud solid punch hitting a human flesh and we all broke apart immediately.

"Papa! Stop it!" He didn't do anything!" I shrieked, horrified at this sudden violence from my gentle father. I ran to JJ, who was doubled over in pain, but Dad roughly yanked me away and swung me in my mother's direction. Mom restrained my arms with her own. I had always known mom's grip was strong but I never knew it could be this strong.

"This is the last time I'll be telling you this, the next time I see you around my daughter, I promise you'll either end up in prison or be carried out in a body bag."

Something in me shattered, leaving me cold and numb as I watched Jacky remain curled up where he was on the floor. No one moved to help him as I struggled against Mom's viselike hold, desperate to go to him.

Cayest stood staring in shock too. She must have found it hard to believe that our father was capable of physically hurting anyone, and with the pound he carried, the punch he landed on Jacky must hurt a lot.

I was trapped and forced to watch JJ struggle to his feet.

It was dark but there were very few people walking along the street and when some of them saw this, they stopped to watch.

"Please, Papa," I whispered, pleading for I don't know what. For permission to go to JJ? For him to leave JJ alone? To go back to the gentle father I once knew?

JJ slowly straightened up with his face still curled in pain. He looked defiantly at my family, but he said nothing, he didn't even try to claim his innocence in all these, my parents saw what they wanted to see. He turned his eyes toward me for a moment, and I wanted to go to him, but I couldn't. He turned around and limped away until he disappeared out of sight.

I knew the worst wasn't over yet, so I braced up.

★ ★ ★ ★ ✝ ★ ★ ★ ★

The distant whine of the vacuum filled my room, its vibrations shaking the walls and rattling my windows. Trying to seem somewhat productive as I wiped the excess tears from my eyes. I just had a feeling that at any minute my parents would come in to finish lecturing me on how I wasn't being the daughter that they used to know. And how "That boy" and my uncontrollable hormones corrupted what image they had been perfecting for years.

Wheeling the vacuum under my bed, I reached out to steady myself against the bedpost. Then, over its low rumble, I heard the unmistakable voice of my little sister from my door. Quickly pressing my foot against the vacuum's off switch, I invited her in.

My room door opened and Cayest came in adjusting the sleeves of her spongebob night gown with furrowed brows.

"What is it Caye?" I asked roughly, coiling up the cord connected to the vacuum.

"What happened with you and Mama earlier, when you stormed out. Where did you go?" She asked, approaching me bare footed on the cold wood floors.

"Nothing and nowhere. Don't worry about it Caye, it's none of your business." Wasn't worth saying anything. I already knew my parents fed my little sister's head with lies of me doing the worst. It would be a miracle if they ever let me out the door again after this. I wouldn't be surprised if they decided that I'll be homeschooled.

Before Cayest could respond, hard knuckles rapped at my open door. We flinched in unison as Dad loomed in the doorway, Mom close behind with her hands on her hips in full disciplinarian mode.

"Sidell, get in the car, we are going to the hospital," My father said immediately.

I scrunched my face, "Hospital? For what?"

"Don't question your father and do as he says," my mother said sharply.

My gut churned with anxiety as I sat silently in the passenger seat, wondering where we were going and why it had to be just Dad and me. I breathed a sigh of relief that at least Mom wasn't here too — I'd probably strangle myself if forced to share this tiny space with her.

Dad kept his eyes fixed straight ahead as he drove, not even glancing my way. I was clearly in serious trouble, but strangely, fear evaded me. My thoughts centered only on JJ, worrying how he might be feeling after my Dad had punched him.

"Did he touch you?" Dad suddenly asked, his first words since we'd gotten in the van. I stared at him, stunned. Of all the things he could say, that was his opening question?

When I didn't immediately respond, he repeated more forcefully, spittle flying, "I asked you a question, Sidell. Answer me right now — did he touch you?"

"No, he didn't," I said in weirdly steady voice. "But you just had to overreact based on your assumption that he hurt me." I wasn't aware my tone was already rising but I was too far gone. "I got lost and scared out of my mind. I would've been harmed if JJ hadn't shown up to rescue me. But how did you thank him, Papa? With a punch to the stomach."

"Be quiet, Sidell," He ordered in a dangerously low tone. "That boy was no good, and the moment you started acting out, I knew it had to be his influence." He turned sharply into another lane and I would have slammed my head against the side window if I wasn't wearing the seat belt. I knew it wasn't intentional, but it only fueled my anger.

"You go out without informing us and you return home late! You even talk back to your mother now. How do you excuse that?" he yelled, the veins in his neck bulging.

"I wasn't talking back, I only wanted her to hear me, listen to me!"

"But that's no way to talk to your parents and you are even doing the same to me right now!" he growled and I snapped my mouth shut.

Dad pulled into a parking space of the hospital and shutted off the engine.

"I don't know where we went wrong with you, but I will put everything right, even if it's the last thing I do." Dad said, getting out of the car. The car shook as he shut his door. I remained in my seat, arms crossed, watching him as he circled around to the back of the car. Huffing an exaggerated breath, I reluctantly opened my door and followed him to the entrance of the hospital.

The sterile white walls of the hospital only fueled my irritation. About an hour later, I was finally allowed to leave, after the most embarrassing experience of my life. I can't believe Dad actually asked them to check if I was sexually active! I vehemently insisted I wasn't, but he didn't let it go until the doctor confirmed I was still a virgin. I was rushed out with a pamphlet and a bad attitude

On the car ride home, the flickering street lights cast dancing shadows on the windshield. I fumed, replaying the humiliating experience in my mind. And dad didn't utter another word to me. Not even an apology. And when we got home I stormed upstairs to my room slamming the door shut behind me. Ripping the pamphlet to shreds, I tossed it into the trash can near my dresser, then I plopped down onto my bed. Burying my face in my pillows, my emotions started to assault me.

With tears streaming freely down my face, I came to the realization that….I really hated my parents.

Chapter Thirty-Three:
ψψ

My stomach felt like a raging inferno, as if I'd been rammed in by a bull. I gritted my teeth, as I tried as much as possible not to acknowledge the pain, but it consumed me. Curled up in bed, I did my best not to obsess over Sidell's safety. She was with her family now, I reminded myself. But what will they do to her? Surely they wouldn't hurt their own daughter, right? Too many horror stories circulated about deranged fathers who lashed out when they believed their kids stepped out of line. Judging by the way he greeted me with a punch to the gut, it made me un-doubt if he was like that. And If I saw a single mark on Sidell's skin, believe me when I say I'd—

"Jacky?" Grandma called, opening my bedroom door. "Been calling you for nearly thirty minutes. I asked you to come take this tylenol where I could see you. Is everything alright? You ain't done something stupid like throw those pills away without taking them, did you?"

"No... Yeah, sorry," I stuttered, "I have it right here though."

I reached for the water bottle and pills on my dresser, hearing Grandma's shuffling footsteps draw closer into my pitch black room.

She clicked her tongue in disapproval, blindly feeling along the wall for the light switch. "I'll never understand why you insist on sitting in pitch blackness all the time, Jacky." Was she referring to my dark room or my dark state of mind? With a flip of the switch, light flooded the space, causing me to recoil like a vampire exposed to sunlight.

"What the hell -heck!" I quickly corrected my language for Grandma's sake. She paid me no mind, settling herself at the foot of my bed as I shielded my eyes in exaggerated agony.

Grandma watched me to ensure I wouldn't pull a fast one on her. I rattled the bottled pills loudly to prove I wasn't pocketing them. Then I tossed two white tablets in my mouth and chased them down with a few gulps of lukewarm water.

"What happened when you dropped that girl off JJ," she asked, as if she could already sense it.

Removing the bottle from my lips, I resealed the cap, refusing to meet her gaze.

"What's the matter with you? You know I'm right here," she said worriedly. I knew this was coming from a good place but all I wanted in that minute was to be by myself.

"Grandma, I said it already. It was your meat pies I ate earlier." I mumbled.

"Don't give me that bull, I've seen you eat three at a go and you didn't double over like this. Now, what really went on?"

"Nothing, Grandma!" I protested. "Just a stomachache. Maybe it's the flu?"

Her gaze was unwavering, her eyes two dark coals that seemed to penetrate my soul. She wasn't convinced. The silence ballooned between us.

"Alright," she sighed, "If you're not willing to tell me then…" she stood up, leaving the sentence unfinished as she moved towards the door.

"I got punched by her dad," I blurted out, not able to bear the sudden surge of guilt washing over me. I watched as she paused in her stride, her hand hovering above the doorknob.

"What? Why?" She turned back with worry etched into her face.

I shrugged and studied my hands as if they were suddenly the most interesting thing in the world. "

"I don't know, Grandma," I whispered. "When I dropped Sidell off, her dad...well he wasn't exactly pleased to see me."

Grandma's eyes softened, though her lips pressed in to a thin line. "Now Jacky, don't tell me you went acting a fool in these people's neighborhood?"

"Well the first time, I kind of did. But grandma, that's why I wanted to apologize for it today. Sidell's dad had a wrong impression of me that I was trying to change today by apologizing for my past behavior. But things got heated and..."

Grandma clicked her tongue, eyes flashing. "And that man assaulted you out of the blue?"

"Yeah," I said, hanging my head. "I know I can be a hot-head Grandma, but I didn't do nothing to provoke him this time. Honest."

She studied me a moment before the fire left her eyes. With a sigh, she sat back on the bed, the old mattress squeaking under her slight weight."It's going to be alright, JJ. That man just needs a little more grace. I'm sure he's gonna come around eventually."

I barked out a sarcastic laugh. "Oh yeah, I'm sure he'll be inviting me over for Passover dinner any day now."

Grandma shot me a warning look. "Now don't go getting smart with me, boy. I know you're upset, but that attitude won't solve anything."

I took a deep breath,. "Is he really going to 'come around' though, Grandma? I mean, Sidell told me her family is part Russian and Jewish. I guess that explains why her dad hates me so much, but what does it matter? I'm friends with Sidell, it's not like I'm out here making a woman out of her. Why can't her dad accept that? Doesn't he care at all about his daughter's emotions?"

Grandma shook her head sympathetically. "No JJ, you've got it all wrong. That man loves his daughter more than you can imagine. He just wanna protect her, make sure you're the right kind of boy for her to be around. It's a father's job to lay down the law, even if he goes overboard sometimes. He don't want his baby getting hurt, that's all."

"Yeah, well it's a shame how he's so obsessed with controlling her life in the process. I swear, he thinks Sidell's his property or something. It's like he can't stand the thought of her fawning over another man besides himself. That religious front he be putting up is just a cover for his insecurities and possessiveness over her. It's sickening, really." I shrugged as Grandma meditated on her response thoroughly.

"I may not have laid eyes on that man, but I believe his reservations are embedded in a cultural context." She began. "See, them folks might be living in America, but they still hold onto their roots and traditions. It's just how things are done in their family. And ain't no amount of American dreaming gonna change that. They stick to their religion and their old school values, and that's just the way it is. Ain't nothing wrong with that, if you ask me."

Grandma paused to rub her arms while her face dipped in sympathy. "So you see, it ain't as simple as you think. You can't just expect people to see you for who you are without showing them something first. They'll always resort to their assumptions because they don't have the truth written on their foreheads. Actions speak louder than words, JJ. You gotta show that girl's parents that there's more to you than that chip on your shoulder."

"I don't got a chip on my shoulder," I grumbled, crossing my arms.

Grandma gave me a pointed look. "Mmhmm. And I ain't got arthritis in my hands."

I sighed, running a hand through my hair. "Look, I care about Sidell. For real. But I got all this...this crap piled up inside me. Resentment and hurt and..." I trailed off, shaking my head.

"Child, you think I don't see the way you look at her when you think nobody's watching?" Grandma said gently. "Like she hangs the moon in the sky just for you. I ain't miss none of it. Now listen here, Sidell and her faith could do wonders for you, but what I wanna know is if you gon be good for her too?" She paused, giving me a stern look.

I twisted my mouth, not sure how to answer.

"Now baby, if you ain't sure about how to answer that question, then maybe it's best you let her go and just be friends. You can't bring all that drama and bitterness against God into a relationship with that girl. And your own baggage and traumas? Child, leave those at the door. We both know that ain't gonna work out. Don't be playin' games with that girl's heart now, ya hear?"

"Yes ma'am, I hear you," I mumbled, looking elsewhere. Grandma was right, as much as I hated to admit it. I'd never felt this way about someone before, but Sidell deserved more than my silences and cutting remarks. She needed someone who could let her in, not build walls to keep her out.

Grandma patted my hand, "You gotta heal those old wounds first, baby. Can't expect to hold someone else together if you're still broken inside. Just take it one day at a time."

I nodded, her words settling heavily in my chest. I had no idea how to fix myself, but for Sidell, I was willing to try.

★ ★ ★ ★ ✝ ★ ★ ★ ★

What are the odds? Of all the rotten luck, the one day I'm back from suspension, Tony, who would've been my saving grace this morning, got suspended. So I opted to ride the bus, which was not what I was trying to do. Just as suspected, Khyree, his cousin Rayo and the two goons Juice and Smurf came standing near me at the bus stop. They never rode with me before, not when Rayo had his flashy car to show off. No, they only did this to corner me while I was alone.

 I swiftly made eye contact with that snitch, Khyree, his eye blacker than my grandma's Sunday shoes, lip swole up like a balloon. He smiled an evil smile before turning to his cousin, "People be scary when the real fight comes" He bragged loudly. I smiled as I unlocked my phone. He should be the least to be talking. I'll leave him stumbling again with a trail of blood.

When the school bus finally pulled up, I went to get on, but they all rushed in front of me. Walking up the steps, each one aimed their fingers at me like guns. "Bang, bang!" Rayo shouted, as the rest cackled like the mindless followers they were.

I clenched my jaw, allowing more of my peers to get ahead of me. If I'm getting on this bus, they better prayer none of them get their throat closed in.

As I stepped onto the bus, I made eye contact with the bus driver. She gave me a knowing look that said, "I've got your back." I nodded slightly to let her know I appreciated it. At least someone was on my side.

I plopped down in an empty seat and put my earbuds in, blasting music to drown out the idiots' laughter and open threats. Khyree kept glancing back at me, waiting for me to react. I pretended not to notice, staring out the window instead. Inside though, my blood was boiling. I imagined leaping over the seat and wiping that smug grin off his face. But I couldn't give him the satisfaction. Not yet anyway. For now, I'd bide my time and hit him where it really hurts.

The bus driver yelled "That's enough!" as we pulled away from the stop. The pack settled down, but I could feel their eyes watching me, waiting for me to slip up. I smirked to myself. They had no idea what I was capable of.

Sitting in my first period class, my leg bounced uncontrollably under my desk as my eyes darted between the clock and the door, counting down the seconds until my imminent demise.

"Hey man, that fight with you and Khyree was crazy yo!" My classmate JuJu's voice cut through my spiraling thoughts. I rolled my eyes inwardly. Yeah Julius, nothing like a near expulsion and death threat to gain me some street cred with you bozos.

At the front of the room, Mrs. Reed droned on in the same monotone cadence he used every class. Not that I could focus on derivatives and functions when all I could envision was the cold steel of Rayo's glock pressed against my forehead. His beady eyes glinted with malice as he mocked my pathetic whimpering. Nah, I wouldn't even give him the satisfaction.

A muffled bang sounded from the hallway, the blood drained from my face. This was it. I wiped my clammy palms on my Forrest green uniform pants, heart hammering as I braced for Rayo and his goons to kick down the door, guns blazing. The door flew open and in came the security guard with his walkie talkie. "Sorry to interrupt, I need to grab Gavin Hill for a minute," he said before garbling into the static-filled radio. False alarm. But my nerves were too shot for relief.

At this rate, Rayo wouldn't need to pull the trigger. My anxiety would take me out first.

While Gavin gathered his things, I took it as an opportunity to escape. I whistled to the teacher as I rose hand, "Yo, Mrs. Reed, can I go to the restroom?"

Truth is, I didn't need to go. But I needed to bolt off campus before I had a full blown panic attack. As I power walked down the staircase, the empty halls were eerie, my hurried footsteps echoing off the rows of lockers like I was being chased. My mind spiraled with morbid fantasies of Rayo and his crew jumping out to ambush me.

But when I turned the corner, it was Sidell who jump scared me instead.

Except she was halfway down the hall, lost in her own little world as she ran her fingers through her long blonde hair.

I tried to swiftly turn and book it back around the corner before she noticed me, but her head snapped up and our eyes locked. Dang it. Now she definitely saw me see her. Not that I was trying to avoid her, exactly. I just didn't want to risk Rayo catching me with her and her getting caught up in my mess.

"JJ, wait up," she called after me, her light footsteps hurrying to catch up.

I slowed to a reluctant stop, my expression carefully neutral as I turned to face her. Can't let her see how freaked I am.

"Hey," she said softly, searching my face with those bright blue eyes that always saw right through me. I stayed silent, racking my brain for a way to explain myself without spilling about the target on my back.

She stepped closer until she stood right in front of me, and I could smell her floral perfume. "Why are you trying to avoid me?" She asked, folding her arms across her chest.

My jaw tightened, "I wasn't," I said, glancing over my shoulder to the hall behind me.

"Don't insult me, JJ. We both know you were trying too."

I bit my lip as I looked down at my sneakers.

"Did I do something to upset you?" She asked, her voice gentle but laced with frustration as she unfolded her arms.

I sighed heavily. "No, of course not. You didn't do anything wrong." Except be friends with a screw-up like me.

"Then why are you pushing me away?" Her words were gentle but I could hear the hurt behind them. "Is it because of what my dad did to you?"

"No, it's not-, Look, just meet me at lunch, okay? We gotta talk." I asked softly.

"But we're talking now," she insisted, her eyes searching mine.

"I know, but..." I paused, racking my brain for a good reason she'd accept. An involuntary smile crept onto my lips. "It's top secret. And I don't wanna hold you up from your classes, you know."

She sighed, brushing a strand of golden hair behind her ear. "Okay. I'll be in the lunchroom with Dawn."

"Cool beans, see you then," I said with forced cheerfulness, before turning and speed walking away, my shoulders sagging in relief as soon as I rounded the corner.

 While Sidell went through the motions of her first to third period classes, I hid out in the school's Cathedral attic, the safest place in my opinion where I could watch everyone's moves below. I was scrolling through my phone for about an hour until I heard the familiar voices eching from outside.

I peeked out the cobwebbed window and cursed under my breath. Of course it was Khyree, Rayo and the two stooges in tow.

I was so sure I'd escaped them, but nope. There they were, lumbering into the entrance of this sacred building, about to defile it with their presence.

"Shoot. Damn," I whispered, prancing around and patting my pockets nervously. What's my next move here? Make a run for it and hope I don't get jumped?

Too late. When I got to the staircase, I could hear them tromping through the doors, hooting and hollering. They started standing on the antique chairs, popping firecrackers, their raucous voices echoing through the hallowed space. No respect at all for this place. I might not be religious, but even I wouldn't dare disrespect the house of the Lord like this. I desperately wished Jesus would come flip some tables to put the fear of God in these weirdos.

"Smurf, you got the roll up?" Rayo asked one of his goons.

"Man.. don't worry about me, as long as you got the green we straight." Smurf replied smartly.

"Rayo, where we gonna have the smoke sesh at?" Juice, the second stooge, bellowed. "That creepy Jesus statue keeps eyeballin' me. I ain't tryin' to have no holy spirit possess me."

"We can go upstairs to the attic, they have a window up there for circulation," Khyree suggested eagerly, desperate for approval.

My heart dropped to my stomach. Oh hell no, you're not coming up here, I thought, panicking.

"Nah, lil' cuz, too much dust up there and I got bronchitis. Follow me, I got a spot," Rayo replied in his typical bored, arrogant drawl.

I watched from above as Rayo led the three stooges further down the long hallway, their footsteps fading. When I heard a door close behind them, I gently but speedily jogged down the old steps, my sneakers barely making a sound. Once I made it to the entrance, I booked it out of there as the lunch bell rang just in time.

Finally free, I breathed a deep sigh of relief. The usual sea of students and staff surrounded me, masking my escape. I immediately went to search for Sidell, finding her chatting in the crowded courtyard with her friend Dawn. Taking a calming deep breath, I smoothed my clothes, put on a charming smile to hide my inner turmoil, and sauntered up to them casually, restoring my reputation as the smooth guy.

When Sidell saw me approach, she gave me a coy smile while Dawn slipped away knowingly.

"Come on JJ, curiosity is nearly wrecking me. Where is this secret that you're withholding from me?" Sidell asked expectantly.

Eyeing her from head to toe, I closed the distance between us. I gazed into her entrancing eyes, remaining silently mysterious for maximum suspense.

"What are we doing Jacky?" she asked as she watched my lips curl wickedly.

"I'm taking you on our second date. We never got to do that and now it seems like the right time." I gently lifted her hand and brushed my thumb across her palm. "We're getting off this depressing campus and heading to the Carnival down the block.

It was the first idea that popped into my head, despite only having a couple bucks to my name. But to escape the goons, I'd make it work.

Sidell's breath hitched in her throat, her gaze wary yet intrigued. "Are you serious, JJ? You know I can't ditch again?" She glanced down at our hands before meeting my gaze again, her accent disappearing as her tone softened. "I thought we were just going to talk."

Not willing to take no for an answer at the moment, I grasped her hand and gently pulled her towards me. "We can still talk, just somewhere less dreary. I promise we'll make it back by 4th period," I assured her with a roguish wink.

Chapter Thirty-Four: Sidell

Awe-inspiring. That was the only way to describe the scene before us as we stepped through Central Chicago's Carnival Park gates. Lights shone in every corner, rhythmic music punctuated by alluring laughter, rides twisting and flying— it was like being thrown into a world of no restrictions. JJ seized my hand with passionate fervor and I smiled. With such an atmosphere of freedom, anything seemed possible.

We played game after game with each other, our competitive natures forcing us to throw ourselves entirely into it until we were exhausted. A joyful exhaustion. A feeling that no one else could understand in its entirety aside from myself and JJ.

We held out our wristbands at one of the game stands. Bleep, went the scanner. A teenager with the name tag Brian on his red polo shirt squatted behind the counter and returned with two trays. Each tray had five rolling softballs and he set them down before us.

"You get the big bear if you get them all in one go and the little turtle if it takes more than one," Brian monotoned, half of his weary attention on the rowdy people behind us.

I smiled and nodded. "Yeah. Thanks," I said as I looked up at JJ with a glint in my eye. I was determined to show him who's boss.

I looked down and picked up a ball, feeling the weight of it in my hand. It's lighter than it should be, but I was not surprised. These things were always rigged. It just meant I had to throw harder, right?

After a quick check around just to make sure no fists were thrown by accident from my backswing, I rocked back and hurled the ball at the pyramid of milk bottles with all my strength.

It shot over the top without even touching the stack. Irritating. I'd been quite confident I was going to be good at this.

JJ licked his lips as he stepped up to take his turn. "That was cute, but I gotta show you how it's done," he said in a low voice that was full of heat.

I rolled my eyes as he took a ball from the tray and adjusted his stance. He released the ball with enough force to make Brian flinch. The ball collided with the top bottle, causing them to shake but none of them fell. My laughter erupted, unable to be contained.

"Missed it by that much?" I teased in disbelief.
A hearty chuckle rumbled from JJ's chest as he sauntered closer and looked around. "Aye, ain't gonna be none of that," he whispered with a playful smile that pierced my heart like an arrow.

"Yeah, okay buddy," I said, trying to hide the smile on my face. "Let's see you do better."

Looking away, I grabbed another ball, ready for my throw. I tried taking some deep, slow breaths to relax myself when I noticed JJ still watching me intently. Please Jesus, make me like diamonds.

I took a couple steps to my right, took a centering breath, and cut the ball at a diagonal angle, aiming for the center of the bottom row.

The sound was glorious.

The whole thing went down all at once in a loud, satisfying clatter of plexiglass on concrete. I beamed as the explosive noise faded into that of a few bottles rolling around, then into nothing.

"Oh, come on fam, not again," JJ groaned, shaking his head at me with a lopsided grin. "You always gotta one-up me."

I laughed, feeling the adrenaline pumping through my veins. "At least you're getting better at accepting defeat," I threw in with a cheeky tug of his earlobe.

He gently swatted my hand away as he chuckled, "Yeah? Well, maybe one day I'll even be able to beat you." He chewed on his lip in an alluring manner before continuing jokingly, "But until then, I'm content watching you win."

★ ★ ★ ★ ✝ ★ ★ ★ ★

My arms wrapped tightly around JJ's neck as he carried me on his back. His hands cupped my thighs, supporting me as we weaved between the crowds of people. The happiness building in my chest bubbled up like a fizzy drink as our laughter made our lungs burn.

"Sorry!" I giggled over my shoulder after JJ caused a guy to slosh some of his drink on the ground.

"Nah, not really," he added jokingly and I slapped him lightly on the side of the face with the blue teddy bear.

"JJ! Are you trying to pick a fight?"

"Always."

"You know, I'm not really surprised by that."
Handing out tickets to the ticket bearer, we soon escaped the ground as we reached the heights of the Ferris wheel, and it was beautiful. The fairgrounds were already on an elevated part of the city, showcasing the view to stretch farther than the ride would've allowed alone.

Despite the sun, It's colder, too, with the higher altitude and stronger wind. I shivered, cursing myself for not bringing a jacket. Why do I never think these things through? JJ noticed me in a semi-huddled position, arms wrapped around my teddy bear.

"Are you okay?" he asked, lounging casually across from me as if immune to the cold.

"Yeah, I'm fine," I lied through chattering teeth. Clinging tighter to the teddy bear for warmth, I wished I could sink into its plush fur.

JJ raised an eyebrow. "Don't lie to me. You look miserable."
I sighed, rolling my eyes. "Okay, fine. I'm freezing. Happy now?"

JJ grinned, clearly enjoying my suffering. "Well, you could always stand up and do jumping jacks to warm up. Maybe a little dance number?"

"Ha ha, very funny," I said dryly. Though, knowing my clumsiness, I'd probably slip right through the safety bar and plummet to my death.

"Or I could rip the bear open for you and you could wear him like a jacket." JJ mimed tearing the bear's head off.

"Don't you dare!" I laughed, horrified, clutching the bear protectively.

"Or . . . you could come here." Wordlessly, he swung his arm across the top of the bench, leaving his side wide open for me.

I felt stupidly shy at his offer, but after a minute or so, I gave in and closed the distance between us. His arm immediately wrapped around my shoulders. He was so warm that I literally couldn't think of anything else for a good ten seconds.

When the Ferris wheel released us back into the buzzing fair, I was both sad and glad to be let free. At some point during the second round, even with JJ's arms wrapped around me, his heat like a furnace, the chill amplified to the point of discomfort.

Down on the ground — with the crowds and people and lights and barbecues and popcorn stands and lack of wind — the temperature was bearable again.

"I have no idea what I'm doing, Sidell." JJ said.

My head swiveled away from the scenery that enveloped us to look at him. Clutching my bear, I began walking backwards. "What are you talking about?"

"This," He whispered, gesturing between the two of us. "I've rarely ever done this. I don't really know how to be a proper boyfriend or even if that's what I am to you or—"

"Do you want to be?" I asked softly, smiling coyly.

He looked at me like he was taken aback by my directness. I surprised myself, but I could see his mouth slowly curving into a proud smile. "Yeah," he whispered back as he got lost in my eyes.

I smiled bashfully and bit my lip in an effort to quell my blush. "Okay, then you are," I declared definitively. "And you're doing good. Really good."

He moistened his lips and his gaze dropped as he murmured, "That's dope."

Now grinning, I took JJ's hand and pulled him into the first fun house I saw that didn't have a line.

Everything inside was far too small for him, and I giggled wildly when he almost slipped all the way down a cramped staircase, his big feet struggling to catch on the little footholds. He caught himself on the rails just in time, cursing the 'inescapable cheap plastic gerbil-sized torture chamber' over and over again in increasingly creative ways.
The entire second floor was made of mirrors - panels of clear glass, panels of mirrors, and a secret invisible path that led through them to the next and last level. A maze.

I focused all my attention, insisting that I could figure it all out and that JJ just needed to follow. He did at first, but we somehow got separated after a few minutes. Probably because I got too excited and started to venture too far ahead.

"JJ?" I called when I realized he wasn't behind me. The sound bounced off the floor-to-ceiling plexiglass surrounding me. I winced. Does sound carry at all in here? He might've still heard me, just muffled. I tried again. "JJ!"

I thought I heard something in return, but I couldn't tell what it was. I had no reason to even believe it was JJ, and no concept of how far away it came from.

It might've been stupid, but I started to feel trapped. And I didn't like it.

I headed back in the direction I thought I came, but I was no longer sure what that way originally was. I started jogging, switching directions often, but only meeting my own flushed reflection over and over at every turn.

"JJ!"

No answer at all this time. Maybe I should just try to find the exit; the only problem was that I had well and truly disoriented myself even worse than before.
Just pick a direction.

I did. I glared at my reflection every time I'm met with it, hoping every time it'd be a different face from mine. I was constantly disappointed, becoming more and more panicked with every passing second.

I finally stopped altogether and stared at myself. It'd been a good five minutes, at least.

With a sinking feeling, it occured to me that JJ might've simply left.

I kept searching anyway. Eventually I found myself against a front-facing window and looked down, thinking maybe he could be waiting outside as a last resort, but there's no sight of him below.

Right, I thought. Okay. JJ left. He left and I'd been running around here alone like an idiot.

This was basically the perfect place to ditch someone. By the time I found my way out of there, he could've easily been long gone back to school or wherever else. Our separation probably wasn't an accident. It was his way out. A clean ghost. Better for both of us, I guessed.

I started moving through the maze again, figuring that I'd have to stumble upon either the entrance or exit eventually. That's when I rounded a random corner and startled at a misshapen reflection.

"Sheesh," it says. "You not good at this at all."

It was him. JJ. Just standing there.

A million thoughts and feelings flooded me at once. I opened my mouth to say something, but nothing came out.

"I think I'm gonna need to take over from here."
I stared up at him for another moment. Then a big, stupid smile slowly spreaded across my face.

"Cool?" he said.

"Cool," I laughed. "I think so too."

He grabbed my hand. "Good. Come on."

With JJ leading, we actually escaped pretty quickly. I agreed to never, ever do that again. The third and final floor of the fun house was full of random baubles and distortion mirrors and squeaky punching bags - all spread out along a railing that looked down on the channel of moving people outside.
JJ landed a half-hearted kick at a punching bag and I followed up with a hard one.

"Ow." I shook out my foot.

"Those aren't really meant for actual punching. Or kicking."

"Obviously I know that now."

He turned, effectively backing me against a divider.
"I didn't suggest you kick it, Sidell. You did that yourself."

When I snuck a look up at him, he was smiling at me. An unfamiliar thrill rippled up my spine as we now stood close. His smile faded a bit as his eyes drifted down to my lips. Jacky started to move toward me but then stopped himself, and my stomach dropped. But instead of pulling away, his dark brown eyes communicated with my blue ones.

He was waiting on me.

My nod was small. A microscopic movement for what felt like screaming. I couldn't hear the outside carnival chaos anymore, just my own breathing and heart pounding as Jacky carefully closed the distance between us.
I was mid inhale when his chapped lips grazed mine. I stood frozen for a moment, like I was waiting for my clueless self to find a way to ruin this.

But I didn't, and I exhaled against his lips. My eyes fell shut as I pressed my lips against his, and his surprised little hum in response sent a warmth throughout my body.

JJ's hand leaned into the wall next to my face as his other arm tightened around my waist, pulling me closer against him as he kissed me harder. Loud noises came from downstairs; we both ignored it. My stuffed bear slipped out my fingers as my arms made their way to his shoulders to hold him in place as I parted my lips for him.

He had no right to know how to kiss like this, I thought weakly. But I didn't want it to stop. I felt more awake than I'd felt in - maybe ever.

Loud fanfare music blasts through the massive speakers outside. I jumped, knocking my forehead into his. "Sorry!"

"Ladies and gentlemen, boys and girls, we thank you for coming to Chicago's annual Summer of Fun at the Fair. We hope you enjoyed this year's theme, Farm Fresh Festivities. We care about your produce, and we care about your fun!"

"Oh god," JJ groaned. I laughed. The announcer wasn't done.

"Here at the fairgrounds, we care about the environment. On your way to the exits…"

"Wait. What time is it?" I asked, my heart still hammering in my throat.

"...please be sure to dispose of your trash and recyclable materials in the designated receptacles. All attractions are now closed, but don't fear! You can still exchange your..."

"It's 4. They're closing."

"...From everyone here at the fair, we wish you a good night and a great year. Please drive safe and adhere the speed limit in the parking lot. The designated taxis and ride-share pick-up/drop-off is located at the..."

My first two thoughts were "I don't want to leave", and "My parents are going to kill me! Like for real this time!"

"Oh my goodness, JJ! It's the end of the school day!" I groaned, pick up my bear. "Shoot! And Dawn! She was probably looking for me to take me home!"

JJ gave me some space. "Hold on real quick." He pulled his phone out of his pocket. "Let me call her."

"Please do," I said, watching him expectedly.

The phone rang a couple times, before going straight to voicemail.

"Maybe her phone is dead." I suggested, but JJ merely tuned me out as he typed a text message to Dawn. His fingertips hovered over his contact list. "Dawn isn't replying fast enough for me. Let me text Tony-, oh wait, damn... he's suspended."

"Please Jesus help me." I prayed, running my fingers through my hair. JJ powered off his screen then tucked the phone away in his pocket.

"Come on, if we dipped now we'd probably catch her before she leaves the school parking lot."

We ran out the carnival park like our lives depended on it. Making it back out onto Chicago's main streets, JJ assaulted the crosswalk button. When it wasn't operating to his liking, he took my hand in and we illegally ran across street. Our feet transitioned from gravel to concrete, as a cop car missed us by mere seconds.

The moment we finally made it back onto campus, JJ and I hovered over, hands on knees, to catch our breaths. I can practically hear both our hearts beating as we panted desperately. I clutched my chest. My lungs were on fire and I could feel my feet pulsating as they ached. Ignoring the hole in the knee area of my black tights, I stood upright and scanned the area to see if Dawn's car was still there. I sighed in relief at the sight of the silver hyundai sonata with the beetle Juice bumper sticker. "Thank you Jesus." I mumbled.

"Is she…still.. Here. Whew, give me a sec." He wheezed, holding out his hand from his chest as he hovered down.

I laughed involuntarily, and it burned. "Don't you…play football? You guys run…the whole game."

He shot me a mock glare between wheezes. "Aye…we ain't…finna have…none of that…slander…"

I couldn't help the borderline hysterical giggles bubbling out of me. He looked so adorably miffed as he tried to catch his breath. So handsome.

"Alright, enough joking around," he finally said, back in protective mode. "Now lets go find you friend." he said.

We passed the remainder of our peers who were waiting near the drop off zone. And Dawn came walking out the doubled doors just in time. She looked rough and annoyed as she absentmindedly scrolled through her phone.

But she looked up just in time before colliding into us.

"Sorry bestie babes. Didn't mean to make you wait long. That weirdo Ms. Kyefer didn't notify me that I had detention until the end of class. I was going to call you but she confiscated my phone." She dramatically rolled her eyes.

I suppressed an urge to laugh. Dawn was forever the drama queen.

"No problem," I said. "JJ kept me company."

JJ flashed me a subtle smile and I felt my heart flutter. Focus, I told myself.

"Oh hey Jacky," Dawn said, finally noticing him. "I see you called my phone?"

"Yeah, Sidell said you were running late so I thought I'd try to reach you since she doesn't have her phone," JJ explained politely. "Anyway I'll catch you ladies later." He backed away slowly, his warm brown eyes lingering on me. I blushed furiously, praying Dawn wouldn't notice. Just wait until she finds out what happened between us, I thought. I think more fireworks will be going off in her heart as if she locked lips with him herself.

"Jacky, you wanna ride with us?" Dawn offered. "I'll take you home? I know my neanderthal boyfriend isn't here to take you."

"If it's not too much on you? I'd Ppreciate it." he sighed, grateful that he didn't have to catch the late bus.

"Yeah, no problem. You got me on the gas though." She yawned, jiggling her keys.

"For sure, I got you." He laughed, before he snuck beside my side.

As we followed Dawn to her car, I slipped my fingers through JJ's and he gave my hand a gentle, reassuring squeeze that sent tingles up my arm. We held hands until we reached Dawn's car and she spun around unexpectedly. We quickly dropped hands like hot potatoes.

Dawn narrowed her eyes, scrutinizing us. Oh no, she's onto us, I thought, holding my breath.

"Wait - where are your backpacks?" she asked suspiciously.

JJ and I exchanged relieved glances. "Shoot, we both forgot them in our lockers," he covered smoothly. "Can you wait just a sec for us to run back in?"

"Pretty please?" I added, giving her my best puppy dog eyes.

Dawn huffed and rolled her eyes, "Yes with a cherry on top, make it quick guys." she sassed, unlocking her car.

Chapter Thirty-Five:
ѰѰ

That very moment was etched in my memory like a hot branding iron. The intensity of the electricity between us could have lit up the night sky for miles. I hadn't been able to focus on anything else since that first kiss. Every cool glance from her had me captivated like a sailor in the grip of a siren's song. As Sidell and I sat in the backseats of Dawn's car, the universe seemed to be conspiring with us. Each red light and stop sign stretched out like an unending abyss. Once we pulled into my apartment complex, Sidell volunteered to walk with me to the door. The moment we were out of Dawn's sight, I snatched kisses like a thief. Desperate? I was well aware. But how could I not be? I was hooked, captured by the magic that her lips had on mine. I had found a missing part of myself that I didn't even know was gone.

A knock at my apartment door jolted me from my creative zone. Quick as lightning, I threw a cover over my canvas and packed away my art supplies. Ignoring the paint stains on my hands and clothes, I dashed down the hallway, skipping steps two at a time, eager to reach the front door in record time. I was trying to keep the repetitive knocking down so as not to wake up my grandma, who was getting her beauty sleep.

"Who is it?!" I interrogated, but there was no response. Clicking my tongue in annoyance, I started unlocking the door. Probably just Kaluna and her crew playing ding-dong ditch again.

I swung the door open, hopeful of catching them this time. Yet before a single word could pass through my lips, my fingers froze on the door's handle as my whole body fell into paralysis. I began doubting my vision as a breeze fluttered against her chestnut brown complexion, and wisps of her black natural curly hair swayed in the wind. My heart pounded in my chest as I scanned her figure critically, from head to toe.

Grandma hadn't mentioned anything about her daughter paying a visit. The fire in my chest spread to the tips of my toes. Seeing her again in this lifetime was the last thing I expected, let alone having her show up on Grandma's doorstep. I exhaled slowly, locking eyes with my biological mother for what felt like an eternity. She offered a tentative smile. Under my breath, curses slipped out as I stepped back from the threshold, slamming the door shut.

My eyelids flickered, and I halted for a dizzying moment to shake off the sleep fog from my eyes.

After all these years. Look who still finds her way home.
Tears welled up, stinging my eyes, while I inhaled sharply. A weight settled on my shoulders. When I mustered the strength to open the door again, I positioned myself as a blockade, arms casually folded across my chest.

"Hey, Mom," I greeted in a voice that could belong to ten-year-old Jacky, filled with excitement and surprise at seeing his birth mother outside a picture frame."What brings you here?"

She blinked a few times, surprised at the reception.
"Forget something?" I asked, scanning the surroundings with narrowed eyes. "Is it the baby gear? The bibs or maybe the stroller? Ah, yes, you came for the stroller. How could I forget?" My words dripped with sarcasm as a cold smile crept onto my face.

I watched her cautiously inch closer, hands outstretched. "Okay, I understand that you are upset and have every right to feel that way, but that's enough, Jacky Jamison. That's no way to talk to your—" She paused, realizing that the gravity of the next word could cause wars. ". . . a lady."

"I'm mighty pleased that you do realize who you are. A lady, some lady. I don't care what you identify as, but it would be in your best interests to back up right now and head back to whichever punk's crib you're coming from right now. Nobody here wants nothing to do with you," I hissed, all but spitting the words in her face.

She stared at me, held captive by guilt or whatever she tried to convince herself to feel better. "I'm here to make things right, Jacky..."

"Forgive my misogynistic a**, but I had no idea that a baddie like you could double as a plumber. You got a degree or some certification or even an ID to prove that? Cause it's the only way you're going to come into this house."

Her eyelids flutter in surprise as her mouth fell open momentarily, before snapping it shut. "Excuse me?"

"Yeah, you're excused."

There was no end to the snappy comebacks lined up for her, ready to serve them on a silver platter, just so I could watch her hurt as much as she hurt me all those years. Every second she stood there served as a painful reminder of the damage she inflicted on my life. Nothing she said could wash away the scars left by her willful absence.

"Jacky, I couldn't possibly explain how difficult it has been to be away from you. It will take a long time to get over the pain I've caused you. I just want a chance to explain things to you because I desperately want to be a part of your life."

"Part of my life?" I asked slowly, my eyes boring into hers.

"Isn't that what you wanted the last time you stood me up at the diner before going ahead and getting happily married to the man of your dreams like you updated your social media friends with? You have done the most explaining to your social media friends all these years. Why not put it on there too? Because I definitely do not have time for the drama you're about to cause."

"Dear Lord, as I live and breathe— it is my daughter in the flesh," Grandma whispered behind me, astounded. Emotion clogged my throat, and I immediately followed my gut and slammed the door closed.

"Jacky! Get some sense child!" Grandma warned, and I swallowed the rest of my words before turning around to face her.

"Jacky," she began more calmly. "Open the door and let your mother in right this moment." She rubbed her free hand over her bloodshot eyes. Couldn't tell if they were red from lack of sleep or from all the crying she'd been doing.
Releasing a huff, I opened the door swiftly.

"How are you, Laussie? It has been a long time," Grandma said softly, a sunny smile stretching her face. Hard to believe this was the same woman who used to give me ultimatums for my bad behavior. Now she's welcoming the same daughter who left her behind all those years ago.

"Yes, Momma, it has," she whispered, staring straight ahead, as if she's afraid her mother would be raptured the next minute if she took her eyes off her. Against my wishes, Grandma crossed the distance between them and threw her arms around my biological mother, clinging on like a drowning man at sea. My fingers were still clasped on the door handle, watching them with caution.

Tears spilled from my grandma's eyes, painting the picture of a hearty reunion to anyone who didn't know any better. She quickly wiped them away and planted a kiss on the intruder's cheeks. My stomach churned.

"Oh, Laussie, I've missed you so much. Glory be to God who has answered my prayers and brought you home. Indeed, God is good."

A soft chuckle escaped Laussie's lips, and she let Grandma usher her further into the house. I watched like a third wheel as they settled down next to each other on the brown leather sofa.

With her hair falling in loose curly waves around her shoulders and a carefully straightened-out fringe in front, Laussie looked more like my older sister than my mother. I guessed that's to be expected, as she gave birth to me as a teenager. She was slightly shorter than me, had woman curves that seemed to fill out her black cotton pants. And the cream-colored silk blouse she wore with fancy buttons, screamed money, along with matching stiletto heels.

I always knew from the pictures Grandma showed me that my mom was drop-dead gorgeous, but seeing her in person hit me differently. Every time she smiled, I was torn between going over to hug her, fawning over her like some love-starved street kid or lashing out at her.

"So, how you been?" Grandma placed a frail hand on her daughter's arm, eyes sparkling with a joy I couldn't understand.

"I've definitely not been handed the short end of the stick," Laussie whispered, well aware that I could hear her from where I was seated.

I eyed her up and down. "Grandma didn't you say no wearing shoes in the house? She probably brought in a vagabond spirit," I mumbled.

"JJ, hush up nah," Grandma barked and I put my hands up in defense.

Laussie's mouth was agape but was soon replaced with a smile.

"Momma, I got married to an amazing man after barely a year of meeting him."

"Mhmp." Grandma nodded, eating it right up.

"And it was all in such a rush that the invitations got messed up, somehow. My hands were tied, and I'm sure that I sent one out to you guys. But, it didn't really seem like I had the right to disrupt whatever stability you guys had just because I was getting married. It seemed like a selfish thing to do, and I couldn't bring myself to tell Devin the truth about myself at the time."

I had never seen a more accurate depiction of self-control as a fruit of the spirit. Looking up at Grandma now, it's easy to conclude that she was a true Christian and of the household of faith. I couldn't even get paid to maintain my composure.

From years of loneliness as an only child and constantly wondering what could have been so important and tasking that my mother had abandoned me without as much as a yearly visit, to years of listening to Grandma mention her name in her nightly prayers… It was all too triggering to listen to her talk about it in such a lighthearted manner.

My teeth tug at my lips, almost causing them to bleed. "It sounds like your hands were really tied. Oh, wait, maybe those were the wedding knots, Laussie," I spat out, avoiding eye contact.

"Look, I left 'cause I thought you'd be better off with your grandma. I was trying to do what's best for you. Why am I the only goddamn villain here? Your grandmother's been in contact with your father all these years and ain't done anything to make him take responsibility for his son. Yet somehow it's all on me, Jacky? I was a young adult just like you..."

I tuned out the rest of her words. My gaze bounced back and forth between Grandma and Laussie with confused brows. "My father? Been in contact with who? What do you mean?"

"Okay, stop. Let's take a break," Grandma turned to me.

"No grandma, what is she talking about?" I demanded, folding my arms as I leaned in.

Laussie avoided eye contact, fidgeting with her gold bracelets. "Tell him, Mama," she said in a tone devoid of guilt like she wasn't gonna be the one spilling the beans.

"Listen to me, Jacky," Grandma pleaded. "Your father sent a few letters last year. I didn't think it was necessary to get you all worked up and destroy the progress you had made when he hadn't mentioned anything about whether he wanted to be in your life or not. Then those letters stopped coming, and I realized keeping you away from that messy situation was the right move. I'd do it all over again without a second thought."

In a dazed state, I slumped against the couch, staring off into nothing. "It's like a freaking cult in this house. Secrets everywhere." I let out a shaky breath. "I deserved to know, to decide if I even wanted to meet my father or not. Could've used the knowledge that at least one of my parents gave a damn about me." A lump shifted in my throat. "I could've used a hug or even a letter or one phone call from him. All these years, I thought my pops was either dead, locked up, or had no clue I existed. Nobody ever brought him up. Not one mention."

My heart squeezed tight as they sat there in stunned silence. Or maybe it was guilt that was keeping them quiet.

"I'm sorry, Jacky," Grandma finally spoke up. "I just wanted to protect you. Didn't wanna see you hurtin' any more than you already were." She nodded slowly, her eyes filled with tenderness as they locked onto mine. "That's what everyone says. They didn't wanna hurt me, yet they turn around and do the complete opposite without considering how it'll mess me up in the long run. Miss me with that!" I got up, turned around, and speed walked down the hallway to my room. My heart cramped all the way to the door.

I slammed the door shut and climbed onto the bed, shivering slightly. As I settled in, dragging the covers up to my neck.

A quiet tear slid down my face. I wanted to let it go. I wanted to get the weight off my chest, but I had no idea where to start.

Chapter Thirty-Six: Sidell

The day Dawn delivered me home from school well past the usual hour, my parents were on the brink of freaking out. My ever faithful friend, Dawn shouldered the blame with grace, explaining to my flustered parents that her tardiness in dropping me off was due to her unexpected detention. Her alibi was solid, yet what she didn't know was that JJ and I had been ditching off campus and had merely chanced upon her in the parking lot just as she was leaving. My parents seemed partially convinced by her story, but my father laid down the law - if Dawn were to be delayed again, I was to call him from the school office so he could take me home rather than having me loiter around aimlessly.

Yet even amidst this chaos, my thoughts were consumed by the lingering sensation of JJ's lips on mine - a memory so vivid it felt like an ethereal dream. I struggled to keep my exhilaration under wraps but found myself grinning at everything and nothing in particular. My mother noticed my unusual behavior and began dabbing a cool washcloth on my forehead whenever she found me daydreaming, convinced I was running a fever. If only she knew it wasn't a fever that plagued me, but rather a severe case of lovesickness, my heart running as wild as a stampede.

However, I couldn't let my dad get wind of this. After ironing my school uniform, I started putting away the ironing board in the hallway closet across from his office.

"Sidell, come in here a moment," he called over his glasses.

Taking a deep breath, I fixed my expression into one of nonchalance before turning to face him.

"Yes, Papa?" I asked casually.

Dad sat down his glasses with a click and motioned for me to sit. His face was unreadable. "I need to discuss something with you. I know you're in a hurry for school."

Dawn was probably already waiting for me outside. I stood there in my pajamas, my hair a mess. But Dad's tone left no room for argument.

I plopped into the chair with a huff, avoiding his gaze. "Okay. What is this about?"

He studied me for a moment before speaking. "Sidell, I wanted to apologize."

I snapped to attention. "Apologize? For what?"

"I know I've been...overbearing. And I overstepped with that doctor's appointment."

He fidgeted with his watch, avoiding my eyes. "I'm sorry for not trusting you. I promise I'll do better from now on." He met my eyes pleadingly.

I searched his face, torn between wanting to cling to my anger and feeling it slip away. He looked so sincere, so vulnerable. I realized that underneath his overprotectiveness, he really did love me and want what was best for me.

"I'm sorry," he said again, his voice heavy with emotion. "Can you forgive your foolish old man?"

That did it. I felt the resentment drain away, replaced by empathy. Getting up, I circled his desk and wrapped my arms around him. "Of course, Papa," I murmured into his shoulder. "Thank you for apologizing. It really means a lot."

He hugged me back fiercely. After a moment, he pulled away and ruffled my hair with a small smile. "Make sure to fix your hair first. It looks like a family of birds nested in it."

I swatted his hand away with a laugh. "Oh, ha ha. You're hilarious." But inwardly, I felt lighter than I had in weeks. Things were going to be okay between us after all.

★ ★ ★ ★ ✞ ★ ★ ★ ★

"Hey! Get your butt down here, Sidell! We're running late for school and I won't have you ruining my perfect attendance!"

The sizzle of my flat iron ceased as I turned it off, straining to catch the familiar but distant voice. Is it 8 already? I quickly yanked the cord from the wall. Wrapping it up and tossing it randomly I then bounded down the stairs, nearly tripping in my haste. My heart pounded against my ribs like a caged bird as I skidded into the foyer.

There she was - Dawn, standing there, hands on hip with her legs apart in her perfectly pressed school uniform. As usual, she looked ready to step into a fashion magazine.

"Are you going to keep gawking at me or are we gonna roll?" She asked impatiently, breaking me from my daze. She flounced to the couch and sat next to my sister Cayest, who was watching our exchange with unconcealed amusement. Of course Cayest must have been the one to open the door to let her in.

Mom, who was just washing dishes, bustled in the living room, smiling brightly as she dried her hands on a dish towel. "Dawn, sweetie, so good to see you this beautiful morning!"

Dawn rose to her feet and embraced Mom warmly, as if they were long-lost friends, " So good to see you too, Mrs Evermost." she said with the same measure of happiness.

Mom pulled back then eyed me pointedly. "I've been telling Sidell to get ready all morning, but she refuses to listen."

Dawn smirked, glancing at Mom. "I know, Sid can be a pain in the a-" she paused, faking sheepishness. "Behind. But don't worry, I'll always put her back in line," she said, walking over to me, flinging her arms around my shoulders. "Close your mouth, else, flies will get in." she whispered and I quickly snapped my mouth shut. I heard Cayest giggling at the other end of the living room.

When around my parents, I was cautious over what Dawn might say or do next. She had always been the unpredictable one in our duo - Her speech varies from being a devout christian one minute and lukewarm the next. And I've been to many Bibles to understand what the Bible says, about being hot or cold. And since my dreamy first kiss with JJ, I'm well aware that I've been playing on edge with cold. So I'm praying that all three of us, including Tony, will one day be sold out for the Lord.

"Good morning Papa," Cayest greeted. Dawn and I both turned to see Dad at the edge of the staircase.

"Morning Dochka." he said and to Dawn he said, "Good to see you this morning firecracker."

Dawn batted her eyelashes innocently. "It's always a pleasure, Mr. Evermost."

Dad was dressed up more than usual, though his office was at home. "Are you going somewhere?" I asked.

"Yea, I have a meeting with a client," then he added, "You girls better hurry up or you're gonna be really late." As if on cue, I dashed upstairs to grab my bag, grateful that I had already packed everything I needed.

"Come with me Cayest, I'll drop you off at school."

"Yehhh!" Cayest's eyes lit up at Dad's offer, a treat that rarely happened as she was used to the boring rides on the school bus.

Eight minutes later, Dawn and I rushed out, sandwiches in hand. Mom insisted breakfast was non-negotiable.

"Honestly if you keep driving like this, it'll get you a speeding ticket," I warned, my nails digging into the leather seat as we swerved around another car. I know we were late, but at this rate we'd wrap ourselves around a lamppost before reaching school.

"Yes I know, but I can't afford to miss this test." Dawn insisted.

"There's always a make-up test," I reminded her.

"We both know my teacher Mr. Mattews doesn't give make-up tests." she said reasonably. In Dawn's defense, she believed that Mr. Matthews lived to torture her whenever she dared to arrive late.

We were about three blocks away from school, suddenly, a velvet cadillac shot in front of us, missing our bumper by inches. Dawn slammed the brakes, swearing under her breath as we fishtailed to the shoulder. My heart pounded against my ribs. We could've died, thank God for the seat belt, I could've hit my head on the dashboard.

Dawn threw the car in reverse, stopping it at the side of the road. She rolled down the window as the other driver did the same. He wore a black beanie, and his skin was a light shade of brown. He was too far away to see the color of his eyes, but I could feel the intensity of the gaze. Something about his gaze felt dangerous, threatening. Dawn must have sensed it too.

"Why the hell is he staring at us?" she growled.

I shook my head mutely, unable to tear my eyes away from his. After a tense moment, his gaze released me and he drove on. I let out a shaky breath. "Let's get out of here."

Knowing Dawn, she would have got out of the car and raced towards the driver to cause mayhem.

"That wasn't an accident , Sid," Dawn said. "He swerved at us on purpose." She delved her hand into her hair then turned to look at me. "Do you know that creep?"

"No way!" I said. "I've never seen him before in my life."

Dawn nodded slowly, clearly deep in thought. "We need to talk to the boys about this. I'll bet my limited edition Metallica t-shirt they know something."

By the time we arrived in school, the class was totally forgotten. I couldn't focus, my mind racing with questions. Who had tried to run us off the road? Why would someone want to hurt us? I forcibly made my way through lessons, impatience gnawing at me. The shrill bell was my saving grace. I bolted from my seat, desperate for a quiet place to gather my spiraling thoughts. The bustle of the cafeteria would surely push me over the edge, so I made my way to the silent sanctuary of the library.

While I was in the library, skimming through the bookshelves, I happened to see JJ on one of the empty aisles. The whole place was quiet but his presence seemed louder than the bellow of a trumpet. I was so attuned to him that it was scary, it scared me. JJ was dressed in our casual green and silver school uniform, with his trademark neon pink, backwards cap atop his head. I couldn't wait for him to notice me, but he seemed distant and lost in thought, staring blankly at an opened book as if it held all the secrets of the universe. With an exasperated sigh, he slammed the book shut and shoved it back on the shelf, his mind clearly somewhere far away from this vast selection of literature.

Sensing a storm brewing inside him, I steeled my nerves and grabbed ahold of his hand, determined to ease whatever was tormenting him. After what seemed like a lifetime, JJ released a heavy breath. He bowed his head, squeezing our intertwined fingers even harder.

"What on earth happened to get you in this mood, JJ? Talk to me," I implored, watching how his small silver earring sway like a hypnotist's pendulum."Are you hurt somewhere?"

He turned to face me as I stood in front of him. His voice cracked badly when he started speaking, "Just in my heart," he said shakily. "M-my mom, who abandoned me when I was five..She came a-around me and my grandma's apartment yesterday and . . . we h-had a f-fight which led to me finding out that my d-dad is alive and not dead like I'd believed."

I wrapped my arms around him, clutching him till I felt his body heat through his shirt, alongside the thumping of his heart. After growing up in the church nearly all my life, I knew the right words to comfort those who were grieving. But even without being told, I knew there were no words to say to JJ that would make him feel better.

Instead of searching for the right words, I rubbed his neck, down to his back, massaging in deep, circular motions. "Shhh . . . I can't promise you that it is going to be fine, JJ, I just want to remind you that God's got you. And he's going to be with you through it all."

He broke away and peered into my eyes. His eyes were swimming with tears and sorrow. "There is nothing I can do about her presence in our home, Sid. My grandma has made it pretty clear that she is accepted and forgiven, as if it's that simple. I don't care what anyone says, but I'm not forgiving her. That's the last thing I'll do. All those years, Sid. All those years and not a single acknowledgment from the woman that birthed me?"

JJ sagged his shoulders as he leaned against the shelves. "I don't know if they expect me to hold onto her, begging for her attention. I'm past the point when I could have bonded with her like other kids do, so what's the point now? What's the point anymore?" A harsh laugh tumbled from his throat. "Oh yes, let's skip over to the park together and ride the carousel to make up for lost time. God knows how desperate I was to have her in my life. Praying that Laussie would send a card on my birthday. Something. Anything to know she cared. But nothing. And if her returning is God's way of answering those prayers, then he should take it back or something. I'm over this already."

A sad smile lined my lips. Amidst JJ's rant, I found God's plan buried in the obvious. I took a step closer, my gaze not leaving him. He was unlikely to entertain what I had to say next.

"Well, I have to admit, you are sure handling this better than I would have," I said, drawing JJ's gaze to myself. "But I have a gut feeling that there is a purpose to all of this that God wants you to fulfill. So what are you going to do about it?"

"Do about what, Sidell? I don't see options lining up–"

"No," I emphasized, cutting in before he could finish, "you do have options, JJ. Are you doing this God's way, or are you sticking to your way? What are you going to do about God's will? Are you going to trust him enough to let him lead — "

"How do you even know what's God's will in this situation?" he shot back, fury blazing in his eyes. "It's easy to say all of that because you're not the one wearing the shoes."

"It's written in his word, JJ." I said, trying to recall a bible verse that'll be helpful in this situation "Okay, so there's this verse," I began eagerly, "It's from Matthew 18:21-22, and it says: '*Then Peter came to Jesus and asked, Lord, how many times shall I forgive my brother or sister who sins against me? Up to seven times? Jesus answered. I tell you, not seven times but seventy-seven times.*'"

"I'm pretty sure that Jesus did not envision the sin of a mother abandoning her own child when he said that," JJ said, his voice as hard as his eyes.

"Oh! And there's another verse uh…" I muttered quietly, as if waiting for permission from him. I was met with silence, so I went ahead and recited it. "The book of Mark 11:25 says: '*And when you stand praying, if you hold anything against anyone, forgive them, so that your father in heaven may forgive you your sins.*'"

JJ abrubtly turned away before strolling to the other end of the room, as if he was desperate to get away from the verses. I was hurting for him, but I couldn't bring myself to stand there in silence. I had no idea why, but I felt the urge to speak to him about forgiveness.

"JJ, God wants you to cast down that burden. You've been carrying it for too long. Jesus cares for you, and that's why he wants you to hand it over to him."

"She is not even remorseful about any of it. Telling me about how it was in my best interests." JJ squinted.

I inched towards him with my hands on my hips. "She was wrong for it, yes. But all we humans have turned against God one time or the other. And if God did mark iniquities, none of us would stand before him. God saw the gravity of what she did, and still, he wants you to forgive her. Not because she deserves it, but because he did it for you and wants you to repay that favor to the next person. That's why he brought her back into your life."

"I don't have to stand here and listen to this." JJ took large strides out of the aisle and in the direction of the double doors. I moved after him but stopped in the middle of the walkway. I figured that maybe it'd be best to leave him alone.

And when JJ realized that I wasn't chasing after him, he grounded to a stop at the door, sucker-punched by the reality of the situation. He hung his head, fists folded tightly by his sides. He spun on his heel, heading back in my direction. "I've heard everything you said. None of it was lost on me, Sidell." He said apologetically. " I just need time and space to deal with it. Is that okay?"

I nodded understandingly. "Of course."

"There you are," Dawn's loud voice announced from the entrance of the doorway. A girl at the nearby table shot her a scornful glare and whispered "Shush!" but Dawn just rolled her eyes and flipped her off, not giving a care about anyone else's discomfort.

The girl huffed, snapped her book shut, and stomped off to the farthest corner of the library. I sighed. Dawn was clearly in the wrong, but subtlety had never been her strong suit.

She sauntered up to us, chains on her green uniform skirt clinking like windchimes. Tony trailed behind, avoiding eye contact with disapproving glares from other students.

"Guys, we need to talk, now." Dawn announced in her usual loud manner.

I reluctantly followed, wishing she could tone it down a bit. JJ too was, annoyed that our alone session was clearly over.

Our footsteps echoed urgently on the marble floors as Dawn led us out of the library, moving with purpose. We made our way to the secluded sitting area near the brick building, currently empty, giving us some privacy. The cold from the stone benches seeped through my clothes as we took our seats.

Dawn clasped her hands dramatically as she looked at Tony and then JJ, "Sidell and I were almost hit this morning and I'm 99.9% sure it wasn't an accident." She paused, gauging their reactions.

"What?" JJ thundered, right on cue.

"Who was it?" Tony asked through gritted teeth, his protective instincts in overdrive. It was a tad hilarious that they didn't question whether Dawn was driving recklessly. Blind loyalty at its finest.

"I don't know, really. But we know it was a warning."

JJ and Tony exchanged knowing looks, a silent conversation passing between them. "That weirdo," Tony finally cursed, turning away as his hands curled into fists.

"Did you see his face?" JJ asked, all business now.

"Yes I did," I answered nervously. I tried my best to describe the man I'd briefly glimpsed, my voice shaking slightly. By the time I was done, it appeared they both knew who the person was and they both wore a calm glance.

"Yo check it, this is what we will do now," JJ said, looking at us with an air of authority. "Be careful when walking down the hallways, try as much as possible not to walk alone."

"Is someone at this school after us?" I asked in a small voice.

"You remember when I fought Khyree? "

My skepticism deepened. Surely he wasn't connected to this somehow? "Yes..." I said slowly.

"Well, his cousin Rayo sent a message to my apartment the other day, I guess to threaten me? And when I saw him at the laundry mat in my complex, I was gonna confront him about it. I knew they were up to some shady business, but-"

"What kind of shady business?" I asked.

"JJ said they had guns, and are gang affiliated. " Tony offered.

"What??!" Dawn and I said in unison.

JJ nodded shamelessly. Dawn punched Tony's shoulder hard, "Ow! What was that for?"

"What is wrong with your blockhead friend over here?" Dawn fumed at Tony, flinging her arm furiously in JJ's direction. "Fighting a gang member's cousin?"

"Hey I'm just finding all this out too!" Tony said defensively.

Dawn rolled her eyes then looked at JJ, "You can't obviously expect us to start tiptoeing around the school because we are scared someone might harm us," she said impatiently. Fear and anger warred within her, but she refused to show weakness.

"Just be careful, Dawn, don't ditch class without me," Tony said, still rubbing his sore arm.

Dawn exploded. "I heard you quite clearly, but I want to know why Khyree is sending his thug cousin after us." She gestured wildly between me and her. "JJ's the one who beat him up!"

I cringed, glancing around the empty area nervously. "Dawn, shhh, keep your voice down!"

Dawn whirled on me. "We could have died today, Sidell! All because your rageaholic boyfriend can't control himself and picks fights with anyone who looks at him funny."

Before I could respond, Tony stepped in. "It's alright, Dawn. Let's all just take a deep breath."

Dawn clamped her mouth shut, but I could tell her rant wasn't over yet. JJ furrowed his brow, deep in thought. "Just give me some time. I'll figure this out and keep you girls safe."

I wanted to believe him, I really did. But it was hard to trust JJ's methods, which tended to involve fists and fury.

"I think we need to get going, we have another class in a few minutes," I said hurriedly, wanting to escape the tension hanging thick in the air. I sped walked across the grassy field, the wind whipping my hair and uniform skirt.

"Sidell, hold up," JJ shouted. I halted reluctantly, every muscle tense. JJ sauntered over, I crossed my arms protectively across my chest.

"What now?" I asked tightly, unable to keep the annoyance out of my tone.

JJ just smiled, and eyed me head to toe. "You mad at me?

"Don't turn this into something about us," I shot back, my voice sharp. "This is serious, JJ. People could get hurt."

He took a step closer, his smile fading into a more solemn expression. "I know it's serious. I'm not taking it lightly, Sidell. But I'm also not gonna let some wannabe gangsters push me or any of my friends around."

I sighed heavily, the worry gnawing at my insides. "But what if they're not just wannabes? What if they really are dangerous?"

"They probably are," JJ admitted with a shrug that tried to seem nonchalant but didn't quite succeed. "Which is why I'm gonna handle it."

"How are you going to handle it? You're just a high schooler, JJ—not some action hero."

JJ straightened up, and despite the situation, a chuckle escaped him. "You'd be surprised how resourceful I can be when it comes to protecting people close to me." His confidence was reassuring and maddening all at once.

I shook my head, the tension between concern and skepticism pulling at me. "And what kind of connections are those? More people we should be afraid of?"

JJ took a hold of my hand, looking into my eyes with a seriousness that was rare for him. "Trust me, Sidell. I'm not gonna let anything happen to you or Dawn or anyone else. This is my problem, and I'll fix it."

As much as I wanted to believe him, the fear still lingered like a shadow at the back of my thoughts. His world—the fights, the threats—was seeping into mine now, and I wasn't sure how to stop it.

"We need to tell someone," I insisted, breaking away from his hold. "The police, the school—"

"No cops," he cut me off firmly. "You think they can protect us from this? They'd make things worse."

"But—"

"Sidell," JJ said with finality in his tone, "let me handle it. Promise me you won't go to the cops or make this bigger than it needs to be."

I looked at him for a long moment, weighing the options that seemed equally dangerous. Finally, I nodded slowly.

"Okay," I said reluctantly. "But JJ... please be careful."

He gave me a confident grin that didn't entirely ease my fears but had always been his way of assuring me things would be fine.

"Don't worry about me," he said before turning and heading back towards the school building.

But as I watched him walk away, his back straight and sure against the world's troubles, I couldn't shake the feeling that we were all walking on a very thin line between normalcy and chaos. It was just a feeling in my gut that things were about to unravel.

Chapter Thirty-Seven:
♉

After getting punked by his girl Dawn, Tony made it clear to me that he couldn't help me because she fears for his life. But I wasn't tripping. As a true friend, I knew Tony didn't have the guts or fists to back up his trash talk. So anticipating his flakiness, I had a backup ready to go.

The shrill bell rang out, but the classroom remained a mess of chaos. I was practically vibrating in my seat trying to get El-Train's attention. We usually talked briefly in the halls, but outside of that, conversation was dead. But, desperate times call for desperate measures. With all the mess I've gotten into, I'm willing to rekindle this old friendship.

I already told El-Train about Rayo and his boys being out for my blood before class started. Made it real clear I need his help. Now I just gotta seal the deal.

I slouched in the hard plastic chair, my gaze shifting between Mr. Auclair scribbling vocab on the board and the clock ticking above the heavy classroom door. Sweat gathered at the base of my spine, a slow burn that had nothing to do with the stuffiness of the classroom and everything to do with the time slipping away.

El-Train sat next to me, lazily spinning a pen between his fingers. He didn't get it, the urgency pulsing through me. I glanced at the clock again. Forty-five minutes left. Rayo wouldn't wait forever, and neither would the street code we lived by.

"Psst." My voice was barely a whisper over the whirring classroom fan. El-Train didn't budge. I shot another look at the clock. Forty-four minutes. Damn.

"El-Train," I murmured, sharper now. My hand snuck beneath the desk and tugged at his sleeve. His eyes flicked to mine, all casual swagger and half-interest. He leaned back in his seat like he hadn't a care in the world, but I could see the edges of tension in the set of his shoulders.

"Man, what?" he whispered, finally leaning in. His breath carried a hint of mint gum.

I nodded up at the clock again.

His gaze followed my gesture, and for a second, I hoped he'd catch on without me having to spell it out. The second hand ticked steadily, each movement a reminder of the tightrope we walked on the streets outside. Every moment we spent in the supposed safety of these four walls, the outside world kept moving, kept plotting.

"Time's running, man," I said, voice barely above a whisper. "We gotta move, gotta plan."

"Alright, partner up for next week's assignment," Mr. Auclair announced. El-Train dropped his pen and straightened up at the instruction as he looked around with a goofy grin.

"Yo, E? Be my partner?" I insisted. My gaze flicked back to the clock—more minutes slipped away like sand through fingers. "We gotta lock this down tight. Need someone solid at my six, bro."

El-Train was already turned sideways in his desk, clearly about to partner up with our classmate Tayah. I could barely hear Tayah's annoyed huff as El-Train turned his head back to look at me, "Man, I ain't got time for that now," he muttered, nudging his head towards her. "You know how it is."

"Come on, man." I huffed. "This ain't 'bout chasing skirts. We need a plan, a real one."

He glanced at me then, a brief flicker. There was a storm behind those eyes—a mix between two decisions. Tayah always had that effect on him, like she could blind him to the crumbling world around us.

He leaned close to me and whispered, "J, man, I hear you," he sighed, half-distracted, "but Tayah... she's something else. Gotta see where that goes, you feel me?"

Without another word, I slid my backpack off my shoulder and onto the scratched linoleum floor. The classroom hummed with the voice of the teacher's further instructions, but in our corner, a different kind of education was unfolding.

"Look, man," I started, unzipping the bag and reaching inside. "I need to know you're all in on this."

My fingers brushed against the edges of plastic bricks, the remnants of childhood dreams and simpler times. Lego blocks—the currency of our innocence. I pulled out a Millennium Falcon, its gray pieces still clinging together despite the years.

"Remember this?" I said, placing it on his open textbook. A symbol of countless hours spent side by side on bedroom floors, worlds away from the streets that now demanded our grit.

El-Train's brows raised as a smile played on his lips. "Man, you really gonna play the nostalgia card?"

"It ain't just about nostalgia," I countered, leaning in even closer. "It's about what we gotta do. This is part of the deal."

"JJ, you serious?" He picked up the Falcon, his fingers tracing the edges we once built together. "You'd give up your Legos for... what? For me to watch your back?"

"More than that," I said firmly. "For us to watch each other's backs."

El-Train held the Falcon like a fragile relic of a forgotten temple, a testament to a brotherhood that had been unshakeable before life got too real. He rubbed the back of his neck, the memories flooding back to him too, I could tell. He glanced around the classroom, making sure no one was eavesdropping on us.

"JJ..." he began, then stopped, his gaze flicking between the Lego spaceship and my expectant face. "Tayah's fine, man. You know she and I got... chemistry."

"Me and Sidell got Chemistry, but it won't be worth anything if we ain't around to enjoy it," I shot back. "I'm on borrowed time, E. And you know who's collecting."

"Damn," he breathed out, setting the Millennium Falcon down. His eyes met mine, and I saw the conflict raging within him. The weight of decisions that could alter everything.

"Think about it," I urged, the tightness in my chest loosening just a bit. "This is bigger than hookups and high school drama. This is my life, bro. My girl's life."

He was quiet for a long stretch, the seconds ticking by like hours. Then, he exhaled, slow and deep, as if letting go of something heavy. "Alright, man. Whatever," he finally breathed out, and I smiled in relief.

"Sorry Tayah, but JJ's already my partner."

"What the heck El-Roy?" Tayah snapped, kicking him in the shins.

"Tayah, do I need to give you another demerit?" Mr. Auclair snapped. As Tayah offered up a half-apology, El Train went up to move closer to me.

"Good lookin' out," I said, stuffing the spaceship back into my bag.

"I'm with you. But this better be worth missing my shot with Tayah." he said.

"Trust, it is." I leaned back in my seat, a silent thank you hanging between us.

Once everyone shuffled around the classroom and settled with their chosen partners, Mr. Auclair. busied himself grading at his computer. Our peers murmured amongst their groups, halfheartedly brainstorming the assignment. Meanwhile, El-Train and I huddled in the back corner, heads together, voices low.

"We gotta be smart about this, man. Timing's everything."

"Right, right," he nodded, his eyes scanning the room to ensure no prying ears were eavesdropping. "So, what's the play?"

"Rayo's crew hangs at the courts after the street lights come on, right?" I started sketching out a rough map of the apartment complex on the class assignment paper. "We'll blend in, act like we're just there for a game."

"Courts get crowded. Could work to our advantage." El-Train traced the perimeter of the basketball courts with his finger, his brow furrowed in thought.

"Exactly. But once Rayo shows up, we need a spot that's outta sight. Behind the rec center." I pointed to an area shaded by overhanging trees—a blind spot from the main street.

"Back there, though... it could go south real quick, JJ," he warned, his voice dropping lower. The gravity of our plan weighed heavily between us.

"Only if we don't handle our business fast. In and out, E. We talk sense into Rayo or...." I paused to really think about it. "You know what? You right. We can try the courts. But we can't roll deep. Too much attention."

" Just you and me?" He looked up, searching my face for confirmation.

"Less is more. And we look out for each other—no hero stuff, El-Train." My gaze was firm, locking onto his.

"Bet. No heroes, just brothers." He nodded, understanding the stakes.

We sat back as the final bell rang, the sea of students around us oblivious to the silent pact we'd just made. Our chairs scraped the floor in unison as we stood, the fading chatter of the classroom giving way to a tense silence that only we seemed to feel.

"Tommorow night," I murmured as we shuffled toward the door.

"Tommorow night," El-Train echoed, his voice barely audible.

There was no turning back now. We stepped into the hallway, the noise of the school day enveloping us, but it was like we were moving in a different world.

As we made our way through the throngs of students, their laughter and shouts fading into the background, I looked back at El-Train down the hall, and our eyes locked—a silent conversation passing between us. In that glance, there was fear, uncertainty, but above all, determination. We were in this together, come hell or high water.

★ ★ ★ ★ ✞ ★ ★ ★ ★

Tony dropped me off and I kept staring at my phone. Dawn said she'd call when she and Sidell got home safely. And here I was being an overprotective mess, fixated on Sidell's wellbeing like a deranged stalker. She probably wouldn't go home for hours, and I would still be wide awake, waiting.

I fished my keys out of my sneakers and unlocked the apartment door. The lock clicked and I shuffled inside. And immediately I saw my grandma sitting at the dinner table entranced in a conversation with Laussie. I quickly and quietly tried to speed walk to my room, pretending I didn't see them. But with one swift movement, I stubbed my toe on something and an excruciating pain shot through, reminding me how impossible such simple actions could be when you live in such a crammed two bedroom apartment. My cover blown, I submitted myself to my fate as Grandma stood up from the table. My estranged mother was slinking behind her like a shadow. Our eyes locked and pride lodged itself firmly in my throat. A clearing cough erupted from deep within me as I tried to break the silence.

"Can I at least change out of my uniform, for God's sake?" I mumbled to myself, tossing my backpack to emphasize my point. "I don't have the strength to go through any of this drama anymore."

"You better stay on guard, boy." Grandma said sternly, sending shivers down my spine. "Don't you start this mess." Her lips pursed together as she adopted a defensive posture.

My temper flared within me and I swallowed, resisting the urge to snap back at her. My gaze then flicked momentarily in my mom's direction as she sailed from the kitchen to the living room area and took a seat on the couch. I quickly looked away, not wanting to pass the wrong message to her. I had clearly been fine with the way things were going until the both of them had insisted on this ill-timed family reunion.

I headed straight to my room, changed into my pajamas and fell onto my bed. Even though I was on a journey of healing, I'd gone to great lengths to dodge my mom and any chance encounters. I think I was scared to face her and I don't know why.

The door to my hideout creaked open, catching me off guard. I scrambled on my mattress trying to reach for my rubix cube on my dresser. Grabbing it, I started twisting it like I'm deep in thought, hoping to avoid Grandma's gaze. She planted herself firmly at the doorway, her eyes held an intensity I couldn't escape from.

"We need to talk, JJ," her voice trembled slightly, hinting at an underlying concern. "Come meet me in my room."

My eyes meet hers for a split second before darting back to the colorful cube. I swallowed hard as I gathered my courage. "All right— I'll be out in a minute."

As she shut the door behind her, my heart plummeted at the same pace as my sinking stomach. I tossed the toy cube then snatched my phone off the bed, grateful that this conversation was going to be over soon.

"How are you feeling now?" she asked as I slowly dragged my sock covered feet across her carpeted bedroom room. I gave her a slight shrug, settling on the bed with my phone in my lap. I was itching to turn it over and send Sidell a quick message, until I remembered that her phone was still under her parents wraps. Lately, Sidell had been the only thing that has stood between my raging mood swings and the JJ everyone else was used to.

"Nothing that a few hundred-mile distance between me and Laussie won't cure." I yawned.

"It is beyond time for us to forgive and forget whatever your mother did to us both and for her to forgive and forget whatever we've done to her as well. Heck, even your father needs to put this mess behind him."

I refused to speak, to move or even blink. Instead, I just stared at Grandma like she had dropped from another universe. Her chin rose, tilting at me as she continued.

"Boy, listen here. Your mother's took the time out of her day to come around here, she didn't have to do that. Don't you be disrespecting her no matter what your feeling is, now ya hear?"

My breath hitched in my throat. I sat rigid, my gaze unwavering. "Nahhh," I said, "I can't do that, Grandma, no matter how much I wanna let it all go.

It ain't about Laussie deserving anything, it's just that I want to find peace again. But how do you really break away from years of hurt? The best I can do is respect her enough to remove myself from her life instead of antagonizing her. Forgiveness and understanding, was something I couldn't even begin to picture. Especially when you know if the other person wished to be a part of your life, then they would have been.

"You're going to have to try harder, JJ." Grandma said.

"Why?" I grunted. "Why is she here now?"

Grandma hiked a brow. "Why? Because she is your momma and my daughter. We can't turn her away, JJ. Family is family, even when it is hard. And if she retraces her steps back to us it's because she needs us. Ain't nothin' else to it."

"No," I bit out. "Why is she here now? What is her ulterior motive?"

Her gaze narrowed, her wrinkled forehead deep in contemplation. "Child, I thought you knew better than this. We all make mistakes and we all deserve the grace to learn from them. You already got your second chance; show that young lady the same mercy — ain't nothin' more disrespectful I can think of than rudeness, no matter how it comes out your mouth or what you do with your hands." She dropped her chin and studied me, sternly, before adding a gentle, "You know I'm right, JJ. That's the least you can do for her."

I studied her face and whispered. "What do you want me to do now?"

Her gaze locked into place the words that were coming out of her mouth. "She needs closure, and so do you. God knows, we all need each other now more than ever. It's been long overdue, and I don't have a lot of time left."

I sighed heavily and lowered my head, hiding my moist eyes that wandered to the floor's carpet. "This is the absolute last thing I want to do, Grandma." I whispered. "Open up all these wounds that I worked so hard to heal. My mind isn't in the space to move forward without almost losing my entire belief system,"

"Maybe this is God's way of restoring your faith, baby. Sometimes we gotta confront our fears head-on to find peace and mercy in His love."

I lifted my head and she locked eyes with me, and I held her gaze..

"I ain't askin' much of you, JJ." She said, "Just do this one thing for me. Then you are free to go off and do whatever you want. Understand?" She said before exiting the room.

Massaging my forehead with my fingers, I sighed as I pushed myself off of her bed, ready to join her and face the woman in the living room.

Tilting my jaw, I stared down my mom as I sat on the opposite couch from her, determined to make it as difficult for her as I could. Grandma was sitting in her recliner chair, watching me warily of my response.

"If we're gonna talk," I began slowly, punctuating each word, "then it's going to be on my own terms. The first is that we're going to do that alone. And everything that transpires between us stays undisclosed...unless I say otherwise."

I could see the hesitation dancing in Laussie's eyes, the speed of her blinking doubling up. "Your grandma is still my mom, JJ. We're family, and sometimes I need her advice," she muttered, and it took everything in me not to push myself off this couch and into my room like I'd done before now.

Grandma's voice trembled just a touch. "Is that all it takes for you two to have a conversation? Me stepping out of the room?"

I lifted an eyebrow. "It's a good start."

Grandma got up and headed over to my mother's side, leaning in close to whisper something barely audible. I watched my mom's face as her eyes welled up, and then she locked gazes with me.

Once Grandma was done, straightening her back like a soldier ready for battle, she turned to face me. "I guess this is the moment we've all been praying for. I don't think it gets any easier than this." She made her way to me where I was seated. "Just remember to show the same grace you expect from others, JJ."

"Yep," I replied tightly.

My mom didn't budge from her spot even as Grandma made her exit. Her whole body shook with emotion, sniffling louder than necessary for my liking.

"Listen up, Laussie," I said as soon as I heard grandma's bedroom door click down the hall. "I'm only doing this for her. Just for Grandma, and no one else. So let's get it over with, pronto."

This time, my mom met my gaze, her lips trembling like my heart beating against those ribs.

"No, JJ. It's no longer about your grandma. You're doing this because I agreed to your terms. If it was about my mother, she would have remained in the room with us."

I shrugged carelessly, letting my eyes settle on the plain white walls. "Then it's best you get started, lady. I don't have a lot of time."

Her face twisted into a scowl as she rose from the chair, pushing it closer to the bed. My eyes involuntarily followed her moves, wondering where this was going and impatiently waiting to serve up that disdain I'd been brewing.

She had hit me hard by being absent, leaving me vulnerable to all those "Yo Mama" jokes as a kid. Easier to ignore then 'cause I wasn't one of those kids they were aiming at. But then we crossed paths in the school hallways and church restrooms, and she messed up my whole life by ditching me right before her wedding. Like I didn't even matter. She knew better — knew how jacked up that was but went along with it anyway. And now she had the audacity to show up at my doorstep unannounced, blaming some sperm donor I never even met for not being any better than she was. Like it was some damn excuse. My gut twisted with fury.

When my mom had come back into our lives, Grandma had gone along with it as though it was an answer to her prayers, but I was too carnal to let that fly, insisting on making her pay. Guilt churned in my belly. It went against all I'd been taught in Sunday school. It went against the love of Christ that I was experiencing all over again. I should do better. Not for anyone's sake but because God wanted me to.

I watched Laussie get comfortable, shedding her coat and draping it on the back of the couch. As she settled, she leaned her arm on the armrest, cheek propped against her fist. Her eyes closed shut, "So... where do we begin, Son?" she asked, her voice thick with curiosity. "You actually wanna have a grown-up conversation? Or you gonna act all childish and list every damn reason why I ain't allowed to call you that?"

I scoffed. "I wouldn't be wrong either. We don't have that kind of relationship, and I'd be hurting myself even more by agreeing to it. Being my mother involves a whole lot more just popping me out."

"See? Look what you're doing Jacky? — I'm going out of my way to step up and fill in that gap, try my best to catch up on what I've missed, but you won't even give me that chance."

"It's not given. It's earned," I whispered furiously, my gaze dropping to her face.

"How do I even start earning that when you won't even let me walk through the front door? When you do everything to make sure that we're not in the same space at any period of time?"

My eyes shuttered closed, the tears made war against my eyelids, burning till I could no longer hold them back. "Why then?" My voice cracked, which was humiliating - she was never supposed to hold this kind of power over me.

"Jacky—"

"Why did you leave me?"

"I - I didn't—"

"Why would you do that to me, Mom?"

"Because I was lost back then," she blurted out. "Okay? I was continually making a mess of every single thing. I blamed and bled into others since it was easier than admitting I was wrong and had made more than a few bad decisions." She sighed, trembling slightly. "It was all me and had nothing to do with you, JJ. There was no way I could let you be a part of that life. I was so afraid. I had to learn and catch myself each time I stumbled. You did not fit in with me."

"What do you mean I did not fit in? I was your child. Children belong with their parents!"

"I want you to know that I tried," she emphasized. "Nothing could have prepared me for the responsibilities that followed conception at that age, JJ,

and I took the only other option open to me, and I'm sorry. I can't find the words to explain how sorry I am. I might have taken some bad turns, but I don't regret having you." Mom let out a shaky sigh. "I'd like to try this thing all over again," she whispered.

Wiping the tears from my face, I struggled to put my defenses back up before she had the chance to sneak into my head and heart. "How do you plan to go about that?"

She pushed herself up from the couch, then slid her purse on her shoulder.

"I've made reservations for dinner at Amethyst's Hall for four. We could start by getting to know each other better over buttermilk-fried quail or even seafood. We can even have milk ice cream for dessert or any other thing you want, of course."

I raised my brows. "Dinner reservations? You think all those meals you've mentioned will make up for abandoning me?"

"Goodness! Of course not." Her palms shot up. "No, I don't think so, JJ. I just want us to have quiet, hearty conversations, get to meet each other and introduce you to my husband, and I can't think of a more perfect occasion than dinner."

Silently, I stared at her while giving it much thought. Involuntarily, my lips curled into a smile, "Make it five seats, and you have a deal," I said simply.

"It's the least you could do, considering how long you've been away."

I hadn't realized this had been such a big deal to her until she let out a relieved sigh. She bended forward, hiding her face behind her hands as tears leaked out of her eyes.

I looked away, opened my water bottle, and took a sip. I must admit that I was a bit prideful as hope bloomed in my heart.

Straightening her posture again she clasped her hands together and nodded, "That works, too." she sniffed. "Look, JJ, I'd give anything to go back to the start and fix all of my mistakes. Every single one of them."

"Dinner at Amethyst Hall then, five o'clock? Do we have to dress up or something?" I asked, recapping my water bottle.

Chapter Thirty-Eight: Sidell

Dawn made sure of it that me and her boyfriend stayed out of the way to let JJ handle it. In her words, this whole mess was my boyfriend's fault anyway. But I wasn't sure what JJ's plan of handling it was going to be. I already knew that he had a bad temper and knowing that these guys that he was trying to confront had guns, made me worried. It was a bad sign. JJ could get himself killed. It was nerve-wracking, conjuring all the possibilities in my mind. My flip flops smacked against the hallway floor as I ran from my bedroom to my little sister's room. She was lying in bed, her cellphone blocking her vision from me. Her legs stretched out on the sheets below her as one of her hands combed through her brown wavy hair. My entrance startled her.

"What is it, Sidell?" she asked. Not once did she lower the phone to look at me.

"I need to talk to you about something." I said, closing the door behind me. The desperation for eye contact was unavoidable. I wished she would lay down the phone and notice me properly.

"Tell me, what is it?" Cayest said emotionlessly. I knew this wasn't the best way to get advice from her but I couldn't help myself; I continued to rely on her for validation despite knowing things wouldn't go any further with us.

"No Caye, first promise you won't tell Mama or Papa. Please?" I held out my pinky, giving her my most pleading look.

She rolled her eyes but linked her pinky with mine. "Fine, обещание на мизинце. Happy?"

"Thrilled," I said flatly. I sighed, slightly relieved she'd promised but knowing my little sister, her promises didn't mean much if she decided it was for your own good. Still, it was a risk I had to take. I sat at the edge of her bed, the too sweet scent of her strawberry shampoo filling my senses.

"You remember my friend JJ?" I asked.

"Ooo Sidell." She said, drawing out my name. "I thought Mama and Papa said you can't be around him anymore?"

"Caye, stop it. You swore on it." I warned.

"Okay, okay," Cayest relented, her demeanor shifting to a more attentive one. "What about him?"

I took a deep breath, letting the air seep out slowly before I answered. "He's in some trouble—big trouble. And he's being... stubborn about it."

Cayest tilted her head, concern etching her features. "Trouble? What kind of trouble?"

"There are these boys at our school involved with a gang. They're threatening JJ. He thinks he can handle them alone, but… I'm scared he's going to get hurt… or worse."

Her expression turned serious. "What are you going to do? You can't get involved with that kind of stuff, Sidell. It's dangerous."

"I know, but I can't just sit back and do nothing either. I love him, Caye."

She sat in silence for a long while, staring at the patterns of her blanket. Then her brown eyes met mine again.

"I don't know what to say, Sidell. I'm scared and I want to tell Papa-"

"Just forget I even said anything Caye." I said, standing abruptly, my heart pounding in my chest. "I'll figure it out on my own."

I stormed out of her room, leaving the door open.

I stormed out, leaving the door wide open. I knew I shouldn't have told her. She'd just want to run and tattle to our parents like always. But I really thought we'd grown closer? My own sister didn't understand me at all.

Chapter Thirty-Nine:
ψψ

The cracked concrete radiated heat like a furnace beneath my sneakers as I dribbled the basketball halfheartedly. This late at night, the rhythmic pounding of the ball was the only sound piercing the heavy silence. El-Train shuffled beside me, scuffing his feet along the blacktop. We both knew this game was just a front.

My t-shirt clung to my back as nerves twisted my stomach into knots. I bounced the ball harder, trying to ignore the panic rising in my chest. What were we doing here, trying to take on Rayo and his boys by ourselves? We didn't stand a chance against their guns and knives. Sweat dripped down my temples. I should've just walked away, kept Sidell out of this mess. But I couldn't back down now.

"Here they come," El-Train muttered under his breath. I followed his gaze to see three figures emerging from the shadows. Rayo led the pack, sauntering onto the court with his chest puffed out. The other two goons, Smurf and Juice, flanked him on either side.

Rayo's greasy curly hair hung in his eyes, but the smug look on his face was unmistakable. "Well, well," he sneered, "looks like we got a couple of trespassers on our turf."

I squeezed the basketball tightly, willing myself to stay calm. "This ain't your turf, Rayo. It's a free court."

Rayo barked out a harsh laugh. "Free? Nah, everything round here belongs to us. Only a matter of time before you and your little friends fall in line too."

The shadow of the night sky passed over his light brown as he stepped closer to me. His eyebrow scar became evident under lights that surrounded the court. Planting his feet directly in front of me, he eyed me up and down like I was a roach he wanted to crush under his shoe. "So I heard you roughed up my cousin Khyree. Over some white girl."

At the mention of Sidell, rage boiled up inside me. "Don't talk about her like that." I warned through gritted teeth.

"Ooh, look who's getting all protective over his little snowflake," Rayo sneered, his lips curling in a vicious grin."And what if I do?" He took a step closer, his cronies chuckling behind him.

In the back of my mind, I knew I should keep my cool, but he was pushing all my buttons.

I met his glare with steely resolve. "Then we're going to have a problem,"

Rayo laughed to himself, "I kinda see why she like you. 'Cause you're a little soft with her." He air quoted mockingly. "But I know she likes it rough." He leaned in close, his rancid breath hot on my face. "Maybe I oughta show her what a real man can do."

That was it. Before I even realized what I was doing, my fist collided with his jaw. Rayo stumbled back, shock written across his ugly mug. In that split second, I felt a savage thrill of satisfaction. No one threatened my girl and got away with it.

Then everything descended into chaos. Smurf and Juice rushed at us, their fists flying. I ducked and wove, channeling all my pent-up rage into my punches. The sounds of fists hitting flesh and grunts filled the air, but somehow, we were holding our own against them.

But then in an instant guns were pulled out and it was no longer a far fight.

I glanced at El-Train, who had a gun to his head too. He met my eyes and gave a slight nod. My hands clenched into fists.

"Yeah, you thought you was big stuff, huh playboy?" Rayo taunted.

We'd gotten out of worse scrapes than this before, but the cold steel against my forehead made my knees weak. I wasn't about to let Rayo win, not without a fight. But what could I even do?

My eyes clenched shut as the sound of the safeties clicking off echoed in my ears like a countdown to our execution. Heart pounding in my chest, I thought about Grandma, Sidell, and even Laussie - the three women I dared to care about who I might never see again if this went south. I couldn't let that happen. Desperate, my thoughts suddenly spiraled into a prayer, "God, I know we haven't talked much lately, but I'm scared as hell right now. You can't let me die. Call me stubborn, but I know you're not finished with me yet."

At that precise moment, the night air was split by a high-pitched voice. "Y'all better back off from my big brother, or I'mma tell every body in this whole neighborhood what you did!" Kaluna, my energetic and often-annoying 8-year-old neighbor, stood at the edge of the court with her hands on her hips. Her two braided ponytails with beads shook as she stomped her foot for emphasis.

"Kaluna, get out of here!" I yelled, my heart pounding even more at the thought of her getting caught in the crossfire.

"Be quiet, JJ! I ain't scared of them!" she retorted, puffing out her chest and wagging her finger at Rayo, Smurf, and Juice. "Y'all think you so tough with your guns and your mean faces. My mama says you're just bullies!"

Rayo's gun wavered as he stared at Kaluna, his face a mixture of bewilderment and irritation. "This ain't no game, little girl. Go home to your mama," he growled, but there was a hesitance in his voice that hadn't been there before.

"Yeah, I know it ain't no game!" Kaluna shot back with sass that defied her small frame. "But my brother taught me one thing - bullies are just cowards. And you... you're the biggest coward I ever did see!"

I could hardly believe my ears. Here was this little girl, calling out a trio of hardened gang members with more guts than most adults I knew. I could see Rayo's pride was wounded, and for a second, I thought he might do something stupid.

But then, from somewhere behind the buildings, the distant sound of sirens cut through the tension like a knife. Smurf and Juice exchanged panicked glances.

"Man, we gotta bounce!" Smurf said in a hurried whisper, tugging at Rayo's sleeve.

Rayo hesitated for a moment longer before shoving his gun back into his waistband. "This ain't over, Jamison." he snarled at me before turning to leave with his cronies trailing behind him.

The moment they were gone, my legs gave way beneath me and I sank to the ground, the adrenaline leaving my body in a rush. El-Train rushed over to me, placing a hand on my shoulder.

"You good, JJ?" he asked, concern etched across his face.

"I'm alive," I said breathlessly, avoiding his gaze. My pride was wounded. I should have been able to handle Rayo on my own.

Kaluna bounced over, grinning from ear to ear. "Did you see me out there? I was like pow! Take that, bully!" She karate chopped the air. "Saving lives is way more fun than watching superhero shows!"

I stared at her in disbelief. "Little girl, you are eight years old. Do you have any idea how dangerous that was? You could've gotten yourself killed!"

She dismissed me with a wave of her hand. "Danger is my middle name! Well actually it's Janine. But danger sounds way cooler."

Despite himself, El-Train chuckled and ruffled her hair.

"You a straight up warrior! She really your little sis, JJ?"

I almost denied it out of habit before pausing. Images flashed through my mind - Kaluna selflessly throwing herself in harm's way to create a diversion, nearly getting shot in the process. She was no longer just my pestering neighbor. I saw her in a new light — my fearless, unpredictable, utterly maddening little sister. "Yeah," I said finally, a weary smile touching my lips. "She's my sister now." I offered her a fist bump which she enthusiastically returned with a blinding grin.

"You just saved our necks out there, little warrior."

I said, shaking my head ruefully. Having a wild card like Kaluna around would definitely keep me on my toes. But I had a feeling this unpredictable kid, as crazy as she was, would have my back when it really mattered.

As we walked Kaluna home, I made a mental note to keep a closer eye on my wildly reckless new little sister. She was either crazy brave or just plain crazy. But she was family now - and we look out for our own.

Once her safety was secured, El-Train and I departed with a brotherly handshake. As I made my way to my dingy apartment alone, I felt a pang of guilt. In my darkest moments, I'd turned my back on God. But He hadn't abandoned me. He'd sent Kaluna - my guardian angel with braids and a mouth that didn't quit.

"Jesus, I know it's been a minute but...thank you," I whispered, glancing upward. "For not giving up on a fool like me."

I didn't expect an answer. But for the first time in forever, I felt a flicker of faith stirring inside me. Maybe I'd find my way back after all. If an 8-year-old daredevil like Kaluna could believe, then maybe there was hope for me too.

Chapter Forty; Sidell

When Dawn and I arrived at school, she nearly sprinted through the doors without me. I grabbed her arm to stop her, reminding her of our boyfriends' warning—with Rayo's gang after us, we shouldn't split up. "Ugh, I don't need a babysitter," Dawn scoffed, rolling her eyes dramatically. She flipped her hair over her shoulder and struck a defiant pose, as if to say she could "go full reign" if she wanted.

I sighed. Dawn was my best friend, but she can be a headache sometimes. Still, I couldn't let her storm off alone, no matter how invincible she thought she was.

"Come on, Dawn. Don't be difficult," I pleaded. "This is serious."

She let out an exaggerated groan, but eventually caved in, pitying her helpless best friend.

We stayed glued to each other's sides as we navigated the halls, Dawn complaining the whole time. When we found Tony and JJ, the contrast between our boyfriends was stark.

Tony seemed relaxed, giving Dawn a quick peck on the cheek. My boyfriend, on the other hand, was a ball of nerves. JJ's arm tightened around my waist as we navigated the crowded hallway. His eyes darted from face to face, muscles tensing with each person who brushed too close. The memory of his words echoed in my mind: "Just let me handle Rayo." But now, surrounded by the cacophony of slamming lockers and chattering students, my unease grew. What exactly had JJ done?

During free period, we met in the deserted locker room hallway. The smell of sweat and old sneakers hung in the air. I expected JJ to finally address the Rayo situation, but instead he asked about Khyree.

"You swear he hasn't tried talking to you again?" JJ's brows furrowed, his voice low and urgent.

"I swear," I assured him, rising on tiptoes to kiss his cheek. As I settled back, a chill ran through me. Khyree's absence today was unsettling – he never missed class. And not knowing whether his gang-affiliated cousin Rayo was lurking nearby made my skin crawl.

"Why do you keep asking?" I murmured, searching JJ's face.

He sighed, leaning his head back against the cold wall lockers. "I just have this bad feeling he's going to try something now that he knows we're together."

I wanted to reassure him, to say Khyree was over it, but the words stuck in my throat. JJ had known Khyree longer than I had. If he sensed something was off, there was probably a good reason.

"What aren't you telling me?" I asked, my heart racing. "What's really going on, JJ?"

His eyes met mine, a flicker of something unreadable passing through them. Then, unexpectedly, he smiled.

I raised a skeptical eyebrow. "Why are you smiling?" I demanded, genuinely confused.

"A few days ago, my mom and I... we finally talked," he said softly. "Like, really talked. About everything."

My eyelids fluttered, confused by the abrupt topic change. "That's... good?"

JJ nodded, his smile fading. "Yeah. It wasn't planned or anything; I just sort of blurted out everything that's been eating at me since I was a kid. And she listened. Like, really listened. We cried – a lot – and talked about us, about everything that went unsaid for so long." He smiled slightly. "It was like pulling shards of glass from deep inside. Painful but necessary."

"Oh. Well that's good JJ." I stuttered, giving his hand a supportive squeeze. "That's amazing. You've wanted that for so long."

"I know," JJ chuckled, his eyes crinkling at the corners. "And the crazy part is, after all the shouting and tears... my mom invited me and my grandma to dinner with her husband. And she wants to meet you."

"Really?" I leaned in, intrigued despite myself.

"Yeah, so what do you say? Dinner on Friday? It'd mean a lot to me."

"Um?" I shut my eyes, inhaling deeply. "Oh JJ, you know I really want to, but..." I trailed off, gesturing helplessly. "My parents. I'm now only allowed to go back and forth to school."

"That's cool, I'm not tripping. Just thought I'd ask."

He shrugged, but the light in his eyes dimmed. It made my heart ache. I chewed my lip, racking my brain. I had to find a way to be there for him. Then the bell rang, interrupting my thoughts as students flooded out the gym into the hallways. We started to part ways when JJ suddenly grabbed my arm.

"Oh wait, Sidell. There's actually something else I need to tell you."

"What is it?" I asked, pulse quickening at his serious tone.

He shifted his weight, eyes darting around the crowded hall. "Never mind, it can wait."

"No, JJ, what is it?" I pressed, searching his face.

JJ ran his hands through his hair. "Alright, remember our conversation outside the library? When I said I'd handle things with Rayo?"

My stomach clenched. "Yes..." I said slowly. "Did you-," I leaned in close, anxiety rising in my chest. "JJ did something happen?"

He swallowed hard, adam's apple bobbing. He glanced down the hall to make sure no one was paying attention to us. "Me and my friend El-Train had a...confrontation with Rayo and his gang." he paused. "Next thing you know, we fought and.... Train and I had guns drawn to our heads."

The world tilted. Blood roared in my ears as fury and terror collided. "They did what?"

JJ held up his hands defensively. "Yeah, and if it wasn't for my neighbor Kaluna intervening, which I didn't ask for considering that she is just a child, it could have turned out really bad."

I buried my head in my hands, willing myself not to completely lose it on him right here in the hallway. I looked up and met his eyes. "Jacky, what were you thinking?" I seethed through gritted teeth.

"What?" He responded, annoyance flashing across his face.

I wanted to slap him. "Jacky?" I repeated, punctuating each word.

"What Sidell?" He shot back, glare matching my own.

I held my tongue, knowing I'd say something I'd regret if I opened my mouth now. Instead, I simply shook my head and walked away, done with his reckless antics.

"I'm telling Principal Baxster. Getting the cops involved. This has gone too far," I called over my shoulder.

"No!" JJ scrambled in front of me, blocking my path. I barely avoided crashing into his lanky frame.

"You can't. I'm trying to lay low, keep off Rayo's radar. If you bring the 5-0 into this, who knows what he'll do," Jacky pleaded, his eyes darting around as if Rayo was lurking just around the corner.

"JJ, he could have killed you and your friend. And Kaluna?! How can you feel calm, knowing that someone you care can get caught by a bullet any minute—"

"Sidell, don't speak on things that you don't know" His cold response stunned me into silence. What didn't I know? We both knew I was right. "You could have died JJ," I explained. "and innocent Kaluna…"

"Okay but what about your safety Sidell? Since you worried about everybody else. But who's looking out for you?"

"I don't need anyone to lookout—"

"Yes you do Sidell! So stop acting like you know everything!"

The second bell rang and my eyes darted toward the locker room before I walked away from him.

"Sidell."

"I'll see you later, I'm already late to class." I mumbled.

"Sidell, I'm serious. Just let it be," He pleaded, grabbing my hand.

I jerked my hand away, as I was full of anger that I tried so hard to conceal. "I'll think about it."

I stomped off without giving him our usual hug or quick kiss, fuming the whole time.

Chapter Forty-One:
ψψ

At every stoplight, both my knees bounced up and down with manic energy the whole drive to the restaurant. I had nearly made myself late with how many shirts I threw onto my bed, searching for one that was nice but not too nice. And right when I thought I had found a suitable ensemble, Grandma intervened and forced me to wear a gray collared shirt with black dress pants that didn't quite fit my personal style. Despite my protests, she insisted that my mom would adore it; so reluctantly, I obliged.

My hair was another ordeal entirely. That pic comb was insufferable, pulling on my scalp with each stroke. But I persevered, knowing that when meeting my mom's husband, I needed to present the best version of me.

Grandma's car rumbled into the parking lot and I felt a wave of relief when I saw that none of the other vehicles on the street didn't appear to be too new. Most were beat up pick-up trucks and minivans with faded paint jobs, so I knew if I were to get out of the driver's seat I wouldn't get judged rolling in grandma's civil war car.

My jaw dropped as I glided through the glass revolving doors, stepping into the lavish vibe of the high-end restaurant my mom picked. Grandma rolled alongside me, her hand gripping my arm tight. Bright-colored chandeliers dangled from the towering ceiling, blending with the natural light that seeped through the mosaic glass windows. Heavy drapes added a pop of color against the dark wooden floor. The jazz music in the air heightened the whole experience. A quick scan of the place and there it was - our table, occupied by my mother and her husband.

"Isn't this place amazing?" Grandma whispered, dressed to kill in a flare blue dress gifted by Laussie for this special occasion. She blended right into the swanky surroundings.

"Sure is. And you look fly, Grandma," I replied. The corners of her mouth stretched wide and her grip on my arm tightened.

"Thanks, baby. But you think it's too much?" She gestured to the dining room. "We coulda done something more intimate and low-key at home. I coulda thrown down in the kitchen…"

"Nah, this is perfect," I reassured her. "You've cooked enough already. Just enjoy this change." A shaky breath escaped me, realizing that I had been holding it in all this time. Meeting my birth mother and her man in such a fancy spot was beyond anything I could've imagined.

We approached the table, and Laussie acknowledged us with a nod and a grin wider than Grand Canyon. "Mom, JJ, meet Devin."

"Hey," Devin greeted us with a firm handshake. Bald by choice, his dark skin contrasted sharply against his crisp navy blue suit. We flashed our pearly whites back at him as he eased into our rapidly expanding family circle. I hoped my poker face didn't betray my indifference. I wasn't sure what to expect from this reunion but when the waiter approached to take our orders and talk about the restaurant, I felt a wave of relief. I wasn't ready for the small talk that would lead to bigger conversations.

As the dinner trudged on, boredom and annoyance decided to join the party. My mind couldn't help but wonder how much more enjoyable this experience would be with Sidell by my side. But I skipped school today, consumed with fear for her safety. The thought of Rayo and his gang scheming without me there made my blood boil.

Across the table, Grandma was deep in a hushed convo with her daughter. The jazz music drowned out their words, but I caught snippets of their exchange. The last word that reached my ears was 'applications.' Praying they weren't discussing my future behind my back, I half-heartedly shifted my salmon around on the plate, throwing a smile here and there without really meaning it. Mentally, I was miles away from everything happening around me..

"JJ?"

I looked up at Devin, blinking slowly. "You seemed preoccupied — did you catch my question?" he asked, his mouth half-full of grub. His inquisitive gaze almost made me crack a smile.

"My bad, didn't quite catch it," I mumbled, embarrassed for zoning out.

"What'd you ask?"

"I was wondering about your plans after high school," Devin replied.

"What's your dream job?"

My dream job? Lately, painting had become my passion; though way back when, being a doctor was all I fantasized about. But that dream faded away when Donica got snatched away too soon. Trying to push away those dark thoughts, I focused on responding to Devin's question.

"Used to wanna be a doctor," I said. "...used to yap about it all the time. Now, I ain't so sure."

"Used to?" Devin quizzed, shoveling more pasta into his mouth.

"I think I outgrew that dream," I shrugged, avoiding the painful truth. The real truth was that it reminded me of my best friend, who now rests six feet under. "Just going through the motions now. Hopefully, I'll figure something out. What about you?"

"What about me?" he asked, pouring steak sauce onto his plate.

"What's your dream? Did you make it happen?"

Surprise flickered in his eyes for a hot second, and he glanced past me towards the exit. "Well, it was to be an athlete. Ended up as a sports psychologist."

"Well, that's not too far off," I replied, smiling when he nodded in agreement. "How do you like it?"

Devin frowned. "I'm not sure. The paperwork drains me dry. But apart from that, I love it. Helping players deal with their mental baggage before a game gives me a deep insight into the world of sports and the lives of athletes."

"JJ, why don't you tell him you on the football team?" Grandma butted in, patting my back. My body froze in surprise.

I took the last bite of my prime rib slowly while they waited for more information. "It's not important. I barely made the team for the last game and ended up in the hospital with an injury. Ain't nothing worth mentioning."

"It happens to the best," Laussie chimed in. "We can arrange for coaching if that's what you want."

"I'm not sure yet," was all I said, although it was a lie. Besides painting, football was the only future I could envision for myself at that moment.

"Still, we'd be thrilled to make it happen for you, JJ," Devin said. "You deserve it."

I gulped hard, my appetite vanishing in an instant. Dropping my fork onto the plate, I wiped my mouth with a napkin and forced a smile.

"I don't want it, Devin. Appreciate the offer," I said in a hushed voice without even glancing at them.

Laussie didn't seem to understand. "You should just try, JJ. If you still dislike it after, then you can let it go."

"I said I don't want it. I really appreciate your offer."

"This is a once-in-a-lifetime opportunity, JJ. You enjoy playing football," Laussie said, poking at the casserole dish of ribs. "What other hobbies do you have?"

"I can't think of anything."

"There you are, then." She heaped more ribs onto my plate alongside a generous serving of fondant potatoes, but I didn't budge. "You'll like it there and meet other boys your age who you can form real connections with."

"Why aren't you listening to me? I don't want it," I snapped, my voice low and menacing. "No matter how y'all try to sell me on this idea, I ain't interested." I stared straight at her, guilt prickling me as her face twisted with hurt.

"Then let's just eat. We'll talk about this later," she suggested.

"I'm not in the mood to." I warned in a low growl. "Just let it go."

Her eyebrows shot up at me. "What's the problem? I've said you don't have to address it now if you don't want to. I understand how you probably feel about this whole issue and…"

"No! No, you don't!" I exploded, slamming my hand onto the table, splashing drinks onto the linen cloth. "I'm not interested in anything other than you explaining why you introduced us to him without first introducing Devin to us. Does he even know that I'm the son you abandoned for seventeen straight years? I don't want to have small talk over fancy dishes when that wasn't the point of coming here in the first place!"

"JJ?" Laussie cried out, her shocked expression flitting from me to her husband, whose eyes looked like they were gonna pop out.

"Dear Lord, sweet baby Jesus," Grandma yelped, scrambling to push away from her seat.

The restaurant fell into silence, even the jazz music took a breather. My gaze remained on Devin as he started coughing, his startled eyes darting around. He looked as thunderstruck as I felt. But instead of calling me a liar or demanding an apology, he rose from his seat, turned slowly, and walked out of the restaurant.

I blinked at my mother, feeling numb. Who was this woman? Surrounded by half-eaten grub and abandoned wine glasses, I stared at the table, anger bubbling up inside me. Staring at those plates for what seemed like forever, I wished they'd disappear and the table would go back to how it was before.

"I'm so stupid," I croaked, tears burning my eyes as I thought about how much this meal cost Devin and how many more expenses he had to bear.

Laussie's face was smudged with mascara running down her cheeks. "What the hell did you do that for, JJ?" she asked in disbelief.

"How far is too far for you, Laussie? Where do you draw the line? Do you ever ask yourself what will become of you when you're old and weak if you keep deceiving people?"

"You're my child, and I'll not have you speak to me in that manner. Can't you see that I had to do what was needed if I was going to be there for you like you wanted me to?"

Too exhausted and lacking the hate to tell her to burn in hell like I wished, I lowered my eyes to the ground. I dug deep inside myself, searching for the strength to confront the woman I foolishly called my mother.

"Be real," I began, "I've tried to make room for you in my life, only to have it thrown back in my face. I can't take it anymore. You're on your own from here on. Don't come back home. I'll take care of Grandma like you should have. I've done my bit for years now and will do more as I come of age. But you? Stay away from the house and Grandma, or else you'll be hearing this conversation again in court!" My heart pounded as I pushed back from the table and stormed off.

"You selfish little cow!" Laussie's words chased after me. It was crazy how they ignited a fire inside me that I didn't even know was there. Despite my efforts to suppress it, the sting only intensified.

Tears welled up, prompted by my anger as everything seemed to explode around me. Swallowing past the lump in my throat, I dragged myself out the door. The thought of seeing Grandma at home wasn't comforting, so I kept walking, wiping at my tears aimlessly. Navigating through busy Chicago traffic, police sirens blared, filling the night air with desperate cries for attention. Red and blue lights flashed in a chaotic blur. This city was as much of a mess as I was.

My hands trembled as I rubbed my knuckles anxiously.

I remembered my school was a few blocks away. I could make it if I pushed past the pain throbbing in my feet from these damn dress shoes.

I needed to talk to Sidell. She was the only one who could help me process the disaster zone formerly known as our family dinner. If only she had been there. Maybe then I could have made it through dinner without completely breaking down. Sidell would have picked up on my trigger sooner and helped me avoid causing a scene.

Wrapping my arms around myself, I took a deep breath. "God, did you just throw all of my emotions into a blender when you created me?" I muttered miserably. "Nothing makes sense or lines up the way it should. My whole internal psyche is a scrambled mess from birth. Why? Make it make sense."

All I wanted was for this nightmare to end.

Chapter Forty-Two: Sidell

I was so angry at JJ after our discussion in the locker room hallway.

His refusal to talk to the cops made no sense to me. Why would he want to let Rayo off the hook after he purposely tried to kill him? Who cares about being labeled a "snitch"? I love JJ, but I was starting to feel like I cared more about his life than he did. Like he could care less about his salvation.

My mind was at war, wondering if I was in the wrong somehow. Am I the one not seeing things clearly? I chewed my lip, doubt creeping in. Am I speaking from my flesh by pushing on JJ what I wanted? Should I trust that God will take care of everything in His own way? My faith clashed with my desire for justice, leaving me torn and unsure of how to proceed.

I found myself beside my bed on my knees that night, seeking guidance from the only one who could provide it. Tears streamed down my face as I confessed my sins and pleaded for clarity. Between rebelling against my parents and worrying about JJ, I needed the Lord's wisdom desperately.

"Lord, I'm so lost and frustrated and I need clarity. Should I turn Rayo in, even if it means betraying JJ? Please, give me a sign of what to do." I whispered into the silence of my room.

The only answer was the neighborhood dogs barking excessively outside my window. I waited, hopeful for some divine sign, until my knees ached and my eyes drooped with the heaviness of a day spent in turmoil.

Eventually, I rose, still uncertain but feeling slightly lighter, as if the mere act of prayer had lifted some of the weight from my shoulders. I shuffled over to my bed and sank into it, letting the familiar comfort enfold me. I had to cling to the hope that prayer itself was enough for now. Surely the Lord would send me a sign soon.

★ ★ ★ ★ ✝ ★ ★ ★ ★

My heart hammered in my chest as I pushed open the heavy door to Principal Baxster's office. Mr. Baxster looked up, his face a mask of concern molded by years of dealing with high school crises.

I took a deep breath. You can do this. Be strong.

"Principal Baxster," I began, my voice barely above a whisper, "I need to tell you something. It's about three boys that go to this school." I cleared my throat and tried again, anger rising hot in my chest. I would not let them intimidate me. "They're planning to hurt my boyfriend JJ. They have guns. I think...I think they want to kill us."

As the words tumbled out, I watched the principal's expression shift from concern to alarm. He rose swiftly, reaching for the phone on his desk. "Thank you for telling me, Sidell. You did the right thing."

Within minutes, the wail of police sirens pierced the usual morning chatter of the school corridors. My stomach churned as I realized there was no going back now.

Officers swept through classrooms with a brisk efficiency that left no locker unchecked, no backpack unturned. The clattering echo of metal lockers being opened and closed filled the halls, mingling with the murmurs of curious students peering out from behind classroom doors.

"What's going on?"

"Is this a drill?"

"Oh my God, are those real guns?"

The whispers grew louder as the search intensified. Then came the sharp exclamations of discovery as the officers uncovered the hidden stash: guns with a cold metallic sheen and small packets of drugs tucked away in the depths of Rayo's, Smurf's, and Juice's belongings.

"Hands where I can see them!" an officer barked, and the shuffle of feet and jingle of handcuffs followed.

Dawn appeared at my side, as did a few students and staff. My breath caught in my throat as I saw them—Rayo and his cronies—being led away in cuffs. They were supposed to be just high school kids, but the items in their possession told a different story.

Yet, it was Rayo's face that seized my attention. His eyes locked onto mine, and even shackled, he radiated a twisted confidence. His smile was slow, deliberate, and bone-chilling.

"We'll finish this later, cheerleader," he snarled, his voice dripping with venom. "You and your pretty boy are dead."

The officers dragged him away, but that wicked grin lingered like a bad omen. I shuddered, a cold finger of fear trailing down my spine.

"He's just talking trash, Sidell," Dawn said, trying to reassure me with a gentle squeeze of my shoulder. But her words did little to steady the tremor that had taken hold of my hands.

"Stuff like that sticks, you know?" I replied, my voice quavering. "He's not going to forget this. None of them are."

Dawn gave me a determined look. "We'll deal with it. Together," she said with a conviction that I wished I could feel. "They're going to be locked up for a long while."

It felt as if a shadow had fallen over me. The rest of the day passed in a daze. Teachers gave me sympathetic glances and students whispered as I walked by, their eyes flickering with a mixture of awe and fear. Nobody expected Sidell, the soft-spoken cheerleader, to be at the center of such an explosive revelation.

The final bell rang, jolting me from my spiraling thoughts.

"We can have a sleepover at my house tonight?" Dawn suggested brightly as we walked to her car. "I'm sure your parents will say yes. We can paint our nails, eat ice cream, and watch cheesy rom-coms to take your mind off everything."

I managed a small smile, despite the dread churning within me. "That sounds nice." I was grateful to have Dawn as my best friend, though I doubted even a carefree girls' night could banish the unsettledness that had taken root inside me.

Dawn's piercing hazel eyes, outlined in smoky eye shadow, darted over to me as she pulled out of the parking lot. "It's going to be okay, Sidell. I promise."

I nodded, wishing I could believe her. But the encounter with Rayo had shaken me more than I wanted to admit. Would I ever truly feel safe again?

Maybe I shouldn't have snitched. JJ was right.

JJ.

JJ?

"Dawn, is that JJ walking?" I asked leaning closer to the windshield to get a better look.

Dawn followed my gaze, squinting against the glare of the setting sun. "Where?" she asked, her voice tense with concern.

"Just there, by the corner," I said, pointing at the solitary figure trudging along the sidewalk.

I remember him telling me that he was going to have dinner with his mom today. He must've just left the restaurant, but he didn't look as ecstatic as when he first told me about it. His hands rested on his head and Dark stains blossomed over his gray collared shirt.

All the possibilities swirled around in my head. His mom had to be responsible for whatever this was, which made me even more furious at myself for not going with him this evening.

Dawn pulled into the auto shop parking lot behind JJ. As the car rolled to a stop, I cranked the window down. "JJ!"

He turned, surprise flickering across his face.

"I'll be right back," I told Dawn, fumbling with my seatbelt. The door slammed behind me as I rushed over. With each step, my heart pounded faster. I nearly tripped twice in my hurry.

Up close, the stains looked like wine, marring JJ's perfectly pressed shirt, hugging his lanky frame. Old scars on his elbow were apparent, which made him more real. Gauging his looks while he was in obvious distress was ridiculous, but I couldn't help it.

I wrapped my arms around him as soon as I reached him, ignoring his weak protests. He fumbled with his hands, which had been tucked into his pockets, before returning the hug.

"Sidell," was all he could manage, unable to hide the tremor in his voice.

"What's wrong? How did the dinner go?"

"It went well." His voice was barely a whisper, hot tears searing their way down his cheeks.

"Oh no Jacky. Listen to me, It's going to be okay." I soothed.

"I'm a mess. Drinks spilled on my shirt, and I probably need a shower and ..."

"It's going to be okay." I interrupted. "Come on, Dawn will take you home." I took his hand to walk him to the waiting car.

JJ's pace became molasses. "No, I don't wanna go home."

"Well where do you wanna go?"

"I don't know Sid. I just-" he rubbed his face like he was frustrated.

I sighed, "Okay, come on. Will figure it out."

JJ slid into the backseat, his shoulders slumped in defeat. I climbed into the passenger seat and before I rebuckled myself, I leaned over to Dawn, lowering my voice.

"Dawn, I said you'll take him home, but he doesn't want to go home. I don't know where to take him."

"He can come to my house. You already said you're staying the night too right?" she asked.

"Yes…. but are you sure?" I asked, still not used to my best friend's unstructured household.

"Yeah, my mom won't care and my brother is at his girlfriend Ashley's house." Dawn said before looking back at JJ in the backseat. "Jacky, do you wanna stay the night at my house?."

JJ hesitated, his eyes flickering between me and Dawn, searching for some kind of reassurance. He took a deep breath, as if gathering the shards of himself scattered by the evening's events. "I... yeah, Please? Thanks, Dawn," he said.

Dawn started up the car again and pulled out onto the road, the hum of the engine filling the silence that stretched between us. We drove with only the soft crackle of the radio in the background, filling the tense quiet.

Turning onto our street, Dawn flicked a glance at JJ in the rearview mirror. "You can crash in my brother's room or the couch, whichever you want," she offered

I turned to look at JJ again. His head rested back against the seat, eyes closed, but now there was a slight softening around his tense jawline. I reached back, my fingertips brushing against his hand; he gripped it out of reflex and held on just a tad bit longer than necessary.

When we got out of the car, I intertwined my fingers with JJ at the same time I watched my house. I was praying that my parents weren't spying out the window.

We followed Dawn up the creaky porch steps to her house next door. She fumbled to unlock the front door, keys jangling.

"You can take a seat on the couch," she told JJ, motioning inside. "Sidell and I will be back. We're going to ask her parents if she can stay the night."

JJ gave a slight nod, his hand slipping from mine as he entered the house.

I pleaded with Mom and Dad to let me spend the night at Dawn's, but they shot me down quick, citing my grounding and the fact it was a school night. As they rambled on with chores I could be doing instead, I sighed and slumped in my seat, knowing it was useless to argue.

But Dawn uses her witty, theater charm to change their minds. Dawn comes up with a fabricated story of how her mom has been drinking like crazy and doesn't have time to spend time with her. And she continued her exaggerated tale, saying that her boyfriend Tony was being possessive and she needed me there for support.

I played along, nodding solemnly as she spun her web of deception.

Mom and Dad ate it up, sympathy overriding their discipline. They granted permission, but not before lecturing me about schoolwork and telling me to come straight home, the next day after school.

Dawn's eyes sparkled with victory as I packed my overnight bag with my homework neatly tucked between my pajamas and toothbrush.

Once back at Dawn's house, we guided JJ to the spare bedroom where he could take a moment for himself. The room was sparsely furnished but clean; random posters adorned the walls - bands and movie stars from another era. A twin bed sat pushed against one corner under a window that looked out over the backyard.

"I'll get you some fresh clothes," Dawn offered as she ransacked her brother's dresser for something that would fit my boyfriend's taller frame.

"And I'll... um... put your clothes in the washer," I mumbled, feeling helpless yet wanting to do something—anything—to ease his discomfort.

We left JJ alone to shower and change while we moved to the kitchen. Dawn tore open a fresh box of sodas lukewarm.

"Do you think he'll actually tell us what happened?" I asked quietly. I slid the laundry room door closed, muffling the sounds of the rumbling dryer.

Dawn shrugged, her face impassive as she stacked cans in the fridge. "If he wants to talk about it, we're here. If not..." Her voice trailed off, but her gaze lingered on me knowingly. "we're still here.

The sound of running water stopped upstairs indicating JJ had finished showering. Not long after, thuds sounded on the stairs. Dawn and I peeked out the kitchen doorway to see JJ settling back down on the couch. His body damp and face scrubbed clean of tears. He wore one of Dawn's brother's oversized shirts that hung loose on him.

"Here's a charger for your phone, since it's dying," Dawn offered JJ as I settled beside him on the couch. He looked at his phone as if he hadn't even noticed. He then smiled warmly at Dawn, receiving the charger cord in his hands.

"Thank you, Dawn," he said, his voice hoarse from the long drive. "I really appreciate it."

"You're welcome. I'll give you guys some space." She said, before walking back into the kitchen.

He gave a nod before turning to look at me. My whole body faced him as I placed my head on my elbow resting on the couch cushion. My eyes were watching him sleepily. His hand rested on my thigh as my legs were folded beneath me where we sat on the couch.

"Feeling any better?" I yawned, gently rubbing his arm.

"A bit. Thanks for... everything." He grimaced, probably worried about infringing on our space. But I pretended not to notice and patted his hand instead before standing up off the couch.

"Come on. We can hang out in the kitchen with my Dawn. Are you hungry?"

"I'm not gonna lie, Sidell," JJ said, his words dripping with exhaustion and defeat. "I could just stay put right here. A little peace and quiet to help me wrap my head around things. Thank you though. Seriously."

"That will not do," I announced, grabbing his hand till I tugged him up off the couch. "You need to eat something, and I'm not going to make exceptions for you." I dragged him towards the kitchen, with JJ frowning the entire way there.

I wandered into the kitchen, glancing back when I noticed he hadn't followed. Curling my finger at him, he stepped inside. I hastened straight to the fridge, gathering what was needed to make the three of us chicken salad sandwiches.

Dawn sat three cups of ice and three cans of soda on the table. JJ's fingers broke the tab off two of them and ritualistically handed them to Dawn and I, before getting to work on his own.

We sat and snacked on our sandwiches in silence. JJ and I helped Dawn clear the kitchen table after we finished. When done we all stared at each other for several long minutes. Dawn's mom, Ms. Tipton, had returned home from the bar with yet another random, sleazy man. Their drunken giggles filtered in from the living room.

Dawn rolled her eyes dramatically. "Ugh, let's bail and watch TV upstairs before I puke." she said, before getting off the stool. Resting my elbows on the table, I leaned in towards JJ, "Do you wanna head upstairs to watch a movie with me and Dawn?"

He glanced towards the hallway where the off-key duet drifted in.. "Yeah, I think we're intruding in their space. Let's go."

We climbed off the stools, wandering out of the kitchen following Dawn.

The blue glow of a television flickered under the door of the guest bedroom, spilling into the dark hallway. It was after 1 a.m., and Dawn had drifted off halfway through our favorite show, mouth agape, limbs splayed at odd angles. One of her biggest pet peeves was falling asleep when she had guests over, but I knew she'd be out cold for hours.

"Is she going to saw logs all night?" JJ whispered.

I stifled a laugh, knowing Dawn would be mortified if she knew we'd seen her like this. "It's just her sinuses. The snoring means she's in a deep, peaceful sleep," I reasoned.

"I need to get her some nasal strips or a crate of Nyquil," JJ said. I almost choked out a laugh before back handing him on the chest.

"You're so dumb, JJ." I leaned over and patted Dawn gently."Dawn, it's okay if you wanna fall asleep on me. I won't mind." I said. With that, Dawn jolted upright, her hair sticking out in all directions like she'd been electrified. "Ugh, thank you Jesus," she said, cocooning herself in her blanket. "Goodnight!"

I chuckled and shook my head as she shuffled off to bed, leaving me and JJ alone.

After a while, I turned down the volume of the tv for the sake of Dawn and her mom being asleep, so JJ and I had to really focus as we sat on the bed, snuggled in each other's arms. He ran his fingers along my spine in a soothing, trancelike manner while the other stayed on my shoulder blade as we watched the action drama series that played on the dresser-mounted TV.

JJ stayed perfectly still for a few moments as he tried to decipher the subtitles. The ginger throw blanket sheltered us both from the chill of the room. The faint musky-sweet smell of his cologne was still present even after he had showered, as if it were his signature scent. It wafted in my airways as his breathing was soothing and calm where it fanned out his throat. Cozying into him further, I let out contented sighs, which made him pull me closer to him in an effortless embrace. His comforting warmth was starting to lull me fast asleep.

"You smell good," I murmured as I looked up at him.

A smirk tugged at JJ's lips. "Yeah, well. I shower sometimes," he joked badly, but I still giggled anyway. I'm sure his hand on my back could feel my laughter reverberate throughout me, more real than what he could hear.

"You ever heard of soap?" he joked again, just so he could make me laugh one more time. And it was even better the second time because I was laughing so hard that my head was thrown back and my body shook with it. JJ's hand held me steady, not wanting me to escape him.

"I'm glad you shower," I said, smiling at him. "Otherwise, I might not be able to stand being this close to you."

"Oh, really now?" he teased, his voice low and husky. "I think you secretly love being this close to me."

I rolled my eyes in response, but there was no denying the truth of his words. After a beat, I asked him the question that has been nagging at me since we last spoke."JJ, are you still mad at me about the whole Rayo thing?"

"What? No, Sidell, I…"he stuttered "No, no. I'm not and I wasn't. You should be mad at me."

"No, I'm sorry that—"

"You have nothing to apologize for, Sidell. Please," he begged. "I can't be mad at you, especially not when you're going to do the right thing," he promised.

"I already did it," I whispered, and he clenched his eyes shut.

"And?"

"The police came to the school and locked him up.."

"Well, that's good," he offered, but knew his gut told him that this was a bad sign.

"You think it was a bad idea." I said.

"I was just worried about your safety. It's not a bad idea." If I were anyone else, He would've told me it was a great idea. But since I'm me. All he wanted was to wrap me up in his arms and keep me safe from harm. "It's not. It's a brave one."

"Goodness JJ, I hate it when people throw around that word. I'm not brave. I simply sent away a bully to where he belonged.."

"Fine. You're tough, then," He said, and I giggled.

"No forreal, Sid. You're the last person I'd mess with. Anyone who stays as calm as you were while dealing with all my chaos was nothing to be messed with."

"Oh my Goodness," I groaned.

"Plus, I'm positive you inherited your Dad's self-defense training, so who knows what you can do?"

"I can give you a punch that hurts more emotionally than physically," I joked, and he bursted out laughing. I'm just glad to see him smiling again after the wreck he was in earlier..

"Hey, Sidell?" he whispered.

"Yeah?"

"I'm really sorry. My reaction whenever I'm scared is to try and take control of the situation, and I'm going to work on that, okay?"

"JJ, it's fine."

"It's not fine. You mean everything to me, and I can't hurt you. I don't want to make you upset ever again, alright?"

"Okay."

Suddenly, the room fell silent, save for the muffled sound of the movie playing. Even after we stopped talking, I couldn't look away. I breathed, my lungs inflating a little jagged but strong. His hand found its way to my hair, trailing down my neck until a blush crept up onto my face. Unable to
meet his stare anymore, I averted my gaze and switched off the TV before getting up off the bed.

"Why'd you turn the movie off? Where are you going?" JJ's voice held a teasing lilt. "Scared you can't control yourself if we stayed like this?"

I widened my eyes in mock surprise and smirked back at him. "I think that's more your problem than mine," I quipped. "And for your information Mr. Jamison, it's late and I am going to bed."

"Wait, hold on. C'mere." JJ begged with a smile as he clumsily shuffled off the bed in one quick motion and grabbed my hand, tightly squeezing it against his heaving chest. He didn't break eye contact with me as I felt his heart beating wildly under my fingertips. "Just messing with you, Sidell," he said, a chuckle escaping his lips.

I pressed my tongue in my cheek watching him. "Sure you were."

"Nah, seriously though. I still wanna wish you a good night since I won't be here when you wake up tomorrow." His thumb stroked my knuckles.

"And besides, I don't want you catching a cold without me here to keep you warm."

I smiled and leaned in for a quick kiss on his cheek. "Don't worry about me, I'll be fine."

His lips grazed my forehead before he let go of my hand and watched as I made my way towards the door. Just before I turned the doorknob to leave, he called out to me again, "Meet me at school tomorrow, second period, by room 346?"

"Whatever you want." I grinned at him one final time before stepping out into the hallway and closing the door behind me. Despite it being late and the house being quiet, sleep was far from my mind.

The fear that had settled in my gut proved that I didn't have a solution for his family matters that he refused to talk about.

Chapter Forty-Three:
ՀՀ

My life was turning into a tragic comedy. Last night, needing to clear my head, I ended up at Dawn's house. I didn't want to overstay my welcome in her spot, so around 2AM, I quietly slipped outta bed and grabbed my clothes from her dryer. Creeping back upstairs, I was hoping to bid farewell to Sidell, just in case she was up. But nah, she was out cold, curled up on her side with her hair spiraling wildly around her face as she laid next to Dawn.

"Sidell," I half-whispered, careful not to step in Dawn's bedroom. No response. I tapped on the door and gave it another shot. "Sidell?" Still nothing.

Exhaling with a smile, I marveled at the peaceful sight of Sidell sleeping. It filled me with an indescribable feeling - both wonderful and painful. I turned the doorknob softly as I left the room. Sneaking down the grand staircase of the dark house, I slipped out the front door.

Without money for a bus pass or a uber, I walked for miles through parks and empty streets. The morning fog hung low, blanketing the air with a damp chill that slapped my face awake, wiping away any remnants of drowsiness. By the time I made it back to my apartment, I was just as drained as when I dipped from Dawn's place. Crawling beneath my own covers, I discovered that falling asleep during a tragedy was surprisingly easy. Your soul may be shattered, yet your body still finds the energy to drift into a deep slumber after a good cry.

Around 5AM the daylight sun broke through my window, forcing my eyes open. Listening to the echoes of neighborhood kids playing outside, I spent the next few minutes trying to piece together my life.

Thoughts of self-harm floated through my mind but vanished when I heard Grandma singing a hymn as she started her day. Reality hit me hard.

In my reality, my world had been upturned by the truth, and I had been left to die in the ashes. The weight of powerlessness felt like a thousand tons of steel; an unbearable agony. No child expects their mother to use them as a pawn to con an honest man for his hard-earned money, especially in their presence. I couldn't believe she was gone. I couldn't believe who she turned out to be despite my reservations about her character. My head felt like it would crack open with all the questions I wanted to ask her. But right now, I got out of bed and removed the sheet from my freshly painted canvas. This was the woman I'd expected Laussie to be; not the sharp-tongued viper I'd ended up with.

"I wished you knew how much your actions hurt me," I said to her smiling face in the painting. "It hurts beyond description. I would never have done that to you. I would never have used you for financial gains or hid the fact that I'm your son from anyone."

I stepped out of my bedroom towards the kitchen for a drink of water, finding Grandma sitting quietly at the dining table, her bible opened in front of her. The look on her face when she raised her eyes told me what she was thinking. When I returned with a bottle of water, her head was resting on her bible.

Taking a swig of the water, I pulled out the chair next to her and dropped onto it. "She played every last one of us." Grandma didn't respond, forcing me to continue even though my throat was raw from sobbing all night and into the early hours of the morning. "There was no way you could have known that she was about to deceive us, except you had a problem with giving people second chances.".

"JJ." Grandma pushed herself up and leaned in to give me an awkward hug. The display of affection threatened my composure and false bravado, forcing me to blink back another round of tears. "It's amazing how you've been handling this whole mess. My heart goes out to you, even though I know I ain't done right by pushing you to accept that girl."

I swallowed and rose, wrapping my arms around her. We remained in that position for some minutes until I spoke again. "Maybe this was supposed to teach me a lesson about forgiveness. Maybe God knew that this was the only way I could ever learn to let my grudge against her go; finding out who she truly is and that nothing would have stopped her from doing what she did the first time."

"I want to believe that God has other plans for us, JJ," Grandma murmured against my chest. "Better plans that do not include Laussie. Boy, this is a hard pill to swallow. I've kept praying over the years, asking him to bring her back so we could be a complete family."

"Then, maybe the lesson might have been for you. God's way of telling you to stop bugging him and see things for what they truly are?" I said jokingly, kissing her forehead.

"I'm going to report her if she ever comes near here again." I said, untangling myself from her embrace.

"I told her the same before leaving. She ain't welcome here no more," she said, wiping away tears. "It's a reasonable decision."

Inhaling deeply, I returned to my bedroom. The memory of Sidell's blushing face brought a welcome smile to my face. I felt bad about leaving her so early and getting her worried without telling her what happened at the dinner. But I was relieved that I'd get to see her again at school in a few hours to explain myself.

I showered, brushed my teeth, and changed into my school uniform. Returning to the kitchen, I found Grandma still seated at the table, her hands clasped together in front of her.

"Are you still thinking about Laussie?" I asked softly.

"That girl's drifting in and out of my mind," she admitted. She smiled weakly before getting up to walk over to the stove, returning with a plate of French toast and a cup of orange juice.

I dug into my meal, more concerned about keeping it down than anything else. "Is there anything else you'd like me to get you when I'm out?"

"I don't think so." Grandma stared off into the distance, probably grieving over her daughter all over again.

After finishing eating, I washed my plate and returned to grandma. "Well, if you remember anything just hit me up. You think you're tech-savvy enough to do that? Or are you needing a bit more time to catch on?" I teased with a smirk.

She cracked a smile. "I'll send you a text, JJ. I know how to do that. Thank you."

"What are you thanking me for? You made breakfast, and all I did was wolf it down without even saying a prayer, I should be thanking you, Grandma. You're the MVP." I kissed her forehead before leaving the room. With my backpack on my shoulders, I felt her eyes following me all the way to the
door.

"JJ?" she called, stopping me at the door. I glanced over my shoulder at her.

"I love you." she said in a surprisingly steady voice. The moment I gazed into those soulful brown eyes, "I love you too."

Chapter Forty-Four: Sidell

The pros about being a cheerleader were being able to leave second period class early to practice. I hated Calculus anyway. And though my grades had been suffering a bit, I made a goal for myself that I'll get them back up before report cards were sent out to my parents. I still haven't received my phone back from them, which makes me afraid that they just might keep it once they find out I'm cruising on C's and D's. Finishing up our new cheer routine's, I changed from my cheer uniform into my school uniform. Sliding on my green blazing I twisted the combination lock on my cheer locker. I waved my goodbyes to coach Sherrie and my teammates before making my way out of the locker room to meet up with JJ as we had discussed. But as I reached for the door, Dawn pressed her car keys into my hand.

"Can you do me a solid and put my cheer bag in my car?" she asked.

I opened my mouth to make an excuse, but she cut me off. "Please bestie babes? Remember when I covered for you and JJ and got myself detention to buy you guys time to return to the school?"

My face flushed scarlet. "What?! You knew?!" I sputtered.

"I might be seventeen but I'm not naive, Sidell. Besides, I was literally within earshot when you guys decided to ditch campus together to go to the carnival."

"Oh my goodness Dawn, you should have told me. Let me guess you found out we kissed too?"

Dawn gasped dramatically. "What? You guys kissed!"

I huffed.

Laughing, Dawn dropped the act. "I'm just teasing! You two were making eyes at each other the whole ride back. It was obvious."

I felt my cheeks burning again. Time for a subject change. "Just give me the dumb bag so I can get this over with," I said, making a grab for her cheer bag. The sooner I helped Dawn, the sooner I could leave.

It was oddly warm outside. The sun was peeking through the clouds even though it was supposed to rain all morning. And the swooning butterflies in my stomach weren't making it any better. In my mind I was still baffled that Dawn knew about JJ and I's first kiss. But by the way my goofy full teeth smile was on full display right now, how could she not have known. I giggled to myself all the way to the parking lot, but it slowly disappeared when I noticed a familiar license plate:

TW 18357

Slowing my walking pace, I took in the sight of that eerie velvet cadillac, parked alone. I'd recognize that car anywhere—it was the same one Rayo used to run Dawn and me off the road. The engine purred menacingly, but no one was present in it.

My heart pounded wildly and my hands trembled as I adjusted the heavy cheer bag on my shoulder.

Was I losing my mind? Rayo couldn't be out already...could he? Don't be paranoid, I told myself. But the possibilities swirled in my head—what if he escaped? What if he was coming for me?

Telling myself that didn't calm the panic rising within me. I was being paranoid. Rayo couldn't be out already. It's only been a few days. But what if he escaped?

I began picking up the pace now, my head on swiveling as I did so. It took me a few minutes to work up the courage to reach Dawn's normal parking spot. I threw my hands over my head, and forced a deep breath. It was okay. It was just a coincidence to see the exact model and color of the car. He wasn't following me.

Unlocking the car, I placed Dawn's cheer bag on the backseat. The rapid slap of footsteps on pavement made my heart skip. I should've run back toward campus—fight or flight, right? Instead, I fumbled Dawn's keys, metal jingling as they hit the ground. By the time my fingers closed around them, a force slammed me back against the car, knocking the breath from my lungs.

I tensed, ready to fight, only to freeze in shock when I saw who it was.

"I left you alone, Sidell!" Kyhree's face twisted with rage, inches from mine. "And you lied to the police about Rayo?"

"What are you doing, Kyhree? Let go!" I shoved against his chest, not as hard as Dad taught me, but enough to break his hold. "I didn't lie!"

His hand clamped around my wrist, yanking me off-balance. Before I could steady myself, he shoved me back. My head cracked against the car door, pain exploding behind my eyes. I swayed, but his hand found my throat, pinning me in place.

"You psycho b****!" he snarled, fingers digging into my skin.

Maybe I'd been hanging out with Dawn too much, because I heard myself quip, "Look who's talking."

Wrong move. His grip tightened, and he slammed my head back again. A shrill ringing filled my ears—was it a car alarm, or just the sound of my brain rattling in my skull? The edges of my vision darkened, the world blurring.

"I haven't done anything to you," Kyhree hissed, "and you go and ruin—"

"Be quiet!" I choked out. "Your cousin tried to murder my boyfriend—"

The word 'boyfriend' sparked something in his eyes. His hand pressed harder, cutting off my air. "Do you ever," he growled, "ever shut up?"

As spots danced across my vision, I saw something in Kyhree's eyes. Something cold and merciless, completely unlike how he used to look at me. There was nothing behind those dead eyes. No humanity, no empathy. Just raw, murderous anger.

He'd kill me. He wanted me dead. But my faith whispered to me: Fear not those who kill the body but cannot kill the soul. Fear only Him who can destroy both soul and body in hell.

With the last of my breath, I rasped, "Do it. Do it, you coward."

He froze. His hands stayed around my throat, still squeezing, but not adding any more pressure. "You can't, can you?"

The challenge was met with his thumb digging into the indention below my jaw.

"Do it," I said again, locking eyes with him. His hands loosened. "

You want to take me out? So, do it!" Every word out of my mouth burned, and the only things that weren't blurry were his confused eyes. "Or did you finally realize how dumb it would be to kill a girl you couldn't have??"

Nothing he could do would hurt me as much as the truth hurt him.

I didn't resist when his palm slammed back into my windpipe. I just let my eyes fall shut. Breathing burned. My neck felt numb.

At least it would all be over soon.

Somewhere in the distance, I heard a scream.

"Do it," I begged before sucking in a desperate breath . . . the last one I might ever take. I could feel the tears burning their way down my cheeks. My whole body felt hot yet numb. The ringing was still so loud. I just wanted it all to stop.

"Sidell!" That was Tony's voice. The rest of the screams weren't as clear. "Oh my Gosh dude!"

The pressure on my throat vanished. I crumpled to the ground, gasping.

"Sidell? Crap, someone help me!"

Hands grasped my shoulders, voices swirling around me.

"What happened?!" A voice resembling Dawn asked.

"Khyree was strangling her!"

My eyes flashed open, my mind finally snapping into focus. The phantom pressure of Khyree's hands still lingered on my throat, a chilling reminder of how close I'd come to death. But I was alive. God had the final say.

The green, white and black uniforms all flashed in front of me in a blur, and I couldn't quite make anyone out until I locked eyes with Khyree. Two students from the football team had him pinned against a nearby car. Tears glistened in his eyes.

"No!" I screamed, lunging forward. Someone grabbed me, and I tried to jerk out of their grasp. "No! You don't get to cry!" My voice didn't even sound like mine. It was rough and frantic, a scream too broken to be my own.

"Sidell, calm down!" Someone shouted, but their words barely registered.

Hot tears streaked down my cheeks as I thrashed against whoever held me. "He doesn't get to play the victim!" Each word was sandpaper in my throat, but I couldn't stop. "He tried to kill me!"

Rage pulsed through me. I wanted to hurt him, to make him feel a fraction of my pain. It was only fair. But as I lunged toward him, my world tilted. Something was wrong. I couldn't keep my balance, and a high-pitched ringing filled my ears. My legs gave out.

Someone caught me, wrapping their arm around my stomach to keep me from plunging head first into the pavement.

"Sidell," Dawn's familiar voice cut through the chaos. I sagged against her, relief flooding through me.

"He... attacked... me," I choked out, my words a desperate plea.

"I know," Dawn soothed, her grip tightening protectively.

"I didn't... do anything." The injustice of it all threatened to overwhelm me.

"Shh." Dawn's hand gently tilted my face up. Through my blurred vision, I could make out her features – a beacon of safety in this nightmare. "You're okay now."

Dawn and Tony carefully steadied me, but the world continued to spin. Nausea rose in my throat.

"Sidell!" It was a distant scream, but one I recognized right away.

"JJ." I whispered, jerking my head in his direction. But my head screeched in pain as soon as it turned, and then the dark blur in my vision grew until I couldn't see anything. I was falling again, and then it all went black.

Chapter Forty-Five:
♉♉

Something was wrong. Sidell wasn't here to meet me. I waited for her, but she didn't show up. I turned my phone back on and called Dawn. They had to have rode to school together, the two were inseparable. It rang and rang until I was hit with her voicemail that was mostly her giggling when messed up what she was trying to say.

I power walked past the building outside, my walk turning into a full-on sprint when I saw a crowd of students around Dawn's car.

"Dawn! Sidell!" I yelled as loud as I could. When I got closer, I could see Sidell's body go slack before she began falling. I couldn't get to her fast enough. But Tony did, catching her before she slammed into the ground. "No, no, no, no," I huffed. I helped Tony and Dawn lower her to the ground, cradling her head the entire time.

"She's okay. She just fainted," Tony told me, but she was anything but okay. I patted her cheeks, but she wouldn't open her eyes. When my gaze drifted down, I spotted her neck. The normally pale skin was littered with red marks, almost like someone tried to…

I jerked my head around to look for Khyree, finding him pinned against a car by El-Train and some other boy named Nick. No one caught me in time to save Khyree from the first punch across the face. El-Train let go of Khyree to hold me back. When I tried swinging again, I missed my mark and only grazed his jaw.

"I'm going to kill him!" I growled. "Let me go!"

Tony helped yank me back, pinning me to Dawn's car while Khyree nursed his cheek. Tony gripped my face, scowling at me. I tried to jerk away, but Tony just held me in place, forcing me to look at him. His face had a red mark on it too.

"Did Khyree hit you?"

"No, Sidell did on accident," Tony huffed, shaking his head. "Now, calm down!"

"I can't—"

Tony smacked my face, shocking me into silence. "Sidell passed out. We're getting help. I am barely keeping it together, so calm the hell down!" he yelled.

"She didn't just pass out," I pointed out. Before Tony could say anything, a group of coaches emerged from the athletic building and started sprinting towards us with Coach Davis in tow. Tony let go of me to stand next to Davis while he took a look at Sidell. Tony quietly told him what happened.

"I saw them first. I had just got here to school because I woke up late this morning. But anyways when I parked my car, I saw that Khyree had his hands around her throat. I think she hit her head too. She was real dizzy and kept losing her balance."

El-Train gave me a warning look before letting go of me, and I held my hands up defensively. I wasn't going to attack Khyree again. Now that I had a moment to think, I knew that I shouldn't have. Khyree deserved it, but I wasn't that kind of person. Actually, I no longer wanted to be.

When I looked over at Khyree, two coaches were pulling him away from the growing crowd. Half the school was out here now, most watching from the sidewalk.

Principal Baxster came sprinting up to us, keys in hand. "Get Latimore into my office!" he yelled at the coaches.

"Hey," The school Nurse Evette whispered, and someone pulled me back before I could run over to Sidell. From over Tony's shoulder, I could see Sidell blinking up at Evette. "How are you feeling?" Someone tugged me back again, but I kept my feet firmly planted, waiting to hear Sidell say she's okay. "Can you tell me your name?"

"Sidell. Sidell Evermost." I let out a relieved breath.

"Good, good."

I felt my entire body relax. Sidell would be okay. Her brain was still working just fine.

"Alright, how many fingers am I holding up?" Evette asked, holding two up right in front of her.

"Stop moving and I'll tell you," she groaned, and my stomach dropped. Evette wasn't moving her hand at all.

"Students, I'm going to need all of you to clear out," Baxster shouted as he weaved his way through them.

It was Tony who ended up making me move, pushing me toward the sidewalk as I watched Baxster and Evette from over my shoulder. They were slowly helping her to her feet and moving her toward the car that Baxster pulled up in.

I felt so helpless as I watched Baxster and Evette drive off with Sidell. I should be with her. I should have been there when this happened. There had to be something I could've done.

★ ★ ★ ★ ✝ ★ ★ ★ ★

I got halfway through my third class before getting called into the principal's office. There, Dawn, Tayah, El-Train and a few of the others from this morning were sitting, all looking about as horrible as I felt.

"What's going on?"

"They're talking to the witnesses," Tayah explained.

"And trying to figure out if someone punched Khyree," El-Train said. "But none of us saw it happen." I narrowed my eyes at him. He was literally holding Khyree down when I punched him. When I looked around at the others, who all knew exactly what I did, they just shrugged or shook their heads.

Tony walked out of Kyepher's office, followed by Headmaster Kyepher, who had a murderous expression on her face.

"Oh cool. JJ is joining in on the fun," he snorted as he plopped down next to Dawn.

"Mr. Daye, this is a serious situation. Students were hurt today."

"Student. Singular. Khyree Latimore is fine," Tony spat.

Kyepher's eyes met mine, and she beckoned me into the office with a small flick of her head. I held my breath as I followed her in. "Khyree said you punched him," Kyepher said as she shut the door.

"Khyree also assaulted Sidell, so I don't think he's a credible source," I snapped, plopping down on the couch.

"Are you saying that you didn't punch Khyree Latimore?" she huffed. "Need I remind you that lying is an honor code violation."

Which meant everyone sitting outside would get busted with one if I told the truth, which would mess up all their college applications. If I had any intention of coming clean, which I didn't, that alone would have kept me from it.

"I'm saying that my girlfriend was just attacked in your school's parking lot and instead of asking for what I witnessed about that, you're interrogating me about something that the boy that strangled her had said."

Before Kyepher could say anything else, the door swung open and banged into a cabinet. I whipped my head around to see Sidell's dad storming in, wearing a leather jacket, jeans, and his gold wedding band.

"Uh, if you could just give me a second—"

"My daughter just got strangled on your campus. What could possibly be more important than—" He finally saw me on the couch, his eyes narrowed in confusion. "What are you doing here?"

"I'm just talking to the witnesses of the altercation," Kyepher said at the same time I blurted out, "She thinks I punched Khyree Latimore."

"Did you?" Sidell's dad asked, his lips turning up in a smile.

"No," I lied.

"Mr. Evermost—" Kyepher started.

"Garren," he corrected gruffly.

"Right, Mr. Garren." Kyepher fidgeted with her clunky glasses. "Look, I have to do a thorough investigation whenever there is an allegation of—"

"Allegation? Allegation?!" Garren interrupted. I sunk farther into my seat, as Garren braced his hands on Kyepher's desk and loomed over her. "I'm sorry, but I thought the school's policy said when one student accuses another of attacking them but there are no witnesses that you give a warning and hope it doesn't happen again. Or is that just your policy when the victim is female?"

"That's not—"

"Or is it a racial issue? Because you were fine to look the other way when the alleged attacker was a rich black boy, but it seems to me that JJ isn't getting fair treatment. So, which is it? Are you sexist or racist?"

"Oh snap." I heard Tony laugh in the main office, clearly eavesdropping.

Kyepher furrowed her brows in confusion. "What? He's black too—" She paused and whispered to me urgently, "JJ, could you step outside?"

I practically sprinted for the door, not needing to be told twice. As soon as it swung shut, Garren's muffled shouts erupted again. "Do you have any idea how many different ways I could sue you right now?" I ducked my head and took a seat, listening to the satisfying sounds of Kyepher getting chewed out.

None of the others said a word. Occasionally, another student would walk by the office, staring at them with wide eyes. There's no doubt that the entire school knew what happened by now.

"They got Khyree in Mr. Baxster's office," Tony whispered, leaning toward me. "Waiting on his mom to get here to bail him out."

"Ain't no way that's finna be happening."

"Probably not. With Sidell's dad coming in threatening to sue and Sidell straight up snapping on Khyree. The Evermost's aren't messing at all."

"Wait, what?"

Tony's eyes flickered over to meet mine. "I don't know what that was. I've never seen her like that, I swear. I don't know what would have happened if I didn't catch her." When I looked over at Dawn, Tayah and El-Train, they were exchanging an odd look, like they knew exactly what Tony was talking about. "That girl wanted to hurt him."

Before I could ask anything else, Kyepher's door swung open. Garren locked eyes with me and gestured with his head for me to follow as he walked out of the main office.

"Are you okay?" he asked as soon as we were out in the hallway.

"Nah, are you?"

"No. But Sidell will be. She's looking at a concussion but nothing is broken. Only God can do such miracles," he sighed before pushing back his hair. "Were you there? How did this happen?"

"I, uh, I wasn't. I was waiting for her near my classroom like I usually did." It felt weird admitting that to her dad, considering that we didn't exactly get along. "When I got there, it already happened. Tony actually saw it."

"Tony?"

"Uh, the guy sitting next to me in there," I said, gesturing with my head back at the office. "He's my bestfriend and Dawn's boyfriend."

"Oh, Tony. Yeah, okay." he nodded.

"So, he saw them when he got out of his car." I continued. " Khyree had his hands around her neck, and then Tony and a few others came running to help and got him off her. I got there right when she passed out." I took a deep breath before admitting, "And then I punched Khyree." I felt a little better saying it out loud.

I wasn't sure what kind of reaction I was expecting from Garren, but an amused snort certainly wasn't it. "Good." He leaned against the wall with a sigh, and I shoved my hands into my pockets. I wasn't sure why that reaction rubbed him the wrong way.

"Do you know why this happened? Was it anything that had to do with you?"

"I, yeah, but…" I stuttered as his eyes lit up with concern. I took a deep breath before I structured the right words to say. "I got into a fight with Khyree, then he got his gang member cousin Rayo involved. And a lot of things went down, leading to Rayo threatening both Sidell and I's lives. So Sidell decided to tell principal Baxster and as a result, the cops were called and Rayo was turned in. But I guess Khyree found out."

Garren let out a loud exhale. "I've never felt so helpless in my life. Seeing my firstborn daughter in the hospital like that… And then, I can't even get your ridiculous Headmaster to agree to expel Khyree."

"He's not getting expelled for this?" I snapped, and Garren just shrugged.

"She said they are looking into alternative solutions. Whatever the hell that means."

I fell against the wall beside him, feeling my chest burn like it did when I found Sidell. There was no way the school could let Khyree get anywhere near her after this. No. It wasn't possible. Especially not when there were witnesses.

"If you want to stop by the house after school, I know Sidell would be happy to see you."

"Yeah, I want to see her too." Tears pricked my eyes, but I fought them off. Just thinking about Sidell lying in a hospital bed, all bruised and disoriented, it ripped my heart into two. It was like the Donica incident all over again. I should've gotten to Sidell faster. I should have known this would happen. I should have protected her.

"Okay. I got to get back," he said, clapping his hand on my shoulder.

I stood there for a while, long past when the doors swung shut behind him. Eventually, Tony came out and stood with me. Not saying a word, which was odd for him. But it was nice not being all alone for a few moments.

★ ★ ★ ★ ✞ ★ ★ ★ ★

After school hours, I called my grandma, letting her know my whereabouts, before booking an Uber to Sidell's house. My phone was blowing up with texts from Dawn, Tony, and El-Train asking for updates on Sidell. I turned it off when my Uber parked in Sidell's driveway.

Mrs. Evermost opened the door before I even got to the porch. Her hair was thrown up into a messy bun, her eyes having dark circles beneath them. "Come on in," she said, forcing a smile.

We didn't say another word to each other as she led me up the stairs.

The upstairs of their house wasn't as clean and perfect as their downstairs. Garren in his office, flipping through a stack of papers. Sidell's little sister, who I haven't actually met, was in her own room doing homework. There was a hamper out in the hallway, overflowing with pieces of Sidell's uniform. A stack of tubs blocked one of the doorways. Sidell's door was covered with cutouts from a magazine, forming a collage. It felt more like a home up here.

"Hey, Sidell?" Mrs. Evermost whispered as we stepped into Sidell's room. It struck me that I had never actually been in here. It was the room where Sidell called me from that night after the big game. It made stepping in here feel so much heavier. "Jacky's here."

Sidell was lying in bed, head propped up on three pillows. She didn't even open her eyes. She just whispered, "Yeah?" with the corners of her mouth turning up.

Mrs. Evermost patted me on the back before stepping out. "Hey, Sidell," I said as I walked up to her bed. Slowly, she blinked those blue eyes open. And despite everything, I smiled . . . because seeing those eyes was easily the best thing that happened to me today.

"What? No kiss?" she whispered. With a chuckle, I leaned down and pressed a careful kiss to her lips. As I pulled away, my eyes drifted down to her neck where the bruises had begun forming. I jerked my gaze away as I sat down on the bed beside her. Sidell held her hand out to me, wiggling her fingers impatiently until I took it.

"How are you feeling?" I asked as I interlaced our fingers.

"Tired. And my head hurts."

"And your neck?"

"Really hurts." At least in the dark of the room Sidell couldn't see my pained expression. "What happened after I left?"

My fingers stroked her palm as I took a deep breath. "All of us got dragged into the principal's office. But it was Ms. Kyepher's, not Mr. Baxster. She wanted to know what we all witnessed, if I punched Khyree, and if there was anything they were missing. And then when Baxster got back from the hospital, he wanted to meet with each of us too, have us talk to the counselor, and really just make sure we were okay."

"Did you just say you punched Khyree?"

I froze, and Sidell weakly squeezed my hand. Right, she wasn't conscious for that.

"Yeah, I did," I admitted. "Right after I found you." I watched her face closely, looking for any sign of panic or worry. Sidell wouldn't be happy that I hit Khyree again. But I was terrified that it might make her scared of me, especially after what Khyree did to her today. "I shouldn't have done it," I added in. "I had just figured out what he did to you and I—"

"Did it hurt?"

"What?"

"Did it hurt him?"

"Yeah."

Her eyes fell shut. "Good." Some hair had fallen into her face, so I pushed it behind her ear. "Tell me something, JJ."

"I was so scared, Sidell."

"No, not that. No more talking about that for today," she sighed.

I leaned back against her headboard and started talking about the essay I pulled out of my brain today. One hand was still firmly holding onto Sidell's. The other was mindlessly playing with the ends of her hair.

"Tell me something," she whispered as soon as I stopped talking.

"Aren't we supposed to take turns?" I chuckled.

"I can't. I have that, uh, head thingy."

"Concussion?"

"Yeah, that," she remembered.

I launched into talking about my grandma's new interest in Home Depot, and the variety of paints that she loved.

As soon as I finished it got to the point where Sidell stopped reminding me to tell her something and I just talked and talked about anything that entered my thoughts. Anything except the one thing that was eating away at me.

I knew she was only half listening. There was only so much she could keep up with in her current state. But there was a small, closed-lip smile on her face as I spoke, like she just wanted to hear my voice. So, I kept going until I looked out the window and saw it was getting dark.

"I have to get home so my grandma won't worry too much," I sighed, and Sidell's eyes shot open.

"You're leaving?" she panicked.

"I'm sorry, but I have to. And you need to rest." I leaned down to kiss her cheek, but as soon as I did, Sidell stuck her chin out like she always did when she wanted one on her lips. I chuckled quietly and gave her a chaste one, earning that little hum that always made my heart stutter.

I hated leaving her. If I had it my way, I'd stay here all night, all week even.

"Hey, do you want to hold onto my hoodie?" I asked, and the sweetest little smile formed on her lips. I tugged it out of my backpack and laid it over her. Sidell immediately put her arms into the sleeves, wearing it backwards. "It'll be just like I'm here," I promised.

"I'll still miss you. You'll come back tomorrow, right?"

"I promise." I gave her another kiss, this one slower than it should have been, but I couldn't help myself. Ten hours ago, I had no idea if I would be able to do this again. I thought I had lost her just as soon as I found her.

I made my way down the stairs but paused at the bottom when I heard Mr. Evermost and his wife talking.

"They have their behind's covered, Yaheli. I can't come up with anything," Mr. Evermost huffed. "Let's just press charges."

"You don't understand, Garren. I did some research and two years ago, a senior girl got raped by her boyfriend, and when she pressed charges and brought all that negative press to the school, Westwood retaliated. All her college scholarships were rescinded without explanation. The headmaster made her out to be a whore and a liar. We can't risk that for Sidell."

"I'm taking off," I called out, alerting them to my presence. Both sets of feet came padding toward the front door to meet me.

"Uh, if anything else happens, will you let me know?" I asked.

"Of course," Yaheli said, darting up to me, pulling me in for a hug. I froze for a second before returning the hug, a bit confused by the sudden gesture. It's not that Yaheli wasn't cold to me before, but I didn't take her for a hugger type. "And you'll come see her tomorrow, right?" When she pulled away, there were tears in her eyes, the same panicked tears I had been seeing all day.

"Yeah, and I told Sidell that too. I just got to get back home and check in with my grandma," I explained, and Yaheli nodded along before looking back at Garren.

"Alright, you get going then," Garren said with a nod. My eyes flickered up the stairs one last time before I walked out the door.

I zoned in and out of the city bus ride back to my Apartment Complex. Vaguely made note of the different sights of the city but mostly my mind was blank. Once inside, I kissed grandma goodnight, before going to my own room, mumbling something about Sidell being okay.

The apartment was silent. Grandma had fallen asleep in her recliner, not even accidentally leaving Family Feud on the living room TV this time. I stared at my phone, longing to hear the voice that had become my lifeline during that school year. But hopefully Sidell was fast asleep now, wearing my hoodie to make her feel safe.

"Dear God, it's me…JJ. I could have fallen apart again. Could have cursed you to your face for all that's happened. But somehow, someway, I can see things differently now. Thank you. Thank you for opening Sidell's eyes and giving her another chance. I love her."

Didn't even have to think about it despite those words never popping up in my mind before now. I admitted it as easily as I would if God were to ask if I liked the color blue. No deliberation needed. I just did.

Maybe it was all the movies I had seen that made me think this should be a bigger realization. A light bulb moment where everything changed because I realized I loved Sidell Evermost. But that wasn't how it was for me.

I didn't have a clue when I fell for her. Logically, I knew I couldn't claim that I had always loved Sidell. That's just not true. But it felt like it. Like she had always held this special place in my heart, even before we knew each other. My heart felt so full with warmth and life now that it was hard to remember when it was cold and empty, just waiting for someone like Sidell to come along and fill it.

"I love her," I repeated once more. Nothing changed at that moment, but it felt good to finally put words to describe the stuttering of my heart. Just seeing her today, looking into her eyes, brought me a sense of peace and contentment that I never thought possible.

Chapter Forty-Six: Sidell

Up until one random day, I realized that I didn't like sleeping alone. That night, my phone was still in my parents possession, which meant that I couldn't call JJ to help me fall asleep. And as much as wearing his hoodie kept me calm, it wasn't going to be enough to make me feel safe.

"Mama?" I called out, but I instantly regretted it because my mom came sprinting out of her bedroom in a panic. I hoped there would be a time where my mom didn't have to be so scared for me all the time. She's a good mom. She didn't deserve what I was putting her through.

"Hey, sweetie. You okay?" she asked.

"Could you sleep in here tonight?"

"Yeah, of course. Let me just go tell your father I'm sleeping in here."

I drifted in and out of consciousness as my mom got ready for bed. Not much had changed about her routine. My mom still put on that cucumber melon lotion right before bed, the same one seven-year-old me would sneak upstairs and put on before diving into my mom's closet and trying on her heels. There was a moment as my mom climbed into the bed beside me that I forgot what year it was. For that beautiful moment, I was just that little girl who just wanted to be close to her mom . . . not the scared seventeen-year-old who still felt those hands around her neck.

Sleep came easier than usual. But the sleep itself was restless, echoing with dreams that weren't quite nightmares yet were jarring enough to keep jerking me awake.

The third time it happened, I sat up too quickly and groaned in pain.

"Sidell?" I heard my dad whisper. I followed the sound of his voice, seeing him lying on the floor beside my bed. Cayest was fast asleep beside him, as he had made a little bed for them on an old quilt and dragged a few pillows in from his room. "Are you okay?"

"When did you guys come in here?" I asked. They definitely weren't in here when I fell asleep earlier.

"About an hour ago. I kept getting up to check on you, so I figured this would save me the walk. Caye then followed."

I layed back down before my dad saw the tears forming in my eyes. I threw my arm over my eyes, soaking the sleeve of JJ's hoodie with my tears. That's the kind of thing my family would do. In that moment, being surrounded by my family's love and protection, I felt grateful to God for blessing me with them. Despite the way I've treated them lately, they were there for me in my time of need without hesitation or complaint.

This time when I fell back asleep, I stayed asleep until my alarm clock started blasting "Every Praise". I had never considered just how not concussion friendly that song was until now. Dad got to it before I did, mumbling a hundred times under his breath in Russian. He collapsed back on the floor, and my mom started laughing, waking Cayest up. It was that low, very unladylike cackle that was so funny sounding that I couldn't help but laugh along too. It kind of hurt my head to laugh, but the rest of me needed it.

★ ★ ★ ★ ✝ ★ ★ ★ ★

The first day went by in a blur. Both Dad and Mom took off work and Cayest from school. I managed to eat some yogurt but drew the line at toast. I had no idea what anyone did all day, including myself. The first time I bothered to look at my clock was at one in the afternoon.

Only two noteworthy things happened: JJ stopped by, and I saw myself in the mirror for the first time since being strangled.

Seeing JJ was easy. A lot of holding hands and listening to him talk. What about? I wasn't quite sure. I struggled to listen, but I liked having him there.

Facing my reflection wasn't easy. Up until then, I hadn't been turning on lights as I went into rooms. The bulbs were all too bright and hurt my eyes. But I wasn't thinking about it when I walked into the bathroom. Just flicked on the light like I always did, squinted my eyes while using the restroom and washed my hands, and then froze in abject horror when I saw my own reflection.

It wasn't the bags under her eyes or how red they were. It wasn't my unbrushed hair that I let go unwashed a little too long before all this happened. It was my neck. Bruise after bruise blossomed across my skin. All angry and purplish black, like a violent storm breaking across my throat. Just a simple graze from my fingertip made me cry out in pain.

I looked broken.

I couldn't stop checking my reflection, sometimes forcing myself out of bed even when I shouldn't to see if it had gotten better or worse. Even though it hurt, I kept poking at the swelling, as if checking to see if it was real. I hugged myself in JJ's hoodie before I fell asleep that night, pretending that if no one could see the marks, then they weren't there.

★ ★ ★ ★ ✞ ★ ★ ★ ★

The second day was full of visitors. Our new family Docter, Dr. Phee made a house visit. I really didn't remember what they talked about, but I overheard Phee tell my mom that I was still in shock. Principal Baxster stopped by, but I didn't get to see him because I was taking a nap.

At four, I heard the doorbell ring and brushed my hair before JJ saw me like this. But it wasn't JJ that showed up in my room. It was Tony carrying flowers in one of my mom's nicer vases.

"Did you bring me flowers, Tony?" I giggled as I looked around the room for somewhere to put them.

"Dawn told me people bring flowers when someone gets hurt. I don't know," he shrugged before dropping them off on my desk. "So, uh, how is everything?" he asked, awkwardly gesturing toward me in a circle.

"Good. I'm not dead, so I've got that going for me."

Tony laughed and combed his fingers through his hair.

"What's going on at school?" I asked.

"Same old same old. Dawn is bugging the crap out of me and JJ is being a jerk. And everyone's asking about how you're doing."

"Does everyone know what happened?"

"Yeah. Half the school saw you ride off to the hospital, Sidell."

I didn't remember any of that. Or really anything after I tried to lunge at Khyree. I wasn't even sure who was there other than Tony and Dawn.

"Kyepher kept the seniors after the assembly yesterday to talk about it. She didn't use either of your names, but everyone knew."

I instinctively closed my eyes. I just knew that when I'd return to school, there wouldn't be a person in that school who didn't know exactly what happened to me.

"You said they're asking about how I'm doing," I whispered, trying to find the right words for my question. But there were no words to make it sound less horrible than it was. "Is there anyone out there asking about Khyree? Like maybe they think I did something to—"

"No," he cut me off. "No one thinks it's your fault."

I hadn't really cried since I got home from the hospital, but right as Tony stopped speaking, I broke into a sob. I didn't know why this made me cry. Maybe I was just relieved. But I heaved into my blanket, and a very uncomfortable Tony just stared at me in a panic.

"Are there tissues in here?" he huffed, his head on a swivel looking for them. "Or do you want a hug? Wait, no. We don't hug. Freak, what do I do right now?"

I dabbed my eyes with JJ's hoodie and laughed a little. "You got Khyree off me without hesitating but it's my tears that make you freak out?" I teased.

"Tony, what did you do?" JJ groaned as he came into my room. I didn't even hear him come in the house.

Dawn came in behind him, punching Tony's shoulder.

"Ow!" Tony yelped, rubbing his arm and glaring at her. "I didn't do anything!"

I laughed, "He really didn't guys," I promised with a watery smile, pointing to the flowers resting on my desk. "He just brought me flowers." I snuck a glance back at Tony, catching his lips turning up for half a second.

"Flowers, huh?" JJ raised an eyebrow. "Didn't take you for a flower kind of guy."

"I'll have you know I can be quite the gentleman when I want to be," Tony huffed, his ego clearly bruised. "I just prefer to maintain my aloof bad boy image most of the time." He ran a hand through his artfully messy hair.

Dawn let out an exaggerated gagging sound. "Yeah right, you got your one romantic gesture of the year from me," She smiled, wrapping her arms around Tony's neck. After planting a kiss on his reddened cheek, she flopped on my bed and pulled me into a warm hug. "How are you feeling, bestie babes? For real though, not just pretending to be fine."

I sighed, relaxing into my best friend's embrace, soaking in her familiar apple honey body spray. "I'm alright, I guess," I mumbled into her shoulder. "Just trying to push through everything, you know?"

"Don't listen to the lies the enemy whispers in your ear, okay? Just remember we're here for you. And Jesus got you, don't lose faith." she said, giving me an extra tight, supportive squeeze.

"Okay."

She released me and stood up from the bed. "Welp, Tony and I are going to bounce before you and JJ start making out or whatever."she winked.

JJ squinted his eyes as he plopped down on my bed. Dawn then headed out the door, and Tony was close behind.

"Hey, Tony?" I called out. He turned around, resting his shoulder against the doorframe. "Thanks."

"For the flowers?"

My smile faltered as I tried to make myself thank him properly for seeing me, for coming to my rescue, for stopping me from doing anything stupid, and for being the voice I recognized when everything else was blurry and confusing. He intervened when I had given up.

God used Tony as a vessel to fight for my life, reminding me that I needed to fight for it too.

"Yeah, those too," I sighed. Tony blinked a few times before nodding and turning into the hallway. As soon as I heard the stairs creak, I scooted over on my bed, patting next to me. JJ raised an eyebrow and smirked. "Come here. I want you to hold me," I pouted, and his smirk transformed into a full-on smile.

"How did we go from you nervously asking if I would, to you straight up telling me to?" he snickered as he propped himself up against my headboard. I groaned as I curled into his side, carefully laying my head on his chest and wrapping my arm around his waist.

"Tell me something," I murmured into his shirt.

"Kyepher figured out I punched Khyree."

JJ had brought up that punch every time he visited me, and I needed it to stop. I didn't want to think about it. What Khyree did to me rattled a lot of people, myself included. Had I not had a concussion, there was no doubt that I would have hurt Khyree myself, so I couldn't fault JJ for having the same reaction. But I remembered God's saying, "Be angry, but sin not."

So I humbled myself, trying my best to represent a true follower of Christ.

"Oh?" I said.

"She gave me a warning."

"Well," I sighed, "you got lucky."

When I looked up at JJ, he was giving me a strange look. He looked like he wanted to say something else, but he didn't. I was relieved when he whispered, "Tell me something."

"Have I ever told you about that time I went to my church's youth camp and decided to change my name and take on a whole new persona?" I asked, and JJ laughed so hard I could feel it in his chest. Whatever scowl was on his face was gone now, replaced with that smile he reserved only for me. Goodness, I loved that smile.

And him.

★ ★ ★ ★ ✟ ★ ★ ★ ★

On the third day, Principal Baxster showed up at the house.

My dad and mom hadn't told me anything about what was going on with the school, but I knew how to read between the lines. It wasn't what they wanted, which was probably the real reason Baxster was here.

Both of my parents fussed over me as me and Cayest made our way down the stairs. Our mom was a surgical nurse. Surely she knew that I was fine to walk now, yet she still insisted on my little sister walking in step with me down the stairs.

Baxster was seated at the kitchen table and rose to his feet as soon as he saw me. "Hey, how are you feeling?" he asked.

I wrapped JJ's hoodie tighter around me as I took the seat across from him. "Fine." I said, as Cayest took a seat by our dad.

Baxster forced a weak smile as he sat back down, and I didn't miss the way his eyes dropped to my neck. His pathetic attempt at a smile fell right off his face as soon as he saw the marks Khyree left on me.

"Principal Baxster brought flowers," my mom said.

"Right, yes. They're from the entire faculty, including Headmaster Kyepher." he stuttered, his eyes finally meeting mine again.

I didn't bother to look. "Thanks," I muttered. "So, is Khyree going to be at school when I go back Monday or not?"

His eyes widened as he looked at my dad and mom. Maybe I was supposed to be more polite and wait for him to get around to it, but I was tired and just wanted to get back in bed.

"Well, no," he said, and my mom fell into the seat beside me with a smile on her lips. "His parents have decided that given recent events—"

"You mean him strangling me?" I snapped.

"Sidell," Mom warned.

"Uh, yes, that. Anyway, Khyree has been admitted into a facility that can help him with some of his mental health problems."

"And what happens when he gets out?" Dad asked.

"We haven't figured that out yet. Sidell's safety at school is obviously our priority, but if there is a way we can ensure that both students get to make it to graduation—"

"You're going to let him come back," I sighed, clenching my eyes shut. "Of course, you are."

"That's not what I said, Sidell. The school and the board believe that Khyree has serious mental health problems. He will be punished for what he did to you, but we don't want to ruin his future over a mistake that was made during a manic episode."

Cayest looked at mom and dad who shared a look that I didn't understand, but neither of them said a word.

"And all of this is hypothetical until he leaves the facility, which could be anywhere between next week to months after graduation."

"Hypothetically if he were to come back, would he still be in Sidell's classes?" Mom asked.

"He'll likely have to drop Photography and AP History, so Sidell will no longer have any classes with him. And we would switch his lunch period too."

"And how do you keep him away from me for the rest of the day?"

"Kyepher and I are discussing that. Right now, we're leaning toward requiring him to spend the time before assembly, his break period, and any other non-class time in our office under supervision. Essentially, if he is on campus, he either has to be in class or with us."

It could work. Their plan would prevent Khyree from ever being alone with me on campus. That's really what I wanted all this time. But he'd still be there lurking around every corner of my mind.

"As for Monday, the faculty met this morning to discuss accommodations. The counselor, Mrs. Jackson will be getting to school earlier and will be staying late in case you need her while on campus." Like I was going to talk to a counselor without being forced. "All of your teachers have been told to excuse you if you need to step out of class for any reason…"

I zoned out as he listed the accommodations. My gaze flickered to the flowers Baxster brought over, all green and white. Our school colors. Tony's flowers were prettier. Carnations of all sorts of colors, still with a Publix price tag on them.

Tony's flowers just felt more honest, unlike Baxster who brought them out of obligation.

★ ★ ★ ★ ✞ ★ ★ ★ ★

My dad and mom drove both my sister and I to school on Monday. They both kept chatting away in the front seat about vacation ideas for the summer. It was clearly a ploy to keep me distracted, but I played along. Threw in a few beaches I liked in the past while staring out the window.

After dropping off Cayest, the car went completely silent as dad pulled into the circle of my highschool. I could feel both my parents searching for some words of comfort, but there weren't any. The only comfort I had was that I knew Khyree wasn't here today. No guarantees about the future. But I was safe today. That would have to be enough. The campus was quiet. It was early enough that only a handful of students would be on campus.

When I entered the building, the nerves I felt jumping around in my chest felt like the same ones I had on my first day at Westwood High.

"Hey?" I jerked upright, turning to see a girl with cherry-red box braids walking up to me. "I'm Cherish, I just saw you from afar and wanted to know if you are okay?"

"Yes, thank you." I smiled. I started to walk, but I forgot where I was going. I stood there for a second, furrowing my brows.

"Are you heading to your locker?" Cherish asked.

Right. My locker. That's always how I started my day.

"Yeah."

"Want me to walk with you?"

I hesitated. I barely knew this girl, but her offer touched me. I guessed I could use a friend right now. "Sure, thank you," I said, managing a small smile.

As we walked through the maze of halls, I snuck glances at Cherish's beautiful and flawless style. She was definitely one of the popular girls that all the boys would make a big deal about. Her uniform was ironed to perfection and her white sneakers looked like they never touched the ground. The gold nose septum and wrist bracelet she wore reminded me of JJ's flashy jewelry tastes. A pang of jealousy pinched me, knowing Cherish's polished aesthetic complimented my boyfriend better than my own style.

Finally, I spotted JJ leaning against my locker and picked up my pace to go meet him. It was when I turned to thank Cherish again for walking with me that I realized she had disappeared from my side. Okay?

"Hey. Welcome back." JJ grinned, and I stood up on my tiptoes for a kiss. His lips met mine with a small chuckle, and for a moment, the morning felt normal. "How are you feeling?"

"Fine," I sighed, nudging him to the side so I could get my books. "Just tired." When I looked over at him, he was giving me a look that said he knew I was lying. "I just want to get through today, okay?"

"Fair enough."

We hung out by my locker for a while, neither of us really saying anything of substance. Just small talk about classes and exams. When we started walking to assembly, there were more students out and about. It started to feel like a normal morning.

And then I stepped into assembly.

The faculty were the first to notice me. Their conversations died as soon as their heads snapped in my direction. JJ nudged me by the back before anyone got a chance to say anything to me.

It wasn't any better inside. The chatter died off in a low wave as student after student spotted me walking to my seat. Laughter and shouts turned into inaudible whispers that somehow felt louder to me. When I got to the senior section, there weren't any whispers. Just silence and about eighty pairs of eyes on me.

Dawn jumped to her feet, arms crossed as she started staring at people boldly as I sat in the chair beside her. She was very protective of me, and will let everyone know it.

"People are complete weirdos." Dawn grumbled, plopping back down. "Bestie babes, are you okay?" she asked softly, and I just nodded mutely.

★ ★ ★ ★ ✟ ★ ★ ★ ★

It kept happening. Everywhere I went, I was being monitored or catered to.

When walking to the study hall, it was Amarah Kincaid who was walking beside me. On the way to lunch, it was my classmate Wayne who powerwalked to catch up with me before asking if I needed notes for Physics.

I didn't know where everyone kept coming from. I never walked beside Amarah Kincaid to class. Wayne took horrible notes and would know that I was better off winging it on my own. And that morning with Cherish was weird too.

The first moment where I actually got to be alone was in the cafeteria. The line was too chaotic and loud, so I just went to my table to enjoy the quiet until the line died down. I pressed my cheek into the cool table and took a deep breath.

Hey Sidell?

I sat up with a gasp.

"Sid, are you okay?" Dawn asked as she dropped her tray onto the table.

"Yeah, I'm fine," I snapped. After a beat, I whispered, "I'm sorry."

"I get it."

"Why is everyone all over me today?"

"Your hair looks nice. Or maybe it's because you almost died last week." Dawn stabbed at the pasta with a fork.

"I didn't almost die. Khyree is an inefficient strangler," I muttered.

"Looked pretty efficient to me." my best friend remarked and my stomach dropped. "Honestly, everyone is all over you because they feel guilty. You should have heard all these weirdos last week. In cheer practice, I had to listen to Emily fake cry, saying how you were such a nice teammate, and how she wasn't there for you."

"Uh, me and you never liked Emily."

"Exactly. She's a clout chaser," she huffed before stabbing another piece of pasta. "No one would shut up about how they had a feeling something was wrong and didn't do anything."

Before I could respond, Tony pulled a chair beside Dawn and JJ dropped a plate in front of me.

"I'm not hungry," I sighed.

"Come on, Sid. You need to eat something," he pleaded, plopping down next to me. I reluctantly took the fork from his hand.

"Sidell's worked up because everyone is all over her," Dawn said.

"It's everyone from Baxster's crew. He asked them all to keep an eye on you and make sure you felt safe when you came back," JJ explained.

"Oh." I ducked my head as I tried to control the overwhelming urge to cry. After a beat, it passed, and I forced myself to take a bite of pasta.

Dawn, Tony, and JJ kept on talking while I focused on eating at least half of what JJ brought me. My gaze kept drifting around the cafeteria, catching classmates and underclassmen I didn't even realize were stealing glances at me.

Chapter Forty-Seven:
♩♩

September 19th. Donica's death anniversary. That was the day I've dreaded for weeks. The reason for my bad attitude. My stomach churned as I huddled over the toilet, spilling my guts out along with any last shred of dignity. Grandma stood watch, murmuring prayers and pats on the back like I'm a toddler with a tummy ache instead of a grieving boyfriend.

"I'm fine," I croak, willing her to leave. She doesn't.

I was a mess. An emotional train wreck barreling down the tracks. But I plaster on a smile as I spotted Sidell at the lockers, my insides shriveling. She had been through enough without my baggage.

My secret sat like a stone in my gut, growing heavier each time I swallowed my words. The perfect moment never comes. Now there's too much at stake. I couldn't just drop a bomb about my dead ex on Sidell's first day back after what that monster Khyree did...well, I couldn't even think about what he did without seeing red.

Maybe one day I'd find the courage to reopen those wounds and tell her everything. But for now, I'd keep pretending I was fine, even as regret ate away at my insides like a parasite. She deserved at least that much. I owe her a rock to lean on, not more heartache. But God, hiding the truth, choking it down until I couldn't breathe...it was killing me.

But I force my lips into a grin. "Hey. Welcome back."

I hated Khyree even more than I did before. That didn't make Khyree special or anything. I hated most people I went to school with. I was surrounded by knotheads who were always at odds with me as if we weren't all trying to get out the city's gutter water, so it was difficult not to resent them all. But my disdain for Khyree was on a whole other level. A fact I hadn't fully grasped until he attacked my girlfriend, Sidell, that day.

Those dark bruises on her slender neck made my blood boil every time I pictured them. And the way her body trembled when I held her close broke me. Reminded me more of my ex Donica when I applied pressure on her bleeding wound as she was dying in my arms.

I knew Sidell didn't want me getting involved in her business with Khyree. And I respected that. I really did.

But when I saw her trying to hide those finger-shaped bruises under my hoodie that evening at her house, I couldn't stop the scenes from that day from replaying in my mind. For as long as I've known Khyree, he had always portrayed himself as the quiet, awkward foster kid who wouldn't hurt a fly. But the truth was, he was an obsessive, cowardly monster with no moral code or ability to see when he was in the wrong. Which was always.

Over the time span Sidell had been absent from school to recover, My friend Tony kept hounding me about my "anger issues" and trying to get me to see the school counselor. But it wasn't anger issues. It was idiocy overload from the morons at this school. They just kept pushing and pushing, trying to get every little detail about what went down with Sidell and Khyree. I was about to snap on all of them. Khyree was actually pretty smart to make himself invisible this week. Because if I saw him, I knew I'd do more than just beat him down this time. I didn't care what the Head Master threatened me with.

On a side note, I was relieved that Cherish and I were able to patch things up. After my thoughtless behavior at the house party—ditching her on the dance floor without explanation—I knew I had to make amends.

It went against my character to be so thoughtless, and the weight of my guilt burdened me for days.

We met in the computer lab after class, the hum of machines providing a buffer for our awkward conversation. I apologized profusely, my words tumbling out in a rush. "Cherish, I'm so sorry. I never meant to hurt you."

Her eyes, usually bright with mischief, were guarded as she listened. I took a deep breath and explained my feelings for Sidell, watching her face carefully for a reaction. To my surprise, understanding dawned in her expression.

"I've been crushing on you all year," she whispered softly, biting down her blush. "But I get it. You can't help who you catch feelings for."

I was shook. How did I not peep game? But instead of being bitter, Cherish showed mad maturity. She even offered to help Sidell when she came back to school, a move that spoke volumes about her character.

As we bounced from the lab, with a newfound understanding between us, I felt grateful for Cherish's realness. It was a bond that I promised to always value and respect.

Chapter Forty-Eight: Sidell

After two long weeks of playing catch up, I was finally back on schedule. Sure, I had to get to the school at 6:30 to take my makeup exams, but now I was home free . . . well, as home free as any senior with a schedule made up entirely of AP classes could be.

Joining my crowd of peers out into the hallway, I nestled between our lockers and caught a sight of JJ. His eyes softened as I watched him, as if he could tell what I was thinking of him, and of how much he made me feel.

And then he opened his arms, and I smiled, earning me one of his adorable dimples in return. I crossed the space quickly, not stopping until I crashed against him, immediately wrapping my arms around his waist. I felt him huff as my head landed on his chest, but then his arms came down around me, and I closed my eyes.

"The exams tore you up, huh?" he muttered into my hair as his hands rhythmically moved along my back. I nodded, my voice muffled by his shirt. "You?"

His voice vibrated through his body as a laugh escaped his lips. "How long would you tease me if I said I barely survived Calculus?"

I had to giggle at that. "At least until graduation,"

Retrieving my backpack from my locker, the two of us started walking down the hallway.

"Hey Sid, are you doing anything tomorrow evening after school?" JJ asked.

"Bible study at church with my family. Why?"

"I got around to organizing my room and just thought you'd finally wanna see those paintings we were talking about?"

"I'd love to JJ but church is very important to me and my family. Especially my dad - he's never missed a day. I doubt he'll let me skip." I said.

"Tell them you're feeling sick and can't go. Isn't church like two hours, three hours long? We'll be back before you know it."

Our hands separated as we passed the Headmaster's office. The snobby woman was probably peering at us through the blinds. We had already been busted for PDA once this week, but Kyepher let it slide with a warning. So now we're attempting to be more careful. "Attempting" being the operative word. Once outside in the parking lot, our hands re-joined like magnets. JJ interlaced his fingers with mine, his palm warm and solid.

"No JJ. I can't keep lying to them," I said firmly, even as my traitorous heart begged me to give in. "And I just can't see myself skipping church to go to your apartment."

"I'll come to church with you," JJ pleaded, his dark eyes boring into mine. "Your parents always saw me as some kind of godless heathen, but they ain't know the real me. But now that they've warmed up to me, I bet they wouldn't object to our relationship if I was a bible-thumping teenager."

I hesitated, hating that he was right. My parents would probably do a 180 if JJ suddenly found Jesus. But the thought of him faking faith for my sake made me deeply uneasy.

"Okay, JJ. Listen, I'm not trying to make things harder for you, really," I said gently. "But I'm going to have to put my foot down about letting you pretend to believe in Jesus. That's going too far. And it's not about us or what we want anymore." I took a deep breath before continuing. "I'm not going to join you in mocking my faith and that of a million other people just because I want to date you."

JJ's face clouded over, his eyes stormy. "Don't judge me, Sidell," he said sharply, releasing his hand from mine and stopping our stroll. "I'm not asking for your permission to play Christian either."

He paused, and I could see him struggling to contain his frustration. When he continued, his tone was measured. "Besides, I've been a Christian for most of my life. I...derailed because of what happened, but that doesn't mean I'm about to commit some unforgivable sin that will doom us both. You need to chill out a bit."

"Chill out?" I shot back, stung. "I'm pretty chill. I just can't see how this is going to work—" I stopped short when a woman's shrill voice pierced the air.

"Where do you think you're going?" a woman yelled. I yanked JJ by the hand and hid behind one of the columns.

"Sid, what are you—" JJ started, but I slapped my hand over his mouth. His eyes widened in surprise.

I slowly peered around the edge of the column, holding my breath.

"I'm not going to sit in there and listen to them talk about my son like that!" A deep voice bellowed in return. Even from this distance, I could see the man's shoulders tense, hands curled into fists.

"Who is that?" I whispered, my voice catching. I had a sinking suspicion, but prayed I was wrong.

"Khyree's parents," JJ confirmed my fears. I clutched his arm, silently begging him not to move. The last people I wanted to see were the Latimores.

"She's just worried. Maybe it's too soon to take him out of—"

"Get in the damn car, Ashanti!" Mr. Latimore cut her off with a growl. "We're leaving."

I didn't need to see his face to envision the scowl, to feel the rage radiating from him. It was a tone I knew too well, one that still paralyzes me.

"No! You can't just throw a temper tantrum every time you don't get your way. Let's just—" Ashanti tried again, stronger this time.

"Ashanti!" Mr. Latimore screamed, his rage palpable even across the parking lot. My entire body shuddered.

That's when it hit me—Khyree grew up immersed in that anger. He learned it from them. This realization didn't erase what he did, but it shifted something inside me. The knots in my stomach loosened ever so slightly.

We stayed hidden behind the column until the Latimores drove off, tires screeching on asphalt. Only then did I let my back relax against the column

"Sidell?" JJ whispered. "Are you good?"

"Yeah." And for once, it wasn't a lie. When I looked up at JJ, I could tell he didn't believe me. I reached down and grabbed his hand. "I'm really okay."

I made a mental note to pray for Khyree tonight. Not because he deserved it, but because maybe someone needed to think about the kid who'd only ever known fury for love.

Chapter Forty-Nine:
♪♪

Agreeing to go to church with Sidell did catch me a little off guard.

But I was slightly offended when she assumed that I was joking about my decision. I seriously wanted to go, but it felt awkward to announce to Sidell that I had started praying again. Of course, I was not ashamed of Christ or his gospel, but being born again did not seem like something that needed to be announced to anyone.

The signs were supposed to tell. And they did.

Sidell had been the product of my prayers and I'd received my answers almost immediately. Almost like Jesus was sitting across the table from me, sipping from a celestial cup of tea, nodding and winking saying, 'I got you, just wait and see.' Sidell was nothing short of a blessing in human form, the sort of blessing that made you wonder if angels took night classes in being human to walk among us.

When I slipped beside Sidell on the pew, her body quivered from the intense effort of restraining her laughter as she tried to keep her face expressionless. The corners of her lips started curling up against their will, but she bit down hard on her bottom lip, as she stared straight ahead at the altar. Her light pink dress accentuated her frame as she glanced over at me once more, her lungs spasmed as a chuckle escaped her and she pressed her hand tightly against her jawbone, desperate to prevent an outburst of hysterical giggles.

I knew I stood out in this stuffy church crowd, but I didn't care. With my charcoal suit, gold chain, and single hoop earring, I was determined to make a statement. Wiping my sweaty palms on my pants, my stomach churned. I loved pushing boundaries, but this time I feared I'd gone too far.

"Let's rise as we take the hymn..." I stood rigidly, hands clasped behind my back. Sidell's eyes caught mine and she snorted, quickly lowering her head.

"Aye, this ain't funny, Sidell Evermost." I hissed through gritted teeth, glaring at her. "You're gonna get us kicked out."

"I can't help it," She whispered back over the sound of the piano. "You look like you're about to explode, JJ, but then that's not surprising. It's likely the resident demons registering their displeasure at the possibility of a deliverance session."

I licked my lips, as I could no longer resist cracking a smile.

"Yeah, I'm sure your parents would like that," I said, looking around to see if they had spotted us, which they hadn't. "Maybe, that's just what we need to do to gain their approval. Put on a show like Christians do all the time," I said quietly.

Sidell's eyes widened in shock, but she quickly composed herself, offering me a tight smile before pretending to study the lyrics on the screen. Damn. That was pretty blasphemous. I realized I had struck a nerve, but Sidell was too polite to call me out on it directly. A pang of regret pierced my chest. I really needed to learn to control my loose lips in church.

I shyly mumbled the lyrics while watching everyone else, paranoid they were judging me with their glares.

That's when I heard Sidell whispering to herself. Scrunching my face in confusion I looked between the big screen and her, realizing that she was not in sync with the rest of the Church. I arched my eyebrows at her but she was too focused to pay me any mind.

That's when I realized she was praying. I couldn't decipher what she was saying but I could tell that she was sincere.

"Sid." I tugged at her fingers as we lowered our bodies to sit after the hymn.

"Uh, d-do you want s-something, JJ?" she asked. The squeeze of her hand made my heart race. My pulse stuttered at her hypnotic effect on me.

"Sidell, I'm sorry–" I began as my hand played with the gold-plated jewelry at my neck. My chest expanded with a heavy breath before my gaze wandered to our intertwined fingers. "Look, I'm an a**hole for saying something like that about your faith while sitting in a Church you tried to keep me from attending."

She blinked sporadically, not sure what she'd heard. "What?"

"I apologize, excuse my language. I was saying that it was stupid and wrong, and I'm really sorry for doing exactly what you'd probably assumed would happen." I expelled a wavering breath. "If it means anything to you, I promise to do better, Sid. I'm hoping you can forgive me so we can move on and we can, you know, be…"

"Better Christians?" she asked with a stern arch of her brow.

A smile teased the edges of my lips. "I was going to say better partners, but yeah, I guess we could do that too, although partners in crime might be more accurate for the description."

"I guess you're right. You're forgiven, Jacky Jamison. After all, that is what Jesus would have wanted me to do." We settled into silence as the Preacher mounted the pulpit.

Our moment was over as we both focused on writing notes and flipping through the pages of my borrowed bible to find the verses. In what seemed like a split second, the end of first service grace was being said and soon the crowd started mingling amongst themselves.

★ ★ ★ ★ ✞ ★ ★ ★ ★

"Alright, you two. I don't want no funny busy on a Sunday morning."

"Papa, come on," Sidell blinked a few times at her dad. But it was understandable. Everything involving his daughter automatically kept him ten toes down.

"I can promise you, Mr. Evermost, we'll stay out of trouble," said JJ.

Mr. Evermost nodded after a moment of taking the prospect of his daughter and her boyfriend skipping mid service into consideration. "If all it takes is mustard seed faith, I trust you, Son, that when you two are not under my eyes, that you'll respect God's watchful eye."

"Yes sir." I pointed a finger at Mr. Evermost. "His eye is always on the sparrow, right?"

Mr. Evermost patted my shoulder and offered a stern smile before directing his attention to Sidell. "Remember the second service curfew?"

"Seven. I know, Papa," she said, leaning into his hug as he planted a forehead kiss on me.

★ ★ ★ ★ ✟ ★ ★ ★ ★

"It's really quiet in here?" Sidell whispered as we entered my apartment. "Is your grandma not home?"

"Oh, no she had church this evening too." I said, looking around as if I didn't already recognize the place. "Did you uh… want anything to drink?"

"Uhm…no I think I'm okay."

"Okay." I patted the pockets of my jeans. "You down to go to my room?"

"Are you sure that we wouldn't be breaking a rule of some sort?" she asked. "You know with your grandma not being here.."

"It's cool, I don't know what you scared of." I laughed, grabbing her hand. "C'mon, Sid. Trust me."

With a gentle tug, I pulled Sidell along with me to my room. As soon as we reached the door, I let go of her hand. She slowly made her way to sit on the edge of my bed while I rummaged through my dresser to find something.

"Here, I got something for you," I said, spotting the small black box amongst the chaos. Sitting beside her, I handed it over with pride. "My grandma helped me pick it out."

She accepted the box and my heartbeat quickened in anticipation. Slowly, she revealed its contents and gasped at the sight before her. Nestled inside was a gold silver necklace, intricately woven with delicate beads and rubies that sparkled like Chicago's city lights.

"It's beautiful!" she exclaimed, fingers grazing over the jewels.

I replied with an easy smile. "Figured you deserved something real nice after everything that went down."

"Thank you, Jacky." She attempted to put it on herself until I intervened.

"Here, I got you." I took the necklace and she turned her back to me as she scooped her hair to the side so I could see better. My heart was beating faster as I felt the warmth of her skin at my fingertips. Trembling, I missed the hook a few times as I pulled the necklace around her. I was so close and it only lasted less than five seconds, but by the time I moved away I had heard how it took Sidell's breath away. Her breathing was rapid until she exhaled slowly as if she needed to remind her brain how to breathe again.

My hands around her neck felt delicious in a forbidden way. I couldn't explain it, but it brought heat to her face again. After fastening the necklace around her neck, we sat in silence.

Sidell's gaze locked onto my face, searching for hints of what I wanted to say next. Under her intense scrutiny, I felt exposed, like an open book waiting to be read. Lost in her hypnotic gaze, I almost forgot why we were there—why I needed to have this conversation. Could she see right through me?

I cleared my throat, grasping for the right words. "There's something that's been weighing heavy on my soul. And honestly, I don't even know where to begin," My confession hung heavily between us. She tilted her head, straining to see my downcast face. But I kept my eyes locked on her, studying every detail like an artist examining a subject.

"Start anywhere. Whatever it is that you want to talk about, just say it. I don't ever want you to feel alone. It would break my heart to imagine you dealing with all you went through completely alone," she urged gently, her words flowing effortlessly without hesitation.

"Man, Sidell. I don't know what to say. Thank you for making this easier to talk about," I grinned, trying to mask my swirling anxiety.

"You're welcome," she cheekily replied, her gaze shifting away from me but still aware of my creepy, unblinking stare. *Restraining order, here I come.*

"You're adorable," I said. She just grinned wider like she found my awkwardness amusing.

"I know and you are, once again, welcome."

I laughed a short laugh that didn't reach my eyes, then I bit my lip, and suddenly the atmosphere in our little corner shifted abruptly. It was time to get real. I had to confront my demons and hope that Sidell could offer some solace, as best as she could.

"So, I get these nightmares," I began, clearing my throat.

Sidell moved the tiny box aside, turning her body towards me with undivided attention. "Ever since your mom..." Her words trailed off delicately, trying not to trigger any painful memories.

I shook my head softly and cleared my throat once again, fingers nervously rubbing against my kneecap. This was unexplored territory for me; no one knew about this. Voicing it aloud was an entirely different monster.

"No. That's not the only reason." I sucked in a breath, then pushed it out. "Sid, when I told you I was going through some stuff...I wasn't unveiling the full truth."

She nodded, encouraging me to continue. My heart hammered in my chest as I left her wondering what else I might be hiding. Deciding to take the plunge, I rose from the bed and headed straight for my closet. With determination, I pulled out a folder that safeguarded my most sacred paintings.

Sitting back down beside Sidell, I took a steady breath before flipping open the folder, even though I didn't need visual reminders to recall her face. "I uh, lost my best friend Donica at fourteen." I confessed, swallowing hard, the weight of my words hung heavy between us. I knew she wouldn't know how to respond; losing a friend at such a young age was a tragedy that you could only imagine from the outside looking in.

"I'm so sorry, JJ," she whispered softly, reaching out to place a comforting hand on my knee. "That must have been really hard, I didn't know."

All I could manage was a nod, handing over the album to her. She scooted closer, her floral perfume invading my senses. I focused on my breathing, in and out, as she flipped through each painted portraits of Donica

"I never believed anyone who said time would heal me," I confessed hoarsely, feeling Sidell's arm gently patting my back in soothing circles. My voice came out as a raw whisper, veiling the emotions that threatened to overwhelm me. "I didn't think anything could bring back even a sliver of the joy we shared through this crazy city life. We had our paths mapped out since we were knee-high — schooling hard, studying to become doctors who followed God's blueprint: saving lives. We never talked about marriage or any romantic ish; it was an unspoken agreement that we were destined for each other. Can't deny it — we were inseparable...Then I got into some trouble. A fourteen year old church boy, trying to act better than I was and I did some people wrong. Donica caught the bullet instead, When it was for me. " A strained chuckle escaped my lips, my pulse racing through my veins.

Sidell extended her arm, offering soothing strokes on my back. I exhaled sharply, my voice a mere whisper as I continued, "I'm ashamed that I blamed God for my faults and in many ways, I felt like that biblical dude Job; like God was testing me to see if I could stay faithful, if I could hold onto him. And hold on, I did. The last few hours of Donica's life, I poured all my time and energy into serving Him, watching every word and action carefully to avoid sinning. I sought His will for my life and when specific answers didn't come, I started fabricating them in my head—especially if they aligned with some scripture. But I gave up on him."

Sidell met my gaze, a touch of pity in her eyes. "You were just a child, Jacky. You need to forgive yourself.," she sighed. "Healing is a miraculous touch of God in our lives and we don't always get miracles, for crying out loud. That's why God says that even when we walk through fire, he will walk with us. Sometimes, walking with God doesn't even spare us from the burn of the fire but in such times, he gives us strength to go through it." She blinked hard several times, attempting not to cry.

"Well, I couldn't recall if anyone else tried, but Grandma did and I wasn't listening. I was so sure that God would heal Donica, while every other verdict was Satan trying to bring down my faith. And then when I got back and found out that Donica had passed on, it wasn't just the pain of losing her that broke me, it was the pain of my destroyed hope that I'd spent a lot of time building. My 'unshaken faith' fell flat on its back." There was a crack in my voice that I couldn't do anything about now.

Sidell wrapped her arms around my back. It brought some sort of relief but I knew that I couldn't sink into that right now. If I didn't say this today, pour it all out, my heart would remain a chalice that held all my haunting memories and raw emotions inside. I couldn't process this on my own.

"I didn't like God very much during that period, but I held out hope, after all, we'd read about how Jesus raised Lazarus and other dead people in the bible, right?"

"Right." she replied breathlessly. "Because he was the same God yesterday, today and forever."

"Exactly. So, when Donica was buried, that's when the bitterness and rebellion started. I couldn't comprehend what life was about. God had let me go through dirt and didn't swoop right in to help me. I got sucked into a black hole where I did things I was not very proud of, but it was either that or deal with the reality that God had let me down, and I'll tell you, being on the wrong side was way easier. I spiraled faster and deeper into this lifestyle, into this person no one could recognize and I used my anger as a shield to shut down the questions and well-meaning advice from family and friends till it stopped coming."

My teeth ground against each other, grinding out the pain and bitterness that had consumed me for so long. "But then fate played a sneaky game and brought you into my life," I continued in a hushed tone. "You became the living embodiment of everything I once cherished... everything I had lost. Of course, I gravitated towards you; you were familiar yet exotic in a way that ignited something deep within me. But the boy who was deserving of you no longer existed." I laughed weakly, licking my lips. "And believe me, I tried to stay away to protect you, to shield you from my world and spare you the pain. But even that didn't work."

Sidell peered up at me, her eyes shimmering with unshed tears. "I'm glad it didn't work," she whispered. "I couldn't bear to lose you, JJ. It would feel like hell on earth."

"I understand you, Sid," I rushed to say. "Because I feel the same way. This entire journey made me realize something profound: I wasn't meant to be where I was. I wasn't one of those chosen few who could stray and find their way back if they pleased. I am part of God's chosen generation, and though I can't comprehend how Donica's death fits into His master plan, I now understand that your arrival in my life, your choices, your struggles – they were all part of a grand design to lead me back to Him. Every single moment was orchestrated for my return."

A smile graced Sidell's lips as she leaned in closer. "You're a peculiar boy, Jacky Jamison," she mused.

I exhaled, the tension melting away from my shoulders as a chuckle danced through the air. "Nah, just a bullhead who dared to defy his creator and got humbled in the most legendary way."

"Don't you ever do it again," she warned playfully. "Don't you ever leave me."

Silently, I raised a pinky finger. "I promise."

"You suck," she laughed as our pinky fingers intertwined.

384

Chapter Fifty: Sidell

"Okay, one more on the porch where we take your first day of school photos," my mom ordered, snapping her fingers in the direction of the front door. I rolled my eyes as I marched outside, followed by my posse of fans - Dad, his camera at the ready, Mom directing the shoot like a drill sergeant, my sisters Cayest and Dawn there for moral support.

I could see the Facebook post now: the picture of me standing with my Winnie the Pooh backpack on the first day of Kindergarten put right next to a photo of me in my cap and gown. I gave the best smile I could, but it erupted into a laugh when I saw Dawn's goofy face behind my mom's camera. "Cut it out!" I yelled at her.

Mom spun around, but Dawn instantly wiped the jack-o-lantern grin off her face and slung an arm around Cayest.

"My phone keeps freezing, stay still Sidell," Cayest complained, snapping her own round of photos.

"I am still." I said, smacking my thigh. "Can we move this along? I only have so much time left."

The senior class didn't have to get there for another two hours, but Baxster emailed me late yesterday afternoon asking me to come in early. I didn't know exactly what it was about, but I had a feeling it had something to do with Khyree.

Mom ended up taking about a hundred more pictures, despite my protests. I must've rolled my eyes in every single one. When she finally put the camera down to fix her hair, I seized the opportunity and grabbed Dawn, bolting for her car before Mom could notice.

As we drove away, I shrugged off my cap and gown in relief. "Step on it before she realizes I'm gone!" I told Dawn. She just laughed and turned up the radio. I glanced back to see Mom, Dad, and Cayest scrambling back into the house, likely realizing that neither of them had showered or dressed for graduation.

"Are you ready to get out of this town?" Dawn asked.

"I'm ready to get out of this school," I replied. But leaving for college . . . that made my chest clench. Not just because I didn't feel ready for it, but also because me and JJ weren't going to the same place.

Three hours might not seem like much, but it was a lot different than seeing him every day like I was used to. I already missed him like crazy.

The school was a ghost town when I arrived.

"I can stay with you if you want?" Dawn offered.

"No, it's okay. I know you're dying to go find Tony right now," I said, smirking.

"He's my boyfriend, I'm not obsessed with him!" she protested, blushing wildly.

"Mmhmm, sure," I teased as she backed away.

"You understand right? Because me and you will be around each other plenty this summer?" she smiled, holding onto the top of her graduation cap.

"Exactly." I laughed, wiping down my graduation gown.

My crystal heels clicked against the pavement as I looked around the quad. Westwood High really was a beautiful school. I never really appreciated it before.

The administration building wasn't entirely empty. A few teachers passed me on the walk to Baxster's office, each offering their congratulations on making it to graduation. It was more by God's grace that I lived to see graduation than it was for me to actually graduate.

Baxster's door was already open, and with no secretary present to tell me to wait, I just let myself in.

"Ah, there's Sidell," Principal Baxster said with a smile. On his couch sat a woman, one I didn't recognize. She was a brown skinned woman with glasses, who wore a plain pantsuit and had a notebook sitting in her lap. "Thank you so much for coming in."

"Is something wrong?" My eyes kept darting between Baxster and the woman on the couch. Baxster's smile didn't match with the hardened look in that woman's eyes and the way she struggled to force a smile.

"No, not at all. Sidell, this is LaTasha Sharma. She's auditing the school," he explained as if that somehow answered why I was brought in. "Basically, it's her job to make sure that everything at Westwood is running how it should. She's looking into our curriculum, our finances, and even our faculty." Baxster stepped behind me to shut the door before turning to close the blinds. "I thought it might be helpful for her to hear from one of our new students what their experience at Westwood had looked like."

For a second, I wanted to protest that I would rather them ask a student whose actually been here for all four years. But as Baxster raised his eyebrows, it clicked. That's why Baxster's brought me here. To tell the auditor directly what Kyepher let slide.

"Principal Baxster, I think it would be best if you stepped out," LaTasha finally said, clicking her pen. Baxster looked at me and nodded. I survived being assaulted and strangled. I could easily survive talking about it.

I settled into the chair across from the couch, wincing slightly when I heard the door click shut behind Baxster. I sat my cap and gown on the desk.

"Before we get to my questions, is there anything specific you would like to share your time here at Westwood?" LaTasha asked, not even looking up from her notebook.

"Earlier this semester, I was strangled in the school parking lot. And in a few hours, I'm graduating alongside the boy who strangled me."

LaTasha dropped her pen as her head jerked up. The blank, bored expression from before was replaced with a look of horror. Baxster definitely didn't warn this poor woman.

"Would you like me to start from the beginning?" I asked, gripping the wooden arm of my chair so hard it felt like it could break.

"Uh, yes," she replied, blinking rapidly as she reached down to grab her pen. "That would . . . yeah, that would probably be best."

"I had a classmate, Khyree Latimore, for the first half of high school. He was . . . obsessed with me," I started. "I just took it as a silly little crush, besides he was nice so I never thought anything of it......"

I watched as LaTasha frantically wrote down every detail, from JJ's fight with Khyree, to Rayo being arrested, to the main incident. I waited for LaTasha's hand to slow down before speaking again.

"Baxster and some of the teachers have been trying to help me recently, but none of them can do much when Headmaster Kyepher kept making compromises with his parents to let Khyree stay," I admitted. "So, that's what I thought I should tell you. What were your questions?"

"Forget my questions," she sighed. "Are you okay?"

"I'm about to spend graduation in the row behind the boy who tried to kill me. No, I'm not okay. But I'm willing to forgive. Not because I want to, but because the God that I serve forgives—"

Before I could say anything else, LaTasha had pulled the tissue box from Mr. Baxster's desk. She took a few and dabbed below her eyes. I shifted awkwardly, not sure what to do. Comforting weeping adults definitely wasn't something I had experience in at all.

"Did you know that Blair Kyepher's contract is up?" she asked. I shook my head, thrown off balance by the sudden change of topic.

"I can't do anything to fix what happened, but I can do something about Kyepher." she sniffed, crumpling the tissue in her fist.

"Really?"

She nodded. "Thank you for telling me all this. It couldn't have been easy."

"Thanks for listening," I mumbled before picking up my cap and gown. "And since you're auditing the school, you should also know that our cheer team is the best."

LaTasha picked up her notebook again, a smirk forming on her lips. "How so?"

"Our routines are original, our stunts are flawless, and our team spirit is through the roof. We boost morale for the entire school, and let me tell you—it's not easy maintaining top grades and dedicating yourself to practice nearly every day. But we manage it. And with all that's been going on… it's like an escape for many of us."

"Noted. Anything else?"

"I could probably get a list to you," I laughed. LaTasha tossed her stuff to the side and stood up, extending her hand out to me and I took it.

"You be careful, okay?" she said. With a nod, I took her cap and gown and opened the door. Principal Baxster was lounging in one of the chairs, picking at his nails. Kyepher was here now, flipping through paperwork. She glanced up at me, her brows furrowed in confusion.

Then, her eyes flickered behind me, where LaTasha was standing. "What brings you to campus so early?" Kyepher asked me, her jaw tense.

"I asked her to come in. Don't worry about it," Baxster replied, all calm.

Kyepher's eyes flashed between Baxster and his office where LaTasha was putting together her notes. Kyepher's eyes landed on me, and for once, she looked scared.

"I'll see you at graduation," I told her before striding past her. My feet hurt like bad in those heels, but it felt so good to leave this office a victor.

★ ★ ★ ★ ☦ ★ ★ ★ ★

JJ was running late for his own graduation. I stepped outside to call and make sure he was on the way. Apparently, he was waiting on his grandma to get ready, which is understandable.

A few parents had started to arrive, no doubt scoping out good seats for graduation. But other than that, it was still blissfully quiet on campus.

I used the back entrance this time, remembering the passive aggressive emails Baxster sent out about seniors needing to remain out of sight before the ceremony. It was the entrance I usually used anyway, the one by all the locker rooms. Normally, it was empty. But I froze as soon as I saw the familiar figure down the hallway.

Khyree was hunched over, bracing his hand on the wall in front of him. He didn't see me. His head was ducked down so far that he didn't have a clue I was anywhere near him. Something was wrong.

In all the nightmarish ways I had imagined today, nothing like this ever came up. I never thought I'd find him all alone, looking about as broken as he had left me that day in the parking lot.

I should go back outside. Use the other entrance. Nothing good could come from being alone when walking past Khyree.

Yet, my feet moved forward anyway. Maybe as an act of rebellion, a statement that my God is bigger, and I only fear him. But that was partly true to what I was feeling.

Khyree never looked up. He should have looked up. He was always scanning the room for me, never missing an opportunity to talk to me.

As I got closer, his labored breathing became audible. Khyree was hyperventilating.

There had been rumors about what happened to Khyree after he strangled me. Some were easy enough to dismiss. Obviously, his parents hadn't sent him off to some military school. But others had a ring of truth to them. Specifically, the one about Khyree trying to kill himself. That one grieved me.

Looking at the boy who was once kind to me, alone and hyperventilating, I knew it was true for him. He had no friends. His parents slap a check onto any problem Khyree had ever had but didn't want to deal with him. The only attention he's ever gotten was from his cousin Rayo, who was locked up.

My cautious pace turned into a power walk as I approached him. Maybe this was a dumb decision, but there was no one else in Khyree life who would ever try to help him. If this was the last interaction we would ever have, then I was going to make it a better one, even if he didn't deserve it. I could help him one last time.

"Put your hands on top of your head," I told him. His shoulders went rigid at the sound of my voice, but slowly, he pushed himself up and did as I said. Khyree's eyes were bright red, his brown skin covered in tears. Something sharp churned in my stomach at the sight. "How many bricks are in the wall in front of you?"

"I don't know—"

"Count," I whispered. Khyree fell back against the wall and quietly counted to himself. My gaze fell to his cheek. It was bruised, like someone hit him.

My eyes darted to the back gym where all the seniors were gathered. I had heard everyone talk after finding out that Khyree was coming back for graduation. A few of the guys said they'd pop him square in the jaw if Khyree showed his face again, but I didn't think anyone actually would.

"Who hit you?" I asked.

"I don't know," he said. "Everyone hates me."

I wasn't taking that bait. Speaking from a fleshly standpoint, he deserved to be hated by everyone here. "Keep counting," I told him. When I heard him start over, I grabbed a paper cup beside the water fountain and filled it up. The back door opened again, and I spotted JJ striding in with his cap and gown on. For a second, he froze, looking between me and Khyree.

As he stormed toward us with his shoulders tense and his eyes panicked, I put up my hand, pleading for him to stay calm. His jaw clenched and it was clear he hated this, but his pace slowed, and he said nothing.

"Drink," I told Khyree, handing him the cup. His hand shook as he took it from me, but thankfully our eyes didn't meet.

"I'm so sorry about what I—"

"Don't," I snapped. "Just drink and keep counting bricks until you're good enough to go back in." I reached back behind me, sighing in relief when JJ's hand found mine, and the two of us walked past Khyree toward the back gym.

"Sidell," JJ whispered.

"Save the lecture," I sighed. "He was having a panic attack."

"I'm not going to lecture you for having a big heart," JJ told me. "I was going to ask if you were okay."

I finally turned to face him. "I think so," I replied. JJ cocked an eyebrow. "No, really. I am." And I meant it this time. Seeing Khyree upset me, sure, but nothing like it used to. "Yeah, I'm okay."

"Good," he grinned before kissing my cheek. After a beat, I put my tassel on the correct side. "Also, my grandma wants lots of pictures of us in our caps and gowns after. Apparently, we robbed her of taking prom photos."

"Huh. My mom said the same thing," I chuckled.

Baxster came in and started barking off orders for everyone to line up. JJ snuck one more kiss to my cheek before leaving for his spot, while I got in mine.

Khyree got in his place in line right before we were about to walk. I didn't miss the way conversation amongst the seniors died down as soon as he came in. Our eyes met, and for a second, I saw the bashful boy who used to smile. Khyree nodded at me before jerking his eyes away.

The song Pomp and Circumstance finally came on, and I gave JJ a little wave as he followed the line out the door. Just a few people behind him was Khyree, who kept his gaze looking forward.

Within minutes, I was walking out into the gymnasium, feeling awkward as I forced a smile. My dad and mom kept waving at me frantically, trying to get my attention so they could get a good photo. Cayest just laughed behind them.

The ceremony was long. Everyone and their mother had to give a speech, none of them particularly good. Tony dozed off. Dawn had a running commentary going on in the row behind me. I poked JJ from behind every time his head started to droop. By the time we all stood up to go get our diplomas, my foot had fallen asleep. The line moved quickly, like everyone couldn't wait to get out of there.

When my name was called, I distinctly heard my parents and Cayest screaming for me. A blush crept onto my cheeks as I took the diploma from Baxster.

Headmaster Kyepher was waiting at the edge of the stage, ready to shake my hand. It'd probably be the last interaction I would've had with this woman.

I forgave her, but I couldn't stomach her congratulations. Instead, I slid my tassel to the other side, ignored her extended hand, and walked right past her. Maybe it was petty. Or maybe I didn't want to ever see a photo of me shaking that woman's hand.

There was a long, awkward pause as I made my way down the stairs. Kyepher should've already called out the next student's name. As I walked back to my seat, she finally resumed reading off names.

My face felt hot, like everyone was still staring at me. As I turned the corner to see the half of the seniors that had already walked staring at me, I realized I was right.

JJ had a huge smirk on his lips while I got to my seat. Dawn, whose row was now standing up, leaned over to whisper, "A middle finger might have been more subtle." I swatted her arm before falling back in my seat.

Within a few minutes, I began to relax. Some girl tripped in her ridiculous heels, so everyone forgot about me stiffing the Headmaster. I zoned in and out of the rest of the ceremony. It was only when the class president stepped up to make his closing remarks that I realized it was over.

JJ and I had made it. Somehow, we made it through all this hell and came out on the other side together.

Chapter Fifty-One:
♉

The sun filtered through the windows of Pete's Music Store, casting a nostalgic glow over the store's rustic interior. Shelves brimming with old records, CDs, instruments, and sheet music were neatly organized in the small space. The soft hum of a classic tune played in the background, filling the store with a sense of timelessness.

Remarkably, I couldn't believe my luck landing this job in less than a few weeks after graduation. It was either that they were desperate for help or they just got tired of me blowing up their phones. I now have something to prove tonight when I'll meet Sidell's parents over dinner. Now that I had graduated, and had no plan to start college until the fall, I for sure didn't want them thinking I was some lazy loser now that their daughter had become mine. Plus, relying on my grandma's weekly allowance for our dates was straight outta the dark ages.

Behind the counter, lost in the pages of my comic magazine, I barely glanced up as the door chimed and a customer strolled in. "Welcome to Pete's!" I called out with forced cheerfulness, without even bothering to look up.

Upon hearing the distinct sound of a rubber ball hitting the ground and bouncing back up, I looked up and offered a bemused grin. "Pretty quiet in here," Tony observed nonchalantly, scanning the store with his eyes.

Closing my book in one smooth motion, I leaned back against the counter and chuckled. "Just wait. It'll get busy soon enough.. But tell me, you got my text or what?"

"Jamison," Tony began, his laughter carrying through every word as he leaned his elbows on the counter. "Getting invited to dinner by your girlfriend's parents is hardly exceptional; quite normal actually – you're merely unaccustomed."

I strolled around the counter, rearranging CD cases on the shelves within easy reach. "Well, that might be normal for you. You know my whole story, Tony. Honestly, I never thought it would go this smoothly." My voice dwindled into a hushed whisper, "This has to be a miracle."

For a moment, silence hung heavy in the store as that music faded into distant static. Tony stopped bouncing his little red ball, giving me a look laced with irony. "Hell yeah, it's a miracle." he admitted, "I never heard of a father compromising on his stance for his daughter's sake."

I nodded in agreement. "Maybe it's because I've started attending church again. I'm grateful I did because now I can see God's fingerprints all over these miracles."

Tony quickly interjected, "Hey man. I'm not saying your spiritual journey isn't legit or whatever. I believe in God too, Jesus and all that stuff. Hell, even Noah's Flood with them chinchillas and that crazy-a** Kraken on that boat. But you gotta tone it down a bit, man. Stop sounding so damn weird. Isn't this just a coincidence?"

I didn't answer right away. This was a side of me Tony had never seen before; he only knew the JJ who shrugged off religion like it was an old coat. So softly, with conviction in my voice, I replied, "Nah man, we all got our own perspectives, and this...this is mine. I believe God had a hand in making this happen. Ain't no way it could be that easy."

Tony looked genuinely concerned, "No, really — what happened to you?"

Casually shrugging my shoulders, hands buried deep in my jeans pockets,

I shot back at him. "Chill, Tony. I ain't askin' you to go grab a Bible to find the verse or start preaching on street corners like some madman. If you can respect my faith like you respect every other part of me, then we still cool as ever."

Tony stared at me, his expression filled with remorse. "My bad, man. I didn't mean to come at you like that. It just feels like everything's changed between us."

Shaking my head in protest, I declared, "Nah, Tony, it ain't true. As long as we show each other respect and honor our boundaries, we good."

"Deal," he responded earnestly, reaching out to perform our signature handshake.

"Now you finna hand me the keys or what?" I asked, my hand remaining open.

Tony fished them out of his pocket. "You're lucky you're my friend because $700 for an 03' Chevy Truck is a pretty fresh deal,"

"Yeah, well it better work right since I'm lucky," I joked.

"You're the only person I know who buys a car the same day before meeting your girl's parents," Tony said, clutching the keys.

"Just know that everyone ain't legendary and can do what I do."

Looking satisfied, he tossed the keys over to me. I caught them smoothly in midair.

"Pleasure doing business with you rockstar." I grinned.

"Yeah, yeah. Anyway, my dad's outside waiting on me. He drove your truck down here. We're going to ride back up in my car."

"Sure thing, drive safe. Tell him I said wassup."

Nodding in acknowledgment, Tony exited the store.

★ ★ ★ ★ ✞ ★ ★ ★ ★

Walking up Sidell's driveway, one of my hands was shoved into my pocket, while the other held a bouquet of yellow roses. Tony may be a *gentleman*, but I can do it better. Before clocking out of my shift, I had hurried and changed into a velvet collared shirt, that once again grandma had picked out. And even though I'll be inside for the evening, I cursed myself for not bringing a jacket. A hoodie would have done the trick. But Sidell kept forgetting to return the one I had left with her last Saturday. And all the other jackets I owned have our school's seal on them. And I didn't wanna be caught in anything issued by that school unless I was actually on campus.

Immediately after ringing the doorbell, the front door swung open to reveal Sidell's dad, a bearded blonde man smiling at me. "Hey, it's nice to see you again Jacky," he said, gesturing for me to come on inside.

"Likewise, and if I didn't forget, Garren, right? . . . I mean, Mr. Evermost," I stuttered. Damn, I had practiced this in my head on the way over and I was already screwing it up. Belatedly, I remembered to extend my hand out to him.

He took my hand with a small smile and said, "Mr. Evermost is fine. Though, I wouldn't mind taking the credit on calling you son. It seems that whoever raised you, raised you right." His gaze shifted towards my shirt and he noted approvingly. "This is quite a nice shirt they've picked out."

How did he know?

I snickered. "Thanks, all credit goes to my grandma. Also, I notice you change the place up a bit."

Mr. Evermost pointed his finger at me with pride, gesturing around the living room at the artifacts and furniture with a smile on his face. "My wife has a real talent for this kind of thing. My only contribution to this house is the new bookshelf that has already started to slant."

"And don't forget about that shed you put together in the back!" Sidell's mom, Mrs. Evermost, called out from another room.

Mr. Evermost ducked his head slightly as he muttered low enough so she wouldn't hear him. "Between you and me, I paid the neighbor's kid to do it."

I tried to force a laugh, averting my gaze.

Mr. Evermost dashed over to the stair railing. "Sidell? Jacky's here!" he shouted, gripping the side of the stair railing firmly with both hands. When he turned back to face me, I extended the bouquet of flowers.

"Oh, and these are for your wife," I said.

He waved them off with a smile. "That's fine, young man. The honors are all yours."

He firmly patted my back, propelling me forward into the archway of the kitchen. Amidst the clatter of dishware and cutlery, Mrs. Evermost's movements were graceful and precise. Her curly brown hair was drawn tightly into a neat bun that accentuated her elegantly angled jawline. She wore a crisp blue floral collared shirt complete with pockets and a pleated skirt that ended just above her ankles.

"Hi, Mrs. Evermost," I said, carefully advancing towards her with the bouquet like some sort of peace offering.

She nodded enthusiastically in my direction, shaking the wetness from her hands after briefly drying them on a worn towel. Her eyes lit up and a broad smile spread across her face as she grabbed the buds with both hands. "Aw, thank you Jacky. These are grand."

I gave a curt nod. "You're welcome," I muttered, scanning around the room.

"Hey, Jacky. I am still preparing dinner, but if you would like some refreshments while you wait, feel free to take something," Mrs. Evermost spoke warmly as her hand was already nursing the refrigerator handle. "We have water, uh, lemonade…"

"That's alright but thank you," I said. Before she could turn around to face me again, a cacophony of footsteps echoed off the ceiling above me. The sound quickly morphed into an intense crescendo of piercing thuds that quickly made their way toward the staircase and into the kitchen where we were.

"Cayest! Quit running around in this house!" Mrs. Evermost bellowed to the young girl with brown eyes who had skidded into the room on her socks, almost losing her footing completely against the porcelain wood flooring.

Her hair was similar to her mother's except it was untamed as it cascaded down her back. "But Mama, somebody turned off the wifi." She spoke out between heavy breaths and held her cell phone as if it were an extension of her.

"Don't you see? It's a sign from God that you should be courteous and attentive. Take a break from that device. We have a guest in our home."

"Not my guest," Cayest grumbled before noticing me for the first time. Her eyes widened. "Oh...uh hi JJ?" She waved shyly, her complexion now bright red from embarrassment.

I lifted my palm in response with a simple, "Whassup Caye?" I received a tiny smirk from Cayest.

"Weren't you on the phone with my sister for 8 hours last night? I kept waking up and hearing you guys talking." she asked blatantly, not hesitating for a moment.

I scratched the back of my head, unsure how to respond. "Uh... yeah," I said slowly, hoping that I wasn't on speaker, because I was being all mushy on the call.

"Caye, go beg your papa to fix the router. And take these flowers and go put them in my room," Mrs. Evermost urged, shooing her daughter out of the kitchen. After she was out of view, she swiveled her attention towards me with a smile.

"And Jacky, don't be afraid. Sit, relax, you're our guest. The living room is available if that puts you at ease."

I slouched on the fluffy cushions of the couch, the soft texture foreign against my skin. It had been a while since I had sat on anything that soft, and I felt like an idiot for sinking down into it. My stiff leg poked out in front of me at a weird angle as I desperately shifted without drawing any notice.

Just then, Sidell descended the stairs, her luminous eyes finding me. She wore her hair half up with the remainder cascading in waves down her back. Her beige dress shimmered with its golden belt buckle, complementing her golden sandals.

The sight of her divine beauty was like a shot of adrenaline; I rose from the couch with renewed vigor.

"Hey," she spoke softly like a symphony playing only for me. I smiled widely with my gaze taking in every feature of hers. She looked gorgeous.

"Hey," I echoed, walking towards her. She met me halfway, wrapping her arms around my neck. I hugged her tightly, feeling her warmth against me. It felt so good to hold her again.

"Sorry it took so long; I changed my dress like a million times," she said as she pulled away slightly.

"It's alright. You look beautiful," I murmured, feeling the sincerity weighing my voice.

A shy smile curved her lips. "Thanks, you don't look too bad yourself," she replied flirtatiously, tugging at the fabric of my shirt. "Your grandma picked this out for you?"

I laughed quietly, glancing down at my chest. "Your dad noticed too."

"I bet he did, that's his favorite color. Anyways, how was he?" she questioned me curiously. "Did he ruff you up?"

I answered honestly. "Nah, he was real light with me today. Probably because I haven't done anything yet," I joked, causing her to laugh softly. "No but seriously, he's a cool dude."

Sidell nodded in agreement. "Yeah, but sometimes he can be a bit much. Especially when he's trying to be funny." She paused, tucking a strand of hair behind her ear. "So, was it trouble getting here on the city bus? Or did you take Uber?"

I decided to play suspense. "Nah, and neither."

"What do you mean 'nah and neither'? Tony dropped you off?"

"Nope."

"Then how did you— Don't tell me you walked all the way over."

A silent smile crept onto my lips as I pulled out a set of jangling car keys in her view. "I drove it all the way here," I proudly proclaimed, winking.

Her face lit up like a summer sky. "No way, I got to see!"

She beamed as she rushed to the living room window and threw back the curtains. At the sight of my new car, her breath caught in her throat. Then she whirled around to catch me in a tight embrace. Her happiness was palpable and I smiled into her shoulder, feeling a deep sense of accomplishment.

"I'm so proud of you, JJ," Sidell whispered, her voice filled with awe and admiration.

"Thank you, I'm glad you like it," I whispered into her ear as I held her close, savoring the moment. It felt like we were in our own little world, away from the pressures and worries of reality. All that mattered was the warmth of her body against mine, the softness of her hair as it tickled my nose, and the sound of her heartbeat, steady and strong.

Her breath exhaled as she pulled away from me, her lips turning up in a knowing grin. "Can I drive it later?" she asked with an impish glimmer in her eye.

My brow furrowed with intrigue. "You can drive now?" I asked in a teasing manner.

Her smile faded as she firmly punched my arm, a reminder of who was truly in control. "Yes! You know this. Dawn taught me. Now can I get the keys, my king?" she replied with a sardonic smirk.

I threw my head back into an echoing laugh. "Alright then, if you must."

This was my first time attending a traditional Russian dinner. We sat around the table which happened to be a glorious sight to behold. Sidell's family embraced me in every vibrant conversation that seemed to echo through the long room. The air was filled with the sweet smells of cabbage, pork and onion pierogies, vereniki dumplings cooked in sour cream, pickled herring, salted salmon, smoky beef stew with pickled mushrooms, and fresh, crusty black bread. Everyone generously passed around plates, glasses clinking in jovial cheers as we toasted to health and happiness.

"I want you to try at least a little bit of this," Sidell told me as she adopted my plate in her hands. Her expression was fierce, like the way she placed the food was an integral part of the experience. Her slender fingers worked feverishly, arranging carefully selected portions of each dish onto my plate. I mustered up a weak protest, but her gaze held me in place more than any iron chains could have. I felt her soft eyes linger upon me long after she placed the plate before me. Though seemingly calm, her parents were watchful from where they sat, so I was mindful not to make it too obvious as my hand lingered on her knee.

Mrs. Evermost sat her wine glass down and gazed at Sidell, a smile playing on her lips. "There is something about seeing you all grown up and ready to date that weakens my knees and makes my heart beat a little faster," she said softly.

Sidell blushed profusely and cut in, "Mama, are you always this persistent when it comes to my love life?"

Mrs. Evermost chuckled. "Only when I see a spark between my daughter and a potential suitor. And I have to say, I see that spark right now." She took a sip of her wine before shooting a knowing glance toward her husband as she spoke wryly, "Your father knows that it's tough raising a daughter that's my replica in words, temper, action and physique."

Mr. Evermost seemed to take pleasure in the challenge. "You don't know half of it. Let's just say I was more than patient when it came to your mother. And JJ..." — he nodded my way for emphasis — "you got your work cut out for you with this one."

I shot him a snicker before shoving a vereniki dumpling in my mouth, my taste buds exploding from the rich sour cream sauce. I replied confidently, "Ain't no worries here sir—I got it handled."

"I'd like to pray so she may be a handful like her mother, but she's worth it," Mr. Evermost added, pointing his folk at his daughter for emphasis.

I smiled, moving my fork around my plate before finally speaking on what I wanted to say. "Mr. Evermost? I wanna apologize for my actions the first few times we met. I'm raised by a godly, accommodating woman who has taught me better, and my behavior the last time was not an accurate representation of the person that I am, my upbringing or my family. I hope that you'll both forgive me and give me a second chance to make a better impression." It's a speech off the dome, but every word comes from the depths of my heart.

"No, forgive me, I didn't trust you Jacky, and I misjudged you. You had a lot of courage that I can now respect." Sidell looked towards me, nudging me as her father continued. "I fell in love with my wife here when I was just as young as you are. I didn't even have the courage to approach her parents because it's not done that way in traditional Russian families. So we threw caution to the winds and went along with the flow, and it brought about a lot of complications, some of which we have yet to sort out to this day."

Mrs. Evermost nodded her approval in agreement as her husband continued. "And Mr. Jamison, forgive me," he clarified, giving me a hard look. "I'm not saying that you would do such a thing, young man. I'm just saying that the majority of young men nowadays think they know best and tend to make impulsive decisions, but you have shown maturity and respect for our family by coming here tonight. So, I thank you for that and hope that our dinner tonight will be the beginning of a beautiful relationship between you and our family."

"Thank you, sir," I gratefully replied and Sidell's cheeks flushed with pride as she listened to her father's praise. She always tried her best to make her parents proud, and tonight seemed to be a success.

After dinner, we headed to the living room where Sidell's little sister Cayest took charge and led us through light-hearted games. We started with a rousing game of Durak, followed by plenty more Russian traditional pastimes. Sidell snuggled up to me, her head resting on my shoulder while I laughed and joked with her family. Each moment felt like a blessing, and I was filled with joy that I could be part of their lives. And though I knew that Sidell and I were still in the early stages of our relationship, there seemed potential for a future between us.

I had gotten used to people always leaving or eventually being left by them. I've been struggling with letting people in, but I was doing better.

And though I hadn't entirely overcome those resistant feelings, I think part of it has been sort of . . . risking it. At a certain point, I realized I had the option to stay hidden or to risk it — kind of like a dare.

I've been daring myself more often because the other side of that dare – the reward – was becoming more and more worth it to me every day. I thought it's been paying off. I was actually pretty happy, for the most part. Maybe happier than I had ever been.

As I intertwined my fingers with Sidell's, I felt grateful that she dared to enter my life. From her I had learned that, when we took a look at our anxieties and acknowledged what they're holding us back from was a great way to reconsider what we wanted, and whether we wanted it badly enough to change our ways, even if it risked discomfort. God had conspired to bring us together, to heal our fragile hearts under this momentous noon sky. With each passing second, I felt my soul brimming with joy, yet disbelief still washed over me at the same time —

Could this be real?

The answers were always there, but none of us possessed the knowledge to make sense of them. He was the only one who knew where everything started and ended. Through our failures, Sidell and I would find a way to form an alliance with him. He'd take us by the hand and lead us down the path of righteousness; we could depend on him to chart the course for our future. Grandma's love, Sidell's love, God's love — each one so different yet so beautiful, healing and divine. They all dared to help me heal and it did, even though I was yet to be perfected.

405

ABOUT AUTHOR

HELLO READER, IT'S NICE TO MEET YOU HERE! MY NAME IS MAKIAH BULLOCK AND THIS IS MY NOVEL, "HELP ME IF YOU DARE." I HOPE YOU ENJOYED IT, AS I TRIED MY BEST TO FILL IT WITH PASSION AND PURPOSE. FROM WHEN I WAS EIGHT YEARS OLD, I DEVELOPED A DEEP LOVE FOR WRITING BOOKS, AND SOON MOVED ONTO POETRY IN MY PRE-TEEN AND ADOLESCENT YEARS. BUT IT WASN'T UNTIL I WAS BORN AGAIN IN CHRIST THAT I REALIZED I HAD TO CHANGE MY APPROACH AND WRITE STORIES THAT GLORIFY HIM. IN THE PAST, I'VE DABBLED IN THRILLERS, COMEDIES, AND MYSTERIES - BUT CHRISTIAN ROMANCE....IT'S NEW WATERS FOR ME.

AND I HAVE TO SAY, WRITING THIS BOOK ABOUT A YOUTHFUL RELATIONSHIP IN A WAY THAT HONORED GOD BROUGHT SOME CHALLENGES. IT'S NOT EASY WRITING SCENES WITHOUT USING WORLDLY LANGUAGE OR IDEAS. BUT WITH FAITH, I KNOW THIS IS ONLY THE START OF WHAT GOD HAS FOR ME -- MORE NOVELS, MORE CHALLENGES, MORE OPPORTUNITIES TO GLORIFY HIM THROUGH MY WRITING. LET'S SEE WHERE HE TAKES ME.

Printed in Great Britain
by Amazon